DEAD
IN THE
WATER

THE DEEP SIX • Book 6

JULIE ANN WALKER

DEAD IN THE WATER
The Deep Six book 6
Copyright © 2021 by Limerence Publications LLC

Limerence Publications LLC
ISBN: 978-1-950100-12-5

To Nikkie, for your big heart, your curious mind, and your never-ending love of family. It's been my honor to watch you grow into the amazing woman you are today.

When you come out of the storm, you won't be the same person who walked in. That's what the storm's all about.
~Haruki Murakami

PROLOGUE

July 29th, 1624...

Dead.
All dead.
And very soon I will be dead too, *Bartolome Vargas thought as he carefully wrapped his journal in oilcloth before placing it in the lead-lined box he had salvaged months earlier from the flotsam washed ashore after the wreck of the grand galleon.*

The Santa Cristina...

Who could have known she would not survive her maiden mission?

Certainly not Bartolome.

The first time he laid eyes on her, anchored in the shipyard in Barcelona with her towering mainmast and hardwood hull gleaming in the sunshine, he had thought to himself, 'Tis a ship to ply the seas long after the good Lord calls me home.

Alas, Mother Nature had made other plans for the magnificent vessel.

Mayhap the galleon could have survived the early season hurricane had she not been weighed down and riding low in the drink with a belly full of treasure from the New World. After all, she had been built tough by Spain's best shipbuilders. A veritable floating fortress.

Overburdened as she had been, however, there had been no hope for her when the seas grew angry and the winds howled like the very hounds of hell.

"'Tis why I made my decision," he said aloud to no one.

Or 'twas possible he said it aloud for the benefit of the ghosts surrounding him. The invisible specters of the men who had sailed and fought by his side. All of them gone now. He, their commander, their capitán, *was the lone survivor of the once heralded crew.*

Of the 224 souls who had sailed the Santa Cristina, *only thirty-six had survived the violence of the big ship's sinking. Thirty-six brave men who had continued to follow Bartolome's commands despite the trials and tribulations they had faced once they found themselves marooned on the spit of mangrove forest and sand. Thirty-six sailors who had continued to prove themselves good and true sons of Spain until, one by one, they too had succumbed.*

Some had fallen victim to the elements or injury. Others to illness. But the last of them had been taken by that merciless demon known as thirst.

After the blue death descended upon their camp, and after Bartolome dumped their water barrels in a desperate bid to keep more of his men from falling victim to the terrible illness, the stingy sky had refused to replenish their drinking supply with even one drop of rain.

Helplessly, Bartolome had watched the last of his crewmen suffer the debilitating headaches and hallucinations brought on by dehydration. His own weakened state had made it impossible for him to stop those who had run into the sea, gulping of the salty water in a desperate attempt to quench their unbearable thirsts.

Of course, their efforts had only expedited their departures into the great beyond.

But mayhap 'twas their intention all along, *he silently mused as he closed the lid on the lead-lined box.* And surely 'tis no sin to hasten death when death is inevitable.

The only thing that had been left to Bartolome then had been to dig their graves with the help of Rosario, the midshipman who had become his right-hand man. And then Rosario, too, had fallen quietly into the arms of death.

With the last of his strength, Bartolome dug Rosario's grave that very morn. Now he lowered the box into the shallow hole beside the midshipman's body.

"Keep this safe, my friend," he whispered, brushing a strand of hair from Rosario's cold brow. For the first time in weeks, the young sailor appeared at peace. No more furrowed forehead. No more pinched lips. No more glint of pain in his dark eyes.

Bartolome had dressed Rosario's body in his very own waistcoat, the buttons of which were stamped with the Vargas family seal. "You now hold the key to the location of the treasure." He gently placed one of Rosario's limp hands atop the precious box.

Bartolome had no idea how long it took him to shovel sand back into the grave, his withered muscles shaking with fatigue. But eventually the deed was done, and he wiped a hand across his brow despite his shriveled body having long ago lost the ability to sweat.

The wooden cross he had carved from the limbs of a mangrove tree found a home at the head of the narrow mound. He pressed his signet ring into the marker until the pattern from the ring was deeply imprinted upon the soft wood.

His hope was that one of his countrymen would stumble onto the remote island, find the graves, and know the significance of the symbol on the cross. If so, and if they had an ounce of intelligence, they would dig up the body with the expectation of it being Bartolome himself, a captain known for his cunning and wits. A captain who would insist on leaving behind a clue, a code, *that only their good king himself could decipher. A code that would pinpoint the location of the* Santa Cristina's *enormous bounty.*

And if not? If no Spaniards arrived to find the grave and the secrets within? Then the massive cache of riches would remain safe in its new resting place. Safe from the covetous hands of Spain's enemies. Locked away in a coral-encrusted tomb for all eternity.

Bartolome dropped his hand atop the hill of sand covering Rosario's corpse. "Rest well, my most trusted and loyal crewman. If there is an afterlife, you deserve all the glory that awaits you."

Dragging himself to the water's edge, he lay on his back and let the surf lap at his legs. The beating of his heart kept rhythm with the warm waves as he stared into the cloudless sky. And then, after a time, his pulse grew thready and the world around him dimmed.

Bartolome couldn't see the bastard, but he knew the instant Death sat next to him.

"'Tis where I wish to face my end," he told the Reaper, his voice a harsh rasp of sound. "Here, on this beach overlooking the watery grave of the Santa Cristina. *The tide will carry my body out to sea where the fishes will pick my tired bones clean. A fitting end for a sailor, me thinks."*

Death did not answer him, of course. But Bartolome thought for sure he could feel a cold, bony hand land upon his shoulder.

4

"I am ready," he declared staunchly. He had lived his life fearlessly. It was only fitting he greet his end with the same courage. "Take me."

With that, Bartolome Vargas, Spain's most celebrated sea captain, breathed his last.

CHAPTER 1

Present Day
6:35 PM...

You ever have the urge to tell someone to shut up even when they aren't talking?"

Dalton "Doc" Simmons frowned at Cami. The toothpick caught between his teeth pointed at the floor. "What the hell? I'm just standing here."

"And silently calling me dirty names. I can *feel* you doing it even if I can't *hear* you." Her lips pursed. Lips that were plush, full, and painted a rich, velvety red. "Which is so much worse. Because then when I call you out for silently calling me dirty names, it makes me sound crazy." She narrowed her eyes. Eyes that were dark, heavily lashed, and tilted up at the corners.

Hands down, Camilla D'Angelo was the most beautiful woman Doc had ever met.

Not that he put a whole heck of a lot of stock in beauty. The Hope Diamond was said to be one of the most dazzling gems ever cut, but everyone who'd ever owned it had died a mysterious death.

Beauty had a way of hiding what was sinister.

Okay. Back up. He wasn't going so far as to say *Cami*'s loveliness came with a curse. But she was a *lawyer*, so…

"But maybe that's your goal. To make me sound crazy." She tapped a ruby-red fingertip on her chin. "You'd love to see me wrapped in a straitjacket. Admit it."

"I'll admit no such thing." He noted how his blood bubbled with pleasure.

Trading barbs with Cami was…*stimulating*. Maybe because she was the only woman whose mouth he'd ever been tempted to simultaneously kiss and tape shut.

Although, having done that first thing, he wasn't stupid enough to attempt it again. Not because it hadn't been good, but because it'd been *too* good. A kiss that'd gone past his lips to sink into a space that, for years, he'd purposefully kept empty.

It'd been an alarming kiss. A dangerous kiss.

A kiss that will not be repeated.

"I wouldn't wish the indignity of a straitjacket on anyone," he assured her. "I'm a firm believer in bodily autonomy. So if it's looking like you're heading toward some sort of unwilling confinement, please know I'll put you out of your misery and smother you with a pillow first."

Her mouth flattened into a straight line. "What a gentleman."

"I like to think so."

He wouldn't have thought it possible, but her mouth flattened further, until her red lips disappeared completely. "Apparently, when it comes to sarcasm, you're tone deaf."

"Oh, no. I picked up what you were laying down. I'm simply being magnanimous and choosing to ignore it." She opened her mouth to come back at him with something scathing, no doubt, but he cut her off by adding, "But since you brought it up, let's address it." He checked his watch. "By my count, that was two hours of stonewalling silence followed up with sarcasm. It's like we've been married for ten years."

"You could only dream of being so lucky. And those two hours of stonewalling silence were a direct result of you accusing me of purposefully making your job harder than it has to be." A fascinating wash of pink stained her high cheekbones. She enjoyed their linguistic tussles as much as he did. "You've called me a witch before, but surely you don't think I'm capable of conjuring up a storm." Her hands were fisted on her hips as she stood with her legs slightly apart to counter the movement of the decking beneath her feet.

The *Wayfarer II* was a large vessel, with a J-frame crane attached to the aft section and a HIAB hydraulic loader on the bow that kept the ship equally weighted in the water. But the approaching hurricane had begun to rile the seas, making the *Wayfarer* bob like a cork.

"I never called you a witch." His tongue worked the fraying end of the toothpick in his mouth. A psych major would probably accuse him of having an oral fixation. But Doc would argue his affinity for the wooden sticks was simply habit. One he'd picked up from his old man because, as a boy, he'd done everything he could to become his father's Mini-Me. "I said you were *witchy*. There's a difference. And I *know* you're not responsible for the storm. But you *are* responsible for having us wait until the reef was submerged before retrieving the treasure."

Her smooth brow lined with frustration. "The *law* is responsible for that. Not me."

Admiralty law, a salvor's best friend, stated it was finders keepers when it came to recovered goods within state or federal waters. Unfortunately, Captain Bartolome Vargas had removed the treasure from the wreck of the *Santa Cristina* and hidden it beneath the reef that protected Wayfarer Island's lagoon from the ravages of the open ocean.

A reef was considered "waters" so long as it was submerged. But if a speck of it peeked above the waves? It was considered land.

Admiralty law didn't apply to land.

"Instead of busting my balls over how tough the last day has been, you should be thanking me for finding the loophole that allows you to keep all of this to yourself as opposed to having to share it with Uncle Sam or the state of Florida," she continued, throwing out an arm to indicate the treasure piled atop the tables in the ship's computer room.

One tabletop held a collection of conglomerates. They were what happened to silver coins when they came in contact with seawater. Corrosion and other maritime accretions fused the currency together into rocky-looking wads that perfumed the stale air inside the room with the briny smell of the sea. But Doc knew as soon as they were electronically cleaned, the pieces of eight—coins like the one that hung on a chain around his neck—would be revealed.

Another table was mounded with doubloons. Unlike silver, gold wasn't affected by its time in the ocean. The doubloons winked under the artificial light as if they'd been minted the day before.

Then there was a small tabletop displaying swords and daggers, each ceremonial and encrusted with gems. A larger table held religious artifacts, all ornamental and heavily bejeweled. And still another was heaped with uncut emeralds that'd been mined from Colombia nearly four hundred years earlier.

Truly, the immensity of the *Santa Cristina*'s treasure was a mindboggling sight to behold. And that wasn't counting the gold bullion and silver ingots the Deep Six crew had already cataloged, packed away in straw-lined boxes, and stacked against the walls of the ship's engine room.

For the first few hours, when Doc and his former SEAL Team members and current Deep Six Salvage partners had hauled up the gems and coins and artifacts from where Captain Vargas had hidden them, he'd marveled at each new piece of wealth. But as the treasure trove had grown, he'd begun to feel an overwhelming sense of surreality.

How could he, Dalton Simmons, a poor kid from Nowhere, Montana, be a one-sixth owner of a lost treasure estimated to be worth nearly half a billion dollars?

And yet…here I am. A millionaire. A multi*millionaire.*

Thanks to Cami and her legal wrangling.

It rankled, but he dutifully told her, "Thank you for finding the loophole that allows us to keep all this." One corner of her mouth hitched up, but it fell into another straight line when he added, "I just would've liked the loophole better if it hadn't meant we had to wait for a king tide smack-dab in the middle of hurricane season."

She shook her head. "All you had to do was wait for a king tide. That the next one happened to occur in the middle of hurricane season didn't have anything to do with me. It was bad luck and worse timing."

"Not true." He lifted a contradictory finger. "There was a king tide earlier in the year, but we missed it while you were poring over precedent."

"Wildly obscure precedent that I would *again* stress is the reason you're able to keep all this. Now"—she pointed toward the hallway—"you see that door? For the love of god, do me a favor and go find out what's on the other side of it."

He felt a chuckle rumbling around in his chest and suppressed it. "For the love of god? I thought you told me you weren't religious."

"I wasn't before I met you. But I've taken to getting down on my knees at night and praying for you to go mute."

One corner of his mouth lifted into a languid, flirtatious smile.

Her eyes narrowed with suspicion. "What's that look for?"

"I'm imagining you down on your knees."

She gasped and left her mouth hanging open long after the sound escaped.

Camilla D' Angelo gave as good as she got when it came to oral arguments—thanks to all the practice her career provided, no doubt. But he'd learned he could beat her at her own game when he tossed in a little sexual innuendo.

It was fascinating how she blinked and sputtered and blushed to the roots of her sleek, black hair when he hinted at anything carnal.

"Oh!" She stomped her foot. "You are the most *aggravating*—"

"Children!" Romeo yelled in exasperation. "I'm trying to count my riches like Scrooge McDuck, and your arguing is ruining the experience for me!"

"Here, here," Uncle John seconded from his seat at the emerald table. He had a jeweler's loupe plugged into one eye, making him look like a Borg off *Star Trek*. Although, his Earnest Hemingway hair and salty seadog beard went a long way toward ruining the sci-fi effect.

Before Doc could respond, the sound of bare feet slapping against the metal decking had him turning toward the computer room's open door. The remaining four members of the Deep Six crew, all still wearing their wetsuits and leaving damp footprints behind, shuffled into the room.

"Water's startin' to kick up out there," Leo "The Lion" Anderson, their former lieutenant and the current head of their salvage operation, said as he folded a fresh stick of Big

Red gum into his mouth. Glancing around the room, he asked in his slow, Southern drawl, "Where's my wife?"

"In the galley making cupcakes for dessert," Cami told him before turning her attention to Brando "Bran" Pallidino. "By the way, I took your lasagnas out of the oven fifteen minutes ago like you asked."

Bran scrubbed a hand through his dripping, wavy brown hair and nodded his thanks. Before he could say anything, however, a larger than average wave rolled beneath the ship.

"Erp." Cami lifted a hand to her mouth, her skin paling instantly. But she was quick to drop her fingers and make a face at Bran. "Sorry. I promise that *erp* has nothing to do with your lasagnas. They look and smell delicious."

Doc crossed his arms and leveled a censorious look on her. The woman got seasick in a bathtub. And somehow she'd agreed to take on a job representing men who made their living on the ocean. "You didn't take that Dramamine pill I gave you, did you?"

She bristled and he imagined her as a black cat, back arched and hair raised. "First of all, you may be a doctor, but you're not *my* doctor. And second of all, Dramamine makes me sleepy. I didn't want to nap my way through all of this." Again, she threw out an arm to indicate the treasure.

"And now you're paying the price." His censorious look deepened. "You are the most *stubborn* woman to ever pull on a pair of pants."

Her chin jutted out. "*You're* calling *me* stubborn? Oh, that's rich."

LT sighed heavily—LT was the nickname everyone used for Leo; it was a nod to his former rank. "Have they been at it like this all afternoon?" he asked Romeo. But before Romeo could answer, he shook his head. "Never mind. It doesn't matter. We have more important things to deal with than the ongoin' animosity between our attorney and our resident malcontent."

"Hey!" Doc objected, snatching the toothpick from his mouth. "I'm not a malcontent. I'm just..." He stopped, searching for the right word.

Perhaps he *had* been a malcontent. Once upon a time. In the years following his tragedy. But recently he'd been feeling so much better.

What had caused the change in him?

When it occurred that the better question was *who* had caused the change in him, he decided it was best just to shut his mouth and leave his sentence dangling.

LT rolled his eyes and turned to Bran. "Go grab everyone and bring 'em here, will you, Brando? We need all hands on deck for this discussion, seein' as how our decision on what to do next is gonna affect us all."

"I take it you weren't able to finish." Doc narrowed his eyes at his former lieutenant.

LT shook his head, causing water droplets to drip from the ends of his sun-streaked hair. "But let's wait to talk about it 'til we got everyone."

Doc recognized LT's tone. It was the same one LT had used *numerous* times when they'd found themselves all the way in harm's way, in the place where metal meets the meat. And hearing that tone now made Doc's stomach sink.

Of their own accord, his eyes tracked over to Cami. She too had picked up on the ominous ring in LT's voice, and the expression on her face pretty much mirrored everything Doc was feeling. He was suddenly hit by the oddest urge to throw a comforting arm around her shoulders.

Then again, maybe the urge wasn't odd. Because as much as she vexed him, he *liked* her.

Liked her swift mind and sharp tongue. Liked the ornery sparkle in her eyes when she was arguing with him. Liked the way her laugh sounded like pure delight when he said something to tickle her.

In fact, were it not for her chosen profession, he could've imagined them becoming friends. The kind of friends to feed each other heaping helpings of shit on the reg, of course. But friends all the same.

And in the eternal words of OMC, he thought, *'how bizarre.'*

With the exception of the wives and girlfriends of his teammates and partners—who didn't really count because they *were* the wives and girlfriends of his teammates and partners—he'd only ever been friends with one other woman.

The woman.

His woman.

Thankfully, he didn't have time to ponder the hows and whys of just what that meant before the computer room filled with people.

LT's wife, Olivia, wore the frilly apron LT had gotten her for her birthday. And considering she was a former CIA agent, as comfortable carrying a loaded weapon as she was wearing a wire to a meeting with international drug dealers, it was an odd thing, indeed, to watch her flitting around looking like Betty Crocker.

Bran's wife, the minuscule Maddy, looped an arm around Bran's trim waist and smiled up at him when he bent to drop a loud, smacking kiss on her temple. There was so much love in Bran's eyes when he looked down at his wife that Doc's own heart melted. Just a little.

Chrissy and Wolf found a spot beside Uncle John at the emerald table. Chrissy's diving skills were as good as any Navy SEAL's, so she'd been helping them haul up the treasure. Her ponytail was still wet from being down at the dive site, and Doc watched as Wolf absently twisted the damp, blond rope around his long, tan fingers.

Mia Ennis, the brilliant marine archeologist they'd

brought on to oversee the excavation, went to sit on Romeo's lap. The couple was still in the honeymoon phase of their relationship, and Doc had to refrain from groaning when they made googly eyes at each other.

And last but not least there was Alexandra Merriweather, the historian they'd hired to study the old documents relating to the Spanish fleet. She broke a strawberry Pop-Tart in two and handed half to Mason.

Peas in a pod, Doc thought as he watched Alex shove her tortoiseshell glasses higher on the bridge of her nose so she could grin up at her fiancé as they both laid into the pastries. Or maybe it was more apt to say Mason and Alex were two sides of the same coin. Because as chatty as Alex was, that's how closed-mouthed Mason was. And yet they belonged together, *complemented* each other.

Glancing around the room then, Doc came to a startling realization.

I'm the last man standing. The only member of my former SEAL Team who isn't head over heels in L.O.V.E.

Of course, that was because he'd been there, done that.

Got the T-shirt and lost it, he thought miserably. *Lost everything, in fact.*

As happened anytime his past reared its ugly head, he felt the terrible void that lived in the center of his chest yawn wide. Felt himself falling into it, traveling back in time to a dirt road. To a pair of wide blue eyes. To the girl he'd loved since the eighth grade.

Lifting his right arm, he ran a reverent finger over the delicate flower tattooed on the inside of his wrist. He'd gotten the ink when he was eighteen years old, the day after he proposed. The day after that blue-eyed girl said yes.

But just like his memories of her, the tattoo was beginning to fade. The flower growing fuzzy around the edges. No longer so bright and pure.

And that hurts worst of all.

That she was paling in his mind. That sometimes he went hours, even a whole day, without thinking of her. Without *missing* her.

Especially recently.

"Sorry! I got stuck in the bathroom. That door lock is like a jigsaw puzzle with pieces missing." The last and newest member of their merry band of misfits burst into the computer room, the sides of her windbreaker flapping like a drunken bird.

Her name was Dana Levine and she worked for the FMC—the Federal Maritime Commission. Cami had brought Dana on to bear witness to the salvage since, according to Cami, *"We need a Fed who will swear under oath that you guys didn't touch so much as a single coin of that treasure while the top of the reef was exposed."*

Glad for the distraction from the melancholy turn of his thoughts, Doc watched Dana slip past LT and plop into a chair next to the table that held the conglomerates. She'd been on deck all day and her wild, windblown hair and slightly sunburned nose attested to the diligence with which she'd taken on the role of witness.

Doc would guess her to be somewhere in her mid-fifties. Her bouncy blond curls were interspersed with threads of gray, and there were laugh lines at the corners of her cornflower-blue eyes.

"Okay. Now that everyone's here, it's time to talk turkey." LT's voice rang with military authority. "We thought we were gonna be able to finish this evenin', but that's not gonna happen."

Doc had pulled the early morning shift at the dive site, so he knew how much work was involved in bringing up the treasure. Knew all about spending hours waving a handheld metal detector over the seabed, waiting for the blinking light to indicate whether he'd found ferrous or nonferrous metals. Knew how tedious the sectioning off and gridding of the area could be, because even though the treasure had been removed from the *Santa Cristina*, it still had to be excavated in an archeological manner. Knew how slow and painstaking the process was of carefully attaching the treasure to lift bags—the vinyl-coated nylon satchels—that did the hard work of floating the riches to the surface.

He wasn't surprised his partners hadn't managed to haul up the last of the booty before they'd been forced to call it quits. No doubt the setting sun had combined with the wave action to make visibility impossible. But he *was* surprised to hear LT add, "And to make matters worse, looks like Julia's gonna hit us after all."

The hairs on Doc's arms lifted in warning. "I thought the meteorologists said she was only going to skim us with her outer edges."

"Apparently she changed her mind and changed directions." LT made a face. "New projections say she'll smack us head-on before turnin' to make landfall somewhere around New Orleans."

"Fuck," Mason muttered. The man was a born and raised Bostonian. When he *did* deign to speak, it was a safe bet the F-bomb would be involved.

"She's currently a Category 2, but they're estimatin' she'll be a 3 by the time she reaches us," LT continued, and Doc gave his earlobe an anxious tug.

As a bona fide landlubber, he'd never gotten comfortable with the tropical storms that crashed through the Straits of Florida and the Gulf of Mexico. Luckily, in the time he'd lived on Wayfarer Island, the biggest hurricane he'd had to weather had topped out at a Category 1.

Even then, he shuddered to remember how the rain hadn't fallen from the sky so much as it'd been flung through the air like watery missiles that'd pummeled his exposed skin. How his hair had whipped around so violently that it'd stung wherever it'd hit his face.

"How much time do we have?" Bran's arm tightened around his wife's shoulders when he asked the question.

"We'll probably start feelin' the winds off her leading edges around noon tomorrow," LT said.

"Which gives us tomorrow morning to finish bringing up what's left of the loot." Bran's concerned expression cleared. "Bada bing, bada boom. Easy peasy."

Bran was a New Jerseyan and couldn't help sounding like an extra off *The Sopranos*.

LT's jaw muscles worked hard against the gum in his mouth. "There's no way we'll be able to outrun the storm in *Wayfarer II* if we wait to leave until the hurricane is almost on top of us. The ship's not fast enough. We'll hafta anchor her on the leeward side of the island and cross our fingers she can ride it out."

"Um." Alex raised her hand, her freckled nose wrinkling. "Is that really the best idea? I mean, what if she sinks? The treasure will go down with her." She frowned. "Not that we couldn't salvage it again. But for the love of all that's holy, what a pain in the ass."

"Which is why I say we sail her to Key West tonight." LT's drawl always grew more pronounced when he was working through a problem.

"And leave what's left of the treasure behind?" One pitch-black eyebrow winged up Wolf's tan forehead. "I know we were thinkin' we got up all but about one, maybe two percent of it today. But two percent of half a billion dollars is still ten million. Are we really okay lettin' the storm come in and scatter ten million benjis across the ocean floor?"

Whereas LT had grown up in New Orleans and spoke with the elongated vowels of the South, Wolf had a twang that was right out of an old Western. He'd spent his formative years on a reservation in northeast Oklahoma.

LT pinned a look on Mia. "You got everything cataloged and recorded at the site for the state, yeah? Everything you need to finish the paperwork?"

The little marine archeologist nodded. "All that's left is to photograph the final pieces once you've brought them up."

LT ran a finger under his chin. "Then I volunteer to stay behind and salvage what's left tomorrow mornin' once the sun's up and I can see what the hell I'm doin' down there. I'll load the loot into Uncle John's catamaran and head west. The sailboat is faster than *Wayfarer II*. I'll sail out of the path of the storm and hang out in calm water until Julia passes. Then we can all meet back here in what? Two days? Three tops?"

Doc opened his mouth to say there was no way in hell he was letting LT stay back to finish salvaging the treasure alone, but Dana interrupted him by asking, "Will the tide still be covering the reef tomorrow morning?"

"Accordin' to the charts it will be," LT assured her. "Plus, Julia will be pushin' the ocean ahead of her. So we should be good to go."

"I'll need to stay to make sure of that, of course," Dana said with a resolute dip of her chin.

"I'm stayin' too," Uncle John piped up. He was dressed in his standard getup of baggy cargo shorts and a Hawaiian shirt that was bright enough to blind a person. "I'm better at sailin' the cat than you are anyway."

When LT opened his mouth to argue, Uncle John—who was technically only LT's biological uncle, but who held the honorary title when it came to the rest of them—lifted a wide, callused hand. "My mind's made up, boy. You know better than to argue with me once that's done."

LT snapped his mouth shut, but a muscle ticked in his jaw.

"I'm staying too," Doc told LT, making sure his tone brooked no argument at the same time he shoved the toothpick back into his mouth. "It'll go faster tomorrow with both of us working."

"And as your lawyer," Cami added, "I'm duty-bound to stay until the very last coin is recovered."

"I'm staying if you're staying," Olivia told LT.

"No." LT shook his head, staring down at his dark-haired wife. "I want you safe in Key West."

Olivia arched an eyebrow. "Safe? The way you tell it, there's no danger. We'll be long gone before Julia hits, right?"

"It's settled then," Doc declared with a decisive nod before LT could throw out any more objections. "The six of us will stay here and finish the job while everyone else makes sure the salvaged ship and the rest of the treasure is hell and gone out of Julia's path."

"Please say we have time to eat before heading to Key West." Alex's Kewpie doll mouth was pursed into a bow. "I'm starving."

"I swear you must have a hollow leg," Chrissy harrumphed.

"Jealous?" Alex wiggled her eyebrows.

"*Yes*," Chrissy declared. But the heat in her voice didn't match the twinkle in her eyes. Chrissy and Alex had become fast friends in the months they'd been working with the Deep Six crew. Probably because they were cut from the same cloth. Both strong-willed. Both independent. Both crazy in love with former fighting men. "Because if I ate half of what you do, I'd weigh six hundred pounds."

Alex shook her head. "Not necessarily. I recently read this interesting article about metabolism that said—"

A font of information. That was Alexandra Merriweather. She chattered on about the article as everyone shuffled out of the computer room, headed to the galley where Bran's famous lasagnas awaited them.

Doc was the last one through the door, but his flip-flops skidded to a halt on the metal decking when he saw Cami standing in the passageway, her head cocked as she stared at him.

"What?" he demanded, ignoring how his heart thudded against his rib cage the instant he realized they were alone.

"I'm wondering why you didn't try to talk me out of staying. You and me, stuck on a sailboat for two, maybe three days? I figured you'd consider that only slightly more appealing than a long walk through the seventh circle of hell."

"Normally that would be true," he admitted. "But I reckon I can pass the time by telling you the latest batch of lawyer jokes I found on the internet. And you'll be too seasick to stop me." He wiggled his eyebrows and the end of the toothpick at the same time.

He expected her to snap and snarl. So he was a little surprised when her wide mouth stretched into a toothy grin. Apprehension had his chin jerking back. "What are you smiling about?"

"Oh, I'm just plotting all the ways I could end you while we're out on that little sailboat in the middle of nowhere."

When she turned and sauntered down the passageway, her hips swishing dramatically, he got the distinct impression the approaching storm was the very *least* of his worries.

CHAPTER 2

11:52 PM...

On the recommendation of a local, William White and his three best friends found themselves at Schooner Wharf Bar in Key West.

"Oysters are good and the beer is better," the old-timer running the souvenir shop had told them.

Will wasn't a fan of Gulf oysters. Too meaty. Too dirty tasting. And their shells were *all stove to hell*, as they liked to say where he was from. A man couldn't suck one of the slimy suckers down the ol' gullet without getting a shard or two of crumbly black junk stuck on his tongue or lips.

Will *far* preferred the clean, bright-tasting eastern oysters found in New England.

But the souvenir shop owner had been spot-on about the beer. It was cold and plentiful, and that's really all Will and his friends cared about. Plus, the band in the corner sang nineties covers, and the clientele was a mix of tourists and Conchs—Will had learned that's what the natives call themselves. So it was a humdinger of a crowd all-in-all.

Not a bad way to spend a few days while the hurricane made its way to the mainland.

And once she's gone, we'll finish what we came down here to do, he thought determinedly, taking a long pull from his pint glass and welcoming the bitter, herbal taste of hops on his tongue.

He barely gave the three guys who grabbed the barstools across from him and his friends a glance when they first sat down. But his ears perked right up when the bartender shambled over to the newcomers and, by way of welcome, asked loudly, "You boys find the *Santa Cristina*'s treasure yet?"

One of the new arrivals, a dark-haired fella who would've looked right at home wearing buckskin and feathers, shook his head and told the bartender, "Not yet. But we're getting closer."

Will glanced meaningfully at Fin, widening his eyes because they both knew the man was lying through his teeth. They had an inside source that assured them the men and women of Deep Six Salvage had located the cache of riches and had planned that very day to bring the treasure up from the ocean floor.

"Julia run you off Wayfarer Island?" the bartender asked the trio.

Another dark-haired dude answered. By the sound of his accent, Will pegged him for a New Yorker. Or maybe a New Jerseyan. "Thought it was best to get *Wayfarer II* out of harm's way. Got her anchored in the marina." The man hitched his chin toward the long dock and piers that ran into the water outside the bar.

Jace shoved an elbow into Will's ribs and it took herculean effort not to grunt. Of the four of them, Jace

24

looked the most like the quintessential New England cod fisherman. He had the full head of wavy hair, the dark beard, the stevedore's build that'd made all the high school hotties spleeny in their younger days.

Then and now, the sonofabitch didn't know his own strength.

Will turned and gave Jace a look that said, *Ayuh. I heard. And how about you go easy on the ribs, eh?* Then he barely refrained from groaning aloud because Brady spoke up, his voice raised theatrically.

"Let's book it after this round!" Brady made a show of downing the beer in his glass. "I'm tired and my hotel bed is callin' my name."

Leaning around Jace's massive frame—Jace and Brady were polar opposites in appearance. As dark and burly as Jace was, that's how blond and spritely Brady was—Will faked a smile at Brady and said through his clenched teeth, "Be cool, man."

"What?" Brady blinked. "I'm cool like ice."

Will rolled his eyes before facing forward again. He had to work hard not to stare at the trio of treasure hunters. He only managed it by concentrating on his beer. *Hard.* So hard anyone looking at him might think the secrets of the universe were floating somewhere inside his pint glass.

Acting was not his forte. It wasn't any of their fortes, come to think of it. And in the ten minutes it took them to finish the pitcher of beer and tab out, he thought it a wonder their body language didn't tell everyone in Schooner Wharf Bar precisely what they'd come to Key West to do.

Namely, pull off a heist.

And who'd a thunk it? Will wondered. Certainly not him. *But desperate times call for desperate measures.*

He and his friends could claim a long line of scrappy New England fishermen as their ancestors. Strong men.

Hardworking men. *Honest* men. But their fathers had begun to struggle even before the four of them graduated high school. Commercial cod fishing had collapsed in their hometown because the persnickety fishes liked cold water, and the Gulf of Maine had been particularly affected by climate change. The water there had risen three degrees in the last decade alone, ninety-nine percent faster than the rest of the oceans.

By the time Will and his buddies were handed their diplomas, there was a distinct lack of opportunity in the area. They'd done the best they could, but it'd been tough to watch as friends and family members, despondent over the lack of jobs, fell victim to the opioid epidemic. And eventually Will and his friends had been forced to move their kids and their wives back into their parents' houses when the cost of a two-bedroom apartment in town exceeded the sixteen dollars per hour they made working at the local cannery.

American Dream my ass! he thought bitterly. The American Dream had driven Jace to try his hand with Lady Luck and bet the deed to his father's house on a horse race. A bet he'd lost, and now here they all were, 2000 miles from home and dead set on turning themselves into criminals.

"It's gotta be on the ship, doncha think?" Fin whispered once they were outside the bar. The warm, moist air smelled familiar, fishy, and it made Fin's auburn curls dance around his head. "I mean, they probably loaded it up and sailed it here to keep it safe from the storm."

"You think they were able to salvage it all in one day?" Brady countered. "The king tide just rolled in last night and—"

"Maybe they didn't get *all* of it," Will was quick to interject. "But we don't want *all* of it, right? We just want some. We just want *enough*."

That was how they'd all rationalized it when Jace came

to them with the plan and begging for their help. They'd leave plenty for the salvors who'd found the loot. *More* than enough.

Jace dragged a hand down his thick beard. "So what do we do now?"

"Let's find the ship first and see what we see." Will gave a decisive jerk of his chin. "*Then* we can decide what comes next, ayuh?"

"Ayuh," all three of his buddies answered.

It didn't take them long to locate the *Wayfarer II*. Most of the vessels anchored in the marina were small fishing boats or pleasure cruisers. The big salvage ship reminded Will of that old *Sesame Street* song. *One of these things is not like the others. One of these things just doesn't belong.*

Adrenaline made his scalp prickle as they slowly made their way down the long pier. The ship's upper hull gleamed a shiny gray in the marina's lights. Her waterline and lower hull were painted a deep, almost blood red. And when the ship's bell rang without the aid of human hands—a bad omen according to pirate superstition—Will ignored the hairs that lifted on the back of his neck.

"She looks deserted," Brady muttered.

Will checked all the windows but couldn't find any sign to make him disagree. Not a single lightbulb burned in the pilot house or lower, in the crew's quarters, galley, or engine room.

"They wouldn't leave all that treasure unattended, would they?" Fin whispered.

"They might if they didn't think anyone would come lookin' for it," Jace countered. "Remember, no one outside their little operation but us and Bernie knows they've actually *located* the treasure."

Bernie Lutz was a fuckup of epic proportions. The dumbest of all Jace's dumbass cousins. A *true* manifestation of a dink—which was the term Mainers used in place of *loser*. But Bernie had certainly come through with this score.

"So what d'ya wanna do?" Brady looked at Will expectantly.

Will was the oldest of the bunch, having been born a whole seven months earlier than Jace, the youngest of them. Which, in the uncomplicated way of children, meant Will had naturally been assigned the role of leader. And he'd maintained that title in all the years since.

"Let's make sure no one's home first," he said.

Brady, always one to jump the gun, cupped his hands around his mouth and yelled, "Ahoy the ship!"

"Jeezum crow, Brady!" Will hissed. "That's not what I meant, and I—"

"Aroooohhh!" A loud bark sounded from the deck and had them all craning their heads up to see the flat, wrinkled face of a disgruntled bulldog. To add to the shock of the moment, the dog's bark was followed by the crow of a rooster. A brightly feathered fowl alighted on the top rung of the deck railing next to the dog.

Apparently, *Wayfarer II* had modeled itself after Noah's Ark.

What's next? Will thought. *A pig? A goat? An elephant?*

"They disembarked about forty-five minutes ago," a low, tired-sounding voice called from behind them.

As a group, Will and his friends turned to the slip next to the *Wayfarer II*. A sixty-something guy stood on the deck of the mid-sized sloop anchored there. He had on slippers and a silk robe that was tied loosely around his waist. Gave off a real Hugh Hefner vibe. "You friends of theirs?" he asked.

"Ayuh." Will was quick to answer. "Heard they'd just pulled into port. We were hopin' to say hello."

Hugh Hefner's twin cocked his head. "You boys are a long way from home. Hail from New England do you?

Maine? Massachusetts? I spent a fair amount of time anchored in North Haven three years ago."

Will's smile was tight. He didn't like the thought of standing out in anyone's mind. He was careful to answer without really answering. "What gave us away? The accent or the Bean boots?"

"Probably both." The man hitched his chin toward the island and added, "Try the Harbor Inn. I overheard the ladies say that's where they're staying for the next couple days."

"Thanks." Will bobbed his head, hoping he looked convivial. *Nothin' untoward here, bub. Appreciate your help and please tie one on tonight so you forget you ever saw us.* "We'll try to catch 'em there."

The man waved a hand and then disappeared through the sailboat's cabin door. Will didn't realize he'd stopped breathing until the sound of the door locking tightly into its frame had him blowing out a blustery breath.

"What now?" Brady whispered from the side of his mouth.

"Now we amble on down the dock a piece like we're headin' to that hotel," Will said quietly. "Once that old fart is asleep, we come back, board that ship, and take what we came to take."

"Think it'll be that easy?" Fin asked.

Will gave the only answer he could. "Lord, I hope so."

CHAPTER 3

The Following Day
11:23 AM...

Cami stood on the end of the long pier that jutted into Wayfarer Island's blue lagoon.

Er...the lagoon *used* to be blue.

The approaching storm's surge had piled the waves over the reef, churning up the sand and silt at the bottom of the shallow body of water and turning the surface a milky-looking gray that was dotted with tufts of white seafoam. The air was heavy with the smell of the sea and burned ozone. Not all hurricanes were preceded by lightning, but Julia had been putting on a show for the last hour.

Craning her head over her shoulder, Cami shuddered at the scene that met her desperate gaze. The storm's towering outer wall obliterated the horizon, and the ocean in front of the hurricane looked fuzzy, distorted by harsh bands of rain. A bright, twisted hand of heaven sizzled through the bank of clouds, seeming all the more sinister because she couldn't hear the accompanying *crack* of sound.

"Come on. *Come on!*" she whispered impatiently, turning back to see the divers climbing the swim ladder at the back of the catamaran. "Come *on!*" she said louder when none of the wetsuited individuals seemed determined to get a move on.

I mean, seriously? she thought uncharitably. *Can't you wait to take off your tanks and swim fins until* after *you've come to get me?*

Doc, LT, and Olivia had been at it since daybreak, working in what could only be described as *unfavorable conditions* to haul up the last of the *Santa Cristina*'s storied treasure. Dana, the bubbly FMC employee, had dutifully remained on the sailboat's deck, fulfilling her role as witness to the legality of the salvage. And Uncle John had been the one to captain the vessel, fighting the ever-angrier ocean in a bid to keep the catamaran positioned correctly for the divers below.

As for Cami? She'd been assigned the role of weathergirl, tasked with staying back at the beach house to monitor the marine channels for storm updates and to keep an eye on Julia via the island's lone laptop for as long as the satellite internet connection held.

And why is it weathergirl? she wondered irritably. *If the person reporting on the barometer has dangly bits, he's a weatherman. So why isn't the term for his female counterpart weatherwoman?*

Or better yet, weatherperson?

Misogyny and the patriarchy hard at work, she decided. *Even here in the twenty-first century.*

And yes, she was purposefully distracting herself from her current situation. Because twice she'd radioed out to Uncle John to inform him Julia had picked up speed. Twice Uncle John had assured her they were almost finished and ready to come get her. And twice he'd called back a couple of minutes later to say, *"Scratch that. Hang on a bit longer. They got a few more items to collect."*

To say Cami was feeling antsy was an understatement. By the time Uncle John had radioed in to tell her it was finally time for her to meet them on the pier, her pacing had cut a path in the beach house's floorboards through the furniture they'd stacked the night before.

The satellite images of the hurricane made it look beautiful. Sweet even. Like the swirl of buttercream icing atop a cupcake. But Cami knew looks were deceiving.

Julia was no confectioner's creation. She was a three-hundred-mile wide roiling ball of wind, water, and fury. And like a bullet that'd been fired from the end of a gun, she was coming. There wasn't a damn thing anyone could do to stop her.

"Oh, thank Christ," Cami breathed when she saw Uncle John point the sailboat's nose toward the break in the reef.

Her relief was short-lived, however. Watching the sailboat lifted aloft on the crest of a wave only to then see it be plunged down into a frothing, watery trough was enough to make her seasick despite standing on the sturdy boards of the pier.

"Erp." She lifted a hand to her mouth when her breakfast threatened a second act.

She'd known it would be rough sailing when she volunteered to stay behind for the last of the salvage. But she hadn't known it would be *this* rough.

Digging into her small overnight bag, she pulled out the package of Dramamine Doc had given her. She'd downed one pill on the jog from the beach house to the pier. But looking at the outraged ocean, she knew one pill wasn't going to cut it. Unless, of course, she wanted to spend her time on the catamaran hanging over the railing and puking her guts into the sea.

Carefully placing the chalky-white disk on her tongue, she did her best to choke it down without benefit of water. Unfortunately, the sucker lodged in the middle of her throat like it came equipped with a set of fishhooks. By the time she managed to work it down her esophagus, she'd used up all the spit in her mouth and the sailboat had motored up to the end of the pier.

Doc, all six-and-a-half lean, mean feet of him, jumped from the deck of the catamaran to tie off the boat just as the wind began to sing. It was a low, melancholy moan that had the hairs on the back of Cami's neck standing stick straight.

Doc's too-long, forever-in-need-of-a-barber hair whipped around his face. The strands were darkened by seawater, but when they were dry they were a combination of colors that spanned the spectrum from medium brown to deep auburn to sandy blond.

He was the calico cat of the Navy SEAL/marine salvor/ arrogant-pain-in-the-ass world. And why she should find his lion's mane so fascinating was anyone's guess. But aside from his eyes, which were sea green and annoyingly enigmatic, and aside from his smile, which was wide and a little crooked, his wild head of hair was her favorite thing about him.

And my least favorite thing about him? she thought. *That's easy. He's a client.*

Camilla D'Angelo never mixed business with pleasure. It was her one hard and fast rule. And she'd always found it easy to follow.

Until Doc came along.

What she wouldn't give to go back to the night they met, before either of them had known who the other was. When she'd simply been a tourist out looking for a good time, and he'd simply been the golden god sitting across the bar. A stranger with a face like a slab of granite that'd been carved by the wind and rain and a look in his eye that told her he knew what it was to suffer.

That's what had prompted her to hop down from her barstool and go introduce herself to him. She'd always been a sucker for a guy who showed a little wear and tear.

And boy oh boy, they'd had fun that night.

Not as much fun as she would've *liked*, considering he'd passed out on the floor of her hotel room before he could make good on all the things his drunken kiss had promised.

But fun all the same.

And then, in the light of day, she'd discovered he wasn't simply a tall drink of water who went by the succinct nickname of *Doc*. He was Dalton Simmons of Deep Six Salvage. Which meant she was his attorney. And *that* meant he was completely off-limits.

Although, even if she had been one to mix business with pleasure, she got the distinct impression Doc would have put the kibosh on anything more between them. All his smoldering looks, dirty innuendos, and flirty smiles aside, ever since he'd learned she was a lawyer, he'd made it clear he held her chosen profession—and *her* by association—in the lowest regard.

And yes, okay, *most* people didn't have very high opinions of those who practiced the law. She blamed slimeballs like Roy Cohn and Rod Blagojevich for painting the lot of them as power hungry con artists. And yet, with Doc, she couldn't help thinking there was more behind his derision.

But whatevs.

Because the long and short of it was they both had their reasons for not finishing what they'd started that first night. And since they couldn't engage in the physical free-for-alls she fantasized about on a weekly basis—*okay, nightly; it was nightly*—she satisfied herself with their verbal skirmishes.

Never in her life had she met anyone with a mind more agile than Doc's. Trying to keep up with him, trying to *best* him, gave her a thrill like no other.

The wind had gone from singing to sounding like the ominous opening score of a horror movie. Where the noise alone lets you know something truly awful is about to happen.

Adjusting the shoulder strap on her overnight bag, she reached a hand toward Doc, needing his help to steady herself as she prepared to step onto the sailboat's undulating...*erp*... deck.

Instead of grabbing her outstretched fingers, however, Doc shook his head. "It's too late!" he shouted above the sound of the waves slapping against the pier's pilings. "The storm's too close! We can't outrun her! We're staying!"

"St-staying!" she sputtered, glancing back at the ramshackle beach house.

She'd heard people use the phrase *my heart sank*. But she'd never experienced the sensation herself. She'd had her heart bruised a few times. And it'd been *broken* twice—the first time when she found out the truth about her father, and the second time when her mother called to tell her that her baby sister had died in a plane crash. But now, she would swear her heart was sitting in the soles of her feet.

"We're staying *here*?" she demanded incredulously. "Are you out of your whole damn mind?"

"Better here than out on the water!" Doc shouted as LT appeared on the sailboat's deck. The head of Deep Six Salvage had a heavy-looking duffel bag thrown over each shoulder. Four more were already piled on the teakwood decking at his feet.

"Catch!" he yelled and Cami realized he was talking to *her* a split-second before one of the blue duffels sailed in her direction.

She squealed but managed to snag the bag before it could hit the weathered boards of the pier. It was even heavier than it looked. Its impact knocked her off-balance and she stepped back to steady herself.

Too late she realized she'd stepped into thin air.

Her right foot was planted firmly on the wooden decking, but her left foot dangled over nothing but fractious waves.

Screwing her eyes shut, she clutched the bag of treasure close to her chest and prepared for the inevitable—a hard crash into the lagoon followed by a struggle to tread water until someone could pull her back onto the pier. But suddenly, inexplicably, her downward momentum stopped.

When she opened her eyes, she saw Doc bent over the side of the pier. He held onto a post with one hand. The other was firmly wrapped around the front waistband of her linen camp pants. She could feel the heat of his bare knuckles pressing against the skin of her lower belly.

Isn't that a weird thing to notice at a time like this? she thought absently as she quickly replaced her dangling foot back onto the pier.

Probably not as weird as noticing how his shoulder muscles flexed with the effort of keeping them both from tumbling into the water.

But his wetsuit fits him like a second skin. How could I not get distracted by all that twisted steel and sex appeal?

All this rumination happened in a split second, of course. Because, with a grunt and heave, Doc pulled her up and into the circle of his arms.

The duffel was between their upper bodies. Her overnight bag hung heavy against her hip. But there was nothing separating their lower halves. Her feet slipped next to his. Their thighs interlocked. And she could feel the uncompromising strength of his legs.

That and the bulge of what he kept *between* them.

Despite the buffeting of the cool wind, every inch of her skin caught fire. Every. Single. Inch. Including her cheeks. Which was why, when she glanced up into his face—*way* up because she was a full foot shorter than he was—she wasn't surprised to find one eyebrow winged up his forehead and that crooked smirk tilting his mouth.

She *hated* that he knew what he did to her. Hated it more that she couldn't help blushing like a schoolgirl around him. But what she hated most of all? His ability to render her speechless with nothing more than a look or a salacious word.

His tone was arrogant when he leaned forward and whispered into her ear, "I'd say this is the part where you thank me for saving you from getting wet." He shifted his leg slightly so that his muscled thigh pressed tight against the juncture of her legs. Her kneecaps nearly liquified. "Except…" His breath was hot against the side of her face. "I think it's too late for that."

She gasped and stumbled out of his embrace.

"Oh!" She snarled at him. "How has no one hit you over the head with a tire iron yet?"

Instead of getting offended, he threw back his head and laughed.

There for a moment, when she'd been safe in his arms, the rest of the world had disappeared. She hadn't heard the gale. She hadn't felt the gusts swirling around her. She hadn't noticed the waves lapping high under the pier. All she'd heard was his deep, raspy voice. All she'd felt was his big body fitted tight against hers. All she'd seen was the seductive, cavalier, downright *cocky* twinkle in his eyes.

It was infuriating how he could make her forget the world. Forget herself. Forget *everything*. eHH

Lifting her voice above the chaos, she snapped, "You

can spend the rest of your life being a dickhole! But since we're about to have to ride out a hurricane in a decrepit old beach house that'll probably blow down around us, I would appreciate it very much if you would take the day off!"

"That beach house has weathered dozens of hurricanes!" LT assured her, tossing the second duffel to Doc, who caught it like it weighed no more than a feather. *Grr.* "She'll weather this one too! Don't you worry!"

Cami didn't respond. What good would it do? They were stuck on the island for the duration and there was nothing she could do or say to change that.

Uncle John darted out of the sailboat's pilot house to help Dana onto the pier. After the FMC employee got her land legs under her, he carefully handed her a third duffel bag.

Olivia was next. She hopped off the catamaran in her wetsuit with the grace and reflexes of a cat. Or a ballerina. *Or maybe a ninja is a better description.*

Cami wondered if the woman had been trained by the CIA to move like that, or if she'd been recruited by the CIA *because* she could move like that.

"Toss one to me!" Olivia yelled to her husband, and LT didn't hesitate to lob a fourth duffel her way. Olivia caught it easily, and all Cami could think was *double grr.*

LT shouldered the remaining two duffels before stepping off the bobbing boat. Without dropping either bag, he untied the catamaran and tossed the securing line back onto the sailboat's deck. A few moments later, Uncle John engaged the engines.

Cami blinked. "Wait! Where's he going?"

"Sailin' her around to the leeward side!" LT explained. "He'll get her anchored and then take the dinghy to shore! Don't worry! This ain't his first rodeo!"

Cami had lived in Miami for years, so Julia wasn't her

first hurricane either. But for the love of god, she'd always evacuated when the weathermen…weather*persons*…told her she should. She'd never tried, never *wanted* to try, to ride out a storm.

Doc must've read the mounting horror on her face because he shoved a toothpick into his mouth—where it'd come from she had no idea; she'd begun to think he conjured the suckers from thin air—and winked at her. "Chin up! This'll be a piece of cake!"

Her scalp prickled with foreboding. "Famous last words," she muttered.

"What?" he yelled. Her reply had been lost on the wind.

Before she could respond, the rain began.

It wasn't a slow drizzle or even a soft shower. It was an instant deluge that drenched everything it touched and made it impossible to see more than a few feet ahead.

"Fuck my life!" she howled before securing the duffel's strap over her shoulder and turning to run down the pier.

Her footfalls made loud thumping noises on the unvarnished boards, and the sound of thunder followed in her wake.

No. Not thunder.

That was the rumble of four people hot on her heels.

When she hit the beach, her sandals sank into the sand and made her feel like she was running in slow motion. Her overnight bag thudded hard against her hip. And there was something sharp in the duffel bag that tried to poke a hole through her ribs. She didn't dare slow down to adjust it. Gritting her teeth, she pressed on and did her best to ignore the pain.

The palm trees dotting the island rattled, their bushy heads waving to and fro. Soon they would be bent nearly sideways, straining desperately to keep hold of the ground. Already, torn palm fronds fluttered in the swirling air.

Cami pounded up the porch steps, grateful for the roof that provided an instant reprieve from the driving rain and slammed back the two dead-bolt locks on the front door. Throwing it open, she ran inside.

With the windows sealed tight by hurricane shutters, and the generator turned off in preparation for the storm—that'd been her last task before heading to the pier—there was no light in the house. No light and absolutely *no* ventilation. The air was already warm and moist and stagnant. Even soaked by the rain, she could feel sweat pop out on her skin.

"Whew!" Doc shook his head like a dog shaking off water. Droplets showered Cami's face and she threw up her hands to ward them off.

"Hey!" she complained, and then wished she hadn't when he stopped doing his best impression of a Labrador retriever and gifted her with an impish grin.

"Seriously?" The end of his toothpick angled down and seemed to mock her. "You look like a drowned rat and you're whining about—"

"I realized it didn't make any sense as soon as the *hey* came out of my mouth," she interrupted. "I'm a little keyed up right now. So maybe go against every instinct you have and cut me some slack, okay?"

His lips—those lips she knew could be soft and firm in equal measure—twisted. "Now where's the fun in that?"

It was his favorite retort.

Or maybe it was the Deep Six Salvage crew's moto, because they all seemed to use it.

"Where do you want the treasure?" Dana Levine asked, which provided Cami a welcome distraction from Doc's magnetic gaze.

"Upstairs," LT answered as he ushered Olivia into the house ahead of him. "The storm surge might reach the bottom level."

"Oh, god." The hairs on Cami's arms lifted at the thought of cowering upstairs while the downstairs flooded. Already the house creaked and groaned, seeming to catch its breath in an attempt to gird itself for what was to come.

"Olivia and I will secure the bags. The rest of y'all gather candles, canned goods, and dry food. We need to fill whatever we can find with fresh water to use for drinking and for flushing the toilet, because who knows if the water tank will survive the storm."

Wayfarer Island's fresh drinking water was housed in a tank on stilts. Which meant those who lived there didn't need a pump. Gravity did the trick of delivering the H_2O to the house. But that also meant the water tank was susceptible to high winds.

"We'll hunker down on the second floor until Julia's well on her way to the mainland." LT finished, making a come-hither motion with his fingers toward the duffel Cami held.

She gratefully handed over the bag, wincing and hissing when whatever had been stabbing into her side sliced painfully across her rib cage.

"What the hell?" Doc absently thrust his duffel at LT while stomping in Cami's direction. "What happened to you?" he demanded.

She shrugged off her overnight bag so she could look down at her side. Two things met her gaze. One, her casual cotton T-shirt was bloody. Two, it'd also gone *completely* see-through, thanks to the rain.

Why had she chosen to wear her most functional and least appealing bra today? Oh, right. Because she hadn't thought anyone would *see* it.

Without so much as a by-your-leave, Doc grabbed the hem of her T-shirt and exposed her entire right side.

"Excuse me?" She slapped at his wide-palmed hand.

"How many times do I have to remind you you're not *my* doctor? Unhand me, villain!"

"Hush, woman." His gravelly voice was low and firm. "How'd you get this?" he demanded.

She ducked her chin to see a small puncture wound between her ribs. Beside it was a short, bloody scrape. "Well, which is it? Do you want me to hush or do you want me to tell you how I got this?"

The look he leveled on her could only be described as irritated.

"Something in the duffel stabbed me," she relented, pointing to the offending blue bag.

LT had already shouldered the duffel, but he easily lifted it off his arm and held it by its strap. Down low on one side, a rusty-looking triangle protruded from the blue nylon.

"It's that ruby-handled dagger we found," LT said.

Doc grimaced. "And its blade is all kinds of nasty. Come on." He grabbed Cami's hand. "We need to get you cleaned up so you don't get infected."

"Wait," she protested, tugging against his grip. It quickly became clear he had no intention of letting her go. And why that should simultaneously give her a thrill and make her mad enough to spit nails was anyone's guess. "We need to help Dana with the supplies and—"

"I'm fine," Dana interrupted, proving herself a complete waste of space when it came to helping a sister escape the clutches of a determined man. "I'll start gathering everything up. John can help me once he gets back. You kids go take care of that cut. It looks like it hurts."

Cami's shoulders slumped in defeat. But that didn't keep her from muttering unkind things about Doc's parentage as he dragged her upstairs and into the bathroom.

It was pitch black inside the cramped space. Miraculously, Doc was able to locate the matches the Deep

Six crew kept on the back of the toilet. He had the three-wick candle sitting in the windowsill lit a handful of seconds later.

"Sit," he told her, pointing to the closed toilet seat lid.

She considered raising her hackles and telling him she wasn't a dog, so there was no need for him to think he could give her orders. But then she decided the quicker she complied, the quicker they could be finished.

And the quicker I can escape this stuffy bathroom.

She could smell that unique scent that always lingered on Doc's skin. It was pine trees and clean mountain air, like his childhood home had imprinted itself into his very cells. And she would swear she could feel his body heat reaching out to her. Curling around her. Rubbing against her.

As if he could read her mind and thought to torment her further, he said, "Hang tight for a sec."

Before she could object, he unzipped the top half of his wetsuit and peeled his arms from the sleeves. He let the empty upper half dangle down behind him. And in the low glow of the candle flame, she got an up close and real, *real* personal view of his tanned torso.

Doc wasn't meticulously cut like Romeo. He didn't have Mason's thick, bulging muscles. What he *did* have was a body that was long and lean and startlingly beautiful.

He was built like an Olympic water polo player. His shoulders were wide. His pectoral muscles were large and well-defined. And his stomach was flat and corrugated.

Unlike a water polo player, he hadn't done away with his body hair. It grew in a brown mat across his chest.

Nestled between his pecs was a silver coin. A piece of eight it was called. All the Deep Six guys wore one. But Cami only pictured what it would be like to have Doc's dangling above her face while he thrust into her.

That little fantasy had her eyes following his body hair as it arrowed toward his waist. Then, farther, as it became a love trail that led to…

Gulp.

He was semi-erect. The wetsuit made it impossible not to notice.

Her body instantly responded. Her skin flushed. Her nipples furled. And despite her best efforts to keep it inside, she gasped quietly.

When Doc chuckled, it was just the bucket of cold water she needed to snap her out of her trance. Ripping her eyes away from his—ahem—*impressive* bulge, she looked up to find him staring down at her, one ever-mobile eyebrow quirked up his forehead.

"See something you like?" He'd lowered his voice until it was little more than a provocative rasp.

This was usually the moment when she went tongue-tied. But maybe it was her fear of the approaching storm, or maybe she was getting used to his flirting, because, to her surprise, she was quick to admit, "I think I made that obvious the first night we met. But like I've told you a million times, I don't shop for meat at the same store that's selling me bread. And besides"—she tilted her head—"you've been very clear that you're all talk and no action when it comes to…" She paused for dramatic effect. "*Amorous congress.*"

He sputtered, "That's just with *you.*"

"Right." She nodded. "Because I'm a lawyer and, as far as you're concerned, that makes me the lowest form of human life."

He didn't contradict her. Not that she thought he would. But, you know, there was always the *hope*. Instead, he turned toward the medicine cabinet.

She sullenly watched him pull out a bag of cotton balls, some antibiotic ointment, and a box of Band-Aids.

"Don't forget the peroxide." She pointed to the brown bottle he'd left sitting on the shelf.

"Contrary to popular belief"—he arranged his haul around the sink before washing his hands in a meticulous manner that reminded her he'd been weeks away from finishing his residency in family medicine at Johns Hopkins before quitting and joining the Navy—"peroxide can actually harm the tissues around an open wound and delay healing. It's best to clean fresh lacerations with mild soap and warm water before bandaging them."

She frowned. "My mom used peroxide for *everything*. Got a scrape? Peroxide. Earache? Peroxide. Bad breath? Peroxide."

He chuckled and the low, warm sound seemed to bypass her ears to swirl around in her chest. "Your mom, my mom, *every* mom who grew up before the invention of the internet and that amazing piece of technological wizardry known as Google."

Kneeling on the tile floor next to her, he reached for the hem of her shirt. "May I?"

"Oh, *now* you feel the need to ask?"

He rolled his eyes. "Just hold the damn candle so I can see what I'm doing."

Dutifully, she did as he asked, and then hissed and tried not to flinch when he tucked the hem of her T-shirt into the side band of her bra so he could pass the bar of Dove soap over her wounded flesh.

"Sorry." His scratchy Kiefer Sutherland voice sounded particularly intimate in the close confines of the bathroom. "We're halfway there."

True to his word, he quickly rinsed, medicated, and bandaged her puncture and scratch. But even after he let her shirt fall back into place, he didn't immediately jump to his feet.

Instead, he stayed on his knees, which put him at eye level. She wasn't sure if it was the light from the candle

45

playing tricks on her, or if she was really seeing a spark of regret in his eyes.

"I don't think you're the lowest form of human life," he said softly. "I think your choice of careers is questionable, but you? As a person? No." He shook his head, and she had such an urge to run her fingers through his messy hair that she had to put the candle back on the windowsill so she could sit on her hands.

Her own voice was scratchy when she asked, "Are you ever going to tell me *why* you hate lawyers so much?"

He was quiet for a while, which gave her time to study his face. The candle flame threw his features into harsh relief. The hollows under his high cheekbones looked more pronounced. The shape of his wide, full mouth appeared more perfect. The jut of his chin seemed more stubborn and unyielding. But most fascinatingly of all, the candlelight made the stubble across his chin and cheeks sparkle.

She'd always thought him good-looking, in a craggy, windblown, and weathered sort of way—he definitely had a young Clint Eastwood thing going. But in the light from the candle, he reminded her of some ethereal creature. He was just so fiercely *beautiful*.

Finally he spoke. "What does it matter? It's not like it'll change anything. You've said a hundred times you don't mix business with pleasure."

She felt her eyebrows pinch together. "I'm not going to be your lawyer for much longer. You realize that, right?"

She would swear the air between them began to vibrate. And the silence inside the little bathroom was a stark contrast to the wind outside, which screamed around the house as if it was furious the structure had the gall to exist.

When he finally shoved to a stand, he did it so quickly her chin jerked back. "It doesn't matter. I can't... *We* can't..." He raked a hand through his hair before gritting his teeth together so hard his jaw muscles flexed.

He wasn't looking at her. She got the feeling he *couldn't* look at her.

Although she couldn't fathom why.

Lord knew she couldn't rip her eyes off *him*.

"*Why* can't we?" she finally asked.

His harsh green stare pinned her then, and she was reminded of her sister's third grade science fair project. Carlotta had collected every beetle native to New York and affixed the dead bugs to a large piece of cardboard with pushpins. Doc's gaze made Cami feel like one of those bugs.

"Because I *want* it too much," he said through a clenched jaw.

Before she could ask him what the hell *that* was supposed to mean, he ripped open the bathroom door and stomped into the hallway. His footfalls were loud on the wooden stairs, and it sounded like he was taking them two at a time as he headed for the first floor.

She realized her heart was fluttering and pressed a hand against her chest in a bid to slow it down.

Why do I suddenly feel like Julia isn't what I should be most worried about?

CHAPTER 4

12:14 PM...

Doc was in the middle of helping Dana load a plastic laundry basket with canned goods and packages of Pop-Tarts from the pantry when he heard Cami walk into the kitchen. He didn't turn to look at her.

He *couldn't*.

He wasn't brave enough to see the question in her dark, hypnotic eyes. A question he knew she would ask aloud if he gave her the opportunity. A question he wasn't prepared to answer because he'd revealed too much already.

He blamed his verbal diarrhea/momentary madness on the swiftness with which she'd admitted to wanting him. The easiness with which she'd suggested they might act on all the chemistry bubbling between them once her stint acting as his attorney was over.

Although maybe he shouldn't have been surprised by her candor.

The legal profession had a well-earned reputation for subterfuge and obfuscation. But in all the months he'd known Cami, not once had he known her to equivocate.

Quite the opposite. Every conversation he'd had with Camilla D'Angelo had been punctuated by a directness that'd left him feeling as if he'd just breathed in a lungful of fresh air and simultaneously suffered a massive myocardial infarction.

The latter was a direct result of him liking her. Like, *liking* her, liking her.

He hadn't *like* liked a woman since Lily.

Lily...

His wife's name echoed inside the confines of his skull and caused the chasm inside his chest to fill with a familiar ache.

It would've been one thing if he'd simply lusted after Cami. Lusting after her was a given since the woman had the kind of beauty that slammed into a guy like a herd of stampeding buffalo. Her face? *Pow!* A combination of Kim Kardashian and Nina Dobrev. Her body? *Wham!* She was the definition of a brick shithouse, with curves so killer it was hard to imagine they were real.

It was amazing his right forearm wasn't twice the size of his left; he'd been giving it quite the workout since he'd met her.

But as sexy as she was, it was her *mind* that really held him in thrall. Her quick sense of humor and snappy comebacks that riveted him and had him coming back for more.

And. That. Right. There. Was why he couldn't take her up on her offer of how things could progress once she was no longer employed by Deep Six Salvage. Because if he *did* take her up on it, if he allowed his fantasies to become reality, then *liking* her and *lusting* after her might grow into something more.

He wasn't ready for something more.

He'd convinced himself he never would be.

Of course, that wasn't to say he'd been a monk in the years since his wife had been taken from him. Au contraire. He'd gone about as far in the *other* direction as a man could go. Burying his grief in a long line of charming, sympathetic women whose names, he was sorry to say, he hadn't bothered to add to the ol' memory banks.

And even though he hadn't been happy—how did *anyone* find happiness after suffering such a loss?—he'd been resigned. Resigned to the idea of being alone. Reconciled with the knowledge he'd never become a father. Accepting of the fact that the sweetest part of his life was behind him even though his newfound windfall meant he'd be able to purchase the ranch he'd been dreaming about since he was a kid. Because, really, what was a thousand acres of pristine cattle country in the coveted Ninemile Valley without the love of his life by his side to share it?

And then Cami had arrived on the scene and things had started to change. *He* had started to change. He'd started to wonder *what if?*

What if all the dreams he'd had as a kid still had a chance to come true? What if there was more of the good life left to live?

But all those what-ifs felt wrong in a million different ways. Which was why he did his best to ignore them. And by association, ignore any possibility of exploring anything more with Cami.

"Anyone mind if I have this last bit of coffee?" she asked, and he finally chanced a glance in her direction.

There wasn't a question in her eyes like he'd thought there'd be. Or if there was, it was camouflaged by weariness. The poor woman looked wrung out.

They'd all been living off adrenaline since they started hauling up the treasure. And with the addition of the approaching hurricane, it was no wonder her limbic system was trying to shut down and encourage her to sleep through the chaos that was to come.

And it was going to be chaos. There was no doubt of that. As unconcerned as he was acting, that's all it was. An *act*.

Maybe it was growing up in Montana, where a spring rain could bring down the side of a mountain or a winter storm could bury you in four feet of snow in a matter of hours, but he had a singular respect for Mother Nature. And there was no question that she was at her most impressive, and certainly her most volatile, when she'd gone and conjured up a hurricane.

Probably should've voiced a nay *instead of a* yay *earlier*, he thought regretfully. Then he winced when it occurred to him Cami had been the only one left out of the decision-making process on Uncle John's catamaran.

When it'd become clear they either had to abandon the last two loads of treasure to beat the hurricane out of Dodge or haul up what was left of the loot and ride out the storm in the beach house, those aboard had taken a vote. But with the clock ticking, they hadn't thought to radio in and invite Cami to join their impromptu assemblage.

It was a glaring oversight. He tried to make it up to her now by saying, "It's all yours. As long as you don't mind that it's cold."

"As stuffy as it is in here"—she pulled out the collar of her stained T-shirt—"I'd love if it were iced."

When she opened the freezer door, it burped out a puff of cold air despite the power to the house having been shut off. Finding an icetray still full, she shot a triumphant fist in the air.

"Score!" She dumped the cubes into a Mason jar and poured the last of the coffee over the ice. Then she took a long, luxurious drink and Doc found himself distracted by the hollow at the base of her throat. He had a sudden and nearly overwhelming urge to flick his tongue inside. "Ahh," she sighed happily, wiping the back of her hand over her mouth. "That's good coffee."

Her New York accent slipped through on that last word, turning coffee into *caw-fee*. He'd noticed that only happened when she was well and truly beat.

"Must not have been made by Uncle John, then," he told her.

John preferred chicory coffee. Which, in Doc's opinion, tasted like dirt. Literal dirt. As if he'd walked outside and taken a bite out of the compost pile John kept on hand to fertilize his marijuana plants.

"Speak of the devil and he shall appear," he added when Uncle John burst through the back door, drenched to the bone but with his hair and beard all wild and windblown.

A gust of warm, soggy air followed John into the kitchen, causing the paper calendar attached to the side of the refrigerator to flap like a dazed bat. Two of the four candles Dana had lit and arranged around the room were instantly snuffed out.

"Lord almighty!" John swore, and the sound of the door slamming tight against its frame was a small comfort considering the wind outside was absolutely *wailing*.

"I'm pantin' like a lizard on a rock," he added in his Southern-fried way while smoothing one hand over his flyaway hair and using the other to tame his salt-and-pepper beard. "Reckon I should cut back on the weed?" Before any of them could answer, he shook his head. "Nah. That's just crazy talk. And speakin' of crazy, there's a ship out there. Saw its outline in the water when I was draggin' the dinghy up the beach. Looks like a trawler."

Doc handed the laundry basket to Dana so he could relight the smoking candles. "Why didn't they put into port somewhere?" he wondered aloud.

"Beats me." John shrugged one soaked shoulder. The rain hadn't muted the colors of his shirt. Inexplicably, it'd made the pattern even *more* eye-bleeding. "But we better radio out to 'em and offer a place to shelter. Soon everything that ain't nailed down is gonna start flyin'."

When John marched toward the living room, Doc grabbed the two newly lit candles and fell into step behind him. He nearly caught the back of Uncle John's hair on fire when John stopped suddenly to place a work-roughened hand on Dana's shoulder. "How you holdin' up, darlin'?"

Doc glanced over his shoulder at Cami and mouthed *darlin'*?

She widened her eyes and shrugged.

Turning back, he caught Dana's reply. "Don't worry about me, John. I'm fine."

"'Course you are. Never doubted it for a minute." Uncle John nodded and took the loaded laundry basket from Dana's hands to set it on the kitchen table. "There's time for that later. For now, let's find out what the hell's wrong with those fishermen that they aren't bellied up to a bar somewhere and havin' themselves a good old-fashioned hurricane party."

When Dana smiled and took the arm John offered her, Doc found himself blinking in consternation. At sixty-five, Uncle John still turned the heads of the women in Key West. They flirted and fluttered their lashes at him. And when John was in the mood, he took them up on what they were offering. But he wasn't gooey about it.

And he definitely didn't use endearments.

But maybe things with Dana are different? Doc thought curiously. *Maybe he's rethinking his stance on remaining single for life?*

Of course, trying to picture Uncle John in a domestic arrangement required more imagination than Doc possessed. John Anderson was the bacheloriest of bachelors. The man lived on tuna salad, macaroni and cheese, and chicory coffee. His evening routine consisted of downing a Salty Dog or burning a joint filled with his own homegrown bud— sometimes both. And his favorite pastime was napping in the hammock in the front yard.

Doc was pulled from his musings when Uncle John pulled down the wooden chair stacked on top of the desk they kept in the corner of the living room. Usually the desk was highly sought-after property since it housed the island's lone laptop, their main connection to the outside world— cell phone service was nothing but a dream this far out. But it wasn't the computer John reached for. It was the small marine radio sitting next to it.

Doc set one candle on the desk and another on the windowsill and watched John fiddle with the knobs on the battery-powered radio before lifting the handset to his mouth. "This is Wayfarer Island callin' the trawler off my west side. Do you copy? Over."

When John lifted his thumb off the push-to-talk button, the radio's speaker crackled with white noise. John frowned and tried again. "Wayfarer Island callin' the trawler off my west bank. You pickin' me up? Please respond. Over."

Static.

"That's weird," John muttered. "Wonder if their radio's out or—"

He was cut off by a tinny-sounding voice from the speaker. "Ayuh. We copy you, Wayfarer Island. We...uh... thought the place was deserted. Over."

"Copy that," John was quick to respond. "We probably shoulda deserted, but it's too late now. What the hell y'all doin' out in this mess? Over."

For the third time, the speaker fell silent except for the hissing sound of open airwaves. John glanced over his shoulder to catch Doc's eye. The look on his face said, *You pickin' up a weird vibe?*

Doc nodded. The captain of the ship should've been overjoyed to hear a friendly voice. Instead, it sounded like whoever was on the other end of the line was surprised, and maybe a little unsettled, to be talking to them.

Finally, the captain answered. "We ran into some engine trouble yesterday. We were dead in the water for about ten hours. Just got her fixed up this morning, and we were hoping to outrun Julia. But she picked up speed and here we are. Over."

Doc realized the muscles in his shoulders had tensed when they suddenly relaxed. What he'd thought was hesitation in the captain's voice was obviously stress. Being stuck in an engineless fishing boat in the path of a Category 3 hurricane was enough to put the fear of god into any man. Even a seasoned seaman.

"Copy that," Uncle John said into the handset. "Well, y'all got a workin' dinghy? You should anchor away and come on to shore. We'll put a roof over your heads until this bitch blows by. Over."

"Uh, that's a negative," the captain came back immediately. "We can't risk losing the boat. We'll stay with her to make sure she makes it. But we'll shelter as best we can here on your leeward side. Over."

"Don't seem like the smartest move, if you ask me," John was quick to object. "If your engine's already on the fritz, you'd best pack up and head on in. Over."

"Appreciate your honesty," came the reply. "But we've made up our minds. Over."

John sat back in the chair and shook his head. "Damn

fools," he muttered. "A boat can be replaced. A life can't." But he didn't say any of this to the captain of the ship when he lifted the handset and depressed the push-to-talk button. "Copy that. We're here if you change your mind. In either case, godspeed, sailor. Over."

"To you too," came the reply. "Over."

John tossed the handset onto the desktop and shook his head again. "Well, I tried."

"That's all you can do." Dana placed a comforting hand on his shoulder.

"They'll be okay as long as their engine holds." Doc was trying to reassure himself as much as anyone. A strange feeling of foreboding had settled across his shoulders. He tried chalking it up to the storm bearing down on them, but he couldn't shake the certainty that there was more to it.

"And if their engine doesn't hold, they're gonna be in a world of hurt," John insisted. "All they'll have is their anchors to keep 'em steady, and that ain't much."

Doc made a face. "As my dear ol' daddy always said, you can lead a horse to water, but you can't make him drink."

John snorted. "Sounds like horses and fishermen are both dumb as dirt."

Doc chuckled, but his response was cut off when Cami let loose with a loud yawn.

"Sorry." She winced, covering her mouth. "I'm not insensitive to the plight of the fishermen. I'm just feeling like I might lapse into a coma."

Doc leaned close to her face and saw her pupils had nearly eclipsed her irises. "Did you get into Uncle John's stash?"

Not that he'd blame her if she had. Getting high on the devil's lettuce was probably the best way to get through a hurricane. In fact, if he didn't feel the need to keep his signals clear in case things suddenly went pear-shaped, he too might try to bum a joint off John.

She made a face. "No. I got into your Dramamine because I *thought* I was going to be spending the next couple of days on a sailboat."

"How much did you take?"

Her grin looked a little drunk. "A double dose."

"For shit's sake, woman! Overdosing on Dramamine can cause hallucinations and seizures."

"There's a difference between double-dosing and overdosing." She pursed her lips. "Or didn't they teach you that in med school?"

He didn't deign to answer. "Now I'll have to monitor you until it wears off."

"Number one"—she lifted a finger—"I'm perfectly fine all on my own. I just need a nap. And number two"—a second finger joined the first—"even if you *did* have to monitor me, why do you make that sound like the worst thing since New Coke hit the market?"

Another question he didn't deign to answer. Instead he turned to Dana and Uncle John. "You two okay to finish gathering everything up? I'm going to take her upstairs before her legs stop working."

"Oh my god!" Cami lifted her hands and let them fall dramatically. "I *told* you I'm fine."

"We can bring up the supplies," Dana assured him. "Go get her settled in."

After nodding his thanks, he grabbed Cami's hand. "Come on. Let's get you into bed."

All her ire disappeared in an instant. It was replaced by a wide, teasing grin. "Oooh. Now you're talkin'. Although, I have to be honest, I don't usually go for guys who run around shirtless all day."

Okay. She was drunk. Or high. Or whatever. Because *he* was the one with the sexual innuendos that rendered her speechless. Not the other way around.

He caught her roving finger and held it tight in his fist. "Cut that out. And what do you mean *usually*?"

She giggled. *Giggled.* Which was totally un-Cami-like. She was a laugher. Maybe even a full-throated chuckler. But a giggler? No.

Sighing heavily, he half dragged, half carried her upstairs and into his bedroom. "Sit." He pointed to the end of his bed while he lit the candle atop his dresser. He set the candle he'd brought up from the desk downstairs on his nightstand.

The dual flames created a cozy, romantic glow.

Not that he noticed.

No sirree, he did *not* notice.

"Is it only me you like to order around like a dog?" Her nose wrinkled as she flopped down on the edge of the mattress. "Or are you imperious and overbearing by nature?"

"Probably a little of both." He knelt in front of her to tackle the buckle on her sandal.

She snorted. "Well, I can't fault you for a lack of honesty."

"Meaning you can fault me for other stuff?"

Like the rest of her, her feet were pretty. Slender and high-arched with toenails that'd been manicured into the perfect shape and painted a ruby red to match her fingernails. When he grabbed her ankle to slip the first sandal free, he noticed how his hand completely encircled the joint.

The thought of snacking on her slim ankle, nibbling his way up her softly muscled calf and thigh, and then burying his face between her legs had his blood pooling in a place it had no business pooling.

With determination, he went to work on her second sandal. His hands stilled, however, and his mouth went bone dry when he felt her fingers slide into his hair.

"Well, there's the whole imperious and overbearing thing. But we just covered that. Plus, sometimes you walk around with a face like a thundercloud, and everyone avoids you then. And also"—she gave his hair a gentle tug—"you need a haircut."

He avoided her thundercloud comment, figuring she was referring to the times when the memories became too much for him, when the empty space in his center became a black hole that threatened to swallow him whole. Instead, he focused on her last comment.

"Needing a haircut is the story of my life. My mother was forever complaining to my dad about me going to the barbershop every two weeks. She used to say my hair grew quicker than the weeds in her vegetable garden."

"Mmm. You've never talked about your parents before." When he glanced up, he found her head tilted slightly, her eyes a little dreamy from the drug. "Are they still alive?"

"Mom is." He pulled off her remaining sandal and pushed to a stand.

The move meant her hand slid from his hair, which was a relief. But it bumped against his thigh on the way down, and that was *not* a relief. It was close enough to his dick that the damn thing got even *more* excited and perked up further.

"My dad passed on eight years ago," he added in a bid to cool his ardor. If anything could do it, it was talk of his father. "He had a heart attack while harvesting fall hay. Died right there on his tractor. Not a bad way to go for a guy like him. Probably how he'd have preferred it, honestly. I take comfort in that."

Since he was still in his wetsuit, and since he didn't think she'd appreciate him shoving his semi in her face— yes, it was still there despite his best attempts to tame it—he spun quickly toward his dresser to pull out a T-shirt and a pair of cargo shorts.

"I'm so sorry for your loss." Her words were full of sincerity.

He nodded, keeping his eyes focused on the pile of clothes in his dresser drawer. "It's been a while. The grief isn't as hard or sharp as it used to be."

"I'm glad." She sighed, and he thought he heard a note of melancholy in her voice.

Glancing over his shoulder, he started to assure her the hurt *did* dull over the years—he somehow knew she was thinking of her baby sister— but he got distracted when he saw her arms lifted over her head as she pulled pins from her windblown bun. With her delectable breasts raised high and proud, and her nipples pebbled into sharp points, he thought she was being intentionally provocative.

Then her bun unraveled, and she didn't do that sexy headshake thing women do when they're trying to seduce. Instead she scrubbed her nails against her scalp, groaned deeply—like his folks' old farm dog used to do when Doc scratched behind his ears—and yawned so wide her jaw popped.

Wonder if she realizes she missed the Jessica Rabbit mark by a country mile, he thought with a secretive smile. Then he frowned because, annoyingly, her *realness* just made him want her more.

He realized he'd pulverized the end of his toothpick into a pulp when she gave her scalp one final scrub and then blinked at him curiously. "Are you close to your mom?"

He'd been so caught up in his musings that the question felt like a sucker punch straight to the gut. He used the excuse of tossing his toothpick into the trash to give himself a moment to think about how he should respond.

He decided on the truth.

"I used to be. But she remarried ten months after my dad died. Randall Thorpe, the man who owns the spread next door. Ever since then, things between us have been..." He tugged on his ear. "I guess the word would be *strained*."

Cami's dark eyes were searching, sympathetic. "Do you think she and this Randall guy—"

"No," he was quick to cut her off. "I don't think Mom cheated on Dad. I just think she was sad and lonely after he died. Randall had lost his wife to colon cancer two years before, and I think he and Mom decided to try to make something good together out of all the bad they'd suffered separately."

"That sounds nice." Her voice was quiet, but her words hit his hide, sharp as a pair of spurs. He must've flinched or made a face or something, because she quickly added, "Or maybe it doesn't?"

"She disrespected Dad's memory by moving on so quickly," he said through clenched teeth. "And I don't know how to forgive her for that." Cami opened her mouth, but he was done with the subject. "What did you do with your overnight bag?" he asked.

A line formed between her eyebrows. "I left it downstairs beside the sofa. Why?"

"I'll go grab you some dry clothes." While he was at it, he planned to stop by the bathroom to change out of his wetsuit. Wearing a rubber skin was *not* conducive to hiding the fact that he pretty much slung wood around Cami twenty-four seven.

She grimaced. "I doubt anything in that bag is still dry."

He realized she was probably right. "How do you feel about wearing one of my T-shirts and a pair of my boxers then?"

She pressed a hand to her chest. "It'll be like being draped in the Shroud of Turin."

"Smart-ass." He bit the inside of his cheek to keep from smiling.

"Never claimed otherwise." She cocked one eyebrow, which he thought was meant to look arrogant. But she was flying higher by the minute, so it only made her look more drunk. Especially because the cocked eyebrow was paired with an eyelid that didn't seem to want to stay up. "Plus, takes one to know one, right?"

Instead of answering—because if he answered, they'd devolve into another round of verbal volleys, and as fun at that was, he needed to get her tucked in before the Dramamine took her out—he turned back to his dresser to find her some dry clothes.

He and the rest of his Deep Six Salvage partners had been living the rice-and-beans lifestyle since they'd spent all their ready cash on the hunt for the *Santa Cristina*. Half his boxers were frayed at the hems and waistbands.

Since his pride couldn't bear the thought of handing her a pair of his holey underwear, he settled on the Christmas jockey shorts Alex had gotten him as a gag gift. Rudolph's red nose was…*ahem*…strategically placed.

He paired the shorts with a plain white tee and handed them to her before saying, "You change in here. I'll head to the bathroom."

"What?" Her grin was impish. "You don't trust that I can resist your masculine wiles if you strip in front of me?"

"I know you can. You've been doing a bang-up job of resisting my masculine wiles for months now."

"The resistance hasn't been all one-sided."

Again, the muscle in his jaw began to twitch. "I know."

All the teasing left her eyes. "Are you going to tell me what you meant when you said we couldn't act on this"—she waved a hand between them—"even after I stop being your attorney?"

And there it was. The question.

"Maybe someday," he submitted cautiously, and then

quickly added, "But not right now." He hitched his chin toward the clothes in her hand. "Go on and get dry. I'll meet you back here in five minutes."

He was to the door when she stopped him. "You know, I think this whole brooding, cynical thing you got going is all an act. Because I swear I detect a twinkle of humanity in you from time to time."

"I told you too much Dramamine can cause hallucinations." He closed the door to the sound of her laughter.

Once he was in the bathroom, he took his time. He didn't want to chance walking in on her half-dressed.

She seemed confident in her ability to resist his masculine wiles, but when it came to *him* resisting her *feminine* wiles? *Uhhh, no.* That see-through T-shirt she had on was bad enough. He couldn't imagine what it would be like to witness her fully in the raw.

Or…maybe it was more accurate to say he'd imagined witnessing her fully in the raw way too often. And if he experienced the reality of it, he might lose his mind.

After draping his wetsuit over the shower curtain rod and slipping into his dry clothes, he made his way back down the hall to his bedroom. The storm battered the house, but he could hear LT and Olivia talking with John and Dana downstairs. The squeak of the pantry door told him they were still gathering supplies.

I should go help, he thought. But then he added the contingency, *after I check on Cami.*

Knocking gently on his bedroom door, he called, "Cami? You decent?"

Silence.

Was she still dressing? Was she already asleep? Was she convulsing on the floor because she really *had* overdosed?

His body flashed hot and cold. Before he could think,

he threw open the door so hard the knob left a dent in the shiplap wall.

"Sweet Jesus doing jumping jacks!" She bolted upright in the bed, pressing a hand to her chest and blinking at him myopically. "What's wrong?"

"Why didn't you answer when I knocked?"

She frowned and waved in a circular motion. "The wind is screaming. The shutter is banging against its locking bar. It sounds like the roof is flexing. And all the joists are popping. I didn't *hear* you."

He blinked when he realized he'd been silly to panic.

"Right." Shaking his head, he walked over to the bed, carefully avoiding staring at the damp clothes she'd draped over the lamp on his nightstand. Particularly because she'd placed her bra and panties on top, and even though they didn't appear to be anything special—just your average, everyday cotton set—they were still *hers*.

Sitting on the edge of the mattress, he peered into her eyes. "How do you feel?"

"Like I could sleep for a decade." She covered her mouth and yawned.

"What in god's name made you think it was okay to double down on Dramamine?"

She shrugged one rounded shoulder before snuggling back into bed. *His* bed.

Camilla D' Angelo was in his bed. Her dark hair was splayed across his pillow. His sheet rested atop her breasts. And her bare thigh was pressed against his hip because she'd done that quintessentially *female* thing of needing one leg out from underneath the covers.

It was such a smooth, shapely, undeniably *edible* leg too.

His mouth filled with saliva.

"I mean…" She yawned again. "I thought it was like

doubling the dose on Tylenol. Not recommended, but not likely to hurt me either."

"And that's what you get for thinking."

Her lips twisted even as her eyes fluttered shut. "Hey Dr. Know-It-All, have I mentioned how much I love the sound you make when you shut your piehole?"

He chuckled despite himself and tried to come up with a pithy comeback. But he realized it was a wasted effort when a deep, resonant breath left her lungs.

The drugs had finally pulled her under.

Without thinking, he tucked the sheet tighter around her shoulders, fitted it snuggly around her hips. Then, of their own accord, his fingers hovered above her bare thigh.

The world disappeared as he dropped his hand lower. Lower. Lower still. Until there was nothing but a hair's breadth between her skin and his fingertip. He went deaf to the sound of the storm. Blind to anything that wasn't the sight of her smooth, lightly tanned leg and—

A knock sounded at the door.

He hopped out of bed like he'd been caught taking advantage of an unconscious woman. And he was ashamed to say, if he hadn't been interrupted, he might have done exactly that.

What is this woman doing to me?

Turning him inside out, that's what. Making him forget himself. Forget…everything.

Running a hand through his hair—why did it feel so much better when *she* did it?—he glanced down to find that neither the knock on the door nor his sudden movement had awakened Cami. Her rosy mouth was open ever so slightly and her chest rose and fell in a steady rhythm.

Tiptoeing across the room, he carefully opened the door. John stood on the other side with a different laundry basket than the one Doc had worked on earlier. It was filled with dry goods and Mason jars full of fresh water.

"Provisions." John shoved the basket into Doc's arms. Then he glanced over Doc's shoulder at Cami and asked, "How's our lady lawyer doin'?"

"Out like a light." Doc moved the candle aside so he could set the basket on his dresser. "But she'll be fine."

"It's a good way to ride out a hurricane, if you ask me."

"A good way to ride out a hurricane is to be two, maybe three hundred miles away from it," Doc countered.

"Pssht." John waved a hand. "Julia only thinks she's big and bad. I've seen plenty of her older sisters and brothers that were way worse."

"Reckon I'll have to take your word for it. How's everyone else doing?" Doc knew LT and Olivia would probably spend the duration of the storm having sex. It seemed to be all they *ever* did when they were alone together in their room. And he tried not to hate them for it while simultaneously wishing there was a way to add more insulation to walls. So his question was really about Dana. He decided to make that clear. "Is Dana okay?"

"I'll keep her with me." John's mustache hid what Doc determined was a shit-eating grin. "She'll be fine and dandy."

"You *like* her." Doc pointed an accusatory finger at John's lecherous smile.

"'Course I do. What's not to like? But before you go givin' me shit for havin' a heart-on for a gal, you better look in the mirror."

Doc choked. "Did you really just say *hard-on*?"

"No." Uncle John shook his head. "I ain't that crude. And I ain't that shallow. I said *heart*-on. I like Dana for a whole helluva lot more than what's she got goin' on between her legs. Same way you like Cami."

Doc quickly glanced over his shoulder to make sure she was still asleep. Turning back, he hissed, "You mind keeping it down?"

"Why?" John snorted. "It's not like it's any big secret. We all got eyes in our heads, boy. We see the way you look at her."

"How do I look at her?"

"Like she's the north star and you're a sailor lost at sea."

"For shit's sake." Doc gave his earlobe a hard tug.

He would've felt better had John said something like, *You look at her like you're a starving man and she's a twelve course meal*. Because *that* would've implied he looked at her with nothing but lust. But the north star and a sailor lost at sea? That meant he looked at Cami like she was his salvation.

"What's holdin' you back, boy?" John interrupted his musings. "Why haven't you made your move yet? And don't gimme none of that crap about her not lettin' you 'cause she's your lawyer. We all know you could talk her outta that in a heartbeat if you tried."

Doc couldn't even begin to explain. All he could do was shake his head.

John sighed and clapped a hand on Doc's shoulder. "I ain't never had a wife, so I can't speak to the loss of one. But I do know somethin' about the human heart. Its capacity to love is endless. Don't go puttin' limits on somethin' that doesn't need to have any. And if it was worth it the first time, like you told me it was, then don't you reckon it'd be worth it a second?"

Before Doc could respond to the hand grenade of profundity John had dropped, John pinched his cheek like he was eight instead of thirty-eight and headed down the hall, whistling a Jimmy Buffett tune.

Shaking his head, Doc softly closed the door and prepared to turn back into the room. Back toward the bed. Back toward the most beautiful woman in the world who just happened to be sleeping there.

But just as he'd feared, no amount of preparation readied him for the impact of Camilla D' Angelo asleep atop his mattress. That shapely thigh was still out, and the temptation to walk over and pick up where he'd left off was unlike anything he'd ever known.

Then, after I've run a hand down her silky leg, I'll join her under that sheet. I'll pull her close and hold her safe while the world rages around us.

At least that's what he *wanted* to do.

Which was why he shuffled over to his closet and took down the shoebox from the top shelf instead.

Sitting in the rattan cane chair in the corner, he opened the lid and pulled out the silk scarf. How many times had he done this? Sat alone with this shoebox in his lap?

Too many times to count. And yet, not at all recently.

The realization made the empty space inside him grow wider, deeper. It renewed the ache that lived there.

Holding the soft material to his nose, he inhaled the familiar scent of his wife. Just that easily, the memory of her was no longer fuzzy. It was as sharp and as shiny as a new scalpel. It cut just as deeply.

Familiar tears clogged his throat. But he screwed tight his eyelids and refused to let them fall.

CHAPTER 5

12:45 PM...

A goddamn pisser if ever there was one."

Will opened his mouth to assure Brady it wasn't as bad as all that. But the words stuck in his throat.

Maybe it *was* that bad. And before he spoke, he needed to think about what to say next. More importantly, what to *do* next.

Tightening his grip on the helm, he kept the trawler's nose pointed perpendicular to the waves. The sea was doing her level best to work herself into a frenzy, and he knew she would succeed at exactly that within the next few hours. But hopefully, here, on the leeward side of the island, they would be protected from the worst of it.

Glancing around the wheelhouse at the others, he noticed Jace looked as determined as ever. Which, of course he did, it was his neck—or, more importantly, his family's home—on the line. Fin's expression was equally unwavering. But

Brady? He was as pale as a ghost.

The man had been spleeny ever since they'd settled on this course of action. But that was probably because, of the four of them, Brady had spent the least amount of time on the water. The approaching storm scared the piss out of him.

If Will was being honest, it scared the piss out of him too. He was no dubber. He knew better than to disrespect Julia's power. But he was confident in the knowledge his father and grandfathers had passed down to him. Confident in his ability to ride out the storm and finish what they'd come to do.

I got this, he silently coached himself. *Just another day on the waves.*

After secretly boarding *Wayfarer II* the night before—and after distracting the bulldog with some beef jerky from Jace's pocket and shutting the rooster in a closet so it'd stop flying at them and squawking—they'd searched every nook and cranny of the abandoned ship for the treasure. And they'd found? A big ol' bunch of *piss all*.

Thwarted but not dissuaded, they'd decided the Deep Six Salvage crew must've left the loot on the island, probably thinking it was the safest place to store it. Because one, they were working under the false assumption no one knew they'd actually found it. And two, they likely reasoned, even if someone did realize they'd found it, who would be crazy enough to brave a hurricane to try to get it?

Four Mainers who'd grown up on the water and who had withstood their fair share of deadly nor'easters, that's who. Four seasoned sailors who knew how to talk a fisherman into leasing them his boat after they'd promised to only fish waters far from the hurricane's path, that's who. Four *desperate* men who were hoping to get their buddy out of a jam and, as a bonus, snatch enough of the rich stuff for themselves to make some sort of future for their families. *That's who.*

"We've come too far to turn back now," Will said through gritted teeth. The engine whined as they rode the crest of a wave. "The plan doesn't change."

"The hell it doesn't," Brady swore. "The island was supposed to be deserted."

"We *assumed* it would be deserted," Will corrected him. "We didn't *know* it would be."

"Doesn't matter." Jace shook his head, his tree-trunk legs braced wide on the rolling decking. "We're here and the treasure is here. So we might have to do things a little dirty. So what?" He shrugged. "We'll wear masks and bring our guns. Wasn't that pretty much the original idea anyway?"

"The original idea, before this wicked wind blew up, was to watch them, find out where they were squirrelin' away the treasure, and then sneak onto the island in the middle of the night when it was darker than the inside of a pocket and steal a little of the loot out from under their noses with no one bein' the wiser," Brady insisted.

"Ayuh." Jace nodded. "But we always knew there was a chance things might get messy."

Yes. They *had* known there was a chance. Will had just been hoping it wouldn't come to that.

His conscience tried to rear its head, but he forced himself to remember three very salient facts. One, his oldest needed new soccer cleats. Two, his poor wife hadn't had a new dress in two years. And three, he *deserved* this, damnit!

He'd struggled for long enough. They'd *all* struggled for long enough.

It's time we get what's comin' to us. What we're due.

Fin had yet to add his two cents. Not an unusual condition with him. He often chose to keep his own council. Which meant, when he finally *did* speak, everyone listened. "Will and Jace are right. The plan stays the same. We'll make our move once the eye is overhead."

CHAPTER 6

3:45 PM...

I *want a time machine! I want to go back and change my vote!*
Dana Levine thought as the winds and the rain continued to
roar around the house.

Julia's leading edges had passed over hours earlier.
Since then, the beach house had been bombarded with a
continuous, nerve-wracking wall of sound that was so loud
she thought it a miracle her eardrums hadn't burst.

Just as LT had said might happen, the storm surge had
pushed seawater under the house. She could hear waves
slapping against the pilings holding the structure up. And the
whole place smelled like the ocean, briny and raw.

I'm on a tiny island in the middle of nowhere riding out
a Category 3 hurricane! What the hell *was I thinking?*

She'd been thinking how exciting it was to witness
the raising of a treasure unlike anything anyone had seen
in decades. She'd been thinking if experienced sailors like

John and LT thought it was safe to stay, then who was she to naysay them? She'd been thinking it couldn't be *that* bad.

Jeez-oh-Pete, was I wrong.

John had pulled a wooden rocking chair close to the bed where she was sitting cross-legged with her back against the headboard. When she glanced over at him, she discovered him looking no different than he'd looked all day. As cool as a frickin' cucumber. Not a whit of worry on his handsome face.

Which should've reassured her.

It only pissed her off.

Or maybe it made her insanely jealous. Because what she wouldn't give for a teensy, tiny bit of his calm.

Her face must've revealed some of what she was feeling, because he yelled above the noise of the storm, "It's okay! Focus on your breathin' and try to relax!"

"I can't relax! Fear and anxiety are the only things keeping me together at this point!"

He chuckled and cocked his head. "You sure you don't want some weed to take the edge off?"

"No thanks! Last time I got high was in college! And I was paranoid for three hours straight!"

"Weed's come a long way since then," he assured her.

She shook her head. "Just keep talking to me!"

They'd spent the last few hours exchanging the standard get-to-know-you fare.

She now knew John was originally from New Orleans. He'd spent summers as a kid working on his dad's shrimp boat alongside his brother James, who was LT's father. As adults, John and James had moved to the Keys to start a salvage business together. But John had quickly tired of the drudgery of the job and so had sold his share of the company to James before opening a bar in Key West. He'd run that bar for twenty-five years before retiring and moving out to

Wayfarer Island to help LT and the others hunt for the storied *Santa Cristina*.

It sounded like an exciting life. Far more adventurous than the one she'd led, having been born and raised in Iowa. She'd grown up thinking everyone knew about "the farmer wave." That single finger salute a person used to acknowledge a fellow motorist on a gravel road that wound through a patchwork of cornfields. She'd told John that it wasn't until she'd moved away to college that she'd realized not every state in the nation had a fair as glorious and grand as Iowa's. And she'd admitted that her perfectionist streak meant she'd been valedictorian of her high school's graduating class, which had landed her a scholarship to Georgetown where she'd studied analytics, and that *that* degree had led to her job at the Federal Maritime Commission working within the legal department— where she'd stayed for twenty-seven years.

It'd been a nice way to pass the time, sharing the Cliff's Notes version of their lives. But she wasn't looking to pass the time now. She was looking for a distraction. She told him as much.

Or rather, she *shouted* as much.

He pushed up from the rocker and found a spot next to her on the bed. "May I?" He lifted his arm as if to put it around her shoulders.

She didn't hesitate. Nodding briskly, she leaned forward so he could wrap her up and pull her close to his side.

She didn't care that he was a relative stranger. For one thing, he smelled nice. Like coconut oil and sea breezes. For another thing, he was warm and solid, which grounded her and kept her from feeling like she was seconds away from doing her very own imitation of Dorothy from the *Wizard of* Oz and getting caught up in the whirlwind raging outside.

"What do you reckon we should talk about now?" he asked.

She liked his voice. It was deep and resonant. His soft Southern drawl worked like a balm on her frayed nerves.

With him so close, she no longer had to shout. It was almost like they were cocooned inside a protective bubble while the entire world threw a tantrum around them.

"You haven't mentioned a wife. Or a family of your own. Were you ever married? Do you have kids?"

"Nope to both," he said succinctly.

"Why not?" She immediately wanted to rip her tongue from her head. She was assuming too much. She blamed it on the failings of her generation, having grown up in a far less enlightened time. "Sorry," she apologized immediately. "I should've said you never mentioned a *partner*. I need to do a better job of not taking for granted that—"

"I like women," he cut her off, his mustache curling around a grin.

A *flirtatious* grin, if she wasn't mistaken.

It was warm inside the house. Not uncomfortably so because the raging storm had cooled the atmosphere. Still, she hoped he mistook the sudden color in her cheeks for the heat and not the fact that he'd discombobulated her with that smile.

He'd also made her very, *very* aware that her entire left side was touching his entire right side.

Swallowing convulsively, she nodded. "Okay. So my original question stands. What stopped you from putting a ring on some pretty woman's finger and having yourself a couple of John juniors?"

When he rubbed a hand over his beard, she wondered if the hair felt wiry or soft. Her fingers itched to find out, so she clasped them together.

"Seems I was always busy startin' a business or runnin' one when I was younger," he mused. "Then I swore I'd never marry 'cause I never wanted to suffer the kinda heartache

James suffered when he lost LT's momma."

When she lifted an eyebrow in question, he went on. "Cancer. Only four months passed from the time she was diagnosed 'til the time she was in her grave. And James never got over it. Loved her 'til his dyin' day. Kinda like Doc with his wife, except the difference between them is no one good enough ever came along to mend James's busted heart. Doc is just pissin' away a damn fine woman, if you ask me."

Dana had wondered what it was that came over Doc's face from time to time. Now she knew. It was grief. And yet, she'd also seen that all it took to wipe the sadness from his expression was one word from Camilla D'Angelo.

"You're talking about Cami?" She didn't wait for John's response before continuing. "The sexual tension between those two is palpable. But I thought *Cami* was the one maintaining their distance. I could've sworn I heard her tell him she never mixes business with pleasure."

"Uh huh." John made a face, and she noticed how the candlelight danced in his eyes, making them look gold instead of hazel. "She's said that so many times, it's lost its meanin'."

"You think it's really *Doc* who's keeping *Cami* at arm's length?"

He nodded. "Doc carries the memory of his wife around like a damn disease, lettin' it eat at him. And he refuses to even consider lettin' anyone try to help him heal."

For a while, Dana was quiet, thinking about Doc's sad plight. Then she experienced a bout of conversational whiplash when John returned them to their original topic, "Anyway, to finish answerin' your question, I guess it's safe to say that what it all boils down to is the right woman never came along for me. And at this point, I *like* my life. Findin' someone who could come into an already good situation and make it even *better*?" He shook his head and she was momentarily distracted by how thick his salt-and-pepper locks looked. Most men her age had lost their hair decades earlier. John's was still as thick and as wavy as a young man's. "Maybe that's just too tall an order, you know?" he finished.

"But you're still looking?" she heard herself ask and once again wondered if she should just go ahead and rip her tongue out of her head.

Oh my god! Now he'll think I'm interested! Think I'm asking for myself!

She blinked. *Am I interested? Am I asking for myself?*

John was older than she was. But she wasn't sure by how much because he was still fit and trim, with wide work-rough hands and heavily muscled legs. His face was timeless. He had that whole Sean Connery thing going. And it was only the deep laugh lines at the corners of his eyes and the gray in his hair that hinted at his number of decades.

"Let's just say I'm open to the possibility," he allowed. "What about you? Ever married? Any kids?"

She used to feel like she'd been stabbed in the heart anytime someone asked her those questions. But no longer.

She'd heard it said that the opposite of love wasn't hate. That the opposite of love was indifference.

It'd taken years, but she could now look back on her marriage—and, more precisely, the *end* of her marriage— with a complete absence of feeling.

"Divorced for nearly fifteen years. And no. We never had any children." Slanting him a look, she added, "Maybe this is TMI, but I have what they call an incompetent cervix. I could never maintain a pregnancy past twelve weeks."

There was sympathy in his eyes, and she noticed how thick and black his eyelashes were. They matched his eyebrows.

"I'm sorry." His words were low. Intimate.

"Maybe it was fate." She shrugged. "I was always ho-hum about the idea of kids. I loved my job. I loved living in D.C. I loved my circle of friends. I loved my *life*. It was David...that's my ex," she clarified, "who was always pushing for a family. And because I loved him, I tried. For over a decade I tried everything the doctors could think of. Then, on my fortieth birthday, I told him I was done trying."

She stopped and waited for the sadness that used to slap her square in the face whenever she thought of that conversation over a cake that looked like it was on fire with forty lit candles, whenever she remembered David's expression of betrayal and how it had quickly morphed into rage. But again, there was only indifference.

"He served me with a petition for divorce three weeks later," she told John matter-of-factly. "Eight months after that he was remarried to a twenty-six-year-old."

"I'm sorry," John said again. Sincerity rang in his voice.

"Don't be. I'm not a victim. I mean, yes, it was hell coming to the realization that the man I'd dedicated sixteen years of my life to loved the dream of having a family more than he loved me. But the heart wants what the heart wants, right?" She shrugged. "Besides, after his young wife gave him two sons, she ran off with her Pilates instructor and left David to raise the boys on his own. Which he has since confided to me is so much harder and less rewarding than he ever thought it would be." She made a face. "Should I feel bad for feeling just the littlest bit vindicated?"

"I wouldn't judge you for feelin' the *biggest* bit vindicated."

She chuckled. "Oh, good. Because I do."

For a while after that, they were quiet. And the sounds of the storm crept back into her consciousness. Just when she was gearing herself up for another panic/anxiety spiral, he asked, "You never remarried?"

"God, no." She shuddered. "The last fifteen years have been the best of my life. I've learned to ballroom dance and I can throw a mean mug or vase on the wheel." When he frowned, she explained. "Pottery. I fell in love with pottery. I do hot yoga on Tuesdays and Thursdays. Wednesdays are porch nights with my girlfriends where we sit outside, drink wine, and play board games. And I'm part of an over-fifty adventure group that gets together on weekends when the weather is nice. We go kayaking or take hikes. We host dinner parties and meet up at concerts. And when I come home at night, I'm greeted by someone who loves me unconditionally."

He arched one of those beguiling black eyebrows, and she explained. "My dog, Rocko." She pulled her phone from her back pocket and thumbed on the screen. After scrolling through her camera roll, she found her favorite picture of Rocko and handed over her cell.

John took one look at her dog and burst into laughter. "Good lord! What *is* he?"

She grinned. "He's half bloodhound, half German shepherd."

John stared again at Rocko's picture. "He reminds me of something, but I can't place what."

"Dobby the house elf from the Harry Potter movies," she said confidently. "It's his ears. They're huge and stick out from his head at ninety-degree angles."

"He's...uh..."

Dana ripped the phone away from him and pretended affront. "The handsomest dog you've ever seen," she finished with a sniff.

John's eyes glinted in the low glow of the candlelight. "So it's you and Rocko rulin' the world, huh?"

"Absolutely. Which means I guess I'm sort of like you." When a line appeared between his eyebrows, she clarified.

"Happy. And not willing to settle. It would take a special man indeed to be better than no man at all."

She nodded and the move caused one of her curls to fall into her face. She lifted a hand to brush it behind her ear—something she did a hundred times a day because her hair was the bane of her existence—but he beat her to it. With gentle fingers, he slowly tucked the recalcitrant curl back into her mess of springy ringlets.

She would swear he'd done it on purpose when his knuckles lightly brushed against her jaw. The little gasp that escaped her lips surprised her as much as the electricity of his touch. It was like she'd come into contact with a tiny bolt of lightning. The hair all over her body stood on end.

Her open mouth drew his eyes, and when she licked her lips, his gaze followed the movement of her tongue. She suddenly felt like a rabbit who'd caught the eye of a hungry wolf.

And maybe most surprisingly of all, she *liked* the sensation.

Is he leaning closer? she wondered a little giddily.

He is!

Is he going to kiss me?

Oh, cheese and rice, he *was* and—

A loud crash followed by a bloodcurdling scream popped their protective bubble.

CHAPTER 7

4:07 PM...

The hurricane was inside the house.

Or at least that's what it felt like to Cami when she was jerked from a drug-induced sleep by the sound of a window breaking.

An instinctive scream burst from her throat. Confusion had her glancing around wild-eyed to see bits of palm leaves and paper flying across the room. The candles had been snuffed out, but the dim light streaming in through the shattered glass showed Doc wrestling with one of the shutters as he squinted against the rain that pelted his face.

"What the hell happened!" a deep voice sounded above the hellish moan of the sustained winds.

Cami found Uncle John had thrown open the bedroom door. Dana peered over his shoulder, and not only were the FMC employees' cheeks chalk white but also her eyes were the size of the apple crumb pies Cami's mom used to pick up from Holtermann's Bakery on Arthur Kill Road on Staten Island.

Cami regretted offering Dana this gig. Regretted putting the woman in harm's way, because it was quite obviously the end of the world. Of course, when she'd approached Dana about the job, she hadn't known there would be a freakin' *hurricane* involved in bringing up the *Santa Cristina*'s treasure!

"The downspout gutter ripped off the side of the house and knocked the lock off the shutter!" Doc yelled over his shoulder.

"Leave it!" John bellowed just as LT and Olivia crowded into the doorway.

Judging by LT's sweaty cheeks and Olivia's rat's nest hair, Cami thought it was a safe bet *they* hadn't been sleeping their way through the storm.

"You'll never get it relocked!" LT yelled. "Just let it go! It's time to relocate!"

"Damnit!" Doc cursed but took LT's advice and released the shutter. The wind caught the wooden slat, slapped it against the side of the house a few times, and then ripped it from its hinges.

Tossing back the covers, Cami readied herself to run to a more secure room. But before she could do more than set her feet on the floor, cannonballs began slamming into the house. No, not cannonballs. *Coconuts!*

Boom! Boom! *Boom!*

It sounded like war.

It *was* war. Mother Nature was trying to kill them!

Instinctively, she curled into a ball, protecting her head because visions of hard, coconuty munitions exploding through the walls and wreaking havoc inside the room danced in her brain.

"Fuck my life!" she wailed as the assault continued.

But her wail turned into a screech of confusion when Doc swooped in to gather her in his arms.

He had her out the door and into the hallway a split second later.

Wham! Uncle John slammed the bedroom door behind them and it created a momentary vacuum. Cami's ears popped. But, blessedly, it was quieter in the hallway, and she thought maybe it wasn't Armageddon after all.

"I think the eyewall is nearly here," LT said. Was Cami hallucinating or did his tone sound almost...*happy*? "Which means we're halfway home. Everybody doin' okay?"

No! she wanted to scream. *I'm not doing okay!* Because even though she'd somehow managed to sleep through the front half of the storm—*thank you double dose of Dramamine!*—the eyewall? Conditions were at their *worst* in the eyewall.

"Ain't none of us doin' as well as you two are doin'," John told LT. Even in the near blackness of the hall, John's white teeth gleamed when he smiled.

"Not sure what you mean by that," LT muttered, and Cami thought she could hear him shuffling his feet. She could sense John opening his mouth to expound on his statement. LT must've sensed it too, because he quickly added, "Doc, you and Cami should make yourselves at home in Mason and Alex's room. And since everyone's doin' okay, we'll see y'all on the flip side." Without waiting for a response, he and Olivia scurried back to their bedroom.

Uncle John waited until their door closed behind them before observing drolly, "Considerin' how much those two go at it, and seein' as how there ain't a single form of birth control on the planet that's one-hundred-percent effective, it's a wonder that woman hasn't been pregnant ten times over by now."

Knowing what LT and Olivia were getting up to...or

rather, getting *back* to…made Cami acutely aware that Doc had yet to set her on her feet.

She tried not to notice how *nice* it felt to be carried as if she were a little thing—for the record, she *wasn't*. She tried and failed. Because no matter how hard she concentrated on anything and everything that *wasn't* the feel of his strong hands wrapped around her back and thighs, the warmth of his wide chest pressed tight against her side, and the sweet smell of his breath—had he eaten a strawberry Pop-Tart?— he made her feel delicate. Dainty. Sort of…*cherished*.

She had the nearly overwhelming urge to grab his stubbled cheeks and lay one on him. A big, sloppy one. A long, *hungry* one.

Instead, she tapped his damp shoulder. "You realize the Dramamine didn't paralyze me, right? I can walk."

His response was a wordless grunt. Instead of setting her on her feet, he stalked down the hallway and pushed open the door to Mason and Alex's bedroom.

His big body moving against hers, the way she was helpless in his arms, had every fantasy she'd ever had about him flipping through her brain like a movie reel set on fast forward.

Would he be the fast and furious type of lover? The type to leave her breathless and feeling as if she'd survived a *human* hurricane? Or would he be the slow and savoring type of lover? The type to make every inch of her body hum before leaving her completely wrung out?

Truthfully? She couldn't say which she preferred. Maybe both. Fast and furious to start, and then slow and savoring to finish.

Just thinking of it had her hands lifting of their own accord toward his face. She'd almost grabbed his cheeks when she remembered herself and curled her fingers into fists.

Could he hear the way her breath caught? Could he feel the way her skin grew warm beneath his hands? Could he recognize the rush of wetness that'd gathered between her legs?

When she wiggled to be let down, he grumbled, "Be still, woman, or I'll drop you."

"That's the whole point," she told him.

"Stop it. We're almost there."

"Were you born this arrogant, or did you take lessons?" She made sure her tone was appropriately haughty so, hopefully, he couldn't hear how hoarse her voice had become.

"Are you always this impatient?" he was quick to counter. "Or is today a special occasion?"

"Oh! You are the most…" She struggled to find the right word and finally settled on, "*bothersome* man to walk the planet."

"Thank you." She could hear the smile in his voice even though it was too dark to see it. "I take that as a compliment."

"Then I must've phrased it wrong."

The urge to lay one on him was replaced by the urge to strangle him when he burst into deep, rolling laughter. And she might have wrapped her hands around his throat, except for she was no longer in his arms.

She was airborne.

"Dalton!" she screamed before she hit the bed and bounced.

"What?" His tone was full of innocence. "You said you wanted me to put you down."

She was up on her knees on the mattress in an instant, staring daggers at him. Daggers he could *see* thanks to Uncle John walking into the room at that exact moment with a lit candle and the laundry basket full of provisions.

"Anyone ever tell you you're cute when you're mad?" Doc's cocky grin stretched his face.

"Keep smiling like that"—she balled up a fist and shook it at him—"and you'll see me get *real* adorable."

His stance, with his legs spread and his arms crossed, looked foreboding. But he threw back his head and laughed again as if her furious visage only tickled him.

Uncle John sighed heavily as he set the candle and the basket on the chest of drawers pushed against the far wall. "I wish y'all would stop this silly one-upmanship and give in."

"You mean give in to the urge to beat him repeatedly about the head and shoulders with a phonebook?" Cami's voice was sugary-sweet. She batted her lashes.

"Nope." John shook his head. "Give in to the urge to bone each other silly."

For a second, she was too shocked to do anything more than sputter. Then, her brazen Italian blood—and the big mouth that came with it—asserted itself.

"Not while I'm still employed by him. But I told him I'd be more than happy to test his suspension, or rather let *him* test *mine*, after the job is done. And do you know what his response was?"

"Cami." Doc's tone held a warning.

She ignored it. "He said we couldn't because he *wanted* it too much. Now you tell me, Uncle John, does that make any sense to you?"

"Not a lick," John assured her and her smile was one of vindication. "But on a different note," he continued, turning to Doc, "just thought I'd remind you that if there's anythin' in your bedroom you wanna keep, you better go grab it before Julia tears the place apart."

Cami blinked when Doc yelled, "Shit! My shoebox!" right before he darted into the hallway.

John watched Doc race away before swinging to face Cami. "Keep workin' on him, darlin'." He leveled a stern look on her. "He could use someone like you."

Before she could ask what he meant by that—*Someone like me?*—he ducked into the hallway and closed the door behind him.

Frowning, she sat back against the headboard. Between John's cryptic statement and Doc's outburst about…*Did he say* shoebox*?*…she was feeling summarily discombobulated.

Her confusion was only compounded when the door burst open and Doc's mile-wide shoulders filled the doorframe. The candlelight glinted off the blond strands in his damp hair, making them shine like the gold coins he'd raised from the seabed, and there were a few new droplets of water standing in his beard stubble.

Julia was doing a number on his room, no doubt. But he didn't seem concerned. Quite the contrary. There was an expression of relief on his face when he glanced down at what was…sure enough. That was a shoebox in his hand.

She opened her mouth to ask, *What's in the box?* But she decided that was too reminiscent of Brad Pitt in *SE7EN*. So instead, she simply lifted an eyebrow in question.

Either Doc didn't see her, or he didn't feel like answering, because he turned his back to shut the door. When he was slow to spin back around, she couldn't stop herself from saying, "Are those, like, ruby slippers or something?"

He frowned at her and then saw the direction of her gaze. Glancing at the shoebox, he shook his head.

It was hard to see in the dim light cast by the lone flickering candle, but she would swear a muscle ticked in his jaw. Then he lifted a hand to tug on his ear—a gesture she'd learned was something he did when he was feeling out of sorts—and she knew there was more to the shoebox than met the eye.

His words confirmed it. "These are souvenirs from my wife."

She felt two things in quick succession. The first was

shock. *He was married?* The second was confusion. *Why didn't I know that?*

Her voice came out sharper than she intended when she said, "I didn't know you were ever married."

He was still looking at the box and running a reverent hand over the lid like it contained treasures more precious than the ones sitting in the blue duffel bags in LT and Olivia's room. And maybe, for him, that was true.

"For eight years," he said softly.

Even though she couldn't see his eyes, she knew there was sadness in them. She could *feel* the sadness in them.

The sadness in *him.*

She tried to imagine him as a husband. And despite him being a brooding wiseass, she decided she could easily picture it.

Dalton "Doc" Simmons was honest and loyal. He was generous and principled. He prioritized the people in his life and, from everything she'd seen, gave respect to and was respected by everyone in equal measure.

In short, he was a good man.

Good men didn't stay on the marriage mart for long. It made sense he hadn't gotten to the ripe old age of thirty-eight without some lucky lady locking her ball and chain around his ankle.

Even so…Cami had known him for *months.* Why hadn't his marriage…his *wife*…ever come up?

Maybe it was because Doc wasn't the kind to overshare. Then again, neither was he particularly secretive or taciturn. For instance, she knew he was an only child. She knew he'd had a buckskin Quarter Horse named Lady growing up, and that when he was sixteen, Lady had fallen into a prairie dog hole, broken her leg, and he'd been the one to have to put her down. She knew he'd graduated at the top of his class in high school and that he'd dabbled with the idea of studying veterinary medicine before finally focusing his schooling on treating two-legged patients instead of the four-legged kind.

He hadn't shied away from sharing any of that with her. And if someone had asked her, she would've said she knew him pretty well. That she hadn't known *this* told her whatever had happened to his wife had been horrific enough for him to keep it locked away behind a wall of silence.

And not just him either. All his partners too. Not one of them had ever even *hinted* that Doc had been married.

A more circumspect woman might have kept her mouth shut. Cami had been absent from school the day they handed out discretion. "What happened?"

He raised his eyes, and it was like someone stabbed her heart with an icepick. There it was. The sadness she'd known was there. But *knowing* his sadness was there, and *seeing* it written all over his face in such haunting clarity were two very different things.

"She died." His voice was always scratchy. Now it sounded like someone had scoured his vocal cords with thirty grit sandpaper.

"How?" She realized she might have pushed her allotment of nosy questions to the limit, so she was relieved when he didn't hesitate to answer.

"She was hit by a drunk driver on her way home from work. She died on impact, and I buried her four days later. Two days after that, I walked away from my residency at Johns Hopkins and signed up for the Navy."

She nodded slowly, an invisible lightbulb flashing over her head.

Finally she knew the answer to something she'd always wondered. Because who in their right mind quits a lucrative medical career only to up and join the armed forces?

Someone who wasn't in their right mind, that's who. Someone who was insane with grief.

"I wanted to join her in the grave," he went on, and Cami wasn't sure she'd ever heard a sadder sentence. "But I was too much of a coward to take my own life. I thought maybe if I became a Navy SEAL, someone would do the deed for me."

Okay, and now it didn't just feel like she'd been stabbed in the heart. It felt like whoever had done the stabbing was twisting the blade.

"Oh, Doc." She shook her head as hot tears pricked behind her eyes. "I'm so sorry."

He didn't say anything to that. Simply nodded as a muscle clenched in his jaw.

"And now?" she asked quietly. Or rather, as quietly as she could and still be heard over the noise of the storm. "Do you still want to—"

"No." He interrupted, and she blew out a harsh breath of relief. "I don't long for death anymore. That passed."

"I'm so sorry," she said again, even though the words didn't come close to capturing the depth of her sympathy. "I know the pain of losing someone. Know what it is for that lost loved one to be the first thing you think about in the morning and the last thing you think about at night. Until, one day, that lost loved one *isn't* the first and last thing you think about. And somehow that's worse. Because it's like losing them all over again."

"It's been over a decade," he said softly.

"As if that matters." She snorted.

His gaze sharpened. The green in his eyes seemed to glow almost gold in the candlelight.

"Yes." She nodded. "I'm not sure I can *empathize*. I've never lost anyone I was in love with. But I can sympathize, because I loved my sister. And it doesn't matter whether it's been two months or twenty years, I will never stop missing her. Never stop grieving her. Never stop wishing I could turn back time and stop her from getting on that damn plane."

She thought maybe his eyes filled with tears. But he turned away before she could be sure.

After clearing his throat, he swung back around. By that time, his eyes were bone-dry. His rugged face was unreadable.

She understood that too. The need to hide the grief because it felt too big to let out. Because it was terrifying to think that if the tears started falling, they might never stop.

Sitting quietly, she hoped he would bring the shoebox over to the bed. She was curious about the woman who had won his heart. Curious to learn what he'd kept as reminders.

To her disappointment, however, he set the box on the chest of drawers before heading in her direction.

When he stood next to the head of the bed, she thought he might reach for her. Reach for comfort. She instinctively sat forward. Ready to take him in her arms. Ready to offer him what solace she could.

But he didn't reach for her. Instead, he sat down beside her. Which was when she realized there wasn't a chair in the room. Unless one of them wanted to stand or sit on the floor, they had to share the bed.

It didn't matter that the atmosphere inside the stuffy room was one of sadness instead of seduction. When the mattress depressed with his weight, and her hip touched his at the same time her shoulder brushed against his warm bicep, her body's responses bypassed her brain. She became instantly, *keenly*, aware of him as a man.

As *the* man she'd been dreaming about for months.

And the fact that he'd had a wife? It didn't change a damn thing.

Or maybe it did.

Maybe it made him *more* desirable because it humanized him. Proved he actually *did* have a vulnerable side. And *that* was Cami's true kryptonite.

She felt the warmth of him everywhere they touched. Smelled that pine trees and clean mountain air scent of him. Couldn't drag her eyes away from the sight of his large, long-fingered hand lying atop the coverlet a mere inch from her bare thigh.

He didn't look at her. Instead, he kept his attention straight ahead as he stretched his tan legs out in front of him and crossed them at the ankles. He'd kicked off his flip-flops and, not for the first time, she noticed how pretty his feet were. Long and narrow, with high arches and neatly trimmed nails.

All of Doc was pretty if she was being honest. He was just so perfectly proportioned. The kind of guy who would never suffer that middle-age spread. Never get a beer gut. Never deal with love handles.

As a woman who gained five pounds just walking by a donut shop, she couldn't help but feel a little envious. A little envious and a *lot* aware of how much she wanted to straddle his lap, run her fingers through his mess of damp hair, and try to take away the pain in his eyes.

The urge to kiss him was back. But it was different from before.

She was no longer hot and horny and looking to scratch an itch. She wanted to *connect* to him. Share a piece of herself and, in that sharing, show him that life went on. That it could still be beautiful despite his loss.

Instead, she fisted her hands into her lap and asked quietly, "What was her name?"

His eyes lingered on her face for so long, she wondered if she had something smudged across her cheek. Then he glanced down at the inside of his wrist, and her gaze followed his to the flower inked there.

She'd noticed the tattoo before. For one thing, it was

incredibly colorful compared to the curly-cue black lettering on his left forearm that read: For RL. For another thing, the flower was unmistakably feminine. Something a woman might get inked onto her hip or shoulder. Not something anyone expected to find on the body of a former Navy SEAL turned rumpled treasure hunter.

When he finally spoke, that colorful flower made perfect sense.

"Lily." The syllables were said with such reverence her heart ached anew. Not out of jealousy. How could she possibly be jealous of a dead woman? But out of sympathy. Sympathy for a young woman who'd been taken from the world too early, and sympathy for the brokenhearted man left behind. "Her name was Lily," he added softly and then tugged on his ear.

"You loved her very much." It was a statement of fact.

His Adam's apple traveled the length of his throat. "Since I was thirteen years old," he admitted with a nod.

Thirteen.

Cami shook her head in wonder. "I can't imagine." When he frowned, she explained. "I mean I've never been in love before. So it's hard to fathom falling in love at such a tender age."

"You've never been in love before?" There was genuine surprise in his face.

It was justified, she supposed. Most people didn't make it to their third decade without having experienced at least *one* head-over-heels tumble into *amore.*

"Nope." She shook her head. "I mean, I've kissed my fair share of frogs. Boy, have I." When he rolled his eyes, she went on. "But none of them turned out to be a prince. Or even just a regular ol' man whom I could imagine building a life with. Building a life *around.*"

When he cocked his head, she went on. "I know I come

across as this ball-busting career woman. And I *am*. I like practicing the law. I can't imagine ever *not* doing it. But I've always dreamed of being a wife and a mother too." A shard of hurt lodged under her heart, nicking the organ with every beat. "Since I was a little girl, I've wanted a big family of my own. Carlotta and I *both* wanted big families. I think maybe because we were so close as siblings. We enjoyed each other so much and had so much fun together that we wanted to compound that. Like that old saying, *the more the merrier*."

She picked at the edge of the comforter, finding a loose thread and pulling at it with her fingernail. That shard beneath her heart grew sharper when she admitted, "And now, with Carlotta gone, and with the relationship with my mother strained and the relationship with my father nonexistent, the longing for a family of my own is even stronger." She swallowed convulsively. "I miss Sunday dinners and Christmas mornings, Fourth of July picnics and sitting around the firepit in the backyard."

His brow furrowed.

"What?" She mirrored his frown.

"I don't know." He lifted one shoulder. "I just always thought of you as this slick New Yorker who preferred sales at Saks and cocktails at the Waldorf over family get-togethers."

"Ha!" She laughed. "First of all, you're stereotyping. Second of all, you're using the *wrong* stereotype. You're thinking of a Manhattanite. I grew up on Staten Island, which is about as provincial and suburban as it gets in that part of the country. And third of all, I'm Italian. Family is everything."

As soon as the last sentence left her lips, she grimaced.

Family *used* to be everything. And then she'd learned her father was a bona fide mobster. A cog in the massive, violent machinery that was the infamous Gambino crime family.

It'd been a devastating blow, to say the least. And yet,

what'd ultimately caused their estrangement had been her sister's death. The bomb that'd taken out Carlotta's plane had been meant for Cami's father—violence begets violence, after all; and *the life* was nothing if not violent. But an illness at the last minute had grounded her dad, and so he'd given Carlotta his seat. Which meant the person who'd ultimately paid the price for Big Tony D'Angelo's wicked ways had been Cami's kid sister. The one human being on the entire planet she had loved more than life itself.

She still kept in touch with her mother. Sort of. Her weekly phone calls home were done more out of a sense of duty than any sense of familial affection.

She couldn't bring herself to forgive her mother for hiding the truth from her all those years. And she couldn't fathom why her mother continued to stay married to her father given his life choices had landed him in prison and had gotten his youngest daughter killed.

Which meant, for better or worse, Cami was alone in the world. And even though she was on every dating app out there, she didn't see that changing anytime soon.

A nameless dread gripped her then. Or maybe it *wasn't* nameless. Maybe it had a name and that name was Childless, Husbandless, Lifelong Loner. Because at thirty-three, it felt like time was running out to make her dream of a big family a reality.

"I swear, woman." Doc pulled her from her depressing thoughts. "Just when I think I've gotten to know you, you go and surprise me."

She made a face. "I am a human onion. So many layers."

"Nah. Layers would imply you're hiding parts of yourself under other parts of yourself. But you're the most forthright person I know."

She frowned. "Why do I get the feeling you think that's a bad thing?"

He rolled his eyes. "Probably because you take offense to just about everything I say."

As if to prove his point, she felt her feathers ruffle. "Could that be because you're usually *trying* to offend me? Have you noticed your level of sarcasm goes up in direct proportion to the amount of time you're forced to be in my presence?"

She fully expected him to rise to the bait and for them to devolve into their usual round of arguments. She was a little surprised when all he did was nudge her with his elbow. "Don't act like you don't like it."

She made a valiant effort to hang on to her pique. But it leaked out of her like she was a sieve. "Fine," she conceded. "I'll admit it if *you* admit it."

"Oh, I admit it," he came back instantly. "You're bossy and obnoxious and you *always* think you're right. But I like arguing with you more than I like laughing with other people. So…" He sighed heavily. "There's that."

She wasn't simply surprised by his admission; she was downright gobsmacked. Which was why her mouth slung open.

When he glanced at her open lips, she thought he'd say something crude. This was usually the point where he would. But instead he lifted his gaze to her eyes. "Anyway, back to my original line of thought. You're no onion with layers. You're a finely cut crystal with facets. Every time I turn you in a new direction, I see the light bouncing off a fresh and captivating side of you."

"Why are you being so nice to me?" She turned her head and narrowed her eyes. "Why aren't you inundating me with sardonic observations about my shady profession or alluding to something overtly sexual in a bid to make me blush?"

He grinned that lopsided grin. "Oh, I still have *plenty* of lawyer jokes in store for you. Don't you worry about that."

She flattened her face Kermit the Frog style.

"As for the sexual innuendos," he went on, "it was all fun and games when I thought I was butting my head up against a brick wall. When I thought you were determined to keep me in the friend-slash-employer-slash-employee zone. But now that I know you'd be willing to"—again, his Adam's apple bobbed in his throat—"*explore* this thing between us at some point, it's not so much fun anymore."

"Why not?"

"Because now I know the thing I've been fantasizing about for months is there for the taking. And I'm tempted." His expression looked almost pained. "God, woman, how you tempt me."

Had the hurricane sucked all the air from the room? She was suddenly having a hard time catching her breath.

"Why do you say that like it's a bad thing?" she managed.

He dragged a rough hand through his hair and she was reminded of how soft those calico-colored strands had felt against her palm when, in her drugged-up state, she'd found the courage to tunnel her fingers through his lion's mane.

She wanted to tunnel her fingers through it again.

"I can't give you what you want, Cami." His words were quiet, but they packed one hell of a punch.

Her chin jerked back. "And what is it you think I want, Doc?"

"Call me Dalton. I like it when you call me Dalton."

Her momentary frisson of wariness became a frisson of yearning.

She wanted him.

She'd never wanted anyone as much as she wanted him. But it was sounding like he wasn't going to allow himself to want her. Or maybe, the more accurate way to put it was that he wasn't going to allow himself to *have* her.

"And what is it you think I want, *Dalton*?" Her heart

pounded so hard she thought for sure if she looked down, she'd see her borrowed T-shirt fluttering.

"You just said you want a husband. You want someone you can build your dreams around." He grabbed her hand. She thought maybe his grip felt a little desperate. But she couldn't say for sure because she got distracted by how warm his palm was. How callused his fingers were. "I can't give that to you because I gave it to someone else a long time ago, and now there's nothing left," he finished hoarsely.

What was he saying? That he would never move on from the death of his wife? That he would never remarry?

And even if he *was* saying that, did it change anything for her?

Yes, she'd wanted him from the first moment she laid eyes on him. Yes, every time he looked at her, her breath strangled in her lungs. Yes, for months she'd imagined what it would be like to stretch out next to his long, lean body and let him do all the things to her that his flirty smiles and dirty innuendos alluded to.

But her mind had never traveled beyond that.

Or maybe she'd never *allowed* it to travel beyond that.

The logistics were a nightmare. Her life and career were in Miami. He had plans to move back to Montana. He hated lawyers and she loved being one. They couldn't be in the same room together without bickering.

She'd always assumed if they ever acted on their feelings, if they ever gave in to their mutual lust, it would begin and end there.

She'd *assumed* that, so why did hearing him say out loud that there was no real future for them have her stomach twisting itself into knots?

The devil in her reared its ornery head. And with the appearance of that little demon, her golden rule lost its sheen.

Her mother had been right when she'd once said, "*The*

quickest way to get you to do something, Camilla, is to tell you that you can't *do it."*

"You're assuming an awful lot," she told Doc with a haughty sniff. "You think when we met that night on Key West that I was hoping to rope you into a happily ever after?"

"No." His eyes narrowed slightly. "That night we were both angling for something quick and dirty."

"So why do you assume I've changed my mind?" She cocked a provocative eyebrow.

"Haven't you?"

She wasn't sure what possessed her to do what she did next. Maybe it was her self-confidence and self-respect that needed appeasing. Maybe it was the dark imp that'd sprung to life inside her.

Or maybe it was a hint of desperation.

Regardless, one moment she was sitting beside him. The next she was straddling his lap.

Just as she'd wanted to do earlier, she grabbed his stubbled cheeks and leaned forward to take his mouth.

Before her lips could land on his, however, he tunneled his fingers into the hair at her nape and made a fist around the strands. The move effectively stopping her forward momentum.

Her throat made an audible *clicking* sound when she swallowed. After lifting her gaze from his beautiful mouth, she instantly got lost in his eyes.

Up close, she could see the flecks of gold around his pupils. And the green turned into an aqua blue near the outer rim of his irises.

"What happened to not mixing business with pleasure?" His voice was so low it was nearly a growl.

"If Julia has her way, we might not survive the day. *Carpe diem*, right? Besides"—she shrugged, sounding breathless because she *was* breathless—"the last of the treasure's been brought up. And since Dana will sign an affidavit swearing you salvaged it legally, I doubt the Feds or the state will try to file a claim. Basically, my work here is done."

For a handful of seconds, he said nothing. And the longer he remained silent, the more worried she became that he might not be on board with her sudden change of heart. Then, his eyes dropped to her mouth and his pupils dilated.

"Once you fire this bullet," he whispered hoarsely, "it won't go back in the barrel."

She shivered at the warning. "Is that a promise?"

He didn't say anything. Instead, he licked his lips, and she saw the muscles in his forearm flex as he prepared to pull her forward. As he prepared to finally, *finally* finish what they'd started the night they met.

It was also when she noticed the blood.

"Doc!" She grabbed his wrist, pulling back from the temptation of his waiting mouth.

"Dalton," he corrected her.

"You're hurt, *Dalton*." She showed him the thin cut through the letter R in his tattoo. Small rivulets of blood beaded on the wound. A few had dripped and left bloody paths down to his elbow. When she glanced down, she saw dark stains on the side of his shirt. "You must've cut yourself on the broken window when you were holding onto the shutter."

"It's nothing." He tried to shake off her grip so he could grab the back of her neck again.

"It's *not* nothing," she protested, hopping off the bed.

When she kissed him again—and it was a question of *when* and not *if*—she wanted to be able to focus all her energy on his mouth. She wanted no distractions. Definitely no thoughts of him contracting some terrible infection that ended in his arm being amputated.

"I'm the doctor," he grumbled when she tried to yank

him to his feet. "If I say it's nothing, it's nothing."

"Remember when I asked for your opinion? Medical or otherwise?" She fisted a hand on her cocked hip. "No? Me neither. Besides, what's good for the goose is good for the gander. You patched me up. Now, let me patch you up."

He muttered something she didn't quite hear. But she was pretty sure it wasn't flattering. When he pushed to a stand, he had to adjust himself.

She was careful to hide her triumphant smile, but some of it must've been revealed in her eyes because he frowned. "Yes. This is what you do to me. I hope you're proud of yourself."

"I am, actually," she admitted cheekily before grabbing his hand and dragging him from the room.

CHAPTER 8

4:39 PM...

I'm a damn fool.

Doc had silently repeated that phrase to himself at least a half dozen times since Cami lit the bathroom candle and pointed for him to sit down on the closed toilet lid. The statement was as true on the sixth repetition as it'd been on the first.

Still, he couldn't convince himself to change course. Couldn't convince himself to tell her that *no*, just because she'd decided there was no longer any reason for them to keep each other at arm's length that *he* was going to throw all his misgivings out the window and go along with her decree.

Because what if he'd been wrong to think if he allowed his fantasies to become reality then *liking* her and *lusting* after her might grow into something more? What if that old saying was true? *We want what we can't have.* And so maybe after he'd *had* her, he'd stop *wanting* her.

Or what if I'm rationalizing because I want her so much I can feel the ache for her all the way from the top of my head to the soles of my feet, and now that I can have her, I just don't have the strength to say no?

"Where is that bottle of peroxide?" she muttered, her head hidden behind the mirrored door of the medicine cabinet.

He knew she was smiling. He could hear the smile in her voice; he was that attuned to every single, subtle nuance that made up the whole of Camilla Jane D'Angelo.

"There you go being a smart-ass again." He feigned a fierce frown when she leaned around the medicine cabinet door and gifted him with an devilish grin.

Her brown eyes looked nearly black in the golden glow of the flickering candle flame. And the expression in them was definitely wicked.

He was once again reminded of that old Eagles song, "Witchy Woman." She had the raven hair and the ruby lips. He wasn't sure her restless spirit was on an endless flight so much as it was a force to be reckoned with. But there was absolutely no question—*none*—that she held him spellbound in the night.

In the day too. And in all the twilight hours in-between.

"Needing a haircut is the story of your life," she said in that delicious voice of hers that hinted at her youth in NYC. "The story of *my* life is being called a smart-ass. My mom always said, *'Cami, you've got a good heart, but that mouth… Girl, it's going to get you into more trouble than you can handle.'*"

The teasing in her eyes faded to sadness at the mention of her mother. Her expression left no doubt that thoughts of the woman who'd birthed her, a woman who'd since let her down, tore at the child that still lived inside her.

He could relate. He, too, missed the days when his

relationship with his mother felt affectionate instead of simply accommodating. *Comforting* instead of uncomfortable. And he couldn't help wondering if that was just the way of the world. The way of growing up.

Did *all* children eventually become disappointed by their parents?

"Okay, let's have it." She made a come-hither motion with her fingers while hitching her chin toward his forearm.

The injury was little more than a surface scrape. Most of the blood had already congealed. He had no doubt it would've been fine to simply ignore it and let it heal on its own.

Nonetheless, he dutifully extended his arm. Mostly because he'd gone a whole three minutes without her touching him and he *missed* the feel of her cool fingers on his heated flesh. Missed the way her perfume reached out to him, fresh and floral, whenever she got close.

Although, thirty seconds later, he was wishing she would put a quick end to her Florence Nightingale routine.

Cami approached doctoring the same way she approached life. With a single-minded focus that reminded him of a bull in a china shop. With her bottom lip caught between her teeth, she scrubbed his scratch with a soapy washcloth as if the wound had personally offended her.

"Good lord, woman." He barely refrained from jerking his arm from her grip. "Now I know why you became a lawyer and not a doctor. Your bedside manner is about as subtle as a sumo wrestler."

"Pfft." She rolled her eyes. "Don't get mad at me for pulling a you on you. You weren't exactly Mr. Cotton Candy Hands when you were doctoring me up earlier. But you didn't hear *me* complaining, did you?"

"The blade that stabbed you was corroded," he said defensively. "I had to make sure there wasn't any dirt or rust left in your wound." And truly, he'd been as gentle as he dared.

Had he hurt her? He hated the thought of that.

"And you think the window glass was sanitary?" She widened her eyes to dramatic effect. Even though she wasn't trying to be seductive, the way the candlelight cast shadows across her high cheekbones and smooth skin was sexy all the same. He felt the familiar stirrings of desire low in his gut.

"Point taken," he was forced to concede.

She blinked. "Are you feeling okay? Has your wound festered? Are you running a fever?" She placed her palm across his brow. "You've never given up a fight that fast."

"When you're right, you're right."

She looked around, patting the sides of her borrowed boxer briefs. "Damn. My phone is in my overnight bag. I was hoping to have you repeat that so I could record it for posterity."

He was suddenly overcome with the urge to pull her into his lap and kiss her until she went cross-eyed. Kiss her until that self-satisfied grin was replaced by a gasp of need.

"Now"—she tossed her long hair over her shoulder as she washed the soap away from his wound with warm water—"be quiet so I can concentrate. And while you're at it, stop bleeding."

Her vigorous ministrations had his scratch leaking anew.

"If only it were that easy," he muttered, sitting stoically through the rest of her ferocious first aid.

She dusted off her hands after slathering antibiotic ointment on his injury and taping a bandage over it. "There. All done. And not too shabby, if I do say so myself. See?" She cocked an eyebrow. "I could've been a doctor. It's not so hard."

"And imagine how much better the world would have been with one less lawyer around."

He'd meant for it to be a joke. Like he *always* joked with her. But there was an unintended sharpness in his voice.

His hope that she hadn't picked up on it was dashed when she fisted a hand on her cocked hip. It was a position he knew well. He'd secretly dubbed it her *sassy pants* stance.

She usually whipped it out right before she laid into him. It was sometimes combined with a smart-alecky head tilt. This time, however, she simply narrowed her eyes.

"Okay. That's it. You either come clean and tell me why you hate my profession so much, or you never make another snide comment about it or tell another lawyer joke again. Because I'm done taking it on the chin with no acceptable explanation."

"You're pretty brave." He mirrored her expression. "Thinking you can unilaterally lay down the law like that."

When she smirked, he knew she was going to come back with something appropriately witty. She didn't disappoint.

"You shouldn't be surprised. Just because I have a vagina doesn't mean my balls aren't still bigger than yours."

"And there's that mouth your momma warned you about," he countered, becoming distracted when talk of her vagina had his eyes unintentionally traveling south, past her smooth neck, past her delicate clavicle bones, until…

If his eyes were tires, they would've left rubber on the pavement. That's how quickly they came to a screeching stop once they hit her chest.

Jesus hopscotching Christ. She's not wearing a bra.

Of course he'd *known* she wasn't. He'd seen it draped over the top of his lamp. But now, with her doing her sassy pants stance, and with the candlelight flickering over the front of his threadbare—thanks to the one million times he'd washed it—white T-shirt, he could *see* she wasn't wearing a bra.

Her breasts were large and teardrop shaped. The outline of her dark areolas cast half-dollar-sized shadows against the thin fabric. And her pencil-eraser nipples made little tents of the cotton.

His mouth went dry. His dick went rock hard. And all the

reasons why he'd been calling himself a damned fool, all the reasons why it was a bad idea to take her up on her offer and take her to bed, fell right out of his head.

"Speaking of your mouth…" He snagged her wrist and pulled her forward until her knees bumped his. Encircling her waist with his hands—and taking a moment to enjoy how dramatically her hips flared—he pulled on her until she was forced to straddle his lap.

The instant her plump, warm ass hit his thighs, he finished with, "Let's put it to a better use than talking."

Twining her arms around his neck, she asked seductively, "And just what did you have in mind for my mouth, sailor?"

He leaned forward until his lips were a hair's breadth from hers. She gasped in expectation. And the sound—the same sound a woman made when a man entered her warm and ready body—had his cock lurching impatiently behind his fly.

"It's best if I show you," he whispered before gently sucking first her top then her bottom lip into his mouth.

She tasted sweet, like something sinful and sugary. Tart, like something decadent and delicious.

"Dalton." Her warm breath bathed his hungry lips. His name sounded musical in her mouth. "I want you."

"You'll have me," he swore. And then he rethought his response. "You've *had* me since the first moment you walked around that bar and cocked that eyebrow at me."

On cue, one sleek black brow arced high across her forehead until…*yup. Witchy woman. There she is.*

"I've been under your spell since that first night," he admitted roughly. "You look at me and I forget my name."

"It's Dalton," she said with a coy tilt of her head. "Dalton Davis Simmons to be precise. Now, shut up and kiss me."

He did.

And damn the consequences.

He'd deal with them tomorrow.

CHAPTER 9

4:41 PM...

Will had been afraid on the water plenty of times.

The sea was a capricious creature, after all, always out to maim and kill those who didn't give her the proper respect. But never had he experienced the kind of terror he felt as Julia's eyewall passed overhead.

For four hours, he'd kept the bow of the trawler pointed toward the prevailing winds. For four hours he'd listened to the main engine roar as the boat rode the waves to their crests before surfing down their backsides. And for four hours he'd never lost faith in the ship or his crew.

But when the most treacherous part of the storm hit, things that'd simply been sliding back and forth across the deck began to fly around and break up. Fin, Jace, and Brady had stopped playing whack-a-mole with the various systems that needed tending and were now hanging onto anything that would keep them steady. And the sound of the bow hitting the bottom troughs of the waves was like a gunshot.

Waves that'd been hills before rose like mountains now, even on the protected side of the island. And the air outside was so full of flying foam, it was impossible to see the ocean around them.

Will had lashed himself to the helm with a rope. And the dynamometer banged off the stops, indicating they were sometimes rolling well over thirty degrees.

Jesus, Mary, and Joseph!

It felt like they were stuck inside some sort of diabolical mashup of a carnival ride and a washing machine. And his only solace was knowing that if the boat was going to fall apart, it probably would've already done so.

There was no longer any pattern to the waves. They seemed to come from all directions. Brady got seasick, barfing up his lunch against the far wall. And the catamaran, which had been double anchored and visible off their starboard side, was now nowhere to be seen.

"God, help us!" Brady cried.

Will figured his friend's plea was useless. The god of the bible, the one they'd been raised to believe in, made way for the ocean gods at times like these.

And if the ocean gods want us, Will thought desperately, *the ocean gods will take us. And there's not a damn thing any of us can do to stop them.*

CHAPTER 10

4:53 PM...

The eyewall was upon them.

Winds that'd been raging against the house were now battering it with everything they had. The *crash* of a nearby palm tree as it lost its battle to hang on sounded above the cacophony of the furious gale. The storm surge slapped at the floorboards on the lower level, and from the direction of Uncle John's bedroom, Dana Levine's whispered words, "Heaven help us," echoed down the hall.

Cami registered none of it.

All she saw was Doc's hungry green eyes. All she felt was his warm breath as he gently cupped her face, leaned forward, and kissed one eyelid, then the other. All she smelled was his clean, mountain man scent when he peppered her face with delicious nips until he once again stopped with his lips hovering a bare inch above hers.

"Cami." Her name sounded like a prayer in his mouth.

And then, all she tasted was him when he finally, *finally* kissed her.

A fluttery sensation winged through her chest as he took her mouth with more care, more softness than she could have imagined. Once again, the word that drifted through her brain was *cherished*.

She'd never known anyone who could so thoroughly combine sweet with sexy. Who could call to her heart at the same time he stoked her libido.

Before she knew it, she'd sunk into him. Melted against him. Luxuriating in the touch of his warm lips, in the slick glide of his tongue, in the soft groan he breathed into her mouth when she matched him stroke for stroke.

It was the kind of kiss seen in the movies, where the main characters get completely lost in each other. The kind of kiss poets wrote about, where two people became one by the simple act of melding their mouths. The kind of kiss songwriters sang about, where even the beat and melody felt like the thrust and parry of eager, hungry tongues.

Cami had been thirteen years old the first time she'd given a boy permission to taste her lips. In the last row of The UA Theater, Dario De Luca had leaned over during a showing of *Blue Crush* and planted one on her.

When she said planted, she meant *planted*. It'd been rough and clumsy and more than a little slobbery. Her watermelon-flavored Lip Smackers lip gloss had smeared across Dario's mouth. And she'd tasted on his tongue the spaghetti he'd had for dinner mixed with the Jujyfruits he'd bought at the concession stand.

Looking back, she was surprised that first kiss hadn't put her off the activity altogether. But, thankfully, things had improved after that. Although, there was a difference between *improvement* and *perfection*.

In her experience, most men, even the ones who were

good kissers, benefited from a little instruction. A little subtle direction on how much pressure to apply. How much tongue to insert. How *little* spit should be swapped.

She was always pragmatic about the process since, to her way of thinking, good kissers were like good wine. They got better with age and the more times she sampled them.

But Doc? Oh, Doc needed no guidance. He was already a top-shelf Cabernet. Delicious and complex. No need to stick him back in the cellar to mature. The man was at his peak.

And he'd managed to catch her off guard. Because after all the buildup between them, she'd expected him to pounce. Attack. Devour. But his kiss was incredibly tender. And *thorough*.

He seemed intent on sampling every inch of her lips, every part of her tongue, all the space inside her mouth.

This, she thought. *This was what it was like the first night we met.*

In all the months since then, she'd convinced herself she'd imagined his skill. Convinced herself she'd been too tipsy and that what she'd perceived as perfection was simply a case of impaired judgment.

But no. He was everything she remembered.

And more.

Her bare toes curled against the cool tile. Her skin grew so sensitive, she could feel the heat of the candle sitting on the windowsill. And the fluttery sensation in her chest moved to her stomach. Then lower. Lower still. Until every inch of her was quivering. Alive. *Hungry.*

"Dalton." She fisted her hands into his still damp hair. The strands were soft and cool at the ends, thick and warm near his scalp.

She pulled him closer. Wanting to absorb him. Wanting to crawl inside his skin. Or have him crawl inside hers.

Which, okay, sounded a little creepy, a little Buffalo Bill-ish—*yes, it will, Precious. It will get the hose!* But it was the only way she felt she could be close enough to him.

Her entreaty was all it took for him to shift the kiss. The pressure of his mouth grew harder. The dart of his tongue grew greedier. His hands left her face to span her waist and rock her forward onto the steely evidence of his desire.

She gasped at the delicious friction, feeling the beat of her heart between her legs.

And yet as delicious as the friction was, it wasn't enough. It wouldn't *be* enough until she popped the buttons on his fly, pulled out his raging erection, and impaled herself upon him. Until he filled the emptiness at her center. Stretched her with his girth. Stroked her with his length. Stuffed her to the brim until the pleasure of having him inside bordered on pain.

She'd always considered herself a lusty woman. But never, *never*, had she wanted a man as much as she wanted Doc.

No. It's more than want. It's need.

She *needed* him.

And Camilla D'Angelo needed no one.

When the thought gave her a moment's pause, she quickly shoved it aside.

She was finally, *finally* allowing herself to take hold of what he'd been teasing her with for months. And she wasn't going to let a frisson of fear stop her.

"Let's go to the bedroom," she whispered.

He didn't need to be asked twice. Palming her ass, he shoved to a stand.

Again, she experienced the thrill of being carried by him. Of feeling small and delicate in his arms. And when his quick movements raked the length of his hardness against her center, it was heaven.

Or maybe it was hell because it just. Wasn't. *Enough.*

"Lord help me, I can feel how hot you are. How *wet* you are," he whispered against her lips.

A less lusty woman might have been embarrassed. But Cami felt no shame in her body's responses. In fact, there was power in it. *She* was powerful. A sexual being. A *woman.*
Hear me roar!

"It's your fault." She nibbled his plump lower lip. "This is what you do to me."

Her words had his dick flexing against her. "And that is what *you* do to *me*." His dark, gritty tone sounded as hungry as she felt. "Now, cross your ankles and hang on."

When she didn't immediately comply, he squeezed her ass. Not painfully. Just as a warning to heed his request.

A new rush of wetness ran between her legs and made them both groan.

Locking her ankles above the rise of his high, tight butt, she swallowed his growl of satisfaction at her obedience. She liked the way the sound rumbled around in her mouth and then slid down her throat.

She didn't know whether to laugh or cry when, once they were in the hallway, Uncle John's deep voice sounded nearby. *Too* nearby. She was pretty sure John stood right next to them.

"Glad you kids decided to heed my advice. But your timin' stinks 'cause the eye is here and we need to do whatever damage control we can before the ass end of Julia starts passin' over. We also need to check on those fishermen. Make sure they made it. And if they did, ask 'em if they've changed their minds and want to ride out the back half with us. Y'all call a timeout and go get your shoes on."

"Why do I suddenly feel thirteen instead of thirty-three?" Cami whispered in Doc's ear.

"It was the part where he told us to get our shoes on."

She giggled, and then did something she'd been wanting

DEAD IN THE WATER

to do since the first night she met him. She rubbed her cheek over his sandpaper stubble.

It was deliciously abrasive. She imagined it would feel even *better* when it was caressing the inside of her thighs.

Her thoughts must've been loud enough for him to hear because she felt his cock flex against her again an instant before his hand tightened on her ass.

"Cut it out, minx." His warm lips were close to her ear.

"Me? You're the one who's reading my mind. *You* cut it out."

"Am I gonna hafta take a crowbar to you two?" Uncle John demanded.

To her immense dissatisfaction, Doc lowered her to her feet. And sweet baby Jesus, it was like ripping two sheets of Velcro apart. By the time she was standing, she felt raw and abraded. As if she were missing her other half.

As soon as the thought whispered through her head, that frisson of fear was back. This time, she shoved it aside in order to face the music.

Or Uncle John, as the case may be.

Taking a deep breath, she swung around to find not only John grinning widely at her, but Dana too.

"No need to be embarrassed," Dana assured her sweetly when her cheeks grew red hot. "We're all adults here."

"Tell that to this one." Cami hooked a thumb toward Uncle John. "He orders us around like we're still cutting teeth."

"Someone's gotta herd the cats on this island," John declared. "Else it'd be pandemonium."

Weak shafts of sunlight slanted in through the slats in the storm shutters and gave the dust motes dancing in the air the look of tiny, golden fairies.

The eye of the storm.

A strangely peaceful space between anarchy and chaos.

"And by the way"—John gave her a wink—"I knew you had it in you."

LT and Olivia saved her from having to respond by stumbling out of their bedroom—Olivia was busy smoothing down her hair, and LT hastily pulled a T-shirt over his head. Both of them were ruddy-faced and looking like they'd run a marathon.

"Time to assess the damage while we got the chance," LT echoed Uncle John's earlier sentiments.

"Let me grab my shoes." Cami tried to turn toward Doc's room to fetch her sandals. And her bra and panties. Even though she wasn't a prude, neither was she an exhibitionist. But Doc stopped her by gripping her shoulders and keeping her directly in front of him.

After sending a questioning glance over her shoulder, she had to roll in her lips to keep from gasping when he pulled her back slightly and the top of her butt brushed against his raging hard-on. A hard-on she would've already unwrapped and gone to work on were it not for the ill-timed arrival of Julia's damned eye.

Never in my life did I think I'd been wishing for those deafening winds to come back, she thought. *And yet here I am.*

Understanding Doc's dilemma, John chuckled. "We'll give y'all a couple minutes to compose yourselves and then meet you downstairs."

He ushered Dana toward the stairway. LT and Olivia followed closely behind them. But LT stopped abruptly once he'd pulled even with Doc. It caused his wife to plow into his back.

"Oof!" Olivia frowned. "You should come equipped with a pair of brake lights, Leo. I swear."

LT ignored her and demanded of Cami and Doc, "Why do y'all need to compose yourselves?" Before either of them could answer, he howled, "Ow! What was that for?" He glared at his wife.

"Just keep on keeping on," Olivia ordered him, shooting Cami a look that said, *Holy geez men are as dense as doorknobs sometimes.*

"But I don't understand what—"

"Move, sailor!"

"Fine!" LT was clearly disgruntled as he let his wife push him toward the stairs. They were halfway to the first floor when Cami heard him whisper, "What am I missin'?"

Olivia's answer was hushed. But with the silence echoing around the house, Cami had no trouble hearing it. "They've finally given in to the inevitable."

"Really?" LT sounded skeptical. "How can you tell?"

"By the beard burn around Cami's mouth and Doc's deer-in-the-headlights look."

Cami glanced up at Doc. "You do sort of look like a deer in the headlights." Her brow wrinkled when a thought occurred. "Please tell me that's because we were caught necking like horny teenagers and not because you're having second thoughts about what just happened."

Something moved behind his eyes. But it was gone so quickly, she couldn't tell what it was.

"Blame this pained, slightly panicked expression"—he pointed to his face—"on the priapism."

"The what?" She wrinkled her nose.

"An erection that won't go down." He gestured toward the bulge that was still very evident inside his shorts.

She would be a liar if she said she didn't experience a thrill at the thought of having rendered him eternally erect. Some of her glee must've flashed across her face because he frowned heavily.

"Stop looking so pleased with yourself. If it lasts more than four hours, it could become a real problem."

"It won't last more than four hours," she assured him with a seductive wink. "In fact, as soon as we're finished helping the others, I'd be surprised if it lasts more than thirty minutes. Forty-five, tops."

He lifted an intrigued eyebrow. "Is that a challenge? It sounds like a challenge."

"Oh, no." She gently cupped his hard-on, loving the sound of his breath hissing between his teeth. "It's a promise."

CHAPTER 11

5:12 PM...

Maybe their radio went out in the storm," Dana said after John tried to hail the fishermen for the second time and got back nothing but static.

Dana Levine's sunniness was one of the first things John had noticed about her. How quick she was to smile. How easily she laughed. How the smallest things seemed to excite her. But now her cheery tone sounded contrived.

When he glanced over, she was unable to hide the look of concern on her pretty face.

He liked that about her too. That she cared about a boatful of complete strangers.

"Probably so." He forced optimism into his voice in hopes it'd wipe some of the worry from her expression.

In truth, he reckoned it was far more likely that if the crew of the trawler wasn't answering their radio, it was because their radio was sitting at the bottom of the ocean right along with their boat.

"Try 'em a coupla more times," Leo said as Doc's and Cami's footsteps sounded on the stairs. "Olivia and I will go check the screened-in porch. See if it's survived so far. Doc?" Leo added as soon as Doc stepped onto the first floor with Cami close by his side. "You and Cami do a quick inspection of the shutters. Make sure they're still secure."

"Copy that." Doc nodded and looked like he had to remind himself not to add in a salute.

Even if John lived to be a hundred years old, he'd never get used to the way Leo's friends were quick to comply whenever Leo gave an order. Then again, anytime John looked at his nephew, all he saw was the snot-nosed kid who used to sit on his brother's knee begging for fried bologna sandwiches and tales of ghost galleons. Not the hardened Navy SEAL who'd led the toughest, staunchest, most loyal group of men John had ever had the honor to know.

How time flies, he thought and experienced a pang of melancholy.

Perhaps it was finding the treasure. Perhaps it was the thought of moving on from Wayfarer Island and only coming back to visit during the holidays and for special occasions. Or perhaps it was simply his age. Whatever the reason, recently he'd been reflecting on his life. On the trajectory it'd taken and the direction he wanted it to go in next.

Sixty-five felt like a milestone, the point where he'd accomplished everything he'd set out to accomplish, experienced everything human existence had to offer, and should be settling in to his lazy, comfortable, twilight years.

Except, he wasn't ready to settle. And he couldn't help wondering if that was because he hadn't *really* experienced everything human existence had to offer.

He'd never been in love.

Oh, there'd been the odd girlfriend over the years

whom he'd *liked* a whole lot and whom he'd grown to care for quite a bit. But an all-consuming, all-encompassing, all-engrossing devotion that made him want to do as the Dixie Cups suggested and go to the chapel? A love like his brother James had felt for Leo's pretty mother?

That had eluded him.

Or he supposed it was fairer to say he'd avoided it. Thinking himself smarter than the Average Joe not to get all twisted up with someone who might end up breaking his heart one way or another.

Lately, however, he'd begun to wonder if it was true what the philosophers said.

Was it better to have loved and lost than never to have loved at all?

Doc certainly thought so.

One night recently, the two of them had stayed up long after everyone else went to bed. Sitting around the beach campfire, listening to the crackle of the flames and the shush of the surf against the fine grains of sand along the beach, John had looked over to find Doc's expression troubled.

It was a look he recognized. A look that came over Doc's face anytime Doc thought of his wife.

"If you'd known how it was gonna end with your sweet Lily," John had asked, "and how much you'd suffer, would you still have gone through with it? Would you still have let yourself fall in love?"

The shadow of memories had still been in Doc's eyes when he'd said without hesitation, "Yes." John's frown had prompted an explanation. "I've had a lot of adventures in life, Uncle John. I've seen and done more than most men. But I swear to you, the best thing I ever did, the thing I'm most proud of, is that I loved a woman with everything in me, with my entire heart and my whole soul. *That* is my greatest accomplishment. My grandest adventure."

Considering Doc was a bona fide physician, Navy SEAL, *and* treasure hunter, that'd been saying a lot. And John was a little embarrassed to admit he'd felt a pang of jealousy.

Or maybe it'd been a pang of envy.

For the first time, he'd admitted there was a part of him that wanted to know what that particular grand adventure was like.

He was pulled from his recollection when Cami heaved open the front door and a gust of fresh air wafted into the living room. She yelped when the wind was followed by a giant palm frond.

Doc valiantly caught the branch before it could tumble in on her. He sent it sailing across the porch and into the front yard with a grunt.

Cami batted her sooty lashes. "My hero. I think I might swoon."

Doc bared his teeth. "Stop your teasing, woman."

"Make me, *Doctor*."

Cami squealed and ran onto the porch when Doc made a grab for her. Then she squealed again when Doc caught her on the steps.

John wondered if it was possible for a man to have *two* great loves in a lifetime, *two* grand adventures.

For Doc's sake, he sure as hell hoped so.

"Looks like we'll have some competition during round two of the storm." Olivia nudged Leo.

"Please." Leo scoffed. "My only competition is myself. And you can bet I'm goin' to beat my last score. How many was that again? Six? Seven?"

"Leo!" Olivia slapped his arm. "Not in front of your uncle!"

"I hate to break it to you, darlin'," John told his niece-by-marriage, a woman he loved to pieces not only because she was smart and capable and kind, but also because she loved his nephew so well. "But your bedroom shares a wall with mine. Ain't nothin' happened in there that I'm not well aware of."

Olivia was usually good at hiding her emotions. *All that CIA training, no doubt.* But she couldn't stop her cheeks from blanching of color.

"Tell me you're joking," she wheezed.

"Wish I was." He tried not to laugh at the look of horror that crossed her face.

"Leo!" She scowled up at her husband. "Did you know the walls between our bedrooms were paper thin?"

Leo had the grace to look chagrined.

"You *did*." She gasped. "Why didn't you *tell* me?"

"Because if I'd told you, you would've stopped lettin' me do that thing that makes you squeal like a—"

She slapped a hand over Leo's mouth. Leo smacked a kiss into the center of her hand and that was all it took to smooth down Olivia's hackles.

"Sometimes I ask myself why I love you so much," she grumbled.

Leo leaned away from her hand. "Because I do that thing that makes you squeal like a—"

"Ahhhhh!" She threw up her hands and ran around the stacked furniture toward the kitchen.

"Where you runnin' off to?" John called teasingly.

"Outside to find a sink hole that'll swallow me up since none seem likely to appear inside the house!" she yelled over her shoulder.

He chuckled and then shook his head when he caught his nephew watching his wife's departure with a predatory interest.

"Put your tongue back into your mouth, boy," he scolded. "Act like you got some raisin'."

Leo was unfazed by his rebuke. "I know it's cliché, but I sure do love to watch that woman go." Growling low in his chest, he took off after his wife.

"My goodness." Dana fanned her face. "This is my first hurricane. Nobody told me they were aphrodisiacs."

"Like most things that get the blood pumpin', I reckon." John winked at her.

"Well…" She cleared her throat. "From the looks of things, you and I are the only ones who won't be spending the second half of the storm naked."

He wiggled his eyebrows. "That don't gotta be the case if you don't want it to be."

When she blushed beet red, he worried he'd overstepped.

He could've sworn she was as intrigued by him as he was by her. Then again, once they'd returned to his room following the broken window incident, she hadn't given him any indication she wanted to revisit the kiss they'd almost shared.

Maybe my romance radar is outta whack, he thought uneasily.

He opened his mouth to apologize and admit to being out of practice when it came to wooing women. Not that he'd given up on sex, of course. When he got the itch, he knew how to scratch it. But the women he took to bed— usually tourists on vacation in Key West—suffered no illusions he was offering them more than a good time for a night or two. Before the words could leave his mouth, however, Dana admitted, "I'm not going to lie. I'm tempted by your offer." Her adorable button nose wrinkled. "But I'm just old-fashioned enough to need at least *one* proper date first."

Warmth spread through John's chest. He recognized it as the glow of anticipation. Of *possibility*.

"Ain't nothin' wrong with bein' a little old-fashioned," he assured her. Then he pinned a serious look on her. "Dana

Levine, it would be my honor to wine and dine you once this damn storm passes. What'd'ya say to some fried grouper and conch fritters? I know just the place."

She beamed at him so brightly, he forgot how to breathe. And he *definitely* forgot what he was supposed to be doing when she caught her lower lip between her teeth and said sincerely, "I'd love that, John."

In the way of women since the beginning of time, her smile turned coy when she realized she'd flustered him. Hitching her chin toward the radio, she added, "Aren't you going to try the trawler again?"

"Oh. Right." He gave his head a shake, hoping to unscramble his brains. "Sure thing."

Picking up the handset, he put out another call to the fishermen. He released the push-to-talk button and...*nothing*. Just the hiss of white noise.

"Damn it." A ball of dread replaced the lovely glow Dana had put in the center of his chest. "Reckon I better go have a looksee. Just in case they're washed ashore or somethin'."

She was quick to volunteer. "I'll come with you."

As much as he'd *love* to keep her by his side—and maybe steal a kiss in the eye of a hurricane?—he felt compelled to warn her. "You'll have to wade through water. Likely knee-high in places."

The storm surge had abated somewhat. But he'd survived enough hurricanes to know it wouldn't withdraw completely until Julia moved on.

"If you can manage it, I can manage it," she assured him.

Her spunk, he thought. *That's* another *thing I like about her.*

"Well, come on then." He offered his arm and couldn't help puffing out his chest when she didn't hesitate to take it. Her cool fingers felt nice when they wrapped around his bicep. And the warmth of her by his side made him acutely aware of how soft her skin looked, how sweet and fresh her bouncy hair smelled, like citrus and sunrise.

Together, they stepped onto the porch, blinking into the weak sunlight.

The sky overhead was cloudless, a beautiful robin's egg blue, but the lateness of the day meant the sun was hidden behind the circle of angry clouds to the west. The island was quiet in the calm of the eye. And the air was fragrant with the scent of the sea.

But that's where the fairy tale ended.

John's heart turned over at the same time Dana breathed, "My god."

Storms like Julia took everything that was familiar and ripped it apart. The destruction to the island wasn't the worst he'd seen, but it wasn't the best either.

Two trees near the house were snapped like kindling. Two others were laid over on their sides with their root balls sticking up in the air. The wind had picked up the fallen palm fronds and blown them around like dandelion seeds before piling them up against the side of the porch.

We'll get her lookin' spick and span again, he thought with determination. *Just like we've done a dozen times before.*

His family had held the lease on Wayfarer Island since Ulysses S. Grant sat pretty at 1600 Pennsylvania Ave. And now that Leo had the funds to buy the tropical retreat outright, it would *truly* be a home away from home for everyone with a last name of Anderson.

John hated seeing the island in such a pitiful state. But having spent his entire life living around the Gulf, he was pragmatic when it came to the storms.

Cleanup sucked. Repairs were a never-ending chore. And each year during hurricane season, all eyes were glued to The Weather Channel like it was forecasting the winners of the Super Bowl for the next twenty years. But the silver lining?

We get to live in paradise.

"Watch your step," he cautioned as he led Dana past some debris that'd piled up on the porch.

They'd barely set foot on the first tread of the stairs when a deep voice he didn't recognize called, "Stop right there!"

Doc and Cami rounded the side of the house. Or maybe *waded* around the side of the house was more apt since the storm surge lapped at their ankles and calves. Their hands were in the air. Cami's face was as white as a sheet. And there was a killing rage in Doc's eyes.

A split second later, when four masked men slipped around the corner with weapons aimed at Doc's and Cami's backs, John understood Cami's paleness and Doc's fury.

His mouth went as dry as the desert wind that time he'd vacationed in the Santa Fe. And he instinctively put himself between Dana and the threat by stepping in front of her.

"We told ya not to move, ya dubbah! Don't make us shoot ya!" one of the masked men yelled.

"John?" Dana's tremulous voice sounded over his shoulder.

He wanted to turn and take her in his arms. Wrap her up and keep her safe. Instead, he lifted his hands and told her, "It's okay, darlin'. Just stay calm and everything's gonna be all right."

He hoped to hell he wasn't lying.

CHAPTER 12

5:34 PM...

S he's not the one you should be worried about," Doc growled when the end of the masked man's gun aimed first at Cami, then at him, and then back at Cami. He was grinding his teeth so hard he thought it a wonder he could open his mouth to speak.

The four gunmen had pulled the ladderback chairs down from the Formica-topped kitchen table, placed them in a line in the middle of the living room, and forced the Wayfarer Islanders to take seats side-by-side.

Easier to keep an eye on us all, Doc reckoned.

"Stop aiming that piece at her and keep aiming it at me and we won't have ourselves a problem," he added to the redheaded assailant who kept swinging his pistol between Doc and Cami. Doc knew the gunman was a redhead because auburn curls peeked from the back of the dude's black ski mask.

"You're not the one in charge here." Red snarled. "So ya can stop givin' me orders."

The last word sounded more like *ahdahs*. Doc noted all four new arrivals spoke with thick New England accents. Although, they sounded different than Mason, so they hailed from somewhere other than Boston.

What the hell are they doing this far from home? And, more importantly, what the hell do they want with us? he silently wondered.

Aloud, he said, "I'm not giving orders. I'm just making it real clear that if you keep waving your gun in her face, the first chance I get, I'm going to grind you up until you're nothing but teeth and toenails."

He meant every single syllable.

Each time the yawning black hole at the end of the dude's Smith and Wesson revolver swung toward Cami, Doc could very clearly imagine himself beating the asswipe into a bloody pulp.

And *enjoying* the exercise.

Especially because Cami posed no threat. Her hands had been secured behind her back with a black zip tie.

"Hands behind your back, bub," said the man who'd already hogtied Cami.

Doc had to hand it to the intruders. They were well organized.

The four masked men had exchanged only a handful of words while ordering the Wayfarer Islanders about. Three of them had automatically moved in front of the group once they'd gotten them seated, spreading out so each of them covered two islanders a piece. And the fourth man, a tall, skinny guy, had moved behind the line of ladderback chairs, tucking his pistol into the front of his pants and pulling out a bouquet of zip ties from his back pocket.

If Doc had been a little less seasoned on this particular

subject, he might have said they were military. That kind of synchronization usually stemmed from hours of training.

But the gunmen didn't carry themselves like soldiers, where every move was a study in efficiency. And the way they handled their weapons told him they weren't terribly comfortable around handguns. Lord knew, by the end of bootcamp, any serviceperson worth their salt considered a sidearm an extension of their hand.

So...what are they? he wondered. *Cops?* Nah. Police were pretty comfortable around weapons too. Not as comfortable as soldiers, but still.

Which leaves civilians? He could see that being the case if these four were life-long friends, guys who'd grown up connected at the hip and, as such, could anticipate each other's moves.

But then the questions remained. *Who the hell are they? And what the hell are they doing here?*

"Wrists together," Zip Tie Guy barked at him because he'd failed to comply the first time.

Curling his hands into fists, Doc lined his wrists up thumb-to-thumb behind the chair. Holding his breath, he waited for Zip Tie Guy to tell him to change his positioning and face his palms together.

One heartbeat became two. Two became three. But the man never said a word. Instead, Doc felt the cool plastic cinch around his wrists.

A surge of satisfaction almost had the corners of his mouth curling up. *As LT likes to say, bingo, bango, bongo.*

And speaking of LT...

When Zip Tie Guy moved on to secure Dana, Doc leaned forward ever so slightly.

LT was at the other end of the line of chairs, but he'd craned his neck around the others so he had an unencumbered view of Doc. The instant their eyes met—and despite the room's dismal lighting thanks to the quickly setting sun making the lone candle sitting on the desk work overtime—a silent exchange passed between them.

Doc: *He doesn't know about the zip ties.*

LT: *Roger that.*

As Navy SEALs, they'd been trained to do…well, just about everything. Whether it was tying knots underwater while fighting someone hell bent on sabotaging their oxygen tanks, making explosives out of common household cleaners, or jumping out of airplanes at altitudes so high the air was too thin to breathe, the SEALs believed that knowledge made for the perfect human war machine.

One very specific segment of SEAL candidate instruction was known as SERE training—survival, evasion, resistance, and escape. It was the brainchild of a bunch of Vietnam POWs.

And talk about some tough sonsofbitches.

Doc had utilized his *escape* knowledge while allowing his wrists to be bound. Now he waited to see if he'd need to put *resistance* and *survival* into action.

The man guarding LT and Olivia spoke up for the first time. "Where have ya hidden the treasure, eh?"

Well, that answers the question of what they want with us, Doc thought, his stomach clinching into a hard ball.

He'd hoped the fact that the gunmen had tied the islanders up and were wearing masks meant that, whatever they were up to, whatever they were doing on Wayfarer Island, they had no intention of *killing* the six of them.

But if the intruders had come for the treasure, there was no way they would leave behind witnesses who'd seen their trawler, who'd heard their accents, and who could give their physical descriptions to the authorities. Unless they were a pack of fools, there was no way they thought they could get away with the heist without offing the islanders first.

Which meant they had tied Doc and the others up so they could threaten and abuse them until they gave up the location of the treasure. As for the masks? Maybe the gunmen simply liked the idea of hiding their faces from their victims. Like executioners of old.

Fuck!

In the matter of a moment, things had gone from bad to the worst-case scenario.

LT had one hell of a poker face. *Usually.* But he couldn't hide his surprise and dismay. It was obvious he'd come to the exact same conclusions Doc had. Still, LT played dumb when he answered, "What are you talkin' about? We haven't found the treasure yet."

"Bullshit," the man spat. "You hauled it up yesterday durin' the king tide."

How the hell do they know that? Did they use a surveillance plane? Doc wondered.

It was possible, he supposed. Except surveillance planes required serious scratch, and by the looks of the gunmen's ragged jeans and work-worn boots, they weren't exactly rolling in the dough.

A drone maybe?

But Doc and his partners had a habit of watching the sky. Call it a survival instinct left over from their time in the Navy when death sometimes threatened from above. If there'd been a drone hovering around the dive site, surely *one* of them would've noticed it.

Is it possible someone from the Deep Six crew let something slip last night in Key West?

That was the easiest to answer. *Hell to the naw.* If his former SEAL teammates knew anything, it was how to keep a secret. For shit's sake, keeping secrets was second nature to men who'd spent most of their adult years working in the black and gray areas of international intelligence and being deployed into just about every combat zone on the planet.

So how? How do these bastards know we brought up the treasure?

Olivia asked his silent question aloud. "Who told you that?" And then, proving you could take the woman out of the CIA, but you couldn't take the CIA out of the woman, she added, "Because whoever they were, they were full of shit."

She made the lie sound like god's honest truth. Spooks were world-renowned for their ability to deceive.

For a moment, Doc thought she might've convinced the gunmen because dread skittered through the man's darting eyes. Then his mouth curved into a nasty frown. "Shut your lyin' trap, missy. The men are talkin' here."

Doc could feel Cami bristling beside him. She wasn't one to put up with anything that even *hinted* at misogyny. He'd found that out the hard way when she'd damn near torn him a new asshole after he told an off-color joke.

But Olivia? She only laughed. "Wow. Does that machismo work on the women in Maine? Because I have to warn you, it doesn't fly down here."

Even though the man's face was obscured by a ski mask, Doc could tell by the look in his eyes that Olivia had scored a direct hit. Not about the feigned bravado, but about where they were from, which answered *another* of Doc's questions.

"I told ya to shut up," the man snarled, taking a step toward Olivia and bringing the evil eye of his weapon closer to her forehead.

The temperature in the room jumped ten degrees. A direct result of the molten anger that rolled out of LT.

John spoke up with a distraction. "Ow! Damn. Not so tight," he told Zip Tie Guy when the plastic cord locked around his wrists. "I'm old. I already got poor circulation."

"You're not *that* old," Zip Tie Guy countered.

John, always one to add levity to a situation, chuckled.

"Thanks for noticin'. Also, you can't blame a guy for tryin', right?"

Zip Tie Guy said nothing to that. When he moved on to Olivia, the dude holding the gun on her turned his eyes on LT. "I'll ask this one more time, shithead. And if ya don't answer me, I'll pistol whip your woman. Where. Is. The. *Treasure?*"

A hard muscle worked in LT's jaw that had nothing to do with the Big Red gum he usually chewed. "Upstairs." The two syllables dripped from his lips like venom. "Room at the end of the hallway. The blue duffel bags."

"That's better." The gunman's smug smile showed through the mouth hole in the mask. "Hurry up and tie this last one," he added to Zip Tie Guy. "Then come around and guard 'em while I run upstairs and grab the treasure."

He appeared to be the leader of the group. The others followed his orders without question.

"Almost done." Zip Tie Guy started to secure LT's hands. But before he could cinch the plastic tight, the ink peeking out from beneath LT's T-shirt caught his eye and had him lifting LT's sleeve. Gasping, he stepped back and pointed. "Holy shit! Check that out."

"What? What is it?" The man guarding John and Dana demanded. He reminded Doc of Mason, about as thick as he was tall. A human wrecking ball. "Jeezum Crow, you know what? I don't have time to check anything out. Hurry up and finish tyin' him. It's already gettin' breezed up out there."

Doc glanced toward the shuttered windows. Weak sunlight still streamed through the slats, but it was obvious Julia's tail end was closing in quick.

The wind along the backside of her eyewall could be heard howling in the near distance. The storm surge running beneath the house made a licking sound against the foundation's supports as the wave action picked up. And the air, which had been blessedly crisp and fresh in the center of the eye, was once more growing dank and heavy-smelling.

"This sumbitch is a Navy SEAL." Zip Tie Guy's voice was wheezy. "That's what the tat means." He pointed at LT's Budweiser ink. "I saw it on a documentary about—"

"Just 'cause he's got the tattoo don't mean he earned it," Wrecking Ball interrupted.

Zip Tie Guy leaned around LT, his eyes wide. "That true? You a poser?"

"What's it matter?" LT came back. "You gonna believe me either way I answer?"

"Secure him to his chair. Just to be safe," the leader of the group instructed.

After binding LT's wrists, Zip Tie Guy also secured LT's elbows to the rungs on the back of the chair.

Damn, Doc thought. *That throws a wrench in the works.*

If LT couldn't escape the ties so the two of them could overwhelm their captors, they'd need to find another way to turn the tide in their favor. Doc ran through possible scenarios while the leader of the masked men disappeared upstairs.

By the time the head honcho came back from his second trip, four of the six duffel bags were stacked on the floor near the bottom of the stairs and Doc had come up with a plan. It wasn't a *good* plan. Everything would hinge on timing. But it was the only way he could see getting Red's gun.

The burn of adrenaline had his heart pumping double-time. Once again, he fell back on his training.

Breath work was a trick SEALs used to slow their heartrate and lower their blood pressure. Doc employed a method known as *box breathing* by focusing on a speck of peeling paint on the wall behind the stairs and visualizing drawing a box around it.

Simple. But effective.

Once he'd repeated the trick twice, his mind was laser-focused, and his heart was metronome-steady.

Turning to catch LT's eyes, another wordless exchange passed between them.

He hitched his chin toward Zip Tie Guy. *Get ready to ram him.*

LT gave a slight nod. *Roger that.*

Darting a quick glance at Red, Doc added, *I'll break my tie and go for his gun.*

LT's left eye twitched in a pseudo wink. *Ready when you are.*

"There are only two more bags upstairs," Head Honcho declared. "Where's the rest of the loot?"

"Not here." LT sounded almost jubilant. And his smile? It reminded Doc of a shark about to bite the head off its prey. "And by that I mean it's not on the island. If you were hopin' to get your hands on the lot of it, you're shit outta luck, my friend."

Zip Tie Guy cursed and Red made an impatient gesture. As for Wrecking Ball, he hitched his chin toward the duffel bags. "How much is *that* worth?"

"Probably somewhere north of six million," LT answered easily. There really was no point in lying and antagonizing their captors further. "We reckon all six bags would ring in at about ten."

Another thing SEALs learned early in training was when it was advantageous to cooperate and when it was advantageous to resist.

"Holy Mary, mother of Jesus!" Wrecking Ball breathed. "Ten million simoleons in six bags. Don't seem possible, does it?"

"It's enough." Zip Tie Guy eyes were wide inside his mask. "*More* than enough. Get the last two bags and let's finish this."

Doc waited until he could hear the leader stomping around upstairs. Then, with a quick, downward jerk of his chin, he told LT it was go-time.

LT didn't hesitate. With the reflexes of a cat, Doc's former commanding officer jumped to a stand, the move made slightly awkward because he was taking the chair with him. LT's roar did his *nom de guerre* proud when he rammed his head into Zip Tie Guy's stomach before Zip Tie could do more than blink in surprise.

"Fuck me!" Wrecking Ball yelled as Zip Tie Guy flew back against the wall beneath the staircase. The dude hit with so much force his head made a sick-sounding *thud* when it smacked into the banister.

Red instinctively turned toward the commotion, and the adrenaline singeing Doc's veins burned his muscles into action. He stood from the chair, lifted his arms as high as he could behind his back, and brought his elbows forward with a hard jerk.

The slack he'd left in the zip tie by keeping his hands thumb to thumb gave him just enough leverage to snap the hard plastic.

A second later, he reared back and punched Red square in the face. *Crack!* The most primitive, primal feeling of destruction rushed through him when the bones of his knuckles made mincemeat of the cartilage in Red's nose.

Red instinctively lifted his hands to protect his face from another blow, and it gave Doc an opening to snatch the pistol. A split-second later, he stepped behind Red, snaked an arm around the man's throat, and placed the cold, steel barrel of the revolver tight against Red's temple.

John, never one to be left out, stood from his chair and charged toward Wrecking Ball. But Wrecking Ball was too quick. He lifted his piece and Uncle John skidded to a stop with the barrel of Wrecking Ball's gun kissing the center of his chest.

At the same time, Zip Tie Guy managed to avoid LT's

second charge. And with a banshee wail, raised his weapon and fired.

Boom!

The sound inside the confines of the house was immense. Dana screamed. Cami gasped. And Doc's head swam with memories of too many battles to count.

Gunfire always brought on the flashbacks.

Luckily, Olivia had had the wherewithal to tip her chair sideways and hit the deck the instant LT began tussling with Zip Tie Guy. Good thing too. Otherwise the bullet might have plowed through her chest. Instead, it blasted through the far wall, leaving a hole the size of a quarter in the wood siding. A shaft of dim sunlight streamed through the breach.

"Olivia!" LT bellowed from where he'd fallen to his knees. Fear made his deep voice crack.

From her sprawl on the floor, Olivia lifted her head and blew a strand of black hair from her face. "I'm okay."

LT shoved to a stand and lowered his chin until he stared at Zip Tie Guy from beneath his furrowed brow. "You motherfucker!" he snarled.

If looks were enough to kill, Zip Tie Guy would be pushing up daisies.

"Stop!" Zip Tie Guy shrieked when LT took a menacing step in his direction. He aimed his weapon around the room at anyone and everyone, as if he didn't know from which direction danger might come at him next. "Nobody move!"

Damnit! Doc silently swore. They'd lost the advantage of surprise. And now he was outnumbered.

Then again, he was no stranger to bad odds. Whether it was treating stage V cancer during his residency or being helo-ed into a warzone during his stint with the Navy, he'd learned the show wasn't over until the final curtain fell.

As long as he had a gun and a hostage, he had leverage.

"You broke my nose," Red wheezed. "I can't breathe."

"Remember what I told you about the teeth and toenails?" Doc whispered next to Red's ear as he listened for commotion from upstairs. Surely the gunshot would bring Head Honcho running. And yet? All was quiet on the second floor.

Was it possible the group's intrepid leader was too cowardly to investigate? Zip Tie Guy certainly looked like he was seconds away from crapping his pants. And Red was breathing rapidly and shaking like a scared rabbit inside Doc's embrace.

None of them were behaving like a band of badasses who had the balls to storm an island during a hurricane and steal ten million dollars' worth of treasure.

Really, who the hell are *these guys?*

The question buzzed through Doc's brain for the hundredth time. And just like the ninety-nine times before, the only thing he knew for sure was that he didn't have the first clue.

"Count yourself lucky all I did was wreck your nose," he whispered to Red. He could smell the iron-rich scent of blood wafting through the material of the man's mask. Turning his attention toward the two gunmen who held his friends in check, Doc said louder, "I'll put a hot ball of lead through your partner's brainpan unless you boys drop those weapons."

He put punctuation to his point by cocking the revolver's hammer.

"Big talk from a guy who's outnumbered two to one," Wrecking Ball countered. The Glock 19 he held against John shook slightly.

Doc knew it'd only take one slip, one accidental squeeze of the trigger, and a 9mm would have John meeting an untimely end. The thought was enough to make Doc's gorge rise. But he gave no indication of that, or that his

JULIE ANN WALKER

disadvantage concerned him in the least.

Instead, he kept his expression filled with steely determination.

The antiperspirant industry coined the phrase *never let them see you sweat*. But SEALs tended to practice something a little different. *Never let them see you flinch.*

"You think you can take out all of my friends before I take out both of yours?" he asked conversationally. "The way *I* see it, the odds are in *my* favor. I, too, am a Navy SEAL, you see. Which means I know a dozen ways to end all three of you. And I bet I could do it by firing only two bullets."

Okay. He was bluffing. He could only take them out with two bullets if Wrecking Ball and Zip Tie Guy happened to line themselves up just right in his sights. But *they* didn't need to know that.

Given Zip Tie Guy's reaction to LT's ink, Doc figured he could use the whole Navy SEAL angle to his advantage.

LT, who stood awkwardly with the wooden chair strapped to his back, played right along. "Do it!" he encouraged Doc. "Don't worry about me and John. Put these bastards down and save the women."

"J-Jesus!" Zip Tie Guy sputtered. "These sonsofbitches are crazy!"

"Crazy is as crazy does." Doc winked, letting his mouth curve into a maniacal-looking sneer even as he listened for any sort of footfall from upstairs. *Still nothing. Maybe Head Hancho is waiting to see how things play out before joining the party.* "I'll give you to the count of three to drop your weapons," he told Wrecking Ball and Zip Tie Guy. "After that, I'm going to start ending lives. One. Two."

He saw it then. The look that came into Wrecking Ball's eyes.

It was a look he knew well. A look a man wore right before he split. Right before he was forced to face both parts of himself. The good and the evil. The light and dark. A look that said Wrecking Ball had made the decision to kill.

"Don't," Doc cautioned, pressing the pistol tighter against Red's head. His heart rate, which had remained steady, ratcheted up a notch.

Wrecking Ball said nothing, but Doc saw the muscles in the dude's big forearm flex as his thick finger tightened around the trigger.

"John?" Dana gasped when Wrecking Ball's intent became clear to everyone in the room.

"It's okay, darlin'," Uncle John assured her. But John cut a look toward Doc that said *Don't make a liar outta me, boy.*

"I said *don't,*" Doc growled again, the hairs on the back of his neck standing stick-straight.

Despite his boasting, he didn't *really* want to kill anyone. No matter how much training he'd received, no matter how hard the Navy had tried to make combat automatic and killing routine, taking a life never set easy on his shoulders. And after bugging out of the Navy, he'd promised himself to go the rest of his days without adding to his tally.

That hadn't worked out, of course. Despite the Deep Six crew having left their Frogmen statuses behind, forces had conspired to make them all continue to fight for their lives. In fact, he'd had to end a man just a few months back.

Sure, it'd been in the service of saving Cami and Mia and Romeo, but it'd been another black mark on his soul all the same. And since then, he'd assured himself, *again*, that *that* death would be the last death to stain the fabric of his being.

Then again, if Wrecking Ball put so much as one more ounce of pressure on that Glock's trigger, Doc was going to send a bullet clean through his skull.

"Brady, you with me?" Wrecking Ball asked.

"Jesus, Jace!" Zip Tie Guy, aka *Brady*, rasped. "How the hell are we—"

Doc stopped listening to the men because, in his mind's eye, he saw Jace's next move. And like a train coming down the tracks, there was no way to stop it short of stopping *Jace*.

Fuck, Doc thought, even as his muscles clenched in preparation to absorb the recoil once he aimed at Jace and scrambled the man's gray matter with a .357 slug. Just as he was poised to point and shoot, however, his ears filled with the sound of Cami's scream. "Dalton! Look out!"

Ah, he thought. *So the man upstairs finally grew some balls.*

Before he could adjust his aim toward the new danger, his head exploded.

CHAPTER 13

5:45 PM...

Cami had heard it said that fear had two meanings. One, forget everything and run. Or two, face everything and rise.

The second meaning came instinctively to her. She had absolutely no thought of herself, no thought of what moving from her chair might cost her. Her only thought was of Doc. Of getting to him.

She didn't remember jumping up, her bound wrists making the move so awkward she stumbled. She didn't remember running to where Doc had fallen. All she knew was that, suddenly, she was kneeling next to him, whispering his name and begging him to move.

The terror pounding through her veins made it sound as if there was a river rushing between her ears. Which meant she was deaf to the fourth masked man's barked orders as he ran down the stairs, aiming his weapon at everyone in the room and gesturing wildly.

"Dalton?" she whispered Doc's name again, panicked tears clogging her throat.

When the fourth gunman had appeared on the stairs above Doc, his deadly black handgun raised high over Doc's head, Cami would swear her soul had left her body. Then when the gunman had brought the butt of the weapon down on top of Doc's head, she'd known her soul had still been very much with her because she'd felt it rip in two.

Doc was a big man. It would've been natural to think he'd timber like a felled oak tree. Instead, he'd just sort of… *wilted*. His knees buckling. His eyes rolling back in his head. Softly sinking to the floor into a loose-limbed sprawl.

For whatever reason, that had been *way* more terrifying to watch.

"Damnit, Fin!" The man who'd bashed Doc's skull in bellowed as he stopped next to Cami. "Grab your gun, man!"

"He b-broke my n-nose!" the redheaded gunman, whose name was Fin apparently, blubbered as he clumsily fumbled for the pistol that'd slipped from Doc's lax fingers.

If only I were strong enough to break my ties, Cami thought, *I'd grab that gun and shoot all four of these fuckers square in the face.*

Riding right behind her fear was a seething rage. She'd never considered herself the bloodthirsty sort. In fact, she liked to think of herself as a pacifist. But she knew a blow like the one Doc had sustained could kill a man. And heaven help her, if Doc was dead—

She couldn't even allow her mind to finish the thought. *He's not dead. He can't be dead!*

She couldn't lose another person she—

Again, her brain screeched to a stop. The word poised on the tip of her thoughts was *love*.

Which was ridiculous. She *liked* Doc an awful lot. She

certainly *lusted* after the man. But she wasn't *in love* with him.

Was she?

"I'm bleedin' like a stuck pig!" Fin wailed after he palmed the weapon and shoved to a shaky stand.

"So am I," the skinny guy named Brady said when he pulled his hand free from under the back of his mask. His fingers came away bloody. He must've cut his scalp when he knocked his head against the banister.

"And the one man who could've helped you both is lying here on the ground!" she couldn't stop herself from snarling up at them.

Fin blinked from behind his mask. His green eyes were bloodshot from tears.

Was she a terrible person for being *glad* he was suffering?

"What's that supposed to mean?" He sounded nasally and congested.

"He's a doctor." She hitched her chin toward Doc who was…

Too still.

Is he breathing?

Her desperate eyes fell to Doc's big chest and the silver piece-of-eight that'd slipped from the collar of his T-shirt to lie in the hollow of his throat. She watched closely for any movement.

One. Two. Three. The antique cuckoo clock hanging on the wall ticked away the seconds.

Nothing.

Or nothing she could see.

She'd fallen hard onto her knees in her haste to get as close to Doc as she could, and pain radiated from her kneecaps. Her shoulders ached from having her arms wrenched behind her back. But when Doc's wide chest didn't move, nothing hurt as much as her heart.

"Thought he was a Navy SEAL," Brady muttered.

"He's *both*, you smooth-brained idiot," she hissed. "And if you motherfuckers have k—"

Her sentence turned into a sob of overwhelming happiness when Doc groaned and pushed up on one elbow.

"You're alive!" she shrieked and wished she could wrap her arms around him. Instead she leaned forward until she was almost unbalanced so she could plant a desperate kiss against his lips. "Thank god, you're alive."

"Mmm." His warm breath was the sweetest thing she'd ever tasted. "When you're six-five, you're not used to anyone getting the drop on you from above." He lifted his hand to palpate his skull.

"How can you joke at a time like this?" she demanded, even as a wobbly smile flirted at her lips.

He was alive. *Alive!*

For the first time in their entire acquaintance, she was grateful he'd been born hard-headed.

"Times like this are when you *should* be joking." He grinned that lopsided grin she saw in her mind's eye when she placed her head on the pillow at night. Then he winced when his probing fingers hit the spot where the butt of the gun had landed. As he pulled his hand from his hair, she wasn't surprised to see his fingers were slick with blood.

"Get up! Get back to your chair!" The fourth gunman toed Cami's flank. Not hard. But he'd hit her puncture wound, making her hiss.

The noises coming from the back of Doc's throat then barely sounded like words. They were more like the growl of a vicious animal. "If you touch her again, I swear on my father's grave I'll rip that gun from your hands, shove it down your throat, and pull the trigger until it clicks."

Cami saw the sincerity in his eyes. The determination. The kind of red-hot anger that came over a person when someone they cared about was threatened.

Warmth bloomed in her chest. Which was ridiculous. It wasn't the time for her to be experiencing thoughts like *he cares about me, he really cares about me*! Nor was it the time to be feeling the effervescent bubbles of joy that realization brought with it.

"It's fine," she assured him. She'd never forgive herself if he made good on his words and ended up getting shot in the process. "I'm fine," she added before awkwardly pushing to her feet and returning to her chair.

Once she was situated, the leader of the group, a man whose name she still didn't know, leveled his gun at Doc. "You too. Get up and get back to your seat. And Brady?" When the tall, skinny gunman blinked in question, the leader added, "Tie 'em *all* to their chairs this time. Arms *and* legs."

Brady of the Bloody Head used his pistol to point LT back to his place in line. Jace of the Giant Arms shoved his gun hard into Uncle John's chest until John, too, retook his seat. And then everyone waited as Olivia awkwardly righted her chair and climbed back into it.

Cami wasn't sure how much time passed while Brady worked his way down the line of ladderback chairs, securing everyone's elbows to the back rungs and cinching their ankles to the wooden legs. By the time he'd finished, the sun outside had been obliterated and darkness had descended over the already dim room. The wind was back to roaring like a freight train, and the air smelled like the sea as the water rose beneath the floorboards.

Jace cursed. "The eyewall is back. We're stuck here until Julia moves on."

CHAPTER 14

6:52 PM...

Doc was concussed.

The momentary loss of consciousness was his first big clue. His second was the incessant ringing in his ears. And the third? He had a headache big enough to drop an elephant.

Fortunately, he seemed to have escaped the blurry vision, nausea, and vomiting that often accompanied a blow to the head. Or at least he'd escaped it for the time being.

Concussions were tricky because they were so subtle. Sometimes symptoms didn't show up for days, weeks, or even longer. But for now, he seemed to be firing on all cylinders—as long as he concentrated on tuning out the head-splitting cacophony of the storm. Because if he *didn't*, he wanted to cry.

Or beg the thieves to get me some damn Tylenol.

The insanity of the backend of the eyewall had moved

on. Now they were simply suffering the incessant moan of Julia's tailwinds as she battered the house, the relentless lash of rain as it pummeled the metal roof, and the rhythmic slap of the storm surge as it licked at the floorboards beneath their feet.

Nightfall had partnered with the gloom of the storm to prompt the thieves to light more candles around the room. Their flames flickered wildly anytime a wisp of wind whispered in through the bullet hole in the far wall. And for nearly an hour—Doc knew it was an hour thanks to the cuckoo clock on the wall—the Wayfarer Islanders had done nothing but sit quietly and watch their captors pace around like caged animals.

Not that the islanders had an option other than sitting quietly since they were all trussed up tighter than cattle on branding day.

For the dozenth time in the span of that hour, Doc felt Cami glance over at him. And for the dozenth time, he caught her worried gaze and winked to let her know he was still okay. That he wasn't about to flatline from a brain bleed.

A wave of relief flooded her pretty brown eyes, but it was quickly replaced by concern when Head Honcho said, "Huddle up," and motioned for his three friends to follow him toward the foot of the staircase.

Doc and Cami were closest to the group of gunmen. Unfortunately, the noise from the storm and the repeated *whack*, *whack*, *whack* of one of the upstairs shutters slamming against its locking bar, meant they could only catch snippets of the thieves' whispered conversation.

Or at least Doc was catching snippets. Cami had closed her eyes and leaned her head back, looking for all the world as if she was trying to enter a meditative state.

And who could blame her? They could all use a little Zen right about then.

Doc ripped his eyes away from the hollow at the base of her long throat, and ripped his mind away from the longing to lick that little divot, when he heard the big guy, the one they called Jace, say, "Why are we hesitatin'? We know what we gotta do."

Yes. Doc had been wondering himself why the intruders hadn't already finished off the islanders. There was no reason to delay the inevitable. Unless, of course, the gunmen were squeamish and didn't want to spend the remainder of the storm stuck in a room with six bloody corpses.

Doc focused on the men with a capital F. But he did his best to pretend he *wasn't* spying on their every word by keeping his eyes trained on the set of chewed-up balusters. Their ragged appearance was thanks to Meat, Mason's fat bulldog, who hadn't figured out the difference between gnawing on a stick of driftwood he'd rescued from the surf or gnawing on a stick of staircase.

From the corner of his eye, Doc watched Brady shake his head. "That's not what we agreed to do. We agreed to try to…" The rest of his sentence was lost in the wind and the ringing in Doc's ears.

Head Honcho raked a hand over the top of his mask. "Come on, Brady. As soon as we heard the island was inhabited, ya had to know it would come to this. There's no way we won't be caught if we leave witnesses and—" Again, the roar of the storm swallowed up what else he said, and Doc barely refrained from growling his frustration.

Red, aka Fin, glanced around at his partners but said nothing. He simply pulled his mask away from his ruined nose in a bid to alleviate the pressure. And long, tall Brady, looking more agitated by the minute as he swayed from foot to foot, swiped a hand over the blood trailing out from under his mask to soak his neck and the collar of his blue T-shirt.

That head lac must be something, Doc mused.

Then again, head wounds were always messy. The scalp was thick and full of blood vessels, so even a minor cut there could make a man look like a murder victim.

"This is one pisser of a…" Jace said, but the end of his sentence was interrupted when what sounded like a palm frond slammed into the side of the house. "But it's what's gotta be done. None of us want it. But we got no choice."

"But there's one problem since we couldn't get back to the boat before the eye moved on," Head Honcho said. "What if the trawler sinks? It survived the front half of Julia because I was pilotin' her. If we off 'em now and then we can't get off the island, we won't be lookin' at grand larceny, we'll be lookin' at murder in the first."

And *there* it was. The answer to the question of why the gunmen hadn't simply shot all of them as soon as they'd got them secured to the chairs.

"We wait then." This from Jace. "If the trawler sank that's that. Game over. But if it didn't, we do what needs to be done and get the hell outta here."

"Dalton?" Cami whispered from the side of her mouth. Her head was no longer tilted back, and her lids were no longer squeezed shut. Quite the opposite, her eyes were huge and full of terror as she pinned him with her dark, desperate gaze.

She'd heard everything he had.

Or maybe more. She was closer to the masked men and she wasn't battling a world class case of tinnitus.

There was nothing he could do to assuage her fear. The only thing he could do was give the subtlest shake of his head, telling her without words to keep quiet. To keep still. To not give their captors any indication she'd heard anything untoward because he had to come up with a counterplan to their murderous intentions, and he couldn't do that if the thieves knew he was onto them.

Her throat worked over a hard swallow, but she firmed her shoulders and nodded subtly, letting him know she'd received his message.

Thatta girl, he mouthed, giving her a small smile that she quickly returned. Although her lips shook with the effort.

She was so damn brave. He'd realized that a mere twenty-four hours after meeting her. Because within those first twenty-four hours, they'd survived a mid-ocean plane crash, a marooning on a desert island, and the arrival on that island of a group of men bent on mayhem. Through it all, she hadn't uttered a single word of complaint. And more than that, she'd kept her wits about her.

Which was more than he could say for some seasoned operators his SEAL Team had worked with.

Looking at her now, so vulnerable yet so tough, he wanted to go back in time and kick his own ass for all the sarcastic comments he'd sent her way. Because truly, what had been her crime?

That she was a lawyer? That she was so smart and sassy and beautiful he couldn't stop thinking about her? That she had him waking up with a skip in his step for the first time in over a decade because he actually looked forward to the day since she was going to be part of it?

That she makes me wonder what if...

That was *really* what he'd been punishing her for, wasn't it? That she made him want. That she made him need. That she made him forget his grief.

Turning his head, he found LT leaning forward. LT's gaze was eagle-eyed on Doc's face and the question in LT's eyes was clear. *What are those bastards up to?*

Doc let his eyes narrow slightly. Let his nostrils flare wide. Let the truth shine in his expression.

LT's nod was subtle. *Message received.* And then LT's eyes darted to his wife.

The look that came over LT's face then was something Doc would remember the rest of his life. It was a look of fear that they might not make it out of this. A look of heartbreak that the woman of his dreams might suffer such a terrible fate. And a look of love so fierce and strong that Doc's own heart ached in sympathy.

"Don't know if I can make it." Fin's clogged voice dragged Doc's attention back to the gathered group of gunmen. "...can't breathe. My head is..." Again Fin pulled his mask away from his face. "...think he sent a bone into my brain."

"And if I keep losin' blood like I am," Brady added, motioning to his head, "then I might not..."

Another palm frond slammed into the side of the house, cutting off the end of Brady's sentence. But Doc didn't need to hear what else was said before raising his voice above Julia's fury.

They'd inadvertently given him an opening.

"I can help with that!"

When the thieves turned his way, he nodded. "I'm a doctor! I can stitch up your head." He looked first at Brady and then turned his eyes on Fin. "And I can set your broken nose."

There was hesitation in Head Honcho's gaze. But that was better than the flat-out suspicion Doc saw in Jace's. Of their four captors, Jace was the one Doc was most worried about. He seemed the most volatile.

"Please, Will," Fin begged Head Honcho. "My nose is killin' me. If he can..."

Again, the sound of the wind swallowed the end of his sentence.

Head Honcho's name is Will, huh? The final piece of the puzzle falls into place.

Except, that wasn't the final piece, was it? The answer to

the question of how Will and his three pals learned the Deep Six crew had pulled up the treasure remained unanswered.

"My medical bag is upstairs," Doc added, wincing when his raised voice made the ringing in his ears increase by about ten decibels. "If you untie me, I can go grab it and—"

"No!" Will barked. "Tell us where it is, and we'll bring it down."

Damnit!

Doc quickly changed gears and pasted on what he hoped was a convincing expression of desperation. "Look, man, I have to piss like a Russian racehorse. Let me hit the head and after I'm done, I can doctor up your friends. They can take turns keeping their pistols pointed at me, and you and Hercules there"—he hitched his chin toward Jace—"can stay down here and cover everyone else."

Will continued to look hesitant, but when Fin whispered something to him, Doc knew the group's leader was going to give in. The indecision in the man's eyes turned to resignation.

Doc was careful to keep the elation off his face when Jace pulled a pocketknife from the front of his jeans and stalked over to Doc. The man leaned close to Doc's face. "Ya make one wrong move, bub, and I'll gut ya like a fish." Doc could smell the sour stench of stress on Jace's breath.

"I'm just trying to help your friends," Doc told him. And even though he didn't have Olivia's skills when it came to the art of deception, he thought he sounded convincing.

Apparently it worked, because Jace nodded and bent toward his ankles. Doc's feet were attacked by pins and needles when Jace sliced through the restraints. But the true relief came when the zip ties keeping his elbows pinned to the back of the chair were cut loose.

Once Doc's hands were free, Jace was quick to tuck his knife away and re-palm his Glock. He leveled the end of the weapon between Doc's eyes. "No funny business. Or I swear to god I'll—"

"I know. I know." Doc slowly stood, rubbing the raw skin around his wrists. "You'll gut me like a fish."

"Nope." Jace gave a quick shake of his head. "I'll put one right between your eyes, ayuh?"

By way of answer, Doc simply lifted his hands and nodded at Brady to lead the way upstairs. He'd barely taken a step when Cami's voice stopped him. "Dalton?"

Once again, his name hit his ears and swirled around inside like a caress. He saw the concern…the *fear*…in her eyes.

He hadn't intended to lean down and press a kiss to the corner of her succulent mouth. But that's exactly what he did. Because she'd bewitched him. And he was *constantly* doing and saying things he never set out to do or say.

"It's okay, sweetheart," he whispered. "You're going to be okay."

I'm going to make sure of it, he silently added.

"Hey!" Will yelled. "That's enough of that! We didn't untie ya so ya could make out. Get your ass upstairs and help my friends, or I'll start takin' out my piss-poor mood on *your* friends."

Doc chucked Cami on the chin and gave her a reassuring wink before following Brady up the stairs. Fin brought up the caboose, keeping his pistol shoved into the center of Doc's back the whole way.

When they got to the restroom, Doc decided his early inclusion in organized sports and the locker rooms associated with them, as well as his subsequent stint in the Navy and the extreme lack of privacy associated with that, worked to his advantage. After he lit the three-wick candle on the windowsill, he had no problem dropping his zipper and relieving himself while two grown men watched his every move.

Thankfully, his bladder was full enough that his earlier *Russian racehorse* comment didn't come off as total bullshit.

Once he was done, he washed his hands and hitched his chin toward the hallway. "My medical kit is in my room."

Fin wiggled his Ruger, telling Doc without words to take the lead and show them the way. As Doc headed down the hall, his mind raced through his upcoming moves.

It was another trick he'd been taught not only in SEAL training, but also when he'd done his surgical rotation. If he could *see* the steps he needed to take, meticulously imagine going through each one, when the time came to implement them, it was a little like muscle memory.

When he turned the knob on his bedroom door, the solid slab of wood was jerked from his grip. The broken window had created a vacuum inside the room, and he was instantly hit in the face with the smell of wet sand, damp wood, and salty air.

Behind him, Brady muttered, "Fuckin'-A."

Doc was glad he was in front of the gunmen. That meant they couldn't see his lips curve into a satisfied grin.

The conditions in his bedroom were even better than he'd hoped. And by *better*, he meant *worse*.

It took a second for his eyes to adjust to the darkness in the unlit room, but once they did, he saw his curtains had been torn into tatters. Bits of storm debris swirled around in the moist air. And Cami's bloodstained shirt was plastered over the back of his headboard.

Seeing it immediately conjured up thoughts of the woman herself.

She didn't deserve to die here on this island in the middle of nowhere. She deserved the life she'd always dreamed of. The house full of kids. The man she could build her world around.

And by god, I'm going to see she gets all of it if it's

the last thing I do, he vowed while staunchly ignoring the little stab of jealousy he felt for whichever lucky bastard eventually won her heart.

Taking a step into the room, he once again forced his mind to go through the motions of his plan.

"My kit is by my nightstand!" he yelled over his shoulder at the two gunmen.

Fin followed him into the room, but Brady stayed behind in the doorway.

"I'll grab it and then we'll head back to the bathroom!" he added, hoping the darkness and the anarchy created by the open window made it impossible for his captors to see the medical kit that *wasn't* next to his nightstand.

His medical kit was actually in his closet. What *was* next to his nightstand—or, rather, taped to the bottom of his nightstand—was his trusty Sig Sauer.

Navy SEALs, even the ones who'd bugged out of the service, squirreled weapons away out of an abundance of caution. Or maybe it was out of an abundance of paranoia.

Either way, Doc was glad he kept his sidearm locked and loaded.

Now, it's all about timing.

Squinting against the dust and debris in the air, his hair swirling around his face and making him wish he'd gotten that haircut Cami mentioned, he knelt next to his bed. Using his left arm to reach between the bedframe and his nightstand, he made sure to employ big movements as a distraction while his right arm bent up slightly so his hand could curl around the butt of his weapon.

He didn't have to fumble to find the pistol. His fingers landed on his sidearm immediately. The metal was cold and damp from the humidity in the room. But palming it felt like coming home.

He'd heard the newest batch of SEALs had switched

from the Sig Sauer P226 to the Glock 19, but he would always remain loyal to his Sig. It'd saved his ass more times than he could count.

He was betting on it saving his ass again.

The Velcro on the holster made a ripping sound while pulling free. But thankfully, the noise in the room meant the sound didn't travel far. Carefully, he curled his finger around the trigger, and then aimed at Fin from under his left arm.

It was a terrible angle. But he'd put enough rounds downfield that he'd gotten pretty good at guessing trajectory. If he was quick and careful, he might just get out of this without taking another life.

Holding his breath—and betting on the gunmen downstairs figuring he'd made a move, after which they'd assume it was their friends firing on *him*—he squeezed the trigger.

Bam!

The bark of his Sig was ear-splitting, even with the sound of the wind screaming in through the open window. The ringing in his ears ratcheted up a notch and it felt like there was a steel spike driving into his skull. But just as he'd hoped, his first round found a home in Fin's gun shoulder.

The redhead stumbled back, blinking in pained confusion as his pistol slipped from his lax fingers and a rosette of inky dark blood spread across the front of his shirt. Behind him, Brady instinctively ducked and then looked around wildly. The pandemonium inside the room masked what'd happened.

Doc used the man's momentary disorientation to his advantage. Jumping to his feet, he aimed and fired a second time.

Bam!

Brady howled in surprised agony when Doc's bullet nicked the meaty part of his gun arm. Unfortunately, Doc's bullet hadn't rendered the appendage useless. Brady had enough wherewithal to lift the weapon in Doc's direction, even as Doc dove toward Fin's dropped pistol.

Boom!

Orange fire blinked from the end of Brady's sidearm, but his aim was shit and the round ranged wide, plowing into the floorboards a foot to the right of Doc's sprawled form.

Doc didn't even flinch. Partly because he was used to being shot at, but mostly because he was one-hundred-percent focused on his next move.

He could've ended both men then and there. With Fin's gun secure in his non-dominant hand—he was still pretty good at firing left-handed; *another* skill he'd been trained on—he was perfectly poised to aim at both men simultaneously and send rounds through the center mass of each of them. But Fin no longer posed a threat since he was disarmed. And Doc knew how to stop Brady without putting a period to the man's life.

And in the confusion and chaos of the moment, that small fact felt like a miracle.

When he squeezed his trigger, his bullet flew true, hitting Brady in his firing shoulder. Brady spun like a top, specks of blood flying in an arc at the same time his gun dropped to the floor with a thud and a rattle.

"Dalton!" he heard Cami yell from downstairs and realized she'd been screaming his name over and over since the first shot. The horror in her voice was enough to shift his focus. He heard the footsteps pounding up the staircase.

It took less than a second to slip Brady's sidearm into a side pocket of his cargo shorts. And half that time for him to note that Brady had slid down into the doorway, a hand pressed to his shoulder wound. Fin was on his knees in the center of the room, ripping his mask off his face so he could hold the material over the blood oozing through his shirt.

Darting over to the wall nearest the door, Doc pressed his back against the shiplap and counted his heartbeats at the same time he counted the approaching footfalls.

Just one set.

Which meant the gunmen had left one of their number downstairs to guard the Wayfair Islanders. That would *seem* like the right thing to do. Keep an eye and a weapon on the hostages. But in truth, it gave Doc the advantage.

In battle, that old saw *divide and conquer* held true one-hundred percent of the time.

With grim determination, he tightened his finger around his rigger.

"Will!" Brady wheezed. His gaze looked dazed as he lifted his eyes to the figure racing down the hall. "Watch out! He's got—"

Doc didn't wait for Brady to finish his warning. He poked his arm and head around the doorjamb and fired.

Bam!

The hallway wasn't as dark as his bedroom, thanks to the candle burning in the bathroom and casting its dim glow into the space. So Doc saw the instant he hit Will.

The man screamed and staggered, his shoulder slamming into the wall and causing two of the framed photographs hanging there to bounce off their nails and fall to the floor, their glass shattering on impact.

With a mighty roar, Doc jumped over Brady and tackled Will to the ground. Using Will's stunned agony to his advantage, he shoved his pistol beneath the man's chin and said softly, "Drop your weapon or I'll blow the top of your head off."

Will's gun made a *thudding* sound when it landed on the wooden floorboards. Doc used his free hand, still curled around Fin's weapon, to push Will's gun out of reach.

Then, slowly, carefully, he shoved to a stand.

Will pushed himself into a seated position with his back resting against the wall. Using his right hand, he covered the wound on his left bicep.

With his adrenaline raging, and while keeping his Sig alternately pointing between Will and Brady, Doc pocketed Fin's gun so he could bend and palm Will's. In less than thirty seconds, he'd gone from having zero weapons to having four.

Not too shabby, if I do say so myself.

"Jesus, Will." Brady panted against his pain. "We're fucked."

Doc didn't wait for Will's reply before saying, "I'll tend to your wounds once my friends are safe. But I swear on all that's holy, if any of you try to follow me down the hall or down those stairs, I won't be merciful when I shoot you a third time. You hear what I'm saying?"

Will nodded limply and Brady whimpered his acquiescence. Doc had barely turned to make his way downstairs to deal with Jace when he heard Cami call his name again.

This time, the fear in her voice had his blood running cold. It was no longer fear for him. It was fear for herself. Fear for the others.

He knew what he'd find before he crept down the stairs.

Even so, he wasn't prepared for the scene that met his gaze. He wasn't prepared to see Jace's pistol pressed tightly against Cami's temple or the terrified tears that'd welled up in her beautiful, dark eyes.

CHAPTER 15

7:07 PM...

Don't move another inch!" Jace yelled with so much force the end of his weapon wiggled against Cami's temple.

Even though she was scared shitless that any second she'd hear the *boom* of the pistol right before her head exploded like a melon, she also felt a wave of relief crash over her when she saw Doc's shadowed form crouched on the stairs.

The light from the flickering candles wasn't much. But that didn't stop her from dragging her eyes over what little of him she could see as she desperately searched for injuries. Thankfully, no dripping blood met her gaze. And his eyes, though fierce and filled with determination, looked blessedly empty of the kind of pain that would accompany a fatal bullet wound.

She didn't know how he'd done it, but it looked like he'd escaped the gunplay upstairs without suffering so much as a scratch.

Hiccupping on a sob of happiness, she could no longer deny the truth.

I love him. I'm in *love with him.*

And she had been for months.

She'd simply been denying her feelings because she'd been operating under the assumption he didn't like her. And who wanted to admit to wanting someone who didn't want them back, much less admit to loving someone who didn't even *like* them back?

She'd been wrong about his feelings, however. He *did* like her. More than that, he cared about her—*that* truth was shining in his eyes and clear in his voice when he asked, "You okay, sweetheart?"

Sweetheart.

It was the second time he'd used that endearment. And hand her the crown and sash for Miss Cliché, because she *liked* it.

Or, rather, she liked it when *he* said it.

"I'm okay," she assured him, happy her voice sounded steadier than she felt.

"She won't be okay in about ten seconds if ya don't throw your weapons down to me!" Jace shouted. "I'm primed to put a bullet through her brain. And with all your friends lined up in a neat row, I might get a two or three-fer! Wha'd'ya think? How many heads can one round get through, eh?"

The mental images that went through Cami's brain had bile burning up the back of her throat.

"There's no reason anyone has to die." Doc's scratchy voice was firm with conviction. "Everyone can keep their lives if you play your cards right."

Jace laughed, but it contained no humor. "Ya killed my friends!" he yelled, the pistol digging so hard into Cami's skull, she winced. "And now ya want me to have mercy on yours?"

"Your friends are alive!" Doc shouted.

"Bullshit!"

Jace said that one word with so much vehemence, spittle flew from his mouth to land on Cami's cheek. She grimaced, wishing she could lean her head to the side and use her shoulder to wipe it away. But any move might have Jace pulling his trigger.

"It's not bullshit," Doc assured him. And then he turned to yell over his shoulder. "Will, Brady, and Fin! I need you all to sound off so I don't have to kill Jace!"

It took a moment before Will's voiced echoed down from upstairs. "We're alive!"

The man could barely be heard above the chaos of the storm, and his tone was pinched with pain. But thankfully, it was enough.

The pressure of the barrel against Cami's temple lessened. "If I drop my weapon"—Jace sounded hoarse, and her heart leapt with elation at that *if*; *if* was a good start—"what'll ya do next?"

"I'll ask you to kick it toward the duffel bags at the foot of the staircase and I'll come down to get it. After I untie my friends, I'll see to yours." Doc's voice was steady. His expression was sincere. "I'm not going to lie to you, Jace. Your buddies are hurt. All of them are shot. But no one needs to die today," he reiterated.

Cami noticed how Doc kept using the man's name. *Smart*, she thought, unsurprised because Doc was beyond smart; he was *brilliant*. That big brain of his was one of the first things she'd fallen in love with.

Right behind his sharp tongue, quick wit, and rugged face.

"I don't *want* anyone to die today," he continued. "I've

seen enough death to last me a lifetime."

And again, for anyone with ears to hear it, the truth rang in his voice. Only this time, it was a *sad* truth.

A lump formed in her throat when she saw his expression had turned haggard. She'd never considered how hard it must've been for him to go from being a doctor, a man sworn to heal people, to a Navy SEAL, a man whose very job description was to mete out death and destruction.

"Ya promise you'll help my friends?" Jace asked shakily.

Doc's answer was immediate. "I swear it on my father's grave."

The relief she felt when Jace dropped his pistol was reflected in Doc's eyes. "That's good, man," Doc told Jace. "That's the smart move. The *right* move. Now set that heater on the ground and kick it over toward the duffel bags."

For a big man, Doc could move with astonishing speed. Before Cami could blink, he'd darted down the stairs, pocketed Jace's pistol, and was marching in her direction.

Her heart swelled at the sight of his determined step. She hoped he would swoop in to kiss her, much like he'd done before going upstairs. Then she realized how silly her desire was when he stopped before he got to her and leveled a look on Jace. "I need your knife."

Jace blinked and shook his head. "Why?"

"Because I don't trust you not to get up to mischief if I leave you alone in here while I run to the kitchen and grab something to use to cut loose my friends."

"Oh." Jace nodded. "Right." He reached into his pocket. But before he handed over the knife, he added in a voice that was little more than a whisper, "What's goin' to happen to us?"

Sticking with his truth telling, Doc shook his head. "I don't know, man. But at the very least, you'll get to live. And where there's life, there's hope."

Jace reluctantly passed Doc the blade.

"Thanks." Doc nodded. "Now, you'll make me a lot less jittery if you take yourself over by the front door while I work on freeing my friends."

Once Jace did as he was asked, Cami braced herself to be cut loose. A second later, her shoulders drooped in dejection when Doc swiftly stalked down the line of chairs and went to work on LT's ties.

Makes sense, she told herself. *Undo the guy who'll have your back.*

Even so, by the time Doc had made his way down the row of captives, cutting through their restraints in quick order, she was nearly vibrating with impatience.

When he finally knelt in front of her, she wanted to throw her arms around him. Unfortunately, her ankle ties were the first to go. Blood surged back into her sandaled feet. Then, he leaned around her to cut her elbows free and the move brought his face close enough to her mouth that she could kiss him.

Four hours ago, she might've fought the urge.

Now she didn't even try.

The skin of his cheek was warm and alive against her lips, his beard stubble deliciously scratchy. "Thank you," she breathed into his ear. "Thank you for saving us all." And then, because she couldn't help herself, but also because he'd come to expect snark from her, she added, "You may not be much to look at, but you have big, clanking brass balls."

As she'd hoped, he chuckled. "Thatta girl. You're learning. Perfect timing for a little gallows humor." But he quickly turned serious. "I'm sorry you were dragged into this in the first place." He slipped the knife's cold blade between her wrists and neatly severed the plastic tie. She could instantly feel her fingers again. "I swear, trouble seems to follow this group."

"Wouldn't have missed it for the world," she assured him, throwing her arms around his neck and hugging him tight because she could.

His wide palm was warm against her lower back when he held her close. She took comfort in the steady thud of his heart against her breast.

It was true that, despite the metric ton of bad luck that'd fallen on her head since agreeing to work for Deep Six Salvage—so much that she might consider wearing a hardhat when she was around them—she wouldn't trade the last few months for anything.

If she hadn't taken the job, she never would have met Doc. And if she hadn't met Doc, she never would have fallen in love. And if she hadn't fallen in love, well…

She'd have been forced to give up her dream of a once-in-a-lifetime romance. Of a family of her own. Of a *home* of her own to replace the one she'd lost when her baby sister died.

A whisper of doubt entered her mind. *Just because you love him doesn't mean he feels the same.*

He leaned back, and she tried to see the truth in his eyes. But all she saw was tired humor when he chuckled. "And here I thought you were smart. Only a fool would choose to live through the misadventures we have recently."

"Eh." She shrugged a shoulder. "Wasn't it Mark Twain who said a person goes to Heaven for the climate but Hell for the company?"

He only shook his head and dug into his pocket to pull out another gun. She'd seen him hand over pistols to LT, Olivia, and Uncle John. And she tried not to freak out when it looked like he was about to arm her too.

"You know how to handle one of these?" he asked.

She swallowed and nodded, wanting to do her part. Wanting to rise to the occasion and figuring *how hard can it be?* But when he handed her the gun, it slipped through her nervous fingers, clattering to the floor.

A line formed between his eyebrows as he bent to retrieve it. When he pushed to his full height, he frowned down at her. "Okay, little lesson here," he said. "The next time someone hands you a weapon and asks if you know how to handle it, you say…"

"No?" Her voice was squeaky.

"Class dismissed." He nodded.

"I didn't want you to think I was a coward."

"Sweetheart…" He caught her chin between his thumb and forefinger. "That's nothing you ever have to worry about."

CHAPTER 16

7:37 PM...

Dana had assumed the worst was behind them once Doc cut their ties and they were no longer victims to the whims of their captors.

She'd been wrong.

This was worse. This was *way* worse.

So much blood. So much pain. So much suffering.

Back in college, she'd been the first to drive up on the scene of a single vehicle accident. It'd been early in the morning, and a tired third shift worker had fallen asleep behind the wheel, running his car off the road and slamming headlong into a massive oak tree.

She vividly remembered the sight of the bent metal, the smell of the smoking engine, the wheezing breath of the driver when she'd wrenched the door open to help him. He'd had a massive gash across his forehead that'd leaked blood into his dazed eyes. The steering column had crumbled against his chest, pinning him to the driver's seat.

For twenty-five minutes while she'd waited on the paramedics to arrive, she'd held his hand. For twenty-five minutes, she'd assured him he was going to live, that he wasn't going to leave his wife a widow and his children fatherless. And for twenty-five minutes, she'd pressed a shammy to his forehead to staunch the flow of blood while simultaneously trying not to throw up at the sight of all that gore.

He *had* survived. And Dana would have sworn to anyone who asked her that she'd seen trauma.

But even as gruesome as that wreck had been, it hadn't come close to the butchery of a bullet.

As a group, they'd made their way upstairs to tend to the wounded men. They'd done it as a group because Doc had insisted on it.

"I'll need as many hands managing blood loss and wound cleaning as possible," he'd said while ducking into his room and coming back out with a big, black medical bag. Like something Dana imagined an old-timey doctor might carry.

Within minutes, they'd gathered the thieves into LT and Olivia's bedroom—it was the largest. They'd lit a dozen candles to give Doc as much light as possible to work by. And they'd closed the door to block out as much of the noise from the storm as they could.

Doc had gone around to each gunman, quickly eyeing their injuries. And then he'd started giving orders in a tone that reminded Dana that all these treasure hunters she'd gotten to know over the past couple of days were actually former military men.

"LT, you and Olivia take Brady," Doc had said. "Use a QuikClot hemostatic dressing on his bicep and make sure the wound on his shoulder is through-and-through. If it is,

QuikClot dressing that too. You might have to use additional gauze to hold it in place, wind it up and over his shoulder and around his chest. If it's not through-and-through, staunch his bleeding as much as possible and wait for me. I might have to dig out the bullet. As for his head lac, clean it up and butterfly bandage it if you can."

"John?" He'd turned to where Dana and John had been standing near the door. "You and Dana tend to Will. His wound looks clean, but it's bleeding pretty good. Use a QuikClot bandage on it and give him twenty milligrams of morphine out of my bag so he'll stop that caterwauling."

The man *had* been carrying on something awful, crying out in pain anytime he was asked to move.

Then Doc had turned to the redheaded man. The one named Fin. *He* had definitely been the worst of the three. Not only was his busted nose five times the size it should've been, but also the mangled feature was an awful shade of purple. Blood bubbled from his swollen nostrils every time he dragged in a breath.

Of course, it wasn't his face that Doc had been concerned about. It'd been the amount of blood he was losing from the wound through his shoulder. Fin's shirt had been soaked in the stuff. It'd even run down to darken the denim on his jeans.

Doc had put him on the bed, cutting off his shirt to get a better look at his wound. But that's where Dana had stopped paying attention.

Instead, she'd done as she'd been instructed and turned her concentration on Will. The gunshot wound through the man's arm hadn't looked like much from the front—a neat hole about the size of a quarter that leaked triple rivulets of blood. But from the back?

Sweet heavens to Betsy.

Talk about a mess. The bullet had exited through the fleshy part of Will's tricep, leaving behind a golf ball-sized wound with ragged edges and exposed muscle.

No wonder he howls in pain anytime he's moved, she'd thought, glad she'd skipped lunch because if she'd had anything in her stomach, she would've lost it when John shoved a wad of specialized clotting gauze into the gaping injury and she'd watched it soak up blood like a sponge.

Will had been sitting on the floor with his back against the wall, and as John had gone to work wrapping the remaining gauze around his arm, he'd groaned and grimaced until tears had leaked from the corners of his eyes and snot had dripped from the end of his nose.

"Get the morphine," John had said, and Dana had scurried over to Doc's medical bag.

It'd taken her too long to locate the pain relief. Doc's kit was stuffed full of things she didn't recognize and couldn't even begin to name. But finally, she'd found the morphine.

Snapping two tablets free from the foil packaging, she'd raced back over to Will and John. And now, she carefully placed the tablets on Will's tongue.

"Swallow them down," she told the dark-haired man.

All the gunmen had removed their masks. Seeing their faces made her realize two things. One, they were young. Barely into their thirties would be her guess. And two, they didn't look like the monsters she'd imagined.

In fact, they looked like average everyday Joes. The kind of guys who'd sell her a car or do her taxes or fill her prescriptions.

Funny. But you always imagine your executioner to be hideous.

And the men *had* been going to execute them. She'd caught that much of their conversation before Doc had pulled his feat of heroism.

She shuddered at the memory. Never in her life had she been so terrified.

And, of course, John had picked up on her horror.

Tied to the chair, there'd been no way for him to offer her a hug of comfort. Even still, he'd scooted his chair close to hers, until their shoulders had touched. And his warmth and steadiness had been the only thing to stop her from crying out in fear or fainting dead away.

"Goddamnit!" Doc yelled now, and Dana turned to look at the scene on the bed.

Doc straddled Fin's waist and his gloved hands looked like they'd disappeared inside the man's chest. There was blood. *Everywhere.* It had soaked through the quilt and was dripping over the side of the bed, creating a terrible, crimson puddle on the floor.

Fin's booted feet scrabbled against the footboard. His head thrashed side-to-side. And the sound coming from the back of his throat reminded Dana of the growling howls of a cat caught in a trap.

"Hold his legs!" Doc hollered at Cami. "I need him still so I can find this fucking artery!"

Cami, who had been beside the bed trying to hold Fin's shoulders down, ran to the foot of the bed and threw herself over Fin's jerking legs.

"More help!" Doc yelled over his shoulder. "I need more help over here!"

The big man, the one named Jace, had been standing in the corner watching the people he'd taken hostage work to doctor his friends. But Doc's cry for help had him racing across the room, his heavy footfalls sounding like thunder on the worn wooden floorboards.

"More! More!" Doc yelled. "I need at least two more sets of hands!"

"We good here?" Dana asked John while eyeing Will. The leader of the band of thieves was quieter now that they'd stopped messing with his injury. And the slow dilation of his pupils told her the morphine was already beginning to take effect.

John shrugged. "Don't know what more we can do for him."

"Okay." She nodded, determined to help Doc.

She pushed to a stand too quickly, however, and the skipped meal combined with her pounding heart to make her dizzy.

"Careful there." When she staggered sideways, John's hand instantly curled around her elbow. "You can sit this one out if you need to." His hazel eyes were filled with concern.

My heavens, he's handsome, she thought. And then quickly followed that up with, *Jeez, Dana. Now's not the time.*

"No." She shook her head, dragging in a few deep breaths until her head stopped spinning. "I'm okay. Let's help Doc."

Doc instructed Jace to hold down one of Fin's shoulders. He had Dana sit at the head of the bed and hold down the other. John became Doc's surgical nurse, reaching into Doc's med kit and pulling out equipment when Doc asked for it.

Dana wasn't sure how much time passed as Doc wrestled with something inside the hole in Fin's naked shoulder, asking for "More gauze! More gauze!" every few seconds in an attempt to staunch the flow of blood. But eventually, Doc crowed in triumph and pulled something from the gaping injury. He barely gave it a glance before flinging it to the floor.

She expected it to be a bullet, to hit the boards with *thump*. But it hit with a weird sort of *click* instead and she watched, stuck somewhere between awe and horror, as the blood dripped away from the object and smooth, glistening white was revealed.

"Is that…" She had to stop and swallow. "Bone?"

She didn't really expect an answer, but Doc gave her one. "The bullet shattered his clavicle. That shard I just pulled out severed his subclavian artery. That's why he's bleeding so much."

Without waiting, Doc shoved his gloved hand back into the wound and Fin let out a sound Dana knew she'd hear in her nightmares. It was half howl, half scream, all *agony*.

"I can't…" Doc grunted as he dug around in Fin's injury. Dana felt her gorge rise when his movements made a squelching sound and filled the room with the metallic scent of liquid life. "Find the end of the damn thing. It's retracted up into—" Doc stopped and a brief look of triumph, or maybe it was just relief, flashed across his sweaty face. "There you are, you slippery little bastard!" He turned his head to the side. "Quick, Uncle John! Grab me those hemostatic forceps!"

John pulled out what looked like a huge set of tweezers from the bag. After he handed them to Doc, Dana turned her head away instead of watching the silver instrument disappear inside Fin's wound.

"Almost there. Almost there." Doc's raspy voice was thin with exertion. "Gotcha!" he cried and Dana turned back to find him sitting back on Fin's thighs.

His elation was temporary.

"Damnit! No!" He leaned forward and pressed two bloody, gloved fingers to the side of Fin's neck.

Dana saw Fin's eyes half-closed and his mouth half open. No more blood bubbled from his ruined nose. No more awful sounds clawed their way up the back of his throat.

"Oh my god." Her gaze darted to Doc's face. "Is he—" She didn't finish her question. She didn't need to. Everyone was thinking the same thing.

Doc was focused on a spot on the wall. But she knew he was blind to what he was seeing. His whole concentration was centered on his fingertips, searching for any sign of a heartbeat.

"Damnit, Fin!" he yelled. "No!"

"What's happenin'?" Will whispered drunkenly.

No one answered him because Doc began shouting orders again. "Get him off the bed! I need him on the floor for CPR!" Dana helped Jace lift Fin's shoulders, but Doc was quick to tell them, "Easy! Don't dislodge those forceps. Uncle John! Help Cami with his feet."

Dana's heart was in her throat as they carefully transferred the redheaded man from the bed to the floor. And it beat so hard it nearly choked her as she stood and watched Doc rip off his surgical gloves and toss them aside before pulling out what looked like a plastic sheet from his medical bag.

She didn't have long to wonder what the sheet was for. Doc quickly unfolded it, placed it over Fin's face, and maneuvered the plastic valve in the center of the sheet into Fin's mouth. He didn't immediately give mouth-to-mouth, however. Instead, he knelt next to Fin's chest and began compressions with so much vigor, Dana was surprised she didn't hear Fin's ribs crack.

She didn't realize she was crying until she felt John's strong arm curl around her shoulders. "Shhh," he whispered close to her ear, his beard lightly brushing the side of her jaw. "It's okay, darlin'. Go ahead and turn away if you need to."

It was good advice. Who would want *this* burned into their memory? Even so, she couldn't wrench her eyes away from the awful scene.

"Someone do mouth-to-mouth for me!" Doc ordered, his words breathless from the effort of the chest compressions.

Before anyone else could volunteer, Cami went down on her knees next to Fin's head. Fitting her mouth over the plastic valve, she blew hard as Doc counted out her breaths.

Will had dragged himself from his place by the wall to grab Fin's boot and shake it. "Fin!" His yell was hoarse. "Come on, man!"

Jace, who was sitting at Fin's head, seemed half his

normal size as his massive shoulders curled in and shook with silent sobs. Tears rolled down his face to get stuck in his bushy beard.

Dana wrapped her arms around John's waist, needing him to ground her again because this... This was the most awful thing she'd ever seen. One man was dying. Another man was working like a fiend to save his life. And three more men were wracked with agony at the thought of losing their friend.

Then, to everyone's astonishment, Fin raked in a ragged breath at the same time his eyes flew wide.

"My god, Fin!" Jace choked, ripping the plastic barrier from Fin's face so he could frame Fin's jaw with his big hands. "We thought we lost—"

"Tell Angie," Fin whispered raggedly, "and the kids that I...love...them. And I'm...sorry." Then his eyes fluttered shut. His breath shuddered out of him. And he grew eerily still.

"No! *Fin!*" Will screeched, tears dripping from his chin as he continued to shake Fin's booted foot.

"Damnit!" Doc yelled. "More, Cami. More mouth-to-mouth."

Cami breathed heavily, not only from the emotion of the moment but also the exertion of having to breathe for herself *and* for Fin. But she didn't hesitate to reapply the plastic barrier, press her lips over Fin's frighteningly pale lips, and begin CPR all over again.

For five minutes, the only sounds in the room were the furious winds of the storm, the *puff, puff* of Cami trying to breathe life into Fin's body, and Doc's grunts as he continued chest compressions.

But eventually, with a roar of frustration, a roar of *anguish*, Doc shoved to a stand. "*Fuuuuuccckkkk!*" The word strained out of him until it ended on nothing but a hoarse whisper.

Dana hiccupped on a sob and felt John's arm tighten around her shoulders. Cami, who'd been a rock through it all, hung her head and let out a sad little bleat of defeat. And Brady, who'd been quiet because LT and Olivia had been working on his arm and shoulder, finally spoke up.

There was such heartbreak in his voice when he said, "Will? Tell me Fin's not—"

Will didn't let him finish. Instead he wrapped a desperate hand around Doc's bare calf. "Don't stop!" he begged Doc, snot leaking from his nose, tears leaving glistening trails down his stubbled cheeks. "Keep tryin'! Please! For the love of Christ, keep tryin'!"

Doc's Adam's apple traveled up the length of his throat. There was such sadness in his eyes that a fresh batch of tears flooded into Dana's.

"I'm sorry." He tugged hard on his earlobe. "He's lost too much blood. His heart won't work."

The whole scene went surreal then. Because there wasn't a dry eye in the room. And it didn't matter that one group had come to rob and murder the other. The fact remained, a man was dead. A husband and a father by the sounds of it. And that was tragic no matter which way you sliced it.

Doc's voice was gruff when he said, "Give the dead his dignity."

Dana wasn't sure what he meant by that. But she understood once John pulled the bloody quilt off the bed.

He was as gentle as if he were wrapping up a newborn when he carefully placed the blanket over Fin's body. Then, with a gesture of kindness she would remember for the rest of her days, he removed the plastic covering from Fin's face and used the edge of the dangling sheet to softly wipe the blood from Fin's chin and cheeks.

Will, Brady, and Jace had all gathered around Fin's

head. Their grief was palpable, permeating the air. But it was Doc's ragged moan that truly shattered Dana's heart.

It was the sound of a man in agony. Not physical, but mental.

Throwing open the door, he stomped out of the room.

"Dalton?" Cami's face was red and splotchy from crying.

John placed a hand on her shoulder. "Come on, kiddo. Up you go." After he'd pulled Cami to her feet, he leveled a look on her. "Go after him. He needs you."

Cami didn't need to be told twice. She darted out of the room, her long black hair swinging and her sandaled feet slapping the floorboards.

John watched her go before turning back to Dana. He used the backs of his knuckles to wipe away the tears trickling down her cheeks.

"Y'okay, darlin'?"

"No," she told him honestly, hiccupping on another hard sob.

She didn't know how much she needed a hug until he dragged her close and closed his arms around her.

CHAPTER 17

8:01 PM...

The bathroom door was closed, but Cami could hear splashing coming from the other side.

"Dalton?" She knocked softly, her eyes slowly adjusting to the blackness of the hallway.

Now that the sun had set, even the faint light that had shined through the slats in the hurricane shutters was gone. And though she could still hear Julia's fury, somehow, not being able to *see* the strobe effect of swirling debris outside made the raging storm seem less scary.

That was a good thing since her nerves were shot.

Once, when she'd been a little girl, a huge nor'easter had pummeled Staten Island with blizzard conditions. The snow had weighed down the electrical lines until the utility pole outside her house snapped in two. She remembered standing in the bay window of the living room, watching the downed powerline drape across a tree and spark against the snowy limbs. *Crack, snap, POW!*

She felt like that downed powerline now.

One wrong move, one wrong *touch*, and she might spontaneously combust.

Or, you know, have myself a richly deserved meltdown.

"Can I come in?" she called with her lips close to the door.

When Doc didn't respond, she pressed her ear against the cool wood. All she heard was more splashing.

Maybe he didn't hear me, she thought. The poor beach house cracked and moaned as it withstood the hurricane-force winds. It wasn't nearly as hellacious as it'd been when the eyewall passed over, but still...

Raising her voice, she called again, "Dalton? Can I come in?"

She waited for him to tell her *yes, come right on in* or *no, fuck right on off.*

She was prepared for either, honestly. If he was half as out of sorts as she was, he might want company with whom to commiserate. Or he might want to process the trauma alone.

What she *didn't* expect was for him not to answer her at all.

Hmm. Stepping back, she gnawed on her bottom lip, unsure what to do next.

Should I take his silence as an invitation or discouragement?

John had told her to go after him. John had said he needed her. But what if John was wrong? What if what Doc needed was...

Fuck it, she decided, never one to tarry long in indecision. *He can always kick me out if he wants to.*

The metal doorknob was cool against her palm. "I'm coming in," she said even as she pushed open the door.

Doc was on his knees beside the tub, vigorously washing specks of blood from his forearms with water from the five-gallon paint bucket the others had filled and left for use in flushing the toilet. The three-wick candle burning on the windowsill cast the small room in a golden glow and highlighted the pink froth Doc had worked up over his wrists.

She could only see his profile. But that was enough to show the muscle in his jaw ticking fast enough to beat the band.

"A-are you okay?" she asked softly, and then quickly retracted her question. "No. Sorry. That was dumb. Of course you're not okay."

"After I left the Navy, I promised myself I'd do everything in my power to never kill again." His voice sounded raw, painful. "I promised myself I'd hang up my handgun. And you've known me what? Five months? Six?"

"Six and a half," she supplied and silently added, *But who's counting? Oh, right. Me. Because every day since the day you walked into my life has felt...portentous.*

She could admit that now. That from the very beginning she'd known he was different from the men who'd come before him.

"And in that time I've killed two more men."

Her mind traveled back to the mid-ocean plane crash and the little island they'd been marooned on afterward. To the boatful of strangers who'd stormed onto the beach. And to the big man Doc had been forced to put down with one fatal shot.

She shook her head. "You didn't have a choice either time."

"There's *always* a choice."

"Okay." She knew her expression looked perturbed. "But when the choice is kill or be killed, I don't think it really *counts* as a choice, do you?"

"I can't get away from it, Cami." When he turned to look at her, a lone tear spilled over his bottom lid to trek down his tanned cheek and get stuck in his beard stubble.

That broke her. Seeing the man she loved broken absolutely *broke* her.

Her own inner turmoil was forgotten and she was down on her knees in an instant. Taking his face into her hands, she gently thumbed away that single tear that was so much more powerful because of its loneliness.

"Maybe killing is like catching the chicken pox or something." He swallowed loudly. "Maybe once it's in your blood, it never really goes away. It just follows you around for the rest of your life waiting to rear its ugly head."

"You don't believe that. *I* certainly don't believe that. Six and a half months ago, you did what you had to do to save me. And tonight, you did what you had to do to save all of us."

"But I didn't *want* to kill him." His voice cracked against a sharp edge. "I just wanted…"

"I know." She took comfort in the warmth of his skin against her palms, the delicious abrasion of his stubble. "You wanted to save *everyone*, including the men who came here to rob you blind and *worse*. I know you heard them. They were going to wait to see if they could escape on their boat, and then they were going to kill us all."

"He had a *family*, Cami. A wife and kids. I took him from them with my bad aim."

"He took *himself* from them when he decided to come here." She shook his face slightly, forcing him to look at her so he could see the truth in her eyes. "You're not the bad guy in this story, Dalton. You're the *hero*."

"I don't feel very heroic. All I feel is…tired." As if to prove his point, he squeezed his eyes shut. "I'm so damn tired, Cami."

The problem solver in her kicked into high gear. "Finish washing up then, and let's go lie down. You were up with the sun and have been going balls to the wall ever since. Plus, your head has got to be killing you."

"No. Not that kind of tired. This is the kind of tired that doesn't go away with rest. The kind of tired that stays in your bones." He let his head fall back and she got distracted by his Adam's apple. Then he straightened, caught her worried gaze, and added, "I'm tired of death. I'm tired of not being able to escape it."

She wasn't sure how she knew he was thinking of his wife. Maybe it was the tenor of his voice. Maybe it was the way his soapy fingers shook as they dangled over the edge of the tub. Or maybe it was the devastation in his eyes.

It made sense. One death inevitably brought up memories of others. And for Doc, the death of his wife was the greatest of all the losses he'd suffered.

She took a deep breath. And when she spoke, she did so slowly, choosing her words carefully. "You *can't* escape death, Dalton. None of us can. There's no life without death. They're two sides of the same coin. Two sides of the same *experience*. Inexorably linked. Like day and night."

His nostrils flared again and she watched him fight to hold back the tears that gathered in his beautiful eyes.

How could she ever have thought to deny her love for this man? This strong, courageous, *gentle* man?

"Is it the lawyer thing?"

Her brow wrinkled. "Is *what* the lawyer thing?"

"Your way with words. Do they teach you that in law school? To be able to lay out an argument that sounds indisputable?"

Some of the anguish had gone from his voice. She took that as a positive sign.

"They *try* to teach it in law school." She donned a

haughty expression. "But I'm not sure it can actually *be* taught. I think some of us are just *born* persuasive." She winked, hoping to diminish his sadness further.

When the corners of his mouth tilted up, she wanted to howl in victory. There was nothing as awful as watching the man she loved suffer, and nothing as gratifying as knowing she was able to put a smile back on his face.

"Guess there's no more denying it then." His sigh was windy. "You were born to be a lawyer."

She wagged a finger. "Ah, ah, ah. Don't say that like it's a bad thing or else you'll have to explain why you feel such animosity toward my profession. Remember our deal?"

He gave her the side-eye.

Good god, he has such long, lovely eyelashes. They were blond at the tips, so it was only when they glinted in the candlelight that she could appreciate their full length.

"I don't remember us striking a deal. The way I recall it, you threw down an ultimatum."

She gave another dismissive shrug. "Toe-may-toe, toe-mah-toe."

He chuckled, and the sound was music to her ears. All too soon, however, he sobered and turned back to rinse and dry his hands. All the levity was gone from his voice when he said, "The drunk driver who killed Lily? He was a lawyer."

"Ah." That one word was out of her before she realized she'd even opened her mouth. She wasn't sure if it was an expression of *ah-ha* or *ah-fuck*.

Maybe it was both.

"Lily and I were living in Baltimore at the time. She'd gotten a job teaching kindergarten while I finished my residency. The man who killed her, Curtis Rienhardt, was the state's attorney there. He was friends with a lot of lawyers and a lot of judges in high places."

"And let me guess." Her voice was hoarse because her

heart had jumped into her throat. "He pulled some strings and got a reduced sentence?"

"Not even that." He shook his head, the candlelight making his lion's mane look more gold than brown. "He and his attorney buddies brokered a deal with a judge who agreed to give him a slap on the wrist. He got behind the wheel of a vehicle when he was too drunk to walk, jumped the median and killed my Lily, and the only consequence he suffered for taking her life was a fine and three years' probation."

"For vehicular manslaughter?" Cami's voice had gone from hoarse to strident in an instant.

He nodded. "I'd already been in the Navy for four months when my mother called me with the news of Rienhardt's *sentence*." He made finger quotes on that last word. "You better believe I spent the next three months dreaming up ways to kill him. The first time I got leave, I parked outside the bastard's house and waited for an opportunity to break in and use the tire iron in my trunk to bash his skull in."

Flames of remembered rage burned in his eyes, even after all these years.

And who can blame him? she thought, easily commiserating.

She knew, no matter how long she lived, she'd never forget her father was the reason her little sister was dead. She might someday work her way around to forgiving him. But because she could never forget, she could never let go of her fury. It would always smolder inside her.

"What stopped you?" she asked quietly.

"Lily." The muscles in his jaw gave one final twitch. "I kept hearing her voice in my head telling me *no*. That what was done was done, and that I would only make a terrible situation worse by killing the man. I couldn't disappoint her."

Cami didn't think she could love him more, but she would swear that last statement made her already full heart pull a Grinch move and grow three sizes.

"I'm sorry you never got any justice for her." She placed a hand on his forearm, feeling his muscles flex at her touch.

"That's lawyers for you." His shrug in no way looked as nonchalant as she figured he meant it to. "They talk big about upholding the law until upholding the law affects them. And then, because they know all the loopholes and all the ways to maneuver, they can break the law so fast it'll make your head spin."

"Not *all* lawyers, Dalton," she assured him.

He sat back on his heels, his eyes roaming over her face. "That's what I'm learning, Cami. That's what you've taught me. But that's why I went from hot to cold on you so fast once I found out what you did for a living. Because wanting you, a *lawyer*, felt disloyal to *her* somehow. I know that probably doesn't make a lot of sense. I mean, you're not—"

"It makes perfect sense actually," she interrupted. "It felt like you were sleeping with the enemy." A thought suddenly occurred. "Or maybe…" She stared hard into his eyes. "Does it *still* feel like you're sleeping with the enemy?"

"We haven't slept together, so how would I know?" He tried for a grin, but it didn't quite work.

"I'm serious, Dalton."

He sighed. "I know." Turning his head, he spent an eternity watching the flames of the candle dance.

Eventually, he looked back at her. When he spoke, her stomach took a nosedive. "The truth is, I don't know. Since Lily's death, I've never had a moment's hesitation about sleeping with any woman. But from that first night, something has held me back from sleeping with *you*. I can't blame that on the lawyer thing, because I didn't know you *were* a lawyer then."

She narrowed her eyes. "I thought we didn't sleep together because you passed out on the floor of my hotel room."

"Yeah." He nodded. "And the last time I let myself get that drunk was my freshman year in college. Come on, you've gotten to know me since. Do I strike you as the kind of guy to booze myself into oblivion?"

She didn't want to admit it, but… "No." She shook her head. "I hadn't thought about it, but no. You don't strike me as that kind of guy."

"Because I'm *not*. I used the whiskey as an excuse." His brow puckered. "I'm not sure I *knew* I was doing it at the time. But in retrospect, it's clear. Even then, something was telling me to pump the brakes."

"Do you…" She had to swallow when her voice came out sounding strangled. "Do you know what it was?"

"Oh, yes." He nodded. "It was because I *liked* you."

She blinked and waited for understanding to set in.

It never did.

"I'm sorry, *what*?"

"I *like* you, Cami." His words were nice, but the look on his face was anything but. He looked almost…*ill*. "I've liked you from the very beginning. We met and it was like…" He shook his head. "I don't know. It's like we're old friends. We use the same pop culture references. We have the same sense of humor, which, in case no one's ever told you, can strike some people as sharp and caustic. We talk and joke like we've known each other for years."

Yes. Despite the massive amounts of alcohol they'd imbibed, she remembered that night as fondly as he did. Which was probably why, despite the acerbic slights he'd started sending her way once he learned she was his lawyer, she'd kept coming back for more.

"I felt the same way," she told him truthfully. "I *feel* the same way. It's just…" She searched for the right word.

"Easy," they said in unison.

She laughed softly. But her humor was short-lived. "See, when I say it's easy, I want to smile." She gestured to her own face before pointing at his. "But when you say it, you can't help but frown."

As if on cue, his frown deepened. "I haven't liked a woman, not *like* liked a woman since Lily. And *like* liking you made me feel disloyal to her."

About halfway through that last sentence, she lost the ability to focus on his face. She was too distracted by the bear trap that'd caught her heart in its metal teeth and clamped down tight. She'd homed in on one word. "*Made*," she asked. "As in, past tense?"

His gaze held hers prisoner, so there was no way to escape the truth in his eyes.

"Ah." That one word shot out of her again. "I see."

She *did* see. But what she didn't *know* was what it meant for them? Where did it leave them?

Does it leave us anywhere at all?

"You're right. My head is throbbing like a bad tooth." He grimaced when he lifted a hand to his scalp. Then he pushed to a stand so quickly, she nearly gave herself whiplash watching him rise.

He moved to the sink. And after wetting a washcloth, he carefully dabbed at his scalp. Once he finished cleaning his wound, he rummaged around in the medicine cabinet until he found the bottle of Tylenol. Shaking a few tablets into his palm, he tossed back his head and dropped the pills into the back of his throat.

It was only after that that he met her searching gaze.

"Should I have kept that to myself? It's definitely not the sexiest thing to admit to a potential lover." He tried to lighten the atmosphere by making a face. "That you like them but you feel guilty for it."

It wasn't what she'd expected to hear. And it certainly

wasn't what she *wanted* to hear. Because if he couldn't get over the past, how could he possibly have a future with her?

Of course, she couldn't say any of that to him. Before she started talking about a future, she'd need to admit she loved him. And how could she do that now that she knew he was struggling with the mere thought of *liking* her?

Her smile was shaky, but she made sure her tone was as irreverent as his. "Eh. It's par for the course, right? When are things ever simple? When do they turn out the way we want them to? I mean, really?" She used the edge of the tub to shove upright. "This whole day has been a shining example that nothing goes as planned, don't you think?"

She'd never *planned* to be the daughter of a mobster. She'd never *planned* to lose her only sister and best friend to a homemade bomb. And she'd certainly never *planned* to be unmarried and childless at thirty-three years of age.

She was suddenly tired. The kind of tired he'd described. And she had an overwhelming urge to break down and cry.

He cocked his head. "Since when did you become the pessimist? You're usually the one assuring all the rest of us that everything's going to be okay. That for every problem there's a solution."

"And what's the solution to you feeling guilty for liking me?"

His eyebrows dipped into a V. "Does there *have* to be a solution? I mean, it's my issue, right? It doesn't affect you, does it?"

Yes! She wanted to scream. *It affects me because I love you, damnit! Because I want to build a life with you! And there's no way for us to do that if you're wracked with guilt!*

Instead she shrugged. "I suppose not." Lifting her chin and hating that the move felt wobbly, she added, "I'm going to go back to Mason and Alex's room. I need some peace and quiet to calm my nerves. I keep feeling Jace's pistol pressed against my head. Smelling blood in the air. Seeing Fin's dead eyes staring up at me." She shuddered.

Doc's expression fell. "Shit, Cami. I'm sorry. I didn't think to ask you how you were holding up. I know that scene in there"—he waved a hand in the general direction of the room at the end of the hall—"was beyond awful. But you handled it like such a champ that I didn't think…" He trailed off before quickly picking back up. "I just didn't think. I should have. I'm sorry," he said again. "Is there anything I can do?"

When he stepped forward to wrap a tender hand around her upper arm, she knew his squeeze was meant to be comforting. But it only brought her closer to cracking.

"No." She waved a hand, hoping the gesture looked unconcerned. "I'll be okay. I just need to get small and still and process."

He ran a hand back through his hair. "I should go check on the patients. But afterward, I can…" Again, he trailed off. And again, he was quick to pick back up. "If you want, I'll come to you after I'm finished."

I only want you to come to me if you can do it wholeheartedly, her heart and soul cried out in unison.

But even though she prided herself on being an honest woman, she couldn't make herself voice the thought aloud. Instead she said, "If you want to."

Before he could respond, she wrenched open the bathroom door and stepped into the hallway.

She was glad it was dark. It meant he couldn't see the tears glistening in her eyes when she turned back to him after he poked his head out of the bathroom and called her name.

"Are we okay?" The tenor of his deep voice was tentative.

She did something she never did then. She lied.

"Sure. Why wouldn't we be?"

CHAPTER 18

8:51 PM...

Life is all about bridges. Deciding which ones we cross and which ones we burn.

Doc's father had loved that quote. Had repeated it many times. And Doc wasn't sure why it came back to him now as he stood outside the closed door of Mason and Alex's bedroom.

Okay. That was bullshit. He knew.

It was because Cami was on the other side of that door. Cami and all the temptations she brought with her.

If he stepped inside, they'd become lovers. And if they became lovers, then what?

What comes next?

Nothing, right?

She was looking for a life partner, and he'd already lost his. She was looking for someone to father the rugrats she dreamed of having, and his chance at fatherhood had died with his wife. She was a *lawyer*, born and raised in New York City and currently living in Miami—an urbanite through and through—and he was a farm boy whose only dream was to go home, raise some cattle, and maybe do a little local doctoring on the side as he watched the seasons sweep over the mountains.

So, yeah, *nothing* came next.

That was something that'd never bothered him with other women. In fact, he'd taken comfort in knowing his liaisons always began and ended in the bedroom. But the finality of becoming Cami's lover and nothing more dismayed him.

Instead of asking himself why that should be—mostly because he was afraid of the answer—he decided maybe his problem was he'd been right all along. Maybe the right thing to do was to *not* give in to her myriad temptations. To keep doing as he'd been doing for months: relegating himself to fantasies of her. To burn her bridge before allowing himself to cross it.

Although, this whole line of questioning might be for nothing, he silently admitted. *She might be the one to light the match.*

The entire time he'd been checking on the wounded men, he'd been replaying their bathroom conversation in his head.

Something about it didn't sit right with him.

It wasn't her words. She'd said all the right things. It wasn't her face, either. She hadn't seemed shocked or mad or upset when he'd admitted to feeling guilty for liking her.

But there'd been something…

He couldn't put his finger on it and decided maybe it was just as she'd said. The events of the day had caught up with her.

Lord knew the events of the day had caught up with *him*.

How many times had he mentally replayed the gunfight? Two dozen? Three? How many times had he admonished himself for not turning and aiming before firing at Fin? At least a hundred.

And yet, if he'd turned and aimed, Brady would've seen him. And instead of being confused, Brady would've immediately returned fire. Who knew if Doc would've been able to dodge that bullet?

If he *hadn't*, if he'd been wounded or worse, he couldn't have saved his friends and—

No matter how many times he went over it, he always came back to the same conclusion. He'd done what he'd had to do.

Even so, he couldn't shake the anguish he felt at having sent another man to meet his maker.

"You tryin' to open it with your mind?"

John's voice pulled him from his swirling thoughts. "Huh?" The candle he carried flickered when he spun around.

Uncle John hitched his chin toward the closed bedroom door. "That there door. You been starin' at it for the last three minutes. You might try *open sesame*. Worked for Ali Baba." John's broad, tan brow wrinkled. "Or maybe it was one of the forty thieves? I forget who actually said it."

"Huh?" Doc asked again.

Uncle John's bearded chin jerked back. "You havin' a delayed reaction to that crack to the skull?"

Doc shook his head, willing his thoughts into some semblance of order. "Sorry. I'm just…" He glanced once again at the closed door. "Distracted, I guess."

Uncle John chuckled. "Yeah. Before all this craziness went down, Cami had whipped you up into a pretty good lather, huh? So what? You nervous about gettin' whipped up again? Don't tell me you, of all people, are havin' performance anxiety."

"It's not that."

"Then what is it?"

"If I knew, I wouldn't be standing out here in the hallway, would I?"

"Hmm." Uncle John crossed his arms over his chest. "You wanna hear my thinkin' on the subject?"

Doc curled his upper lip. "On the subject of sex? No thank you. My old man covered that in trauma-inducing detail the day I turned thirteen."

"No, dummy. My thinkin' on the subject of *life*."

Uncle John had an uncanny way of cutting through the bullshit. So even as Doc nodded for him to continue, he braced himself for whatever might come out of John's mouth next.

"Happiness isn't somethin' that happens to you," John said with a firm dip of his chin. "It's a series of choices you make. And from everything I've seen, Camilla D' Angelo makes you happy. So what's holdin' you back from choosin' her?"

"Choosing her?" Doc felt his brow wrinkle. "You mean like *choosing* her, choosing her?" When John nodded, an uncomfortable laugh burst out of him. "It's not like *that*. There aren't any white dresses and wedding bells in our future."

"Why not?"

Doc wouldn't have thought it possible, but he was even *more* discombobulated than he'd been two minutes earlier. "B-because I already *had* the white dress and the wedding bells," he sputtered.

"And according to you, you don't regret that for one moment. You said it was your greatest accomplishment. Your grandest adventure."

Doc blinked in confusion. "Yeah? So?"

"So who says you can't have another?"

"*I* say," Doc staunchly declared. And then, because he didn't like the thoughts and questions that began darting around inside his head, he turned the conversational tables. "And *you're* one to talk. When are *you* going to get yourself a white dress and some wedding bells, huh?"

To his astonishment, John, the bacheloriest of bachelors, shrugged. "Who knows? It's never too late, right?"

Doc jerked his head to the side and narrowed his eyes. "Are you yanking my chain or just pulling my leg?"

John shrugged again. "I've recently realized there's a reason a windshield is bigger than a rearview mirror. We aren't meant to keep worryin' about what's behind us. We're meant to keep our eyes focused on what's ahead." Before Doc could come up with an appropriate counter-argument to that ridiculous bit of countrified hokum, John turned and sauntered toward the staircase.

"Hey!" Doc called. "I thought you were helping LT keep watch over the thieves?"

"I am," John tossed over his shoulder. "But Dana needs some crackers to settle her stomach and I think there's saltines on the top shelf of the pantry."

"Is she what you're focusing on through your windshield?" Doc asked teasingly.

He expected a flippant reply. Instead, John admitted, "She's definitely *one* of the things."

Two seconds later, Doc lost sight of John—he'd been swallowed up by the darkness—but he could hear John whistling a Jimmy Buffett tune as he continued down the stairs.

Will wonders never cease? Doc shook his head. *John Anderson, willingly looking for a leg-shackle?*

It was like watching a fish walk on dry land or seeing a bird breathe underwater.

Turning back toward the door, John's words replayed

inside his head.

"From everything I've seen, Camilla D'Angelo makes you happy."

"There's a reason a windshield is bigger than a rearview mirror."

"Who says you can't have another?"

Doc had been feeling guilty about possibly *sleeping* with Cami. Imagine the state he'd be in if he was thinking about…

He couldn't even finish the thought. It was too ludicrous. He'd found the love of his life, and she'd died. Period. End of story. A second wife would be…*what*? A consolation prize?

Camilla D'Angelo plays second fiddle to no one, he thought adamantly. *She's someone's first place trophy. Someone's gold medal.*

"Cami?" He knocked softly on the door. "Can I come in?"

All his ruminating and reasoning had gotten him no closer to knowing what to do.

It's time to play the game and let the chips fall where they may.

CHAPTER 19

8:58 PM...

ome in!" Cami yelled, using the excuse of twisting a messy bun onto the top of her head so she didn't have to meet Doc's eyes when he pushed open the bedroom door.

She'd heard.

Heard him assure John there wouldn't be any white dress or wedding bells in their future because he'd already had them. Heard him admit, quite adamantly, that he considered a second chance at love to be out of the question.

And now, she could say she truly understood heartbreak.

It felt similar to death in that the grief came in quick waves. One second she felt like she was drowning. The next she could breathe, and she would tell herself, *It's okay. You're okay.* And then another wave would crash over her head and suddenly there was no oxygen to be had in the whole damn room.

And the worst part? The one person she wanted to tell, the one person who would have brushed away her tears and assured her there were plenty of fish in the sea, was dead.

Carlotta! She silently screamed into the void. *Help me do this! Help me be brave!*

That's what the situation required.

Courage. The mental fortitude to keep all her thoughts and feelings bottled up because it wasn't *Doc's* fault she'd fallen in love with him. It wasn't *his* fault he didn't feel the same way about her. And it *certainly* wasn't his fault her heart was broken.

When he said, "How you holding up?" she hitched one shoulder.

"I'm managing. You?"

"Still dog-ass tired."

She finished with her bun and pressed her back against the headboard. She was glad she'd thrown the coverlet over her legs because they were shaking. So were her hands, so she shoved them under the covers too.

When she finally dared to glance up, it was to see him closing the door and setting a burning candle on the dresser beside the one she'd lit earlier. Then he turned and strode toward the bed.

It took every ounce of willpower she possessed to watch his loose-hipped swagger and not to break down into a puddle of snot and tears at the thought of not getting to see it every day for the rest of her life.

"Mind if I join you?" He kicked out of his flip-flops and waited for her to throw back the covers in invitation.

The mattress depressed under his weight, causing her to slide in his direction until their hips touched. He threw an arm around her shoulders automatically, like they'd been friends for years, *lovers* for years, and that made her want to cry even more.

She bit the inside of her cheek—*hard*—to refocus her mind and latched on to the first subject that came to mind. "How are Will and Brady?"

"They'll live." He grimaced. "Which is good. I don't think I could've handled another black mark on my soul."

She sat forward so she could pin him with a serious look. "Can I ask you a question?"

One eyebrow arced up his forehead. "Sure. But before I answer, I have to know. Am I under oath? You've got your lawyer face on."

"What's my lawyer face?"

"Pinched lips." He brushed a fingertip over her mouth and she shuddered involuntarily. "Laser-focused gaze." His fingertips smoothed over one of her eyebrows. "Somber expression." He booped the tip of her nose at the same time one corner of his mouth tilted up. "It's very intimidating. I bet you're something to see in the courtroom."

"Maybe you'll come watch me some time."

"Maybe." He winked, but she could tell by his tone he had no intention of ever coming to see her in court.

The shattered pieces of her heart were ground to dust.

He mistook her look of despair for one of impatience. Laughing softly, he chucked her under the chin. "Okay, fine. No more conversational detours. What's your question?"

"Have you ever killed someone who wasn't trying to kill you or trying to kill someone you were sworn to protect?"

"Wow." He blinked. "You don't mess around. Just… right for the jugular." He pantomimed stabbing himself in the neck.

"I'm not aiming for your throat," she assured him. "What I'm aiming for is your head. I feel like you have a distorted view of things. And I want to help you see things clearly."

He grew contemplative and the silence stretched. When

he finally answered, his words came out slowly. "You can't understand battle until you've lived it. You know that phrase *the fog of war*?" When she nodded, he continued. "It really is a *fog*. You don't see or remember things clearly. And in a gun battle, so many bullets are flying it's hard to keep track of which ones are yours."

"So the answer is no." She employed her best courtroom voice. "To the best of your recollection, you have never killed anyone who wasn't trying to kill you or those you were sworn to protect. I may be a lapsed Catholic, but I'm pretty sure that means your soul is clean."

The muscles in his jaw began ticking again. "Doesn't feel that way."

"That's because you're mistaking black marks for little rips. Taking a life can tear at the core of you, even when the taking is justified. But black marks are saved for sins, Dalton." She framed his face with her hands so he'd be forced to look at her. To *listen* to her. "For *evils* committed against another person," she went on. "And that, my friend, isn't something you have to worry about."

Something moved behind his eyes. "Are we friends, Cami?"

"*That's* what you focused on?" Her expression matched the exasperation in her voice. "Did you hear anything else I said?"

"All of it. And maybe you're right. Maybe it's tears and not black marks. But tears destroy as surely as stains do. They still make me feel…*less*."

"Less *what*?" she pressed.

"I don't know." He shook his head and the move made her drop her hands from his face. Her fingertips itched with the urge to touch him again, so she once again tucked them under the coverlet. "*Human*, maybe?"

She couldn't give him all her truths, so she was happy

to give him this one. "Dalton Simmons, you have more humanity in your big toe than some men have in their entire bodies."

When he swallowed, his Adam's apple made a *clicking* sound in his throat. Then he cocked his head. "But the question still stands. Are we friends?"

She searched his eyes, trying to think of how to answer. Finally, she gave him another unvarnished truth. "Besides my sister, you might be the best friend I've ever had."

When he blinked in astonishment, she was quick to add, "I mean, you can be brooding and cynical, and you get on my last nerve when you try to yuck my yum. But you're also the only person I've ever met who isn't offended by my sarcasm. Who gets my jokes. Who challenges me intellectually."

He bit the inside of his cheek to keep his self-satisfied grin from growing too big. Then, he asked, "Yuck your yum?"

"Yeah, you know, rain on my parade, burst my bubble. Basically make me want to hit you and hug you at the same time."

"Which do you want to do now?"

He was trying to be playful. But she couldn't manage to join in. Her face and tone were both serious when she asked, "Which do you *want* me to do?"

Suddenly, all the teasing was gone from his eyes too. "I could use a hug."

"Good." Her voice broke. "I could too."

Without hesitation, he circled her waist with his big, warm hands and pulled her into his lap until they were breast to chest. Until her cheek was smashed up against his warm, rough beard stubble. Until she couldn't tell which heartbeat was her own.

"It's been a helluva day, huh?" His scratchy voice whispered in her ear.

"One for the record books," she agreed, unable to hold back a little sob.

She'd experienced the joy of falling in love and the sorrow of having her heart broken all in the span of a few hours. Not to mention the horrors of the storm, the hostage-taking, the gunplay, and the death.

She was half tempted to run into the storm and let it sweep her up and carry her away like Dorothy. But if she did that, she would no longer be safe in the circle of Doc's arms. And despite how much it hurt to hold him and know the end to holding him was somewhere on her horizon, the thought of letting go of him now was unthinkable.

She would soak it up. Soak *him* up. And on those lonely nights to come, she'd take out the memory of this moment and revel in it.

When the thought had another little peep of sorrow slipping from her lips, he pulled back so he could see her face.

"Oh, sweetheart." He brushed a strand of hair behind her ear. "That sound breaks my damn heart."

"I'll be okay." She blew out a shaky breath, glad he thought her sorrow was due to the terrors of the day. "I'm just feeling a little fragile."

"Come here, then." He pulled her into another hug. "Let me hold you together and keep you from breaking."

For a long while that's what he did. That's *all* he did.

He didn't try to kiss her. Didn't let his hand, which was running up and down her back in a soothing path, roam too low to stroke her ass or stray too wide to graze the outer curve of her breast. He didn't try to rub himself against her. He just…lent her his strength.

The gentleness of the act, the *selflessness* of it, had *her* wanting more. More of his strong arms. More of his warm skin. More of his rusty voice whispering in her ear.

More of *him*. *All* of him.

If I kiss him now, I know what'll happen. We'll become lovers. Lovers and that's it, she admitted sadly.

And yet, what was the alternative? To *not* kiss him? To *not* make him her lover? What would that get her?

She'd still be in love with him. She'd still *want* him. The only thing she'd accomplish would be to deny herself the opportunity to know what it was to be with the man who'd charmed her mind, lit a fire inside her body, and stolen her heart.

So for a few hours I'll pretend this Dalton is my *Dalton. And on all those lonely nights to come, I'll have that memory too.*

CHAPTER 20

9:13 PM...

Doc stilled when he felt Cami's warm mouth press over the pulse-point in his neck.

Ever since he'd pulled her onto his lap—and even though touching her made him yearn in ways he'd never known before—he'd done his best to keep his caresses sensitive and not sexual. Comforting and not claiming.

But when her hot breath licked over his throat, and *especially* when her wicked tongue flicked out to taste, he could no more control the groan that rumbled up from deep inside his chest or the erection that throbbed to instant, steely life inside his shorts, than he could control the ferocity of Julia's winds.

"Cami." Her name filled his mouth and he gorged himself on the feel of it rumbling across his vocal cords and sliding across his tongue.

Before he even made the conscious decision to do so,

he'd hooked a finger under her chin and lifted her head to claim her sumptuous mouth.

Her return kiss wasn't tender. It wasn't tentative. It was fierce and ravenous and so deep he wasn't sure whose air he was breathing.

It was the kiss of two people who were starved for one another. Who wanted to eat each other alive. Who'd held back for as long as they could and who couldn't hold back a second longer.

They'd come together, wounded and weary from the day, to offer each other a port in the storm. And now, suddenly, they *were* the storm.

Lust flew through his veins with the force of hurricane winds. Desire swirled low in his gut like a frenzied whirlpool. And the hunger that flashed through his brain was as snarled as a bolt of lightning.

She invaded his mouth. He ravished hers. Her hands were everywhere, his arms, his shoulders, tunneled into his hair. His cradled the mesmerizing flare of her hips, memorized the delicate line of her backbone, pulled her hair down from its confines atop her head to twist the dark strands around his fists so he could control the tilt of her head, the pressure of her greedy mouth.

Then her fingertips skimmed over the laceration on his scalp and she wrenched her mouth away. "I'm so sorry," she whispered, her dark eyes luminous with worry.

"Sweetheart." His voice was scratchier than usual. "I can assure you the only thing I'm feeling right now is you."

A half smile tilted up one side of her kiss-swollen lips as she gently ran her fingers over the bandage on his forearm. Then she pressed her free hand to the wound on her side. "We're a pair, huh? Black and blue and bleeding?"

"Bruised but not broken." He matched her half grin. "It's not so bad given the alternative."

That sleek right eyebrow of hers arched. "Who's the optimist now?"

And there was that wit he admired so much. Although, the devilish sparkle was missing from her eyes.

He missed that sparkle. And since he didn't know how to get it back, he decided to try to make her eyes shine with something else. Something that started with an O and rhymed with *schmorgasm*.

"Come here, woman." He used the hand still wrapped in her hair to pull her forward. "Your mouth hasn't been on mine for the last thirty seconds and that's far, *far* too long."

She didn't resist when he pulled her forward that last inch. And just like before, their kisses were anything but meek and mild. Within seconds he'd made good on his words and was feeling nothing but her, was focused on nothing but her.

"Dalton." Her breath was warm and sweet as she pulled away slightly. "Help me forget this day."

"What do you want, Cami?" He nipped her bottom lip, sucking it into the heat of his mouth so he could lave the lush pad with his tongue. "Tell me."

"I want to not have to think." Her husky voice swirled around in his ears, and he understood the sentiment entirely. He wanted to forget the day too. Forget the gore. Forget the fear. Forget the *death*. "I just want to feel," she added.

He would make her feel.

He'd make her feel every inch of her delicious body as he explored it with his hands and mouth. He'd show her all the ways he'd learned to give pleasure to a woman. And he wouldn't stop until there wasn't a thought left in her head save for bliss and delight and sheer, soul-shaking carnality.

"Your wish is my command," he assured her before reclaiming her lips.

He wasn't sure how long they stayed that way, her

straddling his lap, their mouths eagerly testing and tasting and coming back for more, more, always more. All he knew was that the feverish undercurrent that'd been running below his surface since the first moment he met her jumped its banks and became a flood.

He was caught up in it. Swept away by it. Lost in the power of his want of her. His *need* for her.

When she tilted her hips forward, riding the hard edge of his erection, he slid his hands inside her ridiculous borrowed boxer briefs and palmed her ass, loving the way her ample flesh overflowed his grip. Loving how each luscious globe was warm and firm.

Ignoring the urge to knead, instead he simply held her, his fingertips ten perfect pressure points, and encouraged her to ride him. *Slowly.* A gentle bump and grind that was as old as time.

"Dalton." Her voice caught on pleasure he knew bordered on pain. He knew it because he was experiencing the same thing. The friction of their sexes grinding together was eye-crossing, and yet it wasn't enough.

"Don't rush," he whispered against her lips. "Let's take this as far as we can. As slowly as we can."

She made a mewling sound in the back of her throat that was half acquiescence and half disagreement. And he understood that too. Because for every atom in his being that wanted to drag this thing out, to savor every moment and relish every subtle sensation, there was another atom that said, *Fuck going slow. Take her! Take her now! End this delicious misery!*

He was deliberate as he grabbed the hem of her borrowed T-shirt, trailing his fingers along her ribs as he bunched it higher, higher, higher still. He pulled back from the kiss only long enough to tug the material over her head and watch her luxurious curtain of jet-black hair tumble down around her shoulders. Then her mouth was on his again.

He'd only gotten a glimpse of her simple bra. But it was enough to show him that with breasts like hers, plain cotton was as sexy as see-through lace.

The way she filled out the cups? The way her cleavage beckoned for the glide of his tongue? The way her dark nipples peeked through the film of the fabric?

Fuuuccckkk. It was the very definition of seduction.

With trembling fingers, he pulled each of her bra straps off her shoulders, letting them dangle down her arms. His hands weren't shaking from nerves but from anticipation and the effort it took to hold back from ripping the white cotton clean off her body in a brutal show of force.

She did that to him. Tore away his restraint. Burned off his self-discipline. Turned him into a beast whose only goal was to conquer and claim.

Passion was never something he'd lacked. He loved everything about a woman's body. Everything about the act of physical intimacy. But Cami took his passion and added in a generous helping of jet fuel until the word *passion* wasn't big enough to describe what he felt.

Craving maybe? *Unbridled wantonness?*

Suddenly, he knew the word he was looking for.

Obsession.

He'd been obsessed with her from the start. And having her here in his arms, moving against him and feeding him her fevered kisses, took that obsession and turned it totally animalistic.

It was the animal in him that growled a warning when he ripped his mouth from hers so he could sit back and *see* the moment he freed her breasts from the confines of her bra.

He'd always considered himself more of an ass man—and Cami's butt was certainly grade A. But from the very beginning, he'd been intrigued by her breasts.

They were large and heavy. With that gentle slope from her collarbone that proved they were natural and not the work of some talented surgeon.

He'd fantasized about filling his hands with them. Imagined how they'd feel pressed against his cheeks when he buried his face between them. Jerked off while daydreaming about watching them sway above his face as she rode him soft and slow, her hot, tight sheath milking his greedy dick.

He tipped the cups of her bra forward until her breasts spilled out. And the breath that sawed from his lungs was harsh and hot.

She was even more perfect than he'd imagined. So sweet and womanly. Her flesh soft and smooth and tender-looking.

"My god." The words growled out of him. "You're beautiful."

She had a freckle under the slope of one teardrop-shaped breast. And her light brown nipples pinched into tight points beneath his heated gaze.

He felt an answering pinch low in his gut when she cupped the wondrous globes, her ripe flesh overspilling her red-tipped fingers.

It was sexy as hell. But he realized she hadn't done it to seduce when she softly said, "Gravity has taken its toll."

Dragging his eyes away from the glory of her naked chest, he caught her self-conscious grimace. For three full seconds, he could do nothing but blink in consternation. It was mindboggling to think she could look in the mirror and see anything but perfection.

He told her as much as he gently grabbed her wrists and tugged her hands away. He loved the way her tits bounced when she released them, and his cock wholeheartedly agreed that the sight was erotic as hell.

"You are a *woman*," he assured her. "Absolutely perfect and soft and *real*."

He could feel her wanting to cover them again. So he used one hand to manacle her wrists behind her back. It forced her to arch toward him, and suddenly her succulent breasts were darting out at him like an offering.

He was more than happy to accept their invitation. But first, he did something he'd been wanting to do all day.

Leaning forward, he flicked his tongue into the hollow at the base of her throat. When her head fell back on a moan of pleasure, he tasted her again. Loving the way he could feel her heartbeat against his lips. Loving how delicate her flesh felt against his tongue. Loving the unabashed sounds she made.

Her scent was strong there. That fresh, floral smell that was uniquely her and that would always make him imagine stripping her naked and laying her out in a field of wildflowers.

"I've been dreaming of this part of you for so long," he murmured against her throat. "But it tastes even better than I imagined."

"My throat is what you've dreamed about?" Her voice was husky with desire, but he could hear the teasing smile in it. "Your fantasies must be far more PG than mine."

The thought of her fantasizing about him, of her lying in bed and touching herself, had him moaning. Then he bit the side of her neck in warning and reveled in the sound of her squeal.

"I think I need to show you *exactly* how X-rated my fantasies are." He pulled back from her throat and with his free hand, cupped her breast and plumped it high. Before she could catch her breath from that first touch, he brushed his thumb over the pebbled crest and watched her areola furl tighter.

"You're so responsive." He gently pinched her nipple. Rolling it slightly. "Do you have any idea what it does to a man when a woman's body responds like this?"

"What does it do?" Her dark eyes glittered in the candlelight.

"It makes him hard as a fucking rock." He pressed the edge of his thumbnail into the center of the hardened peak until she squirmed against his steely cock. "See?" He arched an eyebrow.

"Please," she begged. "I need you to—"

He didn't let her finish. He knew what she needed.

Leaning forward, he pulled one eager nub into his mouth, sucking it rhythmically. He loved the feel of the hard point of flesh when he pressed it to the roof of his mouth. Loved more the erotic sound his mouth made against her tender flesh as he settled in and feasted.

When he released her wrists, her fingers instantly tunneled into his hair. Her nails bit into his scalp as he plumped her opposite breast high, flicking the hardened peak with his thumb. He could feel that she touched the cut on his scalp, but there was no pain.

There was only the flavor of her on his tongue. The pleasure of her sultry sex as she continued to ride him. The erotic sound of her crying out, "Oh, my god!"

He felt it then. The rush of wetness between her legs. It soaked through both sets of their clothes and perfumed the air with the sweet, salty scent of a woman in need.

For a moment, he thought maybe she'd cum. But the frantic movements of her hips told him she'd only gotten a step closer.

He'd planned to map out every inch of her body with his hands and mouth. Use every second of every minute of the storm to torment and tease her from head to toe. But suddenly, all he could think about tasting and tormenting and teasing was the part of her that was so hot and wet and needy.

With a snap of his fingers, her bra was gone. A second

later, he'd flipped her onto her back and tugged off Rudolph and his strategically placed red nose.

He took a brief moment to appreciate how fantastically sexy Cami was lying there in nothing but demure white panties, her black hair fanned out on the coverlet behind her head. Then he hooked a finger into the waistband of her panties, and with a quick pull, those were gone too.

"Fuck me," he swore, feeling the muscle in his jaw tighten as his eyes landed on the black triangle of hair that covered the top of her mons.

He liked that she'd kept some of her pubic hair. So many women chose to go completely bare. And while he'd never dream of telling a woman what to do with her own body, he'd always preferred his sexual partners to look like *women* instead of hairless girls.

Cami was woman personified.

Inch upon inch of smooth, lightly tanned skin. Long, silky legs. Round breasts sitting heavily upon her narrow ribcage. Tucked-in waist that flared to dramatically curvy hips. And the most adorable oval belly button he planned to lick until she squirmed.

"Dalton?" She was shocked by the sudden change in him when he hopped off the mattress to tower over her with a predatory gleam in his eye.

He didn't give her time to question, time to object, before he grabbed her behind her knees and dragged her to the edge of the bed.

"Dalton?" she asked again, sounding a little uncertain. But then understanding lit in her eyes when he fell to his knees.

"Lie back, sweetheart." He draped her legs over his shoulders. "I plan to be here a while."

The sound that came from the back of her throat then was half groan and half chuckle. Of course, when he pressed his lips into her delicate folds, instantly finding her swollen clit and flicking it with his tongue, it turned into a whole groan.

The smell of her filled his nose, tangy and sweet. The feel of her soft, wet flesh went to his head, making him dizzy. But the *taste* of her? So salty and delicious? Oh, *that* bypassed his brain and went straight to his dick.

When he softly flicked the swollen bundle of nerves at the top of her sex from side-to-side, she sighed. When he ran his tongue up and down across the hard little nub, he saw her lower belly quiver. But as soon as he slipped a finger into her tight, wet sheath, he knew he'd found the combination that would send her over the edge because she whimpered and her hips bucked up in rhythm to the swipe of his tongue.

He kept up the combo, never breaking stride or pressure because when she said, "Don't stop! Oh my god, Dalton, don't stop!" he took her at her word.

And then her inner walls began to clamp down on his pumping finger.

The thought of how *amazing* those same silky walls would feel rippling along the length of his dick had him reaching down with his free hand to grip his raging cock. He gave it a squeeze through the fabric of his shorts, just to ease some of the ache. And then he reached further to tug at his balls because they'd pulled up tight against his body.

"More," she begged, her head thrashing against the mattress, and he didn't hesitate to shove a second finger in beside the first.

He loved the feel of her stretching to accommodate his intrusion. When he added a come-hither motion at the end of each forward stroke, she cried out and he opened his eyes so he could watch his woman climb the steep slope toward orgasm. Watch her tug at her own nipples in mindless need. Watch her arch beneath his mouth as she reached the ultimate summit.

With the delicious smell of her all around him, with the feel of her inner walls clamping so tight around his fingers that his knuckles ground together, with the sound of her keening voice crying out his name, he pushed her over the edge.

It was only then that he realized what he'd done.

In the silence of his mind, and without a single drop of guilt, he'd thought of her as *his woman*.

His woman.

Fuuuccckkk.

CHAPTER 21

9:40 PM...

Cami realized she'd spiraled down from the glorious heights of release when she felt Doc softly brush his knuckles along the side of her face.

The gentleness of his touch was a sharp contrast to the fevered licking and sucking and stroking he'd been doing only moments before. And maybe such tenderness after such a torrid climax was why her belly instantly tightened.

Or maybe it's that I know what it's like to be intimate with someone I actually love. And it changes everything.

"In case no one's ever told you"—his voice was low and raspy—"you're absolutely stunning when you cum. You get such a pretty blush here." Again, he brushed his knuckles along her cheek. "And here." His fingertips feathered over her chest, lightly stroking when he came to her nipples. "And here." His hand drifted down the centerline of her body until he cupped her still sensitive womanhood.

She moaned as the ache he'd just assuaged returned with a tiny twinge.

He must've felt it. Her eyes were still closed but she heard the grin in his voice when he purred, "And a little insatiable by the feel of it."

"Proud of yourself, aren't you?" She had to fight a grin herself.

"Oh, I think we *both* deserve a trophy for that one, don't you?" When he delicately dragged one finger through her damp folds, she clamped her thighs tight around his marauding hand.

Blinking open her eyes, she saw his face close to hers, one eyebrow quirked in question. "What are you doing?" she panted.

"Giving you what you're asking for," he answered easily. "Or, more accurately, what your *body* is asking for." He pressed his thumb against her still buzzing clit, making her gasp.

"Isn't it your turn?" she asked dazedly.

A line formed between his eyebrows. "I've never liked thinking of sex as quid pro quo. Seems too transactional."

"So how do you like to think of it?"

"As a sport where everyone's on the same team. Your pleasure is my pleasure and vice versa."

Pushing up on one elbow, she caught her bottom lip between her teeth and toyed with the hem of his T-shirt. "Well, teammate. Don't you think we should be wearing the same uniform?"

He chuckled, and the low, warm sound made her nipples furl.

When his glittering eyes homed in on the change, she became intensely aware of her own breasts. The weight of them. The way they swayed gently when she breathed. She was usually self-conscious about them, but the desire in his eyes was so dark and potent she didn't feel the least bit shy.

All she felt was desirable. Sexy. *Bold.*

She stopped fiddling with the hem of his shirt and instead popped the button on his shorts. The zipper made a lovely little *scritching* sound when she pulled it down. Then, she jerked her hand back when the two halves of his fly fell open.

His erection poked above the hem of his boxer briefs. His head was as plump as a plum, the skin so taut it was shiny. And it was clear he was a large man. Which, she'd expected given his height. Not to mention she'd gotten some idea of his size when she'd straddled his lap and indulged in a little high school bump and grind. But there was large and then there was *large*.

Doc was *large* with a capital L.

In fact, she was a little intimidated. But more than anything, she was intrigued. *Impatient.*

The tiny twinge of renewed desire melted into a full-on *ache* of need. Her sex, so recently satisfied, pulsed with renewed lust.

She wanted that thick column of male flesh inside her. Filling her. Stretching her to her limits.

He rumbled approval at her body's response and used his thumb to softly strum her clit. The pleasure was so sharp she nearly went cross-eyed. Her toes definitely curled.

As much as she hated to do it, she gently nudged his hand from between her thighs.

"Too sensitive?" He arched an inquisitive eyebrow.

"That"—she nodded—"and it's *my* turn."

When she lightly scraped her nails over his swollen head, his entire length jumped.

"Take me out," he instructed, already shoving his shorts down his thighs and rolling onto his back. "Touch me."

Her breath caught at his command. She liked a man who

knew what he wanted and wasn't shy about demanding it.

When she pulled his boxer briefs down to his knees, her breath shuddered out of her at the sight of him. He was so long and thick, with angry-looking veins that snarled up his impressive length.

She'd had lovers who'd had pretty penises and lovers who'd had unique ones that bent one way or the other. But Doc's dick was the first she'd seen that was...*aggressive*. That was the first word that flitted through her head.

"Touch me," he said again, and she was more than happy to oblige.

Gently mapping his length with her fingernails, she watched, mesmerized, as his cock bobbed against her touch, begging for more. She gave it to him by wrapping her fist around him—noting how her fingertips struggled to touch—and slowly stroked.

Just one long, luxurious glide from his fat base up the length of his veiny shaft.

His cock was a wonderful contradiction of soft skin covering steely hardness. And he was so hot he nearly burned her. When she reached his swollen tip, a bead of moisture met her exploring fingers.

He growled something low and fierce. Then he hooked a hand behind her neck and dragged her forward for a kiss that made her breath strangle in her lungs.

"I want you, Cami," he moaned into her mouth. "I *need* you."

"Then take me," she told him, more than ready to finally, *finally* be consumed by the fire of her desire for him.

He jackknifed off the bed, shedding his T-shirt and his boxer briefs along the way. When he stood beside the mattress, so big and tall and gloriously *male*, his erection stood out from his body at a ninety-degree angle.

She got the impression it wanted very much to be

upright, to reach past his belly button, but its own weight dragged it down.

Her center melted at the sight, going soft and wet in contrast to all his hardness and heat.

"Come on, Mason," he muttered as he ripped open the drawer on the bedside table. "Don't let me down. Aha!"

He pulled out a roll of condoms, happily ripping off one foil square.

"Here." She scooted to the edge of the bed, taking the wrapped condom from him. "Let me."

She wanted her hands back on him. Now that she knew what it was to hold that part of him, her palms itched to experience the glory again.

He stood before her, unabashed in his blatant sexuality as she tore the foil square and took out the ring of latex. When she lifted her eyes, she found his gaze hot and hungry. Then they both watched as she took him in hand and slowly, ever so slowly, slid the latex down his impressive length.

She grazed her nails over his balls once she reached his base and watched his stomach muscles contract like an accordion.

Scooting back onto the bed, she beckoned him to join her with a crooked finger. He set an Olympic record for speed as he slid onto the mattress beside her. When he leaned forward to kiss her neck, his beard stubble prickled the sensitive skin there.

She pushed on his chest, wanting him to lie back so she could explore his body, wanting to learn every rise of muscle, every length of tendon, all the textures of his scars. But he shook his head.

"Not this first time," he rasped. "This first time I want to explore *you*. Next time, you can explore me."

And then, for long moments, he *did* explore her. His hands ran over every inch of her skin, and his feathery touch made her shudder and moan. He followed the path of his fingers with his mouth, starting with her breasts and paying particular attention to the little freckle under the left one, licking at it like it was made of chocolate.

Then his warm lips left a trail down the centerline of her body. Stopping briefly to pepper soothing kisses around the bandage on her side. He dropped open-mouthed licks to each of her hip bones. Lightly nipped the slight roundness of her lower belly. And then delved his tongue into her belly button.

Desire swirled inside her as fiercely as the winds swirled outside. And tongues of fire licked at her skin everywhere he touched her, everywhere he tasted her.

By the time he'd finished learning the contours of her belly button, her center was throbbing so hard it bordered on pain.

She tugged at his shoulders, whispering commands of her own because her need was so great. He obliged by positioning himself between her spread legs and holding himself aloft on his forearms. Desperation gleamed in his green eyes. Hunger tightened the skin over his cheekbones.

Wrapping her ankles behind his knees, she let her legs fall wide in blatant invitation, feeling the cool air brush against her wet, heated flesh.

Doc eagerly accepted her unspoken request by gripping the base of his dick and angling it down until his swollen tip kissed her hungry entrance.

They both gasped at that first carnal touch. And then she was mewling and moaning as he slowly, so devastatingly *slowly*, began to push inside.

The first inch of him was heaven. The second inch was bliss. The third and fourth? They had her arching under him, eager to receive his full length.

But that eagerness turned to trepidation when he just kept going and going until, with a solid *thud*, the tip of his cushiony cock hit her cervix. She felt skewered by him. Impaled. Every wrinkle was smoothed out by his impressive girth. Every inch was filled up by his powerful length.

In that moment, her body was his to do with as he pleased. And she fully expected him to pump and rut. To *fuck* like most men who'd been denied something they wanted for too long.

To her surprise, however, he scooted higher on her body, adjusting his angle so that when he pulled out of her slightly, his throbbing shaft raked against her greedy clit.

Sensation exploded in her core and caused her breath to shudder out of her.

She'd read about this. It was called the coital alignment technique. But she'd never known a man who knew how to do it.

Doc *definitely* knew how to do it.

When he moved inside her, it wasn't a *stroke* per se. It was more of a rub or a grind. It heightened the closeness of their bodies, increased her pleasure tenfold, and pulled her more deeply into the moment.

It was…*intimate* in a way she'd never known was possible.

His green eyes sparkled like sea glass as he framed her face and watched her surprise melt into astonishment melt into pure, unadulterated *bliss*.

And only when the pleasure became too intense for her to keep her eyes open, did he lower his head and claim her mouth in a slow, deliberate kiss that mimicked the motion of his hips.

His tongue rubbed instead of pumped. His lips ground instead of sucked.

And suddenly, she was once again teetering on the edge.

"That's it," he encouraged. "Cum for me again, Cami. Let me feel that delicious pussy clamp down on my dick."

She did cum for him. The first wave of orgasm washed over her, slow and gentle. The second wave was a little more intense, making her stomach clench and her nipples ache. And then it was just wave after wave of brutal release, her inner walls spasming so hard she wasn't sure if what she was feeling was pleasure or pain.

She was lost. Lost in the moment. Lost to reality. Lost in her body.

She didn't hear the sounds falling from her mouth. Didn't see the way she'd thrown back her head. Didn't feel how he'd scooted down so his cock once again knocked at the entrance to her womb as he held himself utterly still and let her continue to unravel around him.

It was the best, longest, most intense orgasm of her life.

And when her senses finally returned, it was to find him softly nibbling on her earlobe, gently sweeping his tongue inside the hollow. Such a delicate intrusion in contrast to the domineering way his dick filled her to the brim.

"That was amazing." His whisper was guttural. "*You* are amazing. The sexiest thing I've ever seen."

She couldn't answer him. She was too scatterbrained by the intensity of her orgasm. Even when the final ripples of release skittered through her, her pussy continued to throb.

Then she realized it wasn't *her* that was throbbing. It was *him*.

His iron will, the way he held back his own desire to satiate hers despite literally *vibrating* with the need for release, filled her with awe. She'd known he was a generous and selfless man. But *this* much selflessness and generosity was something she'd only read about in romance novels.

If Doc considered sex a team sport, it was high time he got to experience the joy of victory.

Wrapping her legs around his waist and hooking her ankles above his ass, she framed his face with her hands and stared deep into his mesmerizing eyes. Her voice was nearly as gritty as his when she told him, "Fuck me, Dalton. I need you to fuck me now."

The sound he made then was rough and throaty.

Grabbing her hands, he threaded their fingers together and shoved them under her pillow. Then, with unerring certainty, he began to move.

His thrusts were slow and controlled at first. And the friction they created was breathtaking.

Two orgasms was usually Cami's limit, even with a talented partner. But the instant Doc began to move, she knew she'd cum again.

It was the way he filled her. The way each slick withdrawal raked his veiny shaft against the sensitive nerves inside her. The way each solid thrust home abraded the rough patch of skin on the roof of her sex.

His silver piece of eight dangled between them. His chest hair abraded her sensitive nipples. She could feel his muscles quivering as he strained to push her toward the precipice again.

"You feel so good in me," she rasped, placing her bare feet in the crooks of his knees for leverage so she could match his every thrust. "Your cock feels *so* good in me, Dalton."

He rumbled something she couldn't make out. Then his mouth dropped to hers for a bruising kiss and his thrusts became harder, faster.

He'd made love to her before, concentrating on her responses, on her pleasure. Now he was fucking her for himself. Even still, she felt the first telltale tremors of release rippling through her. Felt her inner muscles beginning to rhythmically contract when she squeezed him to keep him inside on the upstroke and then melted and welcomed him home on the downstroke.

"Cami!" Her name was ripped from his lips.

Lightning flashed. Thunder clapped. For a moment, she thought the storm had picked up its fury. Then she realized the storm was inside her body.

"Dalton!" she screamed when the first spark of orgasm burned through her.

He cried out again, hammering home one last time. His release was a rhythmic spurt inside that she could feel even through the condom's latex.

That's all it took to have her own climax expanding, growing, widening, steepening until the pleasure pulsing through her body was stronger than Julia's winds, bigger than the storm itself.

The most devastating, *delicious* natural disaster Cami had ever experienced.

CHAPTER 22

10:15 PM...

Dana's stomach growled for the third time in as many minutes.

She grimaced as three faces turned in her direction. "Sorry. I was about to throw up less than an hour ago, and now my belly button feels like it's rubbing a hole in my backbone. I think those saltines whetted my appetite. It's weird, I know. Who could be thinking of food at a time like this?"

She gestured toward the two would-be thieves lying on LT and Olivia's bed, and the third who was sprawled atop the cot LT had dragged into the room—Jace was staring at the ceiling, but Will and Brady were zonked out thanks to Doc's pain meds. She tried *not* to look at the fourth man, *Fin*, who lay still and cold on the floor beneath the bloody comforter.

She'd watched a man die. She'd seen the exact moment when life left his body. How in the *world* could she be hungry after *that*?

"The human body needs fuel regardless of circumstances," John was quick to reassure her. "Ain't no shame in that."

She sent him a wan look of thanks.

LT had lugged four of the kitchen chairs upstairs. Now, he and Olivia sat in the two he'd placed against the wall near the bed. And John and Dana occupied the other two near the door, holding up their end of the guard duty.

Dana wasn't sure how much help she was in that regard. It's not like she was armed like the others. But she supposed in the off chance one of the unmasked men tried to make a break for it she could throw her body in front of the exit.

After they'd initially sat down, John had encouraged her to go to his room to get some "shuteye." But she hadn't wanted to leave his side. He'd been her anchor through everything, the one thing holding her secure and keeping her from flying apart.

"Why don't you take Dana to get somethin' to eat," LT suggested now, looking at John. "Olivia and I can handle things on our own for a few hours."

"You sure?" John's brow furrowed.

Dana noticed how the expression made him look a little intimidating.

I suppose he is *intimidating*, she silently corrected.

After all, he hadn't hesitated to jump up and charge at Jace when Doc and LT had made their initial bid for freedom. He hadn't blinked when Jace had pressed the end of that evil-looking pistol to his chest. And he'd remained impressively stoic while dressing Will's gruesome wound.

John Anderson tried to come off as some sort of salty island hippy who didn't have a care in the world. But she was learning that beneath his easy smile and his crazy Hawaiian shirts was a backbone forged of pure titanium.

He might not be a former Navy SEAL, but he'd

experienced enough life, enough *adversity*, to give him the same steely resolve. The same grit in his eye. The same ability to remain steady in a crisis.

It was…*hot*.

He was hot.

And yes, the younger generation would probably cut her Feminist Card in half for going all gooey-bellied and googly-eyed over a man just because he was big and strong and courageous.

But so be it. Because…meow.

She suddenly wished she'd encouraged him to try again after their *almost* kiss had been interrupted.

He had *been about to kiss me, hadn't he?* She thought back to his bedroom. To the way his hazel eyes had tracked down to her mouth. She remembered how his tongue had briefly darted out to wet his lower lip.

Yes, she decided. *He'd definitely been leaning in to kiss me.*

The question now became, how did she get him to do it again?

"Go on," LT encouraged John with a hitch of his chin, dragging Dana from her calculations.

"Alrighty then." John pushed up from his chair and extended a hand Dana's way.

She noted how wide his palm was. How marvelously pale the skin was there compared to the tanned flesh that covered the rest of him.

When she slid her fingers into his, she was keenly aware of how strong and firm his grip was when he easily pulled her to her feet.

A little shiver raced down her spine as brief images of what it would be like to have his hands running over her arms, up her legs, and down her back sprang to instant Technicolor life inside her head.

What in the world? Have you suddenly gone man-crazy, Dana Levine?

She was a little embarrassed to admit that, *yes*, when it came to John Anderson, she was losing her head. Which was particularly surprising since, after her divorce, she hadn't had much interest in the opposite sex.

Oh, there'd been dates and a handful of relationships that'd lasted a few months each. There'd even been some sexual partners thrown into the mix for fun and spice. But not *once* had she found herself *wanting* a man.

Not *wanting*, wanting him. Like the kind of want that got into her bones, made her feel drunk with desire, and gave her the urge to throw caution to the wind.

In fact, she'd assumed age and hormonal changes had meant that part of her life was over. Except…

Surprise! It was back.

And with a vengeance too.

Thanks to one Mr. John Anderson.

Just holding his hand made her so excited she would swear her fingernails were sweating.

His bedroom was pitch black when he pushed open the door, but he was quick to light two candles on his dresser. Then he peered into the basket of provisions they'd packed.

"Your choices are Pop-Tarts, canned tuna, a package of dried fruit, or half a bag of Doritos." His deep voice rumbled in the quiet. Even though Julia was still howling outside, it was *much* quieter in his bedroom without the space being filled with the wounded men's snores and LT and Olivia's hushed conversation.

So quiet she wondered if he could hear her racing heart. Or her rapid breaths. Or the way her throat made a sticky sound when she swallowed.

"The dried fruit sounds good," she told him, and gratefully accepted the bag when he handed it to her, shivering when their fingers briefly brushed.

He pulled out a pack of Pop-Tarts for himself and then gestured for her to precede him. She resumed her position on the bed, with her back against the headboard, and then waited, breath bated, for him to snuggle down next to her.

She hid her sigh of disappointment when he chose the wooden rocking chair instead.

For a while, they ate in silence, the smell of sugary sweetness perfuming the humid air. Dana was happy to note some of her shakiness disappeared when the fructose hit her bloodstream.

Maybe my giddiness is partially to blame on low blood sugar, she thought.

Then, out of nowhere, his deep voice cut through her thoughts and had her stomach tightening.

Nope. So much for that argument.

"What gets you excited about life?" His tone was quietly inquiring.

She had a mouthful of fruity morsels and had to awkwardly gulp them down before attempting to answer. "Um…" She blinked. "I've never really thought about it before."

"It's okay if you don't have a ready answer."

"No." She shook her head. "I think…I think I do, actually." When he lifted a dark eyebrow, she continued. "I like experiencing new things. *Learning* new things. That's why I took up pottery and yoga. I like tasting new tastes. Seeing new sights. Which is why I indulge in the tragically un-American habit of taking four weeks of vacation every year to travel."

She popped another piece of dried fruit into her mouth and chewed in consideration. "I like to think of myself as a work in progress. And it's the *progress* that gets me excited, that keeps me looking forward to the future." She donned her most serious voice and lifted an imperious hand as if she were orating in front of a crowd of philosophers. "She who is not busy living, is busy dying."

"Mmm." He nodded. "That's a good answer."

She shrugged, unsure how good or bad it was, just knowing it was her truth. "And you? What gets *you* excited about life?"

"I used to think it was gettin' up every day and runnin' my businesses, visitin' with my friends, meetin' new and interestin' people." He bit into one corner of the Pop-Tart and she was struck once again by the whiteness of his teeth. "Then, when Leo and the boys started the salvage business and I retired to help them, the thought of findin' the treasure kept me hoppin' out of bed each mornin'."

"And now that you've found the treasure?"

He frowned heavily. "I don't rightly know. And the not knowin' has been buggin' the piss outta me. 'Scuse my French. But I keep comin' back to the same question. What's my next big adventure?"

She stared at him thoughtfully. "Anything you want, right? You've got plenty of money. The sky's the limit. You want to buy a beach house in Fiji? Go for it. You want to sail to Antarctica and see some penguins? Who's to stop you? You want to do none of the above and spend the rest of your life fishing off the end of a dock? Well, that sounds nice too."

His low, throaty chuckle bubbled in her ears and then slid down to effervesce in her belly. "Who needs Fiji when I got me a little slice of paradise right here?" He threw out an arm. "And Antarctica?" He shivered. "I've never been one for the cold. Besides, if I wanna see some penguins, I'll go to the zoo. Now, I *do* like to fish off the end of a dock. That's a good way to spend a mornin'. But a life? No." He shook his head. "I want somethin'…different. Somethin' *more*."

He took another bite of Pop-Tart and then completely

caught her off guard by changing the subject. "You reckon you'll get married again?"

She sputtered awkwardly because butterflies fluttered to instant life inside her belly. "Why? Are you asking?"

His smile was indulgent. And the fluttering butterflies multiplied until she could barely catch her breath. "Oh, I don't know. I kinda think marriage is an antiquated institution. But maybe I'm talkin' outta my ass, seein' as how I've never done it before."

"No." She shook her head. "I don't think you're talking out of your ass. Not that I think marriage should be outlawed or anything. I know a lot of people who like the security of being tied to someone by the law. But me?" She shrugged. "I rather like the idea of someone being with me because they *want* to be. Waking up every day and *choosing* me instead of feeling like they're bound to me by a vow they made years ago." She waved a hand. "Which is not to say I'm closed off to the idea of a *life* partner. If someone comes along who wants to spend the rest of their days with me, I'd be open to that."

"Life partner." His tone was thoughtful. "I like the sound of that. A partner to do life with."

"A partner to do life with who makes life *better*," she added, circling back to their earlier conversation.

The wink he gave her was flirty. "Naturally."

"And, uh, speaking of our earlier conversation," she said haltingly. "Were you..." She had to swallow and drum up her courage. She'd never been overtly *forward*. But life had taught her that time tended to pass a person by. And it tended to take the opportunities of the moment with it.

She couldn't miss out on this opportunity.

Something told her it might not come around again.

"Were you thinking of kissing me earlier?" She sounded short of breath. She *was* short of breath.

"Woman, I've been thinkin' of kissin' you since the moment you stepped off that chartered seaplane."

"Oh." She felt her cheeks heat at the same time she envisioned tossing her bag of dried fruit aside and jumping into his lap.

Do it then, a little voice whispered in her head. *You're too old not to go after what you want.*

Not giving herself time to think, she chucked her half-eaten package of fruit to the foot of the bed and scooted to the edge of the mattress.

The wooden rocking chair wasn't wide enough for two. And the arms made hopping into his lap impossible. But she did the next best thing.

Grabbing both sides of his lapel, she pulled him forward.

He wore a grin that looked wholly self-satisfied. And his eyes sparkled with desire as he held her gaze captive, not letting her look away even as she drew him closer. Closer. Closer still.

"I should warn you," he whispered when his lips were nearly touching hers. His beard tickled her chin. His warm breath smelled deliciously of sugar and strawberries. "You open this can and I'm liable to eat it all the way to the tin bottom."

She caught her lower lip between her teeth. "You promise?"

His answer was a low growl. "What about needin' a first date? What about me winin' and dinin' you?"

She pointed to the discarded package of dried fruit. "That covers the dining part. As for the wining part? I much prefer a good cocktail. But we seem to be out of fancy umbrellas..." She shrugged.

"So..." He cocked a provocative brow. "What you're saying is..."

"Kiss me, John," she breathed against his lips.

He didn't disappoint. Wrapping a hand around the back of her neck, he pulled her forward that last inch. And the instant his mouth was on hers, she knew…

John Anderson was going to be the greatest lover of her life.

It was there in his kiss. In the way his mouth moved over hers with such slow, satisfied confidence. In the way he easily transferred her to his lap when he slipped from the chair onto the bed. In the way his big hands framed her face, turning her head this way and that so he could access all the parts of her mouth with his incredibly talented tongue.

When he finally, many, *many* minutes later pulled back from the kiss, her heart was beating a mile a minute. She was intensely aware of all her womanly bits. And her breath came in ragged gasps.

"That was…" He had to stop and clear his throat.

She hid a secretive smile. "Yes," she wholeheartedly agreed. "It was."

He chuckled and then sighed heavily, looking sort of boyish, like a kid who'd just had his lunch money stolen.

"What?" She framed his bearded cheeks with her hands. "What's wrong?"

"Hear that?" He lifted a blunt-tipped finger.

Cocking her ear toward the closed door, she strained to hear what'd snagged his attention. But all she heard was a low, hollow-sounding silence.

She shook her head. "I don't hear anything."

"Exactly." He bobbed his chin and his whiskered cheeks raked against her palms. The friction made her shudder in delight and imagine all manner of naughty things. "Julia has left the building."

"Oh, my gosh!" A relieved breath rushed out of her as reality set in. "You're right! We made it!"

"'Course we did." His mustache twitched. "Did you

ever doubt it?"

She made a face of disbelief. "Uh, yeah. Between the storm surge and the relentless winds and the masked men and the gunplay, there were a few moments there when I thought I'd seen my last sunrise. You asked what gets me excited about life? How about just *life*."

He laughed and she loved the low, liquid sound of it. "It does have a certain ring to it, doesn't it?"

"So now what? What's next?"

"What's next between me and you?" That devilish twinkle was back in his eye. "I got a few ideas."

"Oh, yeah?" She hoped her arched eyebrow looked coquettish. That's what she was aiming for. "Do tell."

"Later." He smacked a quick—an all too quick—kiss on her lips and shoved to a stand. Since she was sitting on his lap, it was either slide onto the floor or stand with him. She chose the latter. "Right now, I need to put in a radio call to the Coast Guard. See if they can send a chopper or a Cutter to take our guests to the hospital in Key West."

Sighing heavily, she smoothed her hair away from her face and grimaced when she felt how huge it'd grown. Humidity was hell for curly-headed gals.

"Back to life," she singsonged. "Back to reality."

His next words had her stomach flipping in anticipation. "But reality just makes the times you get to indulge in fantasy that much more delicious, doncha think?"

Oh, yes. She wasn't sure where this thing with John was headed. If it was headed anywhere other than the bedroom. But what she *did* know was, no matter what, she was going to have one hell of a good time.

Maybe the best time of my life.

And for a woman who was quickly closing in on her sixth decade, that was such a wonderful surprise.

CHAPTER 23

10:48 PM...

Jeezum crow. Will *hurt*!

And not just his arm, although now that the meds were wearing off, that was an agony that defied description.

But what had him tossing his head from side-to-side on the cot was the pain in his heart.

Fin's dead.

His best friend from the cradle. The boy who'd taught him to tie a clove hitch knot. The teenager who'd snuck out of first period with him to spend the day getting drunk on a stolen bottle of whiskey. The guy who'd been the best man at his wedding and who'd cried in happiness with him the night his first son was born.

How am I goin' to tell Angie? Will thought in anguish. *How am I goin' to look Fin's sweet little girls in the eyes and explain to them their daddy's gone?*

And then it occurred to him. He probably *wouldn't* be the one to deliver the news. Because he'd be behind bars.

That thought had a whole new round of suffering rolling through him.

His parents were going to be so disappointed, so *ashamed*. And Sheila? His loving wife for the last ten years? Would she leave him? Would she take their boys and go live with her aunt in Arizona? Would she find another man to warm her bed?

He wouldn't blame her if she did.

How could I have fucked everything up so completely? How could I have let things go so far?

The plan had started out so simple. Slip onto the island in the dead of night and steal the treasure with no one the wiser. Then, when the storm had hit and they'd heard the salvage ship had docked behind Schooner Wharf Bar, it'd seemed even easier, as if the treasure had brought itself *to* them. And even when they hadn't found the booty on the ship and they'd assumed the salvors had left it on the island, even when they'd known they'd have to battle a hurricane to get to it, it hadn't seemed so outrageous.

Then...the island hadn't been deserted. And the instant Will had heard that call come over the radio, he'd known there was no way to pull off their heist without spilling blood. He'd known then and there just what he was capable of.

But even as he admitted it to himself now, he still struggled to believe it. He didn't even like to *hunt*. How in the *world* had he resigned himself to killing someone?

Desperation, he decided. *Desperation and feeling like I'd come too far to turn back.*

A hot tear of remorse and self-recrimination slipped from the corner of his eye to slowly roll down his temple. When his chest shook with a sob, the agony in his arm grew teeth as sharp as a shark's.

"More painkillers," he whispered hoarsely. Not so much because he couldn't stand the physical torment. But more because he sought the oblivion the morphine offered.

When he was unconscious, he could forget the horror of this day. Forget the humiliation and guilt and regret that would be his future.

"Please," he begged and nearly choked on another sob of relief when he heard the floorboards creak as someone crossed the room.

Opening his eyes, he saw in the dim light that the sandy-haired man called LT or Leo, depending on who was addressing him, had begun rifling through the black leather bag that held the medical supplies.

"Thank you," he whispered gratefully when LT handed him a white tablet. He quickly placed it on the back of his tongue.

"You need water for that?" LT asked.

Will shook his head, eagerly swallowing the chalky tablet down and willing it to go to work quickly. Closing his eyes, he tried to clear his mind as he listened to the big man make his way back across the room. But a second later, a knock on the door had him lifting his chin to focus on the older gentleman who poked his head into the room.

"Just got off the radio with the Coasties." Will thought he'd heard the man's name was John. And his drawl heralded his hometown as somewhere deep in the South. "They got a Cutter about an hour north of us. The captain is heading our way to pick up our guests."

Will let his head fall back against the cot. A moan that seemed to have been ripped from his soul sounded in the back of his throat.

There was no more delaying the inevitable. As soon as he and his friends were in the Coast Guard's custody, they'd have to face the consequences of their actions. The

DEAD IN THE WATER

consequences of their ill-conceived plan having gone completely tits up. The consequences of what they'd all been ready to do.

"What the hell am I goin' to do now?"

He realized he'd asked the question aloud when LT answered him. "You'll get patched up and then you'll be arrested."

Once again, he squeezed his eyes closed, wanting to shut out the world. Wanting to shut out reality.

"And who'll take care of my wife and kids while I do time?" More hot tears leaked from the corners of his eyes to slip into the hair at his temples. "My parents don't make enough to take on that burden. God knows Sheila can't work *and* look after the boys."

He didn't expect an answer, so he wasn't surprised when silence met his question.

"How did you know we brought up the treasure?" LT's measured voice cut through the sound of the silent screams inside Will's head.

Opening his eyes, Will saw the severe-looking man had once more crossed the room to stand over him. LT's square jaw worked hard on a piece of gum.

The truth would come out eventually, so there was no reason for him not to answer. "A week ago, Jace's dumbass cousin, Bernie Lutz, told us you'd be haulin' it up on the next king tide."

A deep line appeared between LT's eyes. "Bernie Lutz? Who the hell is that? And how the hell would he know—"

He didn't get to finish his sentence when a hair-raising shriek sounded from downstairs.

"Go!" Olivia said when both LT and John turned toward the noise. "I'll stay here and keep guard." She held Will's own pistol in her lap. And when he turned his eyes on her, she gave it a pat as a warning.

JULIE ANN WALKER

Not that he'd attempt an escape. Even if he didn't hurt too badly to move, he'd never leave his friends behind.

After LT and John shot out of the room, Will closed his eyes and welcomed the warm, floating sensation that came with the morphine hitting his bloodstream.

He didn't care who had screamed. He didn't care *why* she'd screamed.

In fact, he couldn't summon up the will to care about much of anything.

He'd been desperate to change his life, and that desperation had caused him to do something that'd ruined it.

CHAPTER 24

10:56 PM...

John's heart was in his throat when he burst through the open front door. Which was why Dana's name sounded strangled when he called out to her in the night.

Julia's terrible winds had cleaned the air, making the winking stars look brighter and the big moon look closer than usual. Their light highlighted the destruction left by the storm's passing, but John was blind to everything but Dana.

She stood near the far edge of the porch. And when she turned to him, her face filled with chagrin.

"Sorry!" She lifted a hand to her neck. "I didn't mean to scream." She glanced over John's shoulder when Leo skidded to a stop behind him. She included John's nephew in her explanation. "I just went to step off the porch and…" She pointed. "*Look.*"

The fiery panic that'd singed John's veins was extinguished as soon as he saw she was fine as a fiddle. Still, he needed to feel her next to him, which was why he threw an arm around her shoulders and dragged her close as he edged toward the stairs and peered over the side.

Crabs. Loads of them. Pushed up against the steps by the storm surge. Their hard, spindly legs made *scritching* noises as they climbed over and around each other.

"Damn, woman." He held a hand to his heart. "You can't do that to an old man. You nearly gave me a heart attack."

Her pretty blue eyes sparked up at him in the moonlight. "I'll be the second person to remind you today that you're not *that* old."

"Hmm." He grinned down at her. "You wanna head back upstairs and help me put that theory to the test?"

Leo made a gagging noise and John whipped around to scowl at his nephew. "What? It's fine for you to pant after your woman like a steer in rut, but the rest of us aren't allowed?"

Leo scratched his head. "Pant away, Uncle John. But you'll excuse me if I don't hang around for it. It's kinda like watchin' my folks canoodle. Sends a shiver down my spine."

John snorted and gestured down his length. "Take a good look, boy. If you're lucky—and I mean *real* lucky—this is your future."

His nephew cocked his head, glancing between John and Dana. Then he grinned and admitted, "Good point. And yet I'll still be on my way."

Leo could move awfully fast for a big man. His bare feet thumped up the wooden floorboards as he headed back inside to help Olivia watch over the thieves.

"You know what?" Dana mused from beside John. He found a delighted smile tilting up her pretty mouth. A mouth he knew tasted like sugar and sunrises and mysteries he was dying to solve.

"What's that, darlin'?"

"I think I *like* scandalizing the younger generation."

He chuckled. "Yeah. Why should they get to have all the fun?"

"This *is* fun, isn't it?" Her voice was a little breathy, and there was more than amusement in her eyes when she looked at him.

He was too old to play hard-to-get. So he gave her god's honest truth. "I'm havin' the time of my life."

She giggled and he decided it was the happiest sound on Earth. "Oh, good. Me too."

When she went up on tiptoe, he met her mouth with a kiss that left him dizzy. It left her dizzy too if the way she swayed and clutched at his shoulders was anything to go by.

After reluctantly releasing her lips, he glanced at his black diver's watch, noted the time, and cursed.

"What?" Dana blinked. "What's wrong?"

"The Coasties will be here in forty-five minutes. That's not nearly long enough for me to do all the things I want to do to you."

She shivered and bit her lip. Her tone was the definition of flirtation when she asked, "So what do you say to acting like we're kids again and spending the next forty-five minutes making out?"

"I'd say you read my mind."

"Oh good!" She clapped her hands, darting toward the front door. Once inside, she turned back to him because he'd remained glued to the spot, his eyes raking over her retreating form. "What are you waiting for?"

"Nothin'. Just enjoyin' the view, darlin'."

There was that happy sound again. "You and your nephew are a lot alike."

"Mmm. I think it's safe to say we both know a good woman when we see one."

"Come upstairs with me, John." She extended her hand

in invitation.

As he followed her up the stairs, watching her cute, heart-shaped ass tick-tock the entire way, he decided then and there that Dana Levine was going to be his next big adventure.

Maybe the grandest adventure of my life.

CHAPTER 25

10:58 PM...

Lily stood on the porch at the ranch house, the summer sun making her blond hair shine like cornsilk. The cloudless Montana sky matched the blue of her eyes, and the hem of her floral sundress rippled in the soft wind.

"Come here, Dalton," she beckoned with a crooked finger.

His boots made a crunching sound on the gravel drive as he hastened to join her, his whole being full of love and contentment. Except with each advancing step, Lily's image grew fuzzier until, suddenly, it was no longer Lily standing there.

It was Cami.

Cami with her sleek black hair pulled back into a tight ponytail. Cami with her full figure encased in jeans and chambray shirt. Cami with her dancing dark eyes and wide, welcoming mouth. She bounced a drooling baby on one curvy hip, and her free hand smoothed the hair of the brown-eyed boy at her side.

Doc shuffled to a stop, blinking as he glanced around in consternation.

Something odd had just happened. But his muddled brain couldn't figure out what.

Was it always Cami standing there?

Try as he might, he couldn't remember. And the struggle to remember had a deep chasm opening up inside him.

Cami smiled that wicked, witchy smile of hers and there was such love in her eyes when she called out, "Aren't you hungry? I made spaghetti for dinner."

"She made the big meatballs too!" the little boy shouted, shoving a fist in the air. "Just like we like, Daddy."

And just that easily, all Doc's hollowness was gone. In an instant he was full to bursting with pride and adoration, with happiness and satisfaction.

Whatever had made him pause was forgotten. Whatever momentary alarm he'd felt was erased as he broke into a trot toward his waiting family.

Taking the porch steps two at a time, he bent and kissed Cami's warm mouth when he reached the top tread. The drooling baby burbled at him, and the little boy clung to his leg, demanding Doc give him a leg ride inside.

The feel of the boy's trusting weight tugging at his jeans made him grin. His grin stretched into a full-on smile once he stepped inside the house and the rich smells of garlic and browned meat tunneled up his nose.

Home.

His father had liked to quote Ralph Waldo Emerson. "A house is made with walls and beams; a home is built with love and dreams."

Briefly closing his eyes, Doc silently called out, "I did it, Dad. I traveled the world and came back here, to the land you loved, to make my home."

When he opened his eyes, it was to see his son doing a backward somersault off his leg. The little tyke was on his hands and knees when a fluffy Great Pyrenees attacked his face with pink-tongued kisses. The boy giggled, catching the shaggy dog in a headlock.

Doc turned to frown at Cami. "He's supposed to be in the western field with the herd. How's he ever going to learn to be a livestock guardian dog if you keep letting him in the house?"

That ever-mobile eyebrow shot up Cami's forehead. "I've told you a million times, you can take the girl out of the city, but you can't take the city out of the girl. Dogs aren't supposed to be left outside in the cold and rain. They're supposed to be spoiled and coddled and scrubbed behind the ears." Her tone went from haughty directly to baby talk as she bent to scratch the dog's big, block head. "Aren't they? Yes, they are. Oh, yes, they are, you cute, silly, pile of fur."

The canine stared up at her in brainless adoration.

And who can blame him? *Doc thought with a chuckle.* She's adorable. Adorable and smart and sexy and, most amazingly, *mine.*

He sighed and feigned annoyance at her refusal to leave the giant wooly beast outside despite the dog having been bred specifically to withstand the cold and rain. Although, he couldn't hide the skip in his step as he threw an arm around her shoulders and steered her toward the kitchen table.

I have all a man could want, *he thought. And then he added,* I'm happier than I've ever been.

That's when he jerked himself awake.

The peace and comfort of the dream was immediately replaced by a roaring wave of guilt.

How could he have supplanted Lily like that? Even unconsciously? And worse, how could his dreaming brain have gone so far as to feel *happy* about it? *Happier*, even.

It was such a faithless thing.

Stifling a groan of misery, he clenched his teeth together until his jaw ached. He blamed the dream on having taken Cami as a lover and being reminded what it was like to be with someone he cared about. And yet he couldn't regret his decision.

What he and Cami had shared went beyond the physical. It'd been emotional. Spiritual even. Two people who'd communed with more than their bodies.

It'd felt good. So much better than anything he'd experienced since Lily's death. *Healing* even.

So yes, he might not regret taking Cami as his lover, but he could still chastise himself for ever thinking that would somehow make him want her less.

What a joke. It makes me want her more.

To make matters worse, he wasn't sure how he'd ever go back to the vapid, meaningless liaisons he'd been having for over a decade. How could he ever be satisfied with a sexual partner who didn't have Cami's big smile or curious mind or acerbic tongue? How could he ever be satisfied with sex now that he'd been forced to remember what it was to make love?

Cami's head was pillowed on his chest. Her cheek was soft and warm against his skin. In sleep her breaths were deep and even, and he wanted very much to curl his arm around her and pull her closer still. *Keep* her close. Instead, he raised his arm and stared hard at the tattoo on the inside of his wrist.

The flicker of the candles' flames gave the faded ink the illusion of movement. The flower seemed to sway gently in the wind.

Lily, he silently called out. *I'm sorry for the dream. Please forgive me.*

He waited for the sound of her sweet voice to fill

his head, but silence was the only thing he heard. A deep, resounding silence that seemed to echo.

It was a silence that was broken by Cami's voice. "Why didn't you guys have kids? Didn't you want them?"

He'd been so absorbed in his own misery, he hadn't sensed her coming awake. When she reached up to slowly trace the outline of the tattoo, he quickly dropped his arm.

Having her touch the tattoo seemed like a betrayal as much as the dream had been a betrayal. As much as making love to her had been a betrayal.

He hoped to cover up his hasty reflex by grabbing the coverlet and pulling it over them. Only after he'd tucked the material around her did he answer.

"Yeah. We wanted them." He had to stop and clear his throat because it sounded like he had a mouthful of rocks. "But Lily felt like she should establish her career as a teacher first, and I wanted to finish med school. We thought once we were settled, then we'd start planning a pregnancy." He snorted. "What's that saying about making plans?"

"Life is what happens when you're busy making other plans?" she supplied.

"No." He shook his head against the pillow. "I was thinking more…man plans and god laughs."

"I'm sorry." Her voice was soft and low. He could hear the sincerity in it. "For both of you."

"I'm sorry too," he whispered. "For so many reasons. But after all these years, the thing that bothers me the most is that I never got to tell her all the things I wanted to tell her, or that I *should* have told her before she was killed."

Cami went up on her elbow and there was deep compassion in her eyes. "Anything you didn't say, I'm sure she already knew."

A knot formed in his throat. "Lord, I hope so."

"I know so." She gave a staunch dip of her chin. And

then a little line appeared between her eyebrows. He could see a question in her eyes, but long seconds ticked by, and she never asked it.

Finally, he reached up and gently rubbed her frown lines away with his thumb. Women had such soft skin. But the softness of Cami's always surprised him. Maybe because she was so tough in every other aspect that he was shocked when her outer shell didn't match her steely inner resolve.

"What is it?" he asked. "What are you thinking?"

"I heard you talking with Uncle John." Her tone was mildly curious, but he thought he saw more than mild curiosity in her eyes. "You don't think you'll ever remarry?"

Given the closeness of the dream, the *realness* of the dream, he couldn't help but shift uncomfortably. "It would feel disloyal. If I remarried, I'd do it for love. I'd do it because another woman made me happy. But..." He swallowed convulsively. "The pain is all I have left of Lily. I'm not ready to let go of it. To let go of *her*."

Cami's mouth twisted. "The pain isn't all you have left of her. You have your beautiful memories. It's okay to hold onto the past while also embracing the future."

Her words echoed John's windshield observation so closely that the hairs on the back of Doc's neck lifted. "How could I take on a new wife while still mourning my old one? It wouldn't be fair. What woman in her right mind would want to tie herself to a man who can never let go of his first love?"

The line between her eyebrows returned. "Love isn't defined by what we let go of, Dalton, but by what we let in. You can keep the memories and the feelings of sorrow for what you lost while still allowing yourself to find comfort and joy in something fresh and new."

He searched desperately for the flaw in her reasoning. When he couldn't find it—once again, her seemingly irreproachable lawyer logic had muddled his mind—he threaded his fingers through her warm, silken hair and pulled her down for a kiss.

Distraction, that's what I need. Before I say something I'll regret. Before I do something I'll regret.

"I want you again, Cami," he whispered against her lips.

He hadn't fooled her. She knew what he was up to. Even so, her thick lashes lowered, desire ignited in her eyes, and her pink tongue flicked out to wet her lips. "I want you too."

This time when he kissed her, he told himself it would be the last time. Because he couldn't keep doing this. It was far too dangerous to his mental health. Besides, it wasn't fair to Lily. To his *memory* of her.

And it *certainly* wasn't fair to Cami.

CHAPTER 26

11:12 PM...

Cami concentrated on the sensations rippling through her body so she didn't have to concentrate on the thoughts swirling inside her head.

Thoughts like, *After tonight, I won't see him again.* Because the treasure was raised and, except for having Dana sign an affidavit, there was no longer a *legal* reason for her to come to Wayfarer Island. She would go back to Miami, and Doc would buy his ranch in Montana.

Thoughts like, *It's definitely the last time I'll sleep with him.* Because the physical intimacy only deepened her feelings. And they were already too deep. So deep she was drowning in them. So deep she wondered if she'd ever catch her breath again.

Pressing her back into the mattress, he positioned his hips between her spread thighs. For a second, she thought he would enter her. *Condom!* Her mind screamed in alarm. But her apprehension was quickly overcome by another thought.

The thought of getting pregnant. The thought of having the child she'd dreamed of for years. *His* child.

The idea took instant root and began to blossom. She could so easily envision a dark-haired boy who had Doc's sparkling green eyes, or a little girl with his calico-colored hair and slightly crooked smile.

She'd never thought of being a single mom. But if she couldn't have all of Doc, then maybe she could have a part of him? Take a part of him with her?

Of course, the instant she considered the idea, she discarded it. For one thing, Dalton Simmons struck her as old-fashioned enough to insist on making an honest woman of her. And she would never knowingly trap a man into spending the rest of his life with her. For another thing, the alternative would be to keep the child a secret, and that level of subterfuge was anathema to the very heart of her.

So, no. There would be no dark-haired boy or little girl with a lopsided grin.

Cami pulled her mouth from Doc's to remind him to use protection, but she snapped it closed again when he didn't reach down to angle himself toward her waiting entrance. Instead, he left a trail of soft, warm kisses across her jaw.

Burying her fingers in his thick hair—careful of the wound on his scalp—she closed her eyes and focused on the feel of his mouth as he licked his way down her neck to her breasts. She had no idea how long he played with the peaks. All she knew was that by the time he moved on to her belly, her breasts throbbed and ached with pleasure, and her center had gone hot and liquid.

He seemed fascinated by her belly button, swirling his tongue inside over and over again until she pushed on his shoulders, eager for him to use his lovely, talented tongue a little lower.

He chuckled. "So greedy." But it wasn't an admonishment.

He was quick to pepper open-mouthed kisses followed by stinging nips to her lower belly. The sharp edges of his teeth so close on the heels of his soft, hot tongue made her toes curl. And this time, when he draped her legs over his shoulders, she didn't raise her head to watch him press his mouth to her center. Not because she didn't love how erotic the sight was. But because she didn't want him to see the tears standing in her eyes.

Flames of desire licked her from head to toe. And yet her heart was still broken. *Breaking* more with each passing second, because with each passing second she was coming closer to the end of this.

The end of *them*.

Of course, when he wrapped his lips around her thrumming clit, licking it rhythmically, the pain in her heart mixed with the pleasure in her body to create a tsunami of sensation so intense she thrashed her head against the pillow and gave a guttural moan.

Her orgasms usually built slowly, gaining speed as she neared the inevitable cliff. But this time, her climax hit her like a bolt of lightning from the clear blue sky. Before she could catch her breath in surprise, she was electrified. Every nerve ending sparking. Every synapse firing.

She didn't know she'd clamped her thighs tight around his ears or that she'd fisted her hands in his hair. She didn't hear herself scream his name. She was swept up in physical bliss as surely as Julia had swept up the ocean in front of her.

And like the hurricane, Cami felt volatile. Out of control. *Wild* with ecstasy.

It was only after she began to float down from the ultimate heights that she felt the hot, wet trails her tears had burned across her temples.

Doc kissed a path back up her body. And when the mattress beside her depressed with his weight, she threw her arm over her eyes.

She hoped he mistook the gesture for one of rapture. But in truth, she covertly wiped away the wetness that clung to the sides of her cheeks and the tips of her lashes.

"So? Was that good for you?" There was humor in his voice. And when she dropped her arm, she found his lids lowered to half-mast and his eyes sparking in the dim candlelight.

Tell him! a little voice that sounded like her baby sister echoed through her mind. *Even if he rejects you, at least then you'll know you've done all you can.*

I can't, Carlotta! she silently replied. *If I tell him, it'd only be a burden. He already carries enough burdens. Too many burdens.*

Just in case her expression gave her away, she hoped to distract him by steering them back into familiar territory. "Are you giving me shit for my hair trigger, or is this a not-so-subtle fishing expedition for a compliment?"

He was propped up on one elbow. "Maybe a little of both," he admitted.

"Well, I can assure you, I'm more shocked by my hair trigger than you are. As for a compliment?" She arched what she hoped passed as a haughty brow. "I suggest you google 'flattery.' I bet you won't find my name in any of the search results."

"Is it really flattery if it's a fact?"

She rolled her eyes. "You don't need me to tell you that you have a talented mouth. The proof is in the pudding, as they say." She feigned a frown. "Besides, the way you swagger around like you have a dick the size of a redwood, the last thing I want is to say anything that'll further stroke your already outsized ego."

He tossed back his head, his laughter deep and rumbling in the stillness of the room. The pieces of her pulverized heart throbbed with sadness at the thought that soon she'd only hear that laugh in her dreams.

"I mean, it might not be the size of a redwood, but…" He trailed off, wiggling his eyebrows.

She rolled her eyes. "What is it with men and penis size anyway?"

"Part of the issue is that even though you gals like to tell us it's not the size of the boat, but the motion of the ocean, if given a choice between a rowboat or a yacht, we'll choose a yacht every single time."

"It's not the size of the boat *or* the motion of the ocean."

"No?" His eyebrows hitched together.

"Mmm, mmm." She shook her head, happy he didn't seem to have clued in that her teasing was all a ruse. "It's whether the captain can keep his vessel in port long enough for everyone to get off."

This time his laugh burst out of him like a backfire on the I-278. It was such a happy sound that she almost lost control and let a tear fall. *Almost.* She managed to hold it back by turning to the side and blinking rapidly.

"Lord, woman. I know I'm not the first to say it, but you've got one *hell* of a mouth on you."

She placed a hand in the center of his chest, shoving him back onto the mattress. She couldn't keep up her subterfuge. She needed to distract him. She needed to distract herself.

After straddling his hips, she bent so her breasts brushed the hair on his chest. Her mouth was an inch above his when she purred, "Oh, baby. You ain't seen nothin' yet."

And then she claimed his lips.

If this was the last time they were going to be together—and it was; she was determined it was—if she was going to spend the rest of her days wanting him, missing him, *loving* him, then she was going to make sure to leave him with something he would never forget.

Maybe it was vanity. Maybe it was pride. But she wanted him to look back on this night and regret ever letting her go.

Or, at the very least, look back on it as one of the best of his life.

"Mmm," he hummed in approval when she thrust her tongue between his lips. His moan turned into a low, grating growl when she ripped her mouth away only to mimic the path he'd taken down her own body.

She sucked on his pulse point, swirled her tongue inside his ear, and then kissed her way across his chest to his nipple.

Some men didn't like having their nipples played with. They either thought it a turnoff because they only viewed women's nipples as sexual, or their nipples were too sensitive or not sensitive enough. So she started out slow. But to her satisfaction, he hissed when she brushed her fingers over his tan areola, gritted his teeth when she pressed the side of her thumbnail into the center of his nipple, and flexed his hips up involuntarily when she sucked the ruched peak between her lips.

Since she was still straddling him, the move made his cock slide between her slick folds. And suddenly, she wasn't *trying* to distract herself. She *was* distracted.

Distracted by the feel of his most intimate flesh slipping through hers. Distracted by his hardness rubbing against her melting center. Distracted by how good it felt when the crest of his thick head bumped over her clitoris.

But as much as she hated having to lose the sensation of his cock, she had a plan. A destination. And it required her to keep making her way south.

She nibbled on each of his ribs. Slipped her tongue into the shallow oval of his belly button. And bit the muscles that made up his Apollo's belt.

By the time her face was level with his dick and she wrapped her fingers around his meaty girth, he was panting like he'd run a race. She glanced up to find his hands laced behind his head, and his chin tucked to his chest so he could watch her progress. She held his gaze and slowly flicked out her tongue to swipe at the drop of precum sitting proudly on his swollen tip.

His eyelids flickered and a long, shallow breath wheezed out of him. When she wrapped her lips around his heated head, he whispered, "Fuuuuccckkk," and fell back against the pillow.

She could taste herself on him, tangy and salty. And the smell of sex tunneled up her nose. He was too large to take in all the way, but she did the best she could, opening her throat as much as she could, until his plump head hit her tonsils and she had to stop.

She loved the feel of him filling her mouth. Loved the thrum of his snarling veins against her tongue. Loved the way his lower belly quivered when she added just a little bit of suction.

She'd never understood women who didn't enjoy oral sex. Oh, sure. It was no fun when the guy was an asshole by thrusting too hard or pressing on the back of her head until she gagged. But a man who knew how to lie back and let a woman play? Who was secure enough in his manhood to give up control? *That* was sexy as hell.

For long moments she teased, alternating between mapping his cock with her tongue and taking him far into the back of her throat. And only when his fists curled into the sheets beside his hips did she take pity on him and set up a steady rhythm.

Her hand slid over his slick shaft as her mouth kept up a constant suction. Up and down. Suck and stroke.

The sounds her mouth and hand made were a little lewd

and a *lot* carnal.

And it wasn't long before she could feel him getting close. Feel his testicles pulling up tight against his body. Feel his thighs begin to shake.

"Cami!" His voice wheezed out of him. "You have to stop or you're going to make me—Oh, god!" he croaked because she didn't stop. Instead, she redoubled her efforts.

"Cami!" His head thrashed against the pillow and his fingers found their way into her hair.

As she pushed him over the edge, tears filled her eyes.

It occurred to her there were occasions in life when the earth stopped spinning on its axis. When time was suspended, and a person could experience an entire existence in a mere moment. Like when a baby was born or when a loved one breathed their last.

Or when she realized that what she had with Doc, she'd never have with anyone else.

CHAPTER 27

11:41 PM...

"Good lord," Doc panted as Cami kissed her way back up his body only to curl onto her side with her silky thigh thrown over his and her head pillowed on his chest. Surely she heard how his heart raced. There was no hiding his labored breathing. "You win. Yours is the more talented mouth. The *most* talented mouth. Believe me when I say… *day-yum.*"

She chuckled and the delicious sound swirled in his ears before traveling south to squeeze his heart. She had the most wonderful laugh. So low and throaty. It made him happy to hear it.

Happy.

Not a word he'd used to describe himself in quite some time.

"This isn't a competition," she scolded.

"No?" He absently brushed a hand over his eyes because

he wasn't sure if the candlelight played tricks on him or if he was actually seeing stars.

Seeing stars, he decided when white spangles continued to flash and blink in his field of vision.

"It's a team sport, remember? And I was just returning the favor, teammate."

"What did I say about no quid pro quos, woman?"

Before she could answer, a hard knock sounded on the front door and echoed up through the rambling old house. "Coast Guard!" a strident female voice called.

Cami bolted upright, holding the coverlet to her breasts as she glanced around wide-eyed. "Why is the Coast Guard here?"

"Listen." Doc sat up. "The storm's passed." The eerie silence Julia had left in her wake was almost as unsettling as the roar of her mighty winds.

Doc couldn't believe he hadn't noticed the hurricane had moved on.

Okay, that wasn't true. He *could* believe it. He'd been... ahem...rather preoccupied.

"Holy shit. You're right." Cami blinked, and he clocked how delightful she looked with her lipstick all rubbed away and her hair a mess.

She was usually so put together. Bun perfect. Makeup on point. Clothes just so. Seeing her disheveled turned her from a sleek, sophisticated temptress into an adorable, charming partner in crime. And that hollowness that lived in his center yawned wide at the thought of this being the last time he'd ever see her in such a state.

"They got here awfully quick." She swung her legs over the side of the bed and glanced around for her clothes.

"I'm sure LT or Uncle John put in a call as soon as the storm passed. The thieves need to go to the hospital and there's the...uh..." He had to swallow when his voice turned

261

hoarse. "The body to deal with."

For a few blessed hours he'd been able to forget he'd taken another life. Now the reality of it, the horror of it, came crashing back in.

Why can't I get away from death? He asked his question to the universe. But, as was its way, the universe was frustratingly silent.

Maybe in Montana...

Maybe if he was far, far away, surrounded by mountains and wilderness, death wouldn't find him. Maybe in Montana he could finally put the warrior life behind him and become what he'd always wanted to be. Something simple. Something pure.

A rancher. A healer.

And maybe in Montana, with his past all around him, Lily's memory would stop fading.

"We should get dressed." Cami bent to grab her discarded bra from the floor. She was quick to slip it over her shoulders and hook it behind her back. Then she did that delightfully feminine wiggle to adjust her breasts inside the cups.

Seeing that made Doc forget about the Coast Guard. Forget about the wounded men. Forget about his past and the future and death.

Hell, if someone had asked his name, he might not have been able to answer.

All he wanted, all he could *think* about, was dragging her back into bed with him and taking her again.

He didn't realize he'd crawled across the mattress toward her until she lifted a finger and took a step backward. "No, sir. You better stop right there. I recognize that look."

"What look is that?" he said lowly.

"Your *I'm-going-to-eat-you-alive* look."

"Correct me if I'm wrong, but I thought you *liked* it

when I ate you alive."

"Dalton!" This time when she blushed, it extended past her cheeks and chest. Her belly pinkened right along with the tops of her thighs.

Enchanting.

Where was that growling coming from?

Oh, right. From me.

She laughed and danced out of his grasp when he made a swipe for her.

"If you run," he warned, staring at her from beneath his eyebrows. "I'll just have to chase you."

Desire darkened her eyes, but she snatched her borrowed T-shirt and boxer shorts off the floor. "I'm serious, Dalton." She lifted a staying hand. "We have things to take care of. I'm sure the others are wondering where we are."

"They know *exactly* where we are."

"Well, then we've shirked our duties long enough. We need to help them with the thieves, and we need to give our accounts of the evening to the Coast Guard so it's all on record."

"Ugh. Why do lawyers have to be such spoilsports?"

"I don't know. Why are libertines so insatiable?"

"*You* make me insatiable."

He expected her to come back at him with something appropriately saucy, so he was a little disappointed when all she did was hastily step into the shorts. He thought for a moment he saw an expression of…he couldn't be sure… but it kind of looked like *sadness* flitter across her face. Then she pulled the T-shirt over her head and he decided he'd been imagining things.

"Well that's a crying shame," he complained when she pulled the white cotton down over her luscious breasts.

She didn't meet his eyes, simply tossed his shorts and shirt at him. "Clothes, Dalton. Before you put someone's eye out." She made a vague gesture toward his nether regions where, once again, he'd grown hard. Although, as soon as she added, "Tonight's fun and games have come to an end," he felt himself begin to whither.

Did she have any idea how true those words were?

After they dealt with the thieves and authorities, he'd have to explain to her why this night's fun and games would have to be the *only* night of fun and games. He'd have to tell her that they were treading treacherous ground, and that it was better to end it early, before anyone got hurt.

If Cami saw the change in his demeanor as he dressed and slipped into his flip-flops, she didn't say anything. But neither did she reach for his hand when he opened the bedroom door.

They were brought up short when they ran into LT and Olivia escorting the three thieves down the darkened hallway. Both LT and Olivia had their weapons drawn, but neither of them aimed at the men. Instead, they kept their handguns close to their thighs, their trigger fingers resting outside their trigger guards.

In all honesty, they could've put the pistols away. The trio of men were as docile as newborn pups. Will and Brady babied their injuries, and Jace's head hung down in shame.

Once again Doc was overcome with the anguish of Fin's death. And whether or not Cami was right and his soul had suffered another tear, or *he* was right and it'd sustained one more stain, the simple truth was that because of him, somewhere up in Maine there was a wife who'd never see her husband again, little kids who'd hugged their father for the last time.

"Sorry I slept through the end of the storm," he said to LT.

His former commanding officer snorted. "Slept. *Riggghhhttt.*" Then he wiggled his eyebrows before giving

Doc a wink and a nudge.

Doc frowned. "What are you? Thirteen?"

"You know what they say." LT shrugged.

"I'm afraid to ask."

"Growin' old is mandatory. Growin' up is optional."

Doc shook his head but didn't say anything more. Leo "The Lion" Anderson had always been such a serious man. Ever since marrying Olivia, however, LT's whole persona had lightened. It was like his wife had dragged him out of the shadows and into the sun.

Doc couldn't help but feel a little envious.

After the group trudged past, he stepped into the hallway, purposefully keeping his eyes turned away from the open door at the end of the hall and the blanket-covered body lying on the floor inside the room. He didn't need a visual reminder of the night's consequences. The whole, horrible scene was burned into his brain.

He must've made a noise because Cami finally grabbed his hand. As they fell into step behind the others, he curled his fingers around hers, taking comfort in her touch at the same time a lump formed in his throat.

This is probably the last time she'll ever reach for me like this, he thought joylessly.

He hadn't set out for a wham-bam-thank-you-ma'am, but that's effectively what'd happened. And considering Cami was a proud woman, a woman with a heaping helping of self-respect, she wasn't going to thank him for it. In fact, she'd probably give him the tongue-lashing of his life before refusing to ever speak to him again.

It's what's best, he reminded himself staunchly, *for everyone.*

John and Dana had lit half a dozen candles and placed them around on the stacked furniture in the living room—no doubt in preparation for the Coast Guard's arrival. Which meant there was plenty of light to see by. So Doc had no trouble recognizing the tall, severe-looking woman who stood in the center of the room.

"Captain Rachel Mallory." He dipped his chin in greeting. She'd been the one to come to the rescue when he, Cami, Mia, and Romeo had been stranded on the deserted sandbar. Six of her crewmen, all dressed in their blue Coast Guard uniforms, formed a semicircle behind her. "Nice to see you again."

Mallory returned his gesture. "Nice to see you too. Although, you think it's possible we meet under less ominous circumstances next time?"

"Not likely." He shook his head woefully. "Trouble seems to follow me."

She grunted and then included all the Wayfarer Islanders in her next question. "Who wants to tell me what happened here?"

LT was quick to explain what'd brought the men to the island. But before he could get to the shootout, Mallory stopped him.

"Last I heard, you'd found the *Santa Cristina* but not her cargo. You saying I heard wrong?"

LT ran a finger under his chin. "It's not like we were goin' to take out an ad announcin' our discovery."

"Guess that makes sense." Mallory nodded. "Which begs the question, how did *these* guys find out about it?" She gestured toward the trio of Mainers, and Doc's ears perked up when LT answered.

"This one here"—LT shot a finger gun at Will—"says he got the information from some guy named Bernie Lutz who's apparently that one's cousin." LT turned his finger gun from Will to Jace.

A loud gasp echoed through the room, and Doc glanced down to find Cami's dark eyes wide and unblinking. Her perfect mouth was open in a little O and she'd pressed a shaky hand to her chest.

Foreboding had the skin on the back of his neck crawling. "What?" He scowled at her. "Do *you* know who this Bernie Lutz character is?"

Her voice was a raspy wheeze. "My father's cellmate."

Now it wasn't simply the skin on the back of his neck that was crawling. His whole body felt like he'd been attacked by a colony of fire ants. "*What?*" He dropped her hand and took a step back. "You told your *father*—"

"No!" She shook her head, her eyes pleading with him to understand. "I don't even *speak* to Dad. I told you that, remember? I don't know how—" She came to an abrupt halt and all the pink drained from her cheeks.

LT's tone was far more cordial than Doc's when he asked, "What happened, Cami? It's okay. You can tell us."

Doc watched her chin tremble a moment before she covered her mouth. She shook her head from side to side as if she couldn't fathom forming words. But eventually she dropped her hand and answered haltingly.

"I—I told my mother she wouldn't be able to reach me for a few days because I'd be here on Wayfarer Island. When Mom asked why I couldn't take a day to fly up for my cousin Tina's baby shower, I told her it was because Tina's shower was scheduled the same day as the king tide and I needed to be here for that." The more she talked, the faster she talked. "She asked me if you guys had found the treasure." Her eyes pinged desperately from Doc to LT to Olivia to Uncle John. "I mean, everyone knows you're looking for it, right? But I scolded her and told her she knew better than to ask me questions like that. I didn't tell her you'd found it. I swear I didn't—"

"For fuck's sake!" Doc ran a hand through his hair, his gut twisting in knots. But he couldn't tell if they were knots of disbelief or amazement or simply outrage. Maybe all three. For such a smart woman, Cami had made one stupendously *stupid* mistake. A mistake that could've gotten them all killed. "You didn't *need* to come out and tell her. You let enough clues slip that even a third grader could've figured it out."

"But—"

"No." He sliced a hand through the air and the motion reminded him of his concussion. The endorphins from sex had acted as painkillers. But they'd disappeared in the last handful of seconds. His roaring headache was back. Fishing a toothpick from his pocket, he shoved it into his mouth to chew on it angrily. "Your mother told your father, who obviously told his cellmate, who then phoned Jace."

Cami's hand was back over her mouth, but she was no longer shaking her head. She was just staring at him, wide-eyed, as the truth sank in.

LT turned to Jace. "So what? You guys are all part of the mob too?"

"Huh?" Jace blinked, his mouth twisting beneath his beard. "No. Bernie jacked some hot rods to pay for his meth habit. That's why he's doin' time. What's the mob got to do with anything?"

"Her *father* is a mobster." LT hitched his chin toward Cami. "Why would he pass on the information about the treasure to your cousin if not to try to get in good with his old cronies?"

Jace shook his head. "I-I think he was just braggin'. Ya know, proud of his daughter for bein' part of somethin' so big. But Bernie knew I'd gotten into some trouble with a bookie, so he thought maybe the information would help me—"

Doc stopped listening and decided the knots in his stomach were mostly outrage. And they were cinching tighter with each passing second.

It was as if all his hesitation about taking her to bed suddenly made sense. As if all the things he'd jokingly accused her of because she was a lawyer had turned out to be true.

"We nearly *died* because of you," he told her, his voice cold but not nearly as icy as the fist squeezing his heart. "A man *did* die. I had to kill him and now I have to live with that the rest of my—"

"Hang on a second," LT cut in. "I think maybe—"

"No," Doc declared, pulling the toothpick from his mouth and pointing it at Cami.

How could she have done this to us? How could she have done this to me?

The more he thought about it, the angrier he got. It felt like that empty space in his center had filled with nitrogen gas and someone had lit a match.

"I knew you were one big walking red flag the first time I saw you. But you turned out to be an entire bouquet *full* of red flags, didn't you? I mean, for pity's sake. You told your *mother*? What the fuck happened to attorney-client privilege?"

"Dalton." She reached for him, but he dodged her hand.

"I should've listened to my gut when it was screaming at my brain to run away from you as quickly as my feet could take me." He shook his head and began to pace as his mind flew in ten thousand directions. Then he stopped and pointed to her again when a horrible thought occurred. "You're damn lucky all your father did was tell his cellmate. What if he'd done as LT just said and told his mob buddies, huh? What if it'd been the Italian Mafia who came down here to take the treasure"—he pointed to the blue duffel bags that someone had taken from the base of the stairs and stacked against the far wall—"instead of four poor saps from Maine? I guarantee there'd be more than one dead body in this house."

Another thought occurred and his boiling blood bubbled over until he felt diffused with heat from head-to-toe. "What if he *did* tell his buddies?" he demanded. "Who's to say there's not a bunch of Gambino goons waiting to come at us now that the storm has passed?"

"No." Cami shook her head. "Dad wouldn't—"

"What?" Doc knew his expression matched the derision in his voice. "He wouldn't endanger his daughter? Tell that to your kid sister."

Cami stumbled back as if he'd slapped her.

"Doc," LT interrupted. "She gets it. She fucked up."

"I'm so sorry." Tears swam in her eyes. Her words were for all the Wayfarer Islanders, but her gaze was trained on Doc.

There was a part of him—a *large* part—that was tempted to take her in his arms. He'd never been very good at withstanding a woman's tears. But instead he held onto his rage and forced himself to remember that he'd had to kill. *Again.*

His jaw muscles twitched spastically when he snarled, "Yeah. I'm sorry too. Sorrier than you can imagine."

CHAPTER 28

12:02 AM...

C ami wanted to run away and hide. Just turn toward the
door and flee into the damp night so she wouldn't have
to face the look of betrayal, the look of horror on Doc's
handsome face.

But only cowards run from their mistakes.

She was many things—a terrible lawyer being one of
them, as it turned out—but she wasn't craven. She stood
rooted to the damp floorboards, not saying a single word, but
also not able to stop the lone tear that slid hot and salty down
her cheek.

She hastily wiped it away at the same time Olivia caught
her eye. The former CIA agent wore a look of compassion.
And her tone was so kind it was only through sheer force
of will that Cami didn't break down into heaving sobs. "It's
okay, Cami. You didn't mean to—"

"No." Cami cut her off, unable to bear someone trying

to make her feel better. It only made her feel *worse*. "It's not okay. Doc's right."

She glanced over to see he'd turned his back to her.

And who can blame him? she thought wretchedly. *He had to kill again because of my big, Italian mouth and because of my father's ties to the criminal element. A man is dead because I didn't consider how my mother might tell my father who might tell his cronies or his cellmate or any of the other felons he's locked up with. How could I have been so thoughtless? So* stupid?

"This is my fault." Her voice was hoarse with tears. "All I can say is I'm sorry." Another tear broke free to travel down her cheek. This one dripped from her chin before she could wipe it away. "I'm so damn sorry," she croaked.

Silence followed her apology. It was so deafening, she would swear she could hear it throbbing in her ears.

Finally, Captain Mallory cleared her throat. "Um. I suspect the police are going to want to take statements from everyone."

LT shook his head. "Not tonight. We could all use some rest. Plus we have treasure to catalog and an island to clean up. Bill Dixon is one of the detectives with the Key West PD. He knows us. Tell him we'll come in to make statements in a coupla-three days. These guys"—he gestured toward the injured men—"probably won't be out of the hospital until then anyway and—"

"I'll go with Mallory tonight," Doc volunteered. "And I'll take the treasure with me. It'll kill two birds with one stone. It'll get the goods off the island just in case Cami's wrong about her dad telling his mob buddies."

"I'm not," she insisted. Her father was many things, but she felt she could safely say he'd never knowingly put her in danger. Hell, the whole reason he was still locked up was because he'd refused to take the deal the DA had offered him, which would've commuted his sentence, after the head of The Family threatened Cami's life should her father even *think* of turning state's evidence.

"And it'll satisfy Dixon," Doc continued as if she hadn't spoken. "Since I was the shooter, he'll be most interested in talking to me."

She watched his face, hoping beyond hope he'd look at her. Hoping she'd see some glimmer of mercy in his green eyes. But he didn't even flick her a glance as he pulled the toothpick from his mouth and flung it angrily through the open front door.

Was it possible to die from shame and sadness?

"I'll come with you," she volunteered desperately, thinking if she could just get some time alone with him, if she could just explain in more detail what'd happened, then maybe he'd find a way to forgive her. "There might be some legal stuff that—"

"No." It was only one word, but it cut through the air like a sword, slicing off the end of her sentence. "I don't want you."

It was a good thing there was a lump in her throat or else she might have cried out with the pain of his statement. It was clear to anyone with ears that he hadn't simply meant he didn't want her to come with him to Key West. He meant he didn't want *her*. Period. End of story.

Once again, silence descended over the gathered group. This time it was Uncle John who broke it. "Best you stay here with us, Cami. You and Dana got an affidavit to put together, right?"

She sent him a watery smile of thanks and followed it up with a little nod.

"Okay, then." Captain Mallory clapped her hands and turned toward the men spread out behind her. "Lieutenant Peterson, take Ensigns Hernandez and Johnson to get the body. I'm assuming the dead man is upstairs?"

When LT nodded, Captain Mallory made a hand gesture. Three of the uniformed Coast Guardsmen dutifully skirted around her and headed upstairs with a foldable stretcher.

"Ensigns Rodrigo, Davis, and Flores," Captain Mallory continued. "You three grab a duffel each and escort these men out to the Cutter."

Cami stood by helplessly as the thieves were hustled out the front door. Not long after, the remaining Coast Guardsmen appeared on the stairs, balancing the stretcher between them as they descended.

She wanted so badly to look away from the blanket-covered body. But she forced herself to watch its progress down the stairs. Which was why she saw the exact moment the dead man's hand slipped out from under the coverlet to dangle beside the stretcher.

The sob that'd been building in her chest finally broke free.

"Come on now." Olivia hustled over to throw an arm around Cami's shaking shoulders. "Don't go taking all this on yourself. These men came here to commit a crime. They came here armed. And, in the end, they were willing to kill us for the treasure. That's not an innocent man lying on that stretcher."

Cami's chin trembled. "But he wasn't exactly a monster either, was he? He was just a man. Capable of good and bad like any other. And now he's dead because—"

"Because he made a choice."

"Didn't I do the same thing when I told Mom I needed to be here for the king tide?"

Olivia sighed heavily and was quiet for a long moment. Then she shook her head. "If this life has taught me anything, it's that nothing is ever black and white. Everything is a nuanced shade of gray. I'm saying there's blame enough to go around. Don't you go trying to shoulder it all by yourself."

When Olivia gave her shoulders another squeeze, it reminded Cami of how her little sister used to stand next to her and another harsh sob hiccupped out of her.

Somehow, in the span of eighteen months, Cami had lost everyone she'd ever loved. Her parents—even though they were still living they might as well be lost to her. Her baby sister. And now Doc.

She *had* lost him.

That much was obvious in the way he held himself rigid as he shouldered two of the remaining duffels and followed the Coasties through the front door. In the way he couldn't even seem to bring himself to look at her.

CHAPTER 29

Two days later
5:42 PM...

The ocean air was still crisp and clear from the passing of the storm. But Doc didn't notice how sweet-smelling it was as he piloted the dinghy through the still waters of the lagoon.

Neither did he notice how the broken palm trees had been cut up and stacked on the beach, how the sand had been raked, or how the debris from the storm had been placed in trash bags and piled at the end of the pier in preparation for a trip to a dump on the mainland.

His complete focus was on the three people standing near the gently lapping edge of the surf as the sun sank close to the horizon. LT had his arm draped casually over Olivia's shoulders. And Uncle John was barefoot, his canary-yellow Hawaiian shirt shining like a neon light against a western sky that was a kaleidoscope of pinks, purples, and oranges.

Where are Cami and Dana?

As soon as Doc had the thought, a strange feeling took hold of him. It seemed like...*disappointment.*

But, nah. Couldn't be. Had to be relief, right? Relief that he didn't have to see Deep Six's lawyer again?

Because of her, he'd spent nearly eighteen hours in an interrogation room going over every detail of what'd transpired during the storm all while battling the side effects of his concussion. Because of her, a man was dead and a possible trial loomed in Doc's future. Because of her, Lily's memory had begun to fade faster and faster over the past few months, which, if he was being honest, was the thing that bothered him the most.

Yeah. It's definitely relief I'm feeling, he assured himself, studiously ignoring the voice of doubt that lived in the furthest reaches of his mind when it asked, *Are you sure about that?*

After motoring the dinghy onto the beach, his passengers were quick to hop out when he cut the outboard engine. Mason hoisted Alex over the dinghy's rounded rubber edge. Bran followed suit with his own wife and carefully lowered Maddy's sandaled feet to the sand.

"Come on, Meat." Mason snapped his fingers at his fat, wrinkly bulldog.

Meat scrambled over the side of the boat in an ungainly show of piss-poor athleticism. And, right on cue, Lil' Bastard, the colorful rooster who was Meat's unassailable sidekick, flapped his wings and landed beside the panting canine.

The two animals didn't miss a beat before taking off toward the water's edge. Meat to hunt up waterweeds, which he'd ralph onto the floor later that night. And Lil' Bastard to pillage and plunder the tiny sand crabs that occupied the beach's tidal zone.

"Where's the rest of the crew?" LT asked as a seagull squawked overhead, scolding Meat and Lil' Bastard for encroaching on its territory. LT's jaw worked hard on a stick of gum, and his eyes were hidden behind the reflective lenses of his aviator sunglasses.

"Wolf and Romeo stayed back to guard the treasure," Bran answered. "Chrissy had work to do at the dive shop. And you know Mia doesn't go anywhere without Romeo."

LT nodded. "It was good of Captain Bailey to give y'all access to the vault on base. Detective Dixon radioed out to tell us those boys from Maine boarded *Wayfarer II* lookin' for the loot the night before they headed our way."

Captain Mark Bailey was the current commander at the Naval Air Station on Key West. He'd gone through basic training with Romeo. And the two had stayed in touch over the years.

Turned out, the Deep Six crew who'd taken the bulk of the treasure back to Key West before the storm had decided at the last minute it would be safer on the base than hidden aboard *Wayfarer II*. So Romeo had made the arrangements with Bailey and they'd transported the bounty to its new home before they ever even put into port in the marina outside Schooner Wharf Bar.

Life is odd, Doc thought. All it took was one decision to change the course of events and the lives of a dozen people.

What if the thieves had found the treasure on the ship? Would Wolf, Romeo, Mason, and Bran have caught them and killed them all? Or would they have gotten away?

There was a part of Doc that wished the thieves *had* been able to find the treasure on *Wayfarer II* and then disappeared into the night. Because what could they have possibly taken? A few million at most? There would have been more than enough left over for Doc and the rest of his teammates. Not to mention Doc wouldn't have been forced to take another life.

Of course, all his wonderings and what-ifings wouldn't

be necessary if only Cami had kept her mouth shut. If Cami had been just a *little* bit more discreet, none of this would've happened.

Doc gritted his teeth when he stepped onto the beach. It wasn't because of the bitter turn of his thoughts. It was because sometimes, when he changed positions too suddenly, his healing concussion made it feel like some sorry sonofabitch drilled a steel screw into his skull.

LT pulled off his glasses to give Doc the once-over. "Y'okay, man?"

"I'll live," Doc muttered grumpily.

LT snorted. Then he was quick to observe, "Fancy new duds you got there."

Doc glanced down at the T-shirt and swim trunks he'd bought off the sale rack of a souvenir shop on Duval Street. The trunks were bright orange with lime-green palm trees and the T-shirt read: *Key West. Where we salt margaritas, not sidewalks.*

"I left here without a change of clothes. By the time Dixon was done with me, I was pretty ripe, so I improvised."

"And still somehow you're less of an eyesore than Uncle John," LT quipped.

"Hey!" John objected. "You kids don't have any sense of fashion. That's all."

"I always think you look very handsome, Uncle John," Alex told him sweetly, fluttering her lashes.

Bran nudged Mason. "I think you need to take your woman to get her eyes checked. She obviously needs new lenses in those glasses."

"Not a chance," Mason muttered. Then, proving he wasn't always the strong, silent type, he added, "What if she gets a good look at me and changes her mind?"

Alex laughed. "Oh, baby, you could be as ugly as a mud fence and I'd still love you. Especially if you keep doing that thing you did last night where you swirled—"

"*And* that's about enough of that." John lifted his hand. Then he used it to motion for everyone to follow him. "Come on, y'all. Dinner just came out of the oven."

"Tuna casserole again," Olivia warned the group.

"That's fine as long as he didn't use corn flakes in place of saltines this time." Alex wrinkled her freckled nose.

Sniffing in affront, Uncle John said, "I still think y'all made too much of a fuss over that. It wasn't *that* bad."

"It tasted like someone threw a bucket of minnows into a bowl of Post Toasties," Alex objected. And with that, the group trudged through the sand toward the beach house.

For the first time since dropping *Wayfarer II*'s anchor outside the reef, Doc took the opportunity to look around the island. Those who'd stayed behind had worked miracles. Then again, hurricanes had always been a way of life for Uncle John and LT. And he knew from experience that both men turned into fine-tuned machines when it came to cleanup.

"I don't know what I was expecting, but it wasn't this." Alex pushed her tortoiseshell glasses higher on the bridge of her pert nose. "Either you guys have been busy over the past couple of days, or Julia wasn't as big and bad as the weathermen were making her out to be."

"Well you know that's why they're called weather*men*, right?" Olivia said over her shoulder, her blue eyes sparkling with mischief. "Because they're always lying about how many inches you're going to get?"

"Ba-dum-tss." Alex chuckled.

"But, seriously," Olivia added as she lithely bounded up the porch steps. "These two"—she waved a hand to indicate LT and Uncle John—"have been working from sunup to sundown. With a little help from me, Cami, and Dana, of course." She widened her eyes. "Uncle John had Cami

DEAD IN THE WATER

running the chainsaw this morning."

"Our perfectly poised lawyer going all *Army of Darkness*?" Bran laughed. "I'd pay to see that. Please, someone tell me they snapped a picture."

After following the others inside the house, Doc realized he was glancing around furtively when John sidled up next to him. "She's gone," he announced quietly.

"Who?" Doc was quick to come back.

"Cami, of course." Uncle John frowned. "She and Dana took a chartered floatplane back to the mainland about an hour ago to deal with the last of the legal stuff."

"I wasn't looking for Cami," Doc lied. "I was marveling at how good the house looks." It was a valid excuse since the furniture had been unstacked and put back in its place. "It's like Julia was never here."

The expression John wore called bullshit. Thankfully, before he could form the words, LT asked, "So what about our uninvited guests, Doc? Did Dixon tell you what's next for 'em?"

Doc was quick to latch on to the change of subject.

"They're due to be released from the hospital into police custody either today or tomorrow. Dixon says they're looking at trespassing, unlawful imprisonment, and aggravation with deadly weapons charges on top of the attempted grand larceny charges. He suspects their attorneys will advise them to plead guilty to the worst of the offenses in hopes the lesser charges will be dropped."

"Cutting a deal will be good," Olivia said. "It means there won't be a trial."

Doc grimaced and LT said, "Something tells me you've saved the worst for last."

Olivia slipped an arm around her husband's waist and demanded, "Out with it, Doc. Don't keep us in suspense."

Blowing out a windy breath, Doc told them, "Dixon

said because Fin Allen died while he and his friends were attempting to commit a felony, the DA might choose to charge the other three with felony murder."

"Which means there *will* be a trial." Maddy's Texas twang emphasized both syllables of the last word. "There's no way they'll plead guilty to that."

Doc touched his nose. "As LT likes to say, *bingo, bango, bongo*."

"Damn," Olivia muttered. "I was hoping we were done with them."

"Believe me." Doc nodded. "Me too."

A trial meant he'd have to recount and relive Fin's death. Maybe even have to look into the eyes of Fin's widow and children while he did it. It also meant he'd have to see Cami again—no doubt, she'd be called as a witness.

"This is goin' to suck," LT grumbled.

A long silence followed his pronouncement, and Doc counted the seconds ticking by on the cuckoo clock. Then Uncle John clapped his hands together. "Nothin' to be done about any of it now. Let's eat."

"Thank goodness. I'm starving," Alex declared.

"No surprise there." LT chuckled.

Alex sniffed. "Didn't your father teach you not to make fun of people who have conditions?"

"And what are you sufferin' from? Besides motor-mouth-itis?"

"Hypoglycemia!" Alex placed her hands on her hips. "I've *told* you that a million times."

"I'll believe it when I see a note from your doctor."

"Ooh." Alex stomped her foot. "And to think I missed you when I was away."

"Ahhh." LT caught her in a headlock and scobbed her noggin. "I missed you too, pipsqueak. It was awfully quiet around here without your constant commentary. Even Julia had nothin' on you."

"Hands off my woman," Mason growled in mock affront, making both LT and Alex laugh.

A pang of melancholy stabbed into Doc as he watched the antics. These people were his family. Found family, but family all the same. And soon they would be scattering to the four winds.

He was going to miss them terribly.

Close on the heels of that realization was the certainty that, after years of everyone living on top of each other at the beach house, the ranch was going to feel awfully empty. Awfully *lonely*.

But I won't *be alone,* he assured himself. *I'll hire a manager and ranch hands. And if I start a private practice, I'll have my patients.*

It's enough, he told himself staunchly and once again ignored the voice of dissent when it asked, *Are you sure?*

The group shuffled into the kitchen. But before Doc could follow, Uncle John slapped a hand on his shoulder, holding him back.

He lifted a questioning brow.

"Cami was lookin' mighty low when she left this afternoon," John said. "You might think of usin' the sat phone to call her."

"Why the hell would I do that?"

Uncle John's eyes narrowed. "So you can apologize for comin' down so hard on her, that's why."

"I didn't come down too hard on her. A man is *dead* because—"

"Because that man made the decision to try to steal your treasure," John interrupted, sounding impatient. "And boy, you know I love you like family, but it's a wonder you ain't got a nosebleed from that moral high ground you're standin' on. Did Cami mess up by tellin' her momma as much as she did? Sure. But you're treatin' her like *she* was the one who came down here armed to the teeth and with a mind to robbin' you blind. Makes me wonder if you're usin' her mistake as an excuse."

"An excuse for what exactly?" Doc scoffed.

"For pushin' her away 'cause she had the temerity to get too close."

"Temerity, huh? This isn't Scrabble. You don't get extra points for using big words."

Uncle John sounded impatient-bordering-on-pissed. "See, if I didn't know better, I'd say you were intentionally bein' an asshole so I'll drop the subject."

Chagrined, Doc opened his mouth to tell John…what? Lord help him, he didn't know. He *was* trying to change the subject.

John took advantage of his silence. "I've been watchin' you for the last couple years, and I think I finally got you figured out."

All the fight had gone out of Doc. "Well, that makes one of us," he muttered.

The look Uncle John leveled on him then was so shrewd it took all Doc's concentration not to shift uncomfortably.

"I think people lock their hearts away for a lot of different reasons." John's tone had softened slightly. "Some do it 'cause they've suffered a loss so great their heart becomes an empty shell, fragile and delicate. Others do it because they're terrified of gettin' their hearts broken again. I'd say both of those scenarios probably fit you for a while."

"But not now?" Doc was genuinely intrigued.

John shook his head. "Now I think you're hangin' onto your pain because you think it's worth somethin'. Because you think continuin' to hurt somehow gives meanin' to your wife's death."

Doc's heart skidded to a halt so quickly it left him

dizzy. If Uncle John noticed he reached out to steady himself against the newel post, John didn't say anything. He just plowed ahead.

"But that's horseshit, Doc. Lily died and it's awful. But you're still alive, and you don't honor her by hidin' away from what god or fate or the universe or whatever you believe in is offerin' you. You honor her by goin' on livin'. By havin' a happy life. By takin' a happy wife if you can find one who'll have you. By fatherin' a whole bunch of happy kids if that's what you want. You honor her by doin' all the things she can't."

Tears pricked the backs of Doc's eyes. He opened his mouth but, again, nothing came out. Probably because his thoughts were swirling so quickly he couldn't hold onto any of them. Anytime he tried to catch one, it felt too heavy or too big and it would slip through his grasp.

He finally settled on something quippy. "Are we going to have to start calling you Philosopher John instead of Uncle John?"

John twisted his lips until they completely disappeared beneath his beard and mustache. "I've always been a little introspective. But recently I've been doin' even more soul-searchin' than usual. And you know what I've decided?"

Doc was afraid to ask. And yet he heard the word *what* come out of his mouth.

"I've decided that lettin' yourself fall in love takes more courage than keepin' your heart to yourself. That lettin' yourself fall in love is both as commonplace and as miraculous as a sunrise, and it's that dichotomy that makes it so damn beautiful. I've decided I would be a fool to throw it away when it's starin' me square in the face."

"Are you saying you've gone and fallen in love with Dana Levine?"

When John smiled, his teeth blazed white. "If I ain't

there already, then I'm well on my way."

Doc nodded. "Yeah? So how would you feel if she was gone tomorrow? Would you be okay just up and replacing her with someone else?"

Uncle John's brow pinched as he gave the question the consideration it deserved. When he finally answered, he did so slowly. "If I was fortunate enough to meet someone as wonderful as she is? I reckon I'd welcome that woman with open arms and count my lucky stars."

Doc knew the next question he asked was going to sound antagonistic. But he didn't know of another way to phrase it. "You don't think that'd be a slap in the face of Dana's memory?"

"That's what I was gettin' at earlier, son." Uncle John sighed. "What good would it do to stand my ground and honor Dana's memory if it meant I was standin' alone? After all, she's the one who taught me just how sweet fallin' in love can be."

Uncle John's use of the word *son* reminded Doc of his father. Reminded him of a conversation he'd had with his dad a couple months before the heart attack.

His mind drifted back to that balmy summer evening…

"Lily wouldn't want you carrying on this way, son," his father said quietly.

Doc's leave only allowed him to be home for twenty-four hours before he needed to catch a plane in Butte and head back to base in Little Creek, Virginia. He'd wanted to spend that limited time enjoying his parents' company and avoiding heavy subjects. But his old man had never been one to skirt around an issue he felt needed addressing.

They sat in the front porch rocking chairs, and the air smelled of fresh-cut hay and cow manure. As the sun sank behind the mountains to the west, Doc was reminded of the way Lily had always said sunsets were god's poetry, that He painted the sky in silent verses of color.

Lord, how Doc missed her.

Dad just doesn't understand, *he thought sadly.* He's had Mom for over three decades.

Using his tongue to shove his toothpick to the left side of his mouth, he asked, "And what way am I carrying on, Dad?"

"Like you're trying to get yourself killed so you can join Lily wherever she is. You do a disservice to her, my boy, by throwing away your life when she'd probably give anything just to have one more day on this beautiful earth. Besides…" His father's stern face was pointed toward the mountaintops. *"It'd break my damn heart to lose you. And I don't think your momma would ever recover."*

Doc stopped rocking. The only sounds to break the silence then were the subtle squeaks of his father's chair and the gently tinkling knells of his mother's windchimes.

All Doc's irritation leaked out of him. In its place was sadness. Sadness and shame.

He'd been so caught up in his own grief, he'd never stopped to think what his dying would do to his parents.

"I'm sorry, Dad." His voice was so quiet it was nearly lost beneath the sound of a cow mooing in a nearby pasture.

His father heard him though. Rocking softly, his dad shook his head. "Nothin' to be sorry about, son. Just do me a favor and start taking care of yourself, okay? And maybe phone home more often. Your momma worries."

Doc smiled, knowing his mother wasn't the only one. But in the way of rugged men who'd been raised in the West, his father couldn't bring himself to say he *worried too.*

"You know I can't when I'm out in the field. But once I'm inside the wire, I'll do better about calling."

"I'd appreciate it." His father adjusted his cowboy hat and turned to him. Doc was struck anew at how much

the two of them looked alike. Same eyes. Same lines around their mouths, although his dad's were cut more deeply. Same raggedy toothpicks sticking out of their mouths.

"Now, tell me more about Rusty's tangle with that bartender in Bogotá," his father said. "That guy sounds like a hoot."

Doc laughed and launched into the tale of Rusty Lawrence's latest exploits. By the time his mother called them in for dinner, he had his father clutching his stomach and howling with laughter.

Doc snapped out of the memory and ran a finger over the tattoo on the inside of his arm, thinking of how that had been the last time the two of them had sat on the front porch together.

So much loss, he thought. *Lily's gone. Dad's gone. Rusty's gone.*

Uncle John noticed his gesture and cleared his throat. "Death comes for all of us eventually. So do yourself a favor, Doc, and don't go wastin' any more of your life, okay?"

Before Doc could say anything to that, Uncle John turned and headed for the kitchen where the sounds of clinking silverware, conversation, and laughter echoed. But once he reached the doorway, he turned back to Doc. "Aren't ya comin'," he asked.

Doc shook his head. "Save a plate for me, will you? I'm going for a walk."

He needed to think.

Because Uncle John wasn't right about him coming down too hard on Cami. He wasn't right in saying Doc was using Cami's mistake as an excuse to push her away. He wasn't right about Doc doing Lily's memory a disservice by hanging onto his pain.

Was he?

That voice piped up again. *You know he is.*

This time Doc didn't ignore the voice. He *couldn't* ignore it. It had gone from small and quiet to loud and reverberating.

Shit. He turned and pushed out through the front door, not feeling the warm evening air as it swept over his bare arms and legs. *Shit, shit, SHIT!*

If Uncle John *was* right, then there was more than one person he'd been too hard on and who deserved his apology.

CHAPTER 30

The next day
12:47 PM...

Jeez-oh-Pete. Remind me never to witness a crime again. I almost feel like *I* was the one who tried to steal the treasure." Dana plopped down into one of the plastic chairs lining the hallway outside the interrogation room.

She'd expected a police station, even one on a little island like Key West, to be buzzing with noise and activity. That's always the way the movies made it seem. But other than the distant ring of telephones, the only sound to break the silence in the hallway—besides her own words, of course—were the tapping toes or the rustling clothes of the four people who'd gone in to give their statements before her.

John, who sat in the chair to her left, handed her his cup of coffee without a word. She sent him a grateful smile and chugged down half the contents. She didn't care that it was strong enough to walk out of the paper cup on its own or that it was barely lukewarm. She needed the kick of caffeine after the day she'd had.

Scratch that. After the week *I've had.*

Flying down to Wayfarer Island to witness the raising of a lost treasure would've been enough excitement to last her a decade. But add on the hurricane, the hostage-taking, the shootout, the field medicine, the cleanup, and the time she'd spent yesterday evening helping Cami make sure neither the state of Florida nor the federal government could lay claim to the Deep Six's cache of riches by filling out an exhaustive affidavit, filming herself swearing before a judge that none of the riches had been raised while the reef was above the waterline, and basically leaping through every legal loophole Cami could think of, only to hop a puddle jumper first thing this morning so she could fly to Key West to give her statement to a detective named Dixon, and she was ready to *sleep* for a decade.

Maybe two *decades. Just call me Rip Van Winkle.*

"Dixon is tough." John laid an arm across the back of her chair. "But that's what makes him good at his job. And, hopefully, if what he says is true, these statements could be the last of it for us."

"I was in the bathroom when he came out to talk to the group after your interview." She turned to search his face and, not for the first time, found herself suffering butterflies when she looked at him. He was just so darned *handsome*. Earlier, when she'd walked into the police station to find him standing by the front desk, she'd nearly swooned. Seriously. Her knees had buckled, and she'd felt so light-headed she'd had to steady herself against the doorjamb. "So I only caught the end of what he said. Will, Jace, and Brady are going to plead guilty? Which means there won't be a trial?"

"They'll plead guilty to the attempted grand larceny and two of the lesser chargers," he explained, "*if* the prosecutor takes the felony murder charges off the table."

"But?" she asked when she heard a particular tone in his voice.

"But Dixon warned the prosecutor likes to bring down the hammer when he can. Says he takes that whole *tough on crime* schtick to heart."

"Ugh. A trial." Her shoulders slumped, but she was instantly gratified when John moved his arm from the back of her chair so he could pull her close. She reveled in the solid feel of him along her side and the coconutty smell of him that would always remind her of the beach. A dozen memories of the two nights they'd spent together after the storm flipped through her mind like a naughty slideshow, and she felt that telltale pull low in her belly.

"I'm sorry," Cami whispered from Dana's other side, dragging her thoughts from the delicious past to the not-so-delicious present. It was like walking out of a steam shower only to have a bucket of ice water thrown in her face. "It's my fault you're all going through this."

Dana sighed. She was dog-tired, but Cami looked like *death*. And Dana had lost count of the number of times she'd heard Cami apologize.

"You've got to let it go," LT said from Cami's other side. "We're not holdin' it against you, so don't go holdin' it against yourself. Those men *chose* to rob us. They *chose* to hold us hostage. And if they'd had their way, they would've killed us."

Instead of agreeing, Cami simply leaned back until her head rested against the wall. When she closed her eyes, Dana knew she was holding back tears.

Camilla D'Angelo was suffering something awful. And even though she'd been nothing but professional during the legal wrangling the day before, Dana had winced every time she'd found herself looking into the pretty lawyer's eyes.

There was such devastation there. Such…*loss*.

Dana was tempted to grab Doc by the shoulders and shake him silly the next time she saw him. He'd been too hard on Cami, and his condemnation was why Cami was being so hard on herself.

Life-threatening situations and the trauma that came with them stripped away people's veneers and forced them to get to know each other real quick. What Dana had learned about Camilla D' Angelo was that the woman was *good*. Plain and simple. She was good-natured, good-humored, and good-hearted.

A rare combination, in Dana's experience. And for the hundredth time, the words *Doc, you dumbass* drifted through her head.

Aloud, she said, "It's okay," and reached over to give Cami's arm a squeeze. "No matter what happens, whether the prosecutor pushes for the felony murder charges or not, we *will* be okay."

Before Cami could respond, Detective Dixon shoved through the door of the interrogation room. His hair was even messier than when Dana had left him. His suit pants were rumpled from the hours he'd spent sitting and taking their statements. And his scuffed-up loafers made squeaking sounds on the tile floor.

When she'd first met the man, she'd thought his wrinkled shirt and ketchup-stained tie meant he was as bumbling and inept as a character on one of those ridiculous buddy cop movies. But as soon as he'd started taking down her account of things, she'd been disabused of that notion *tout de suite*.

Dixon was as sharp as they came. His mind was a steel trap. And his questions had been as honed and precise as one of Doc's scalpels.

He was followed out of the interrogation room by the prosecutor, a guy whose slicked-back hair and Italian leather shoes pegged him as a mainlander and made him look like

Dixon's polar opposite. But Dana knew what the men lacked in physical similarities, they made up for in other ways. They both had hawkish gazes and rare abilities to cut to the chase.

"We've got everything we need." Dixon bobbed his head. "Thank you all for coming in."

Everyone mouthed their *your welcomes* and *of courses*, and then the prosecutor said, "William White is here at the station. He'd like a word with all of you if you're willing."

"Who's—" Dana started to ask, but then she quickly realized. "Oh, you mean Will."

"None of you have to grant his request, of course." The prosecutor looked stern. "It's totally up to—"

"I'd like to see him." Cami pushed to a stand.

"We'll all go." LT stood as well, dropping a hand to pull his wife up beside him. Then he winced and added, "Uh, sorry. I don't mean to speak for everyone." He looked down the row of chairs at Dana and John. "Blame it on the whole former lieutenant thing. Unilateral decision makin' is a hard habit to break."

"No." Dana stood. "You're right. We should all go."

"Okay then. Come this way." Dixon motioned for them to follow him.

Falling into step in the wake of the others, Dana smiled when John threaded his fingers through hers. His hand was so big and rough and warm.

The memory of how he'd used his hands to make her body sing had her shivering.

My claim to being old-fashioned and needing to be wined and dined went right out the window after the storm passed.

And boy-oh-boy was she lamenting it'd taken her *that* long to give in to John's considerable charms. Sex with him had been...*illuminating*. She'd felt things and done things and *said* things she never had before. Which had forced her to realize she'd spent way, *way* too much of her life sleeping with men who didn't truly understand—or appreciate—a woman's body.

Now that she *had* been with a man who truly understood and appreciated a woman's body? Well, she wasn't sure she could ever go back.

Which was a little scary. Because John lived in Key West and she lived in Washington D.C. How were they going to make it work? Better yet, did he even *want* to make it work?

When she'd been ready to step into the chartered float plane the day before, he hadn't said, *"Wait, Dana. What's next for us?"* He hadn't said, *"Let's talk about what we want outta this before you take off for Miami."* All he'd said was, *"I'll see you tomorrow at the police station."*

"You okay, darlin'?" He leaned in close, making her shiver because his warm breath against her cheek reminded her of all the deliciously naughty things he'd whispered while they were in bed together. John had a rare…*ahem*…gift with words. Particularly those of the carnal variety. "If you've changed your mind about seein' Will nobody'd blame you."

She realized he'd mistaken the frown on her face for an expression of trepidation.

"No." She shook her head. "That's not what—"

She didn't get to finish her sentence. They'd come to the end of the hallway and Dixon shoved open the last door on the right.

"You got five minutes," he said to whomever was inside the room. Then he stood back and nodded for Dana and the others to enter.

She loved how John placed his big hand against the small of her back to usher her in front of him. She loved it more when he took her hand again as soon as they both stepped inside the room.

Love.

It was a big word. Maybe the *biggest* of words. And she'd been using it a lot in reference to him. Which didn't bode well for her since she didn't know the answers to the questions of how they were going to make it work or if he even *wanted* to.

Of course, as soon as Cami moved aside and Dana got a look at Will, all her thoughts ground to a halt.

Will was seated at a table in the center of the room. His injured arm was held in a sling close to his chest but his free hand was wrapped in a silver cuff that was cinched around a metal bar in the middle of the table.

He'd aged ten years in the space of a few days. His face was drawn and haggard. There were deep circles under his eyes. And his skin looked waxy and corpse-like against the garish orange of his prison uniform.

To Dana's surprise, there was no guard inside the room. No lawyer. Just Will.

His chin wobbled a bit, but he didn't shy away from looking all of them directly in the eye. It was only after he'd acknowledged each and every one of them that he spoke.

Dana wasn't sure what she'd expected him to say, but it certainly wasn't, "Thank you."

CHAPTER 31

1:01 PM...

Will had given a lot of thought to what he wanted to tell the people he and his friends had taken hostage. He'd played around with the notion of starting with *I'm sorry*.

Because he was.

So damn sorry.

Sorry he'd ever been tempted by the thought of easy money. Sorry he and his friends had traumatized all these good and decent folks. Sorry he'd considered killing them in order to save his own neck.

But he'd decided saying he was sorry put the focus on him. On *his* feelings. And his victims—yes, he'd come to terms with the fact that they were his victims—didn't deserve that. They deserved the focus to be on *them*. Which was why he started out by thanking them.

"Thank you all for takin' care of me and Brady. The

doctors say Brady's injuries mighta left him stove all to hell if ya hadn't been so quick to patch him up."

The lump that'd formed in his throat the instant Fin died was still there. Firmly lodged into place. He figured it was just part of him now, same as the scars on his arm. But that meant he'd gotten good at being able to talk around it.

"Ya treated us better than we deserved. And I'll always be grateful for that." He swallowed and forced himself to once again look each of them in the eye. Would he *really* have gone through with the plan to kill them? God help him, he would have. And that was the most disheartening revelation of all. That he had that in him. That he was capable of such atrocity.

"And not that it matters one way or the other, 'cause what's done is done," he continued hoarsely. "But I want ya to know how sorry I am. How sorry we all are for what we put ya through. If we could take it all back, we would."

Oh, how I would.

He couldn't stop the tears that pricked behind his eyes any more than he could stop recalling the sound of disbelief in his mother's voice when he'd called to tell her what'd happened. But the disbelief in her voice was so much better than the disappointment he'd heard in his father's voice. Of course, worse than all of that had been the look of betrayal, the look of disgust that'd come over Sheila's face when she'd flown down to visit him in the hospital.

"How could ya?" Her big green eyes had filled with tears when he'd explained what he'd done. "How could ya have done this to us, Will?"

He'd tried to reach for her, but he'd been thwarted by the cuff securing his hand to the hospital bed's guardrail.

"I was trying to do it *for* us, Sheila," he'd said, choking on a sob when she didn't step forward to take the hand extended her way.

"We were *fine*." She'd shaken her head. "We were strugglin', but we were makin' it work because we were all together, ya dubbah. Now you're goin' away for who knows how long, and what are me and the boys supposed to do, huh?"

He'd had no answer for her then. He had no answer for her now.

A part of him wanted to beg her to wait for him. But if the prosecutor went for felony murder, and if he and the others were convicted, they would be looking at life. He couldn't ask his loving wife to lock herself away in a prison of her own making just to stay true to him.

She was still young. She was still beautiful. She still had time to make some other lucky sonofabitch the happiest man on earth. Which meant his boys would be brought up by someone else.

The thought of another man parenting his sons sent a steel boat hook straight through the meaty part of his heart.

But at least I'll still be able to write them letters, he consoled himself. *At least I'll still be able to tell 'em how much I love 'em. Fin can't even do that.*

Every time he thought of his best friend, he broke into tears.

This time was no different.

"Sorry," he croaked when his eyes overflowed. His cuff made a jangling noise against the restraining bar when he leaned toward the table to brush away his tears. "I didn't ask ya to come in here to watch me blubber like a baby. I just wanted to thank ya, and I felt like ya should have the chance to say to me whatever it is ya feel ya need to say." He straightened and blew out a shaky breath, ready for an earful. "Don't feel like ya need to hold back. I deserve anything and everything ya got."

"What you did was wrong." LT's eyes were penetrating

as they held Will's stare. "And you'll pay a price for that. But despite what you were willin' to do to us, none of us wishes to add to your ills. We're happy to let Lady Justice do to you what she feels is right."

Will nodded, unable to speak around the tears in his throat. He'd expected them to scream at him, to call him all the things he'd been calling himself. Somehow, their grace and mercy was worse.

Because it highlighted just how far he'd fallen.

So far there's no way to climb back up.

William White had spent his life thinking of himself as a good man. And now he was forced to face the truth.

He'd only been as good as circumstances had forced him to be. When he'd been tempted by easy money, he'd been willing to do the unthinkable. And that weakness, that inability to avoid temptation, hadn't only ruined *his* life. His parents and wife and sons would pay the price too.

For that, he'd never forgive himself.

CHAPTER 32

1:06 PM...

A fter hours spent breathing in the police station's stale air, John couldn't wait to push through the glass front doors and escape into the sunshine.

Rich, humid air that smelled of flowering plants and hot cement filled his lungs when he raked in a deep breath. The soft ocean breeze whispered over his skin like the touch of a longtime lover. And he turned his face toward the sun's brilliant yellow glow, closing his eyes and letting its warmth bathe away the stress of the last few hours.

"I'm glad that's over." Olivia threaded an arm around Leo's waist and placed her head against his shoulder.

"You ain't the only one," John concurred as Alvaro Martinez, the prosecutor on the case, exited the station's front doors.

"I'm sure you're all glad that's behind you," Martinez echoed their sentiments while sliding on a pair of flashy-looking sunglasses. "And I think you'll be happy to hear I'm not moving forward with the felony murder charges."

John felt a wave of relief even as he lifted an eyebrow. "Really? Why's that?"

Martinez frowned. "My whole case would hinge on the jury being unsympathetic toward the defendants, and that's not going to happen. They're all family men with no priors. I'm not going to waste taxpayer money on a sure shot loss."

"So then it'll just be the lesser charges they'll face?" Cami asked.

The poor woman didn't look like she'd slept a wink since the storm, and John had spent the time Dana had been in with Dixon and Martinez racking his brain for a way to wipe some of the misery off her face. Ultimately, however, he'd decided the only person who could do that was Doc. And the man was 3000 miles away.

Martinez nodded. "Which they've already agreed to plead guilty to. I'll push the judge for the full twenty-year sentence. He'll probably settle on fifteen. And with good behavior, your would-be thieves could be out in as little as ten."

"I know I should be upset by that. They were planning to kill us, after all. But I just can't bring myself to feel animosity toward them." Dana frowned. "I just feel sorry for them. They're pitiable."

John was distracted from Cami's misery by Dana's compassion.

Her cornflower-blue eyes held such kindness. Her springy blond curls bounced as she shook her head. And her sad expression took up her whole face.

He was hit by the nearly overwhelming urge to bend down and kiss her frown away. Probably because he knew just how quickly that frown could dissolve into a moue of passion.

Dana Levine was a *very* responsive lover. Not to mention eager and enthusiastic. And, most charmingly of all, *fun*. He'd never been with a woman who could be orgasming one minute and laughing the next.

Martinez shook his head. "Which is exactly how a jury would feel about them." He glanced down at his watch. "Damn. I'm late. Have a great day."

He gave them a dismissive wave and marched toward a baby-blue convertible Porsche Boxster.

"Seems like a nice guy," Olivia muttered sarcastically after he sped out of the parking lot.

"Prosecutors aren't generally the touchy-feely sort." Cami made a face. Not for the first time that day John thought her voice sounded hoarse. Like she'd spent the night crying. "They have all sorts of political pressures and bureaucratic red tape to get through. Not to mention they get to see just how unfair and arbitrary our justice system can be. I haven't met one who isn't jaded as fuck." She winced. "Sorry. The New Yorker comes out in me when I'm tired."

Taking her cell phone from her giant carryall purse, she thumbed on the screen and then glanced around at the group. "Dana and I have a flight leaving for the mainland in an hour. I'm calling an Uber. Are you guys headed back to the airport too or—" She let the sentence dangle.

"Nah." Leo shook his head. "We didn't fly in. We sailed here on the catamaran."

Cami had been staring at her phone, pushing buttons on the screen, but that had her looking up at Leo and then over to John. "It survived? I thought you said it sank."

"Thought she did." John shrugged. "But she only came loose of her moorings and started driftin' toward Cuba. The Coasties found her and brought her back to me last night. She's fit as a fiddle except for a little damage to her boom basket."

"That's great news." Cami tried for a smile, but the expression hurt John to look at. It was like a smile that'd been shattered into a million sharp pieces. "I know how much you love that boat."

He nodded. "She's a peach."

And then everyone fell into an awkward silence.

Idle chitchat felt trite. But no one wanted to touch the ten-thousand-pound gorilla that was the subject of Doc. Because, really, what could any of them say to someone whose heart was so obviously broken? And by one of their very own?

Thankfully, a black Ford Escape with the lighted Uber sticker in the window pulled up to the curb next to them, proving the car had been close when Cami put in her request. The driver was a young man, no more than twenty-five, who wore his baseball cap backward. He rolled down the passenger window and leaned across the seat to yell, "I'm here for Camilla D'Angelo?"

"That's me." Cami gave a half-hearted wave. "Be there in a sec." Turning back to the gathered group she said, "I guess that's it." Her face looked ready to crumble, like some of the ancient wooden artifacts they'd been unable to save from the *Santa Cristana*'s remains. "Thank you all for letting me be your lawyer. I'm sorry I messed everything up at the end." Her lips trembled. "Turns out I'm one of those people who should use a glue stick in place of ChapStick."

Her attempt at levity fell flat. Mostly because it was so very obvious to everyone that she was absolutely miserable.

"If it's any consolation," she went on. "I don't think anyone will give you a fight over the treasure's jurisdiction. That part I got right. That part I didn't fuck up."

"Cami—" Olivia began, reaching for the lawyer.

"No." Cami held out a hand, shaking her head. "Don't be nice to me. I can't take any more niceness. Just know that it was a pleasure representing you all in this matter."

"Come on, Cami. Don't pull out that professional bullshit like we're nothing more than a job to you," Leo said gruffly. "You've become a friend and—"

"I feel the same way about all of you." She cut him off. "Now, I have to go before I make a fool of myself." She turned away but not before John had seen her face shatter.

Wrenching open the SUV's back door, she quickly slid inside.

Leo sighed and ran a hand through his hair. His words were quiet, meant only for those gathered around him, when he said, "Wish I knew what to say to make her feel better about all this."

"Absolution will have to come from Doc." Olivia echoed John's own conclusions. "And he's in Montana."

"Montana?" Dana blinked incredulously. "He's gone home already?"

"Just for a quick trip," John explained. "He lit out of the house early this morning saying he'd be back in a couple days."

"Oh." She nodded. "Well. I…" She bit her lip, drawing his eyes to her mouth. Once again he was hit with the overwhelming urge to kiss her. "I guess I better get going."

John's stomach dropped. When she started to turn away, he caught her wrist. "Wait. When am I goin' to see you again?"

"I, uh, just remembered I left somethin' in the police station," Leo said.

"I'll come with you," Olivia added, scurrying after her husband.

John watched them disappear through the glass doors and then turned back to Dana. "They're both so subtle." He made a face.

A light breeze tousled curls into her eyes. She lifted

a hand to push them behind her ears, but he beat her to the punch, pinching the springy strands between his fingers before reluctantly dropping his hands from her face.

Touching her was such a treat. She was so warm and soft.

Her eyes searched his. There was a question there, but he wasn't sure what it was. So he repeated his own. "When am I goin' to see you again, darlin'?"

"Do you *want* to see me again?"

His chin jerked back so fast it was a wonder he didn't give himself whiplash. "'Course I do. Did you ever doubt it?"

"I just…" She bit her lip again, and this time he cupped her face with his hand and rubbed his finger over her mouth. "You keep gnawin' on that thing and I'm not goin' to be able to let you leave until you give me another chance to gnaw on it myself."

A pretty blush stained her cheeks, but the look in her eyes was coy. "You don't gnaw. You nip and lick and suck."

Instant desire had his blood running hot. "Hmm. Yes. I do seem to recall that."

She shivered despite the heat of the day, which was how he knew she was feeling everything he was.

Strange to have found his life's passion at the ripe old age of sixty-five.

But I reckon it's true what they say. Good things come to those who wait.

"How do we make this work, John?" There was entreaty in her voice. "You live here. I live in D.C."

"I'm retired," he came back instantly. "I can come visit you anytime you want me to. All you gotta do is invite me."

"You're invited."

Her answer was so quick, he couldn't help but chuckle. And damned if his heart wasn't doing a happy dance. "Okay. When?"

"Now?"

"Oh, darlin', you're killin' me." He held a hand to his chest. "I need to stick around for a bit. We've got to make arrangements for the treasure. How 'bout I fly up over the weekend?"

"That's four days away."

She was adorable when she pouted, and he couldn't stand it a second longer. He bent to claim her lips.

Her mouth was hot and open and eager as she went up on tiptoe to wrap her arms around his neck. He knew they must be a sight. A couple of folks of a *particular age* making out on the sidewalk like teenagers. But he didn't care.

He kissed her with every ounce of passion inside him. And when they finally pulled apart, he was breathing hard and glad his Hawaiian shirt was untucked and hiding what was happening in his shorts.

She rubbed her thumb over his bottom lip where some of her lip gloss had transferred. "Get your ass up to D.C., John." She slanted him a seductive look. "I'll be counting the hours until you do."

When she turned to step into the Uber, he couldn't stop himself from reaching for her. She came willingly back into his arms, but she pressed a finger over his mouth when he bent his head to kiss her again.

"You'll make me miss my plane," she scolded.

"Good." He slid his hand down to the small of her back and pressed her forward so she could feel what she'd done to him, loving the way her eyelids lowered to half-mast when her pelvis bumped his erection. "Then you can help me deal with this."

She giggled and the sound was like bubbles of joy that fizzed and popped in his ears. "Hold that thought for four days."

"Fine." He faked a pout. Or maybe it wasn't fake. "Four days."

After planting a quick kiss on his lips, she danced out of his embrace and slid into the car's back seat. Before she closed the door, however, she leaned her head out and added, "I'm going to miss you, John."

"Darlin'"—he shook his head—"you got no idea how much I'm goin' to miss you."

She blew him a kiss and then closed the door. He hated seeing her disappear behind the tinted glass. Hated worse watching the Uber driver make the gas pedal one with the floorboard as he sped out of the parking lot.

Four days.

John Anderson had waited sixty-five years for Dana Levine to come into his life. Surely he could wait four measly days to see her again. To look into her smiling blue eyes again. To make long, slow, passionate love to her again.

CHAPTER 33

3:31 PM...

Even this far into summer, the tops of the mountains to the west were still crowned with caps of white snow. Doc watched as a golden eagle circled one of the lower peaks. The raptor's lazy, relaxed flight stood in stark contrast to the cauldron of emotions roiling inside him.

"The night I met her, I didn't know who she was or where she was from. But she felt instantly familiar to me. Like I'd known her all my life." He swallowed and turned his eyes to the nearest pasture, where a herd of Angus cattle munched on sweet green grass shoots. "And I think maybe I've been holding that against her ever since. Because the more I got to know her, the more I was unable to shake that sense of familiarity. And the more familiar she became, the further away I felt from Lily." Tears clogged his throat. "I *hate* that feeling, Mom. I don't want to lose Lily. I still love her."

They were sitting on the front porch steps of the ranch house she shared with Randall Thorpe—Doc didn't think of the man as his stepfather; didn't reckon he ever would. And he watched as his mother tucked the ends of her long sundress tighter around her ankles when the soft-smelling breeze tried to push it up her legs. She was staring out at the fields, same as he'd been. But her eyes seemed to be focused on the middle distance.

"For years after your father died, he was the first thing I'd see in my mind's eye when I laid my head on my pillow at night. He was the first person I wanted to run to anytime something sad or scary happened. And when I heard a funny story, he was certainly the first person I wanted to tell." Her voice was low and gentle when she spoke. "And then, one day, he was the second person I thought about at night. And Randall was the one I clung to when I was sad or scared. And all my funny stories got shared with my friends." She blew out a ragged breath. "On that day, I felt like I'd lost your father all over again."

Doc jerked back his chin, and she caught the movement out of the corner of her eye. When she turned to him, her smile was melancholy. "What? You think just because I married Randall that I fell out of love with your father?"

"I—" he started and then immediately stopped. All he could manage was a confused shake of his head.

"When a person loses someone they love with their whole heart, it leaves an awful emptiness inside them," his mother said. He thought of the yawning void at his center and nodded in understanding. "And sometimes a person's instinct is to fill that emptiness with something dark. Like bitterness or loneliness."

Doc had certainly been lonely since Lily's death. Had he been bitter too?

If his treatment of Cami was anything to go by, he was

afraid the answer to that question might be a resounding *yes*.

"Randall and I decided we wanted to fill our voids with love instead," she went on.

"Just like that?" Doc pulverized the end of his toothpick with his teeth. "You could fall in love again just like that? But *how*?"

She shrugged and her expression was self-deprecating. "Most of my thinking comes from a lifetime of farming and ranching. So maybe I tend to oversimplify things. But…I think love blooms where it's planted. And I think a person can choose where to till the soil and put down seeds. I chose Randall. He chose me. We planted love together in a new field. But that doesn't mean either one of us loves our first spouse any less or that we don't still tend to those original fields and visit the love still growing there. We do. Every day."

He was quiet while letting her words sink in.

She took advantage of his silence by asking, "You're worried about Lily's memory fading?"

Unshed tears stung the back of his nose when he nodded.

"Son, that's bound to happen regardless of whether you let someone else into your life. Regardless of whether you open your heart to new love." Her smile was sad. "Time takes all things. The vibrancy of youth dims. Memories fade." She gave him a meaningful look. "Even the stars wink out and die."

"I feel like I should try not to let that happen. That I should try to hold onto her. Like I owe it to her. To our love."

His mother brushed his hair back from his forehead, just like she'd done when he was a boy. Closing his eyes, he admitted to himself how much he'd *missed* her. "*Should* and *owe* are dangerous words, Dalton. I suspect Lily would hate to hear you utter either one in reference to her."

The tears that'd been burning the back of his nose

welled up in his eyes. He used the excuse of flicking his toothpick into the flower beds to turn away and give himself the opportunity to wipe them away.

When he swung back to her, his eyes were dry, but his voice was wet-sounding. "Okay, so what if I do as you say? What if I till the soil and plant the seeds? Will that be fair to Cami?"

His mother frowned and he appreciated how the years had etched lines into the corners of her eyes and feathered streaks of gray through the blond hair at her temples. Even at sixty-one, she was still a handsome woman. "What do you mean by *fair*?" she asked.

"I mean at least with you and Randall, you'd *both* suffered losses. You were *both* having to share space in the other's heart with someone else. Is it fair for me to ask Cami to share space with Lily when I won't have to do the same?"

He realized what he'd said and tugged on his ear. "Of course, that's assuming she *could* love me after the way I behaved. After the things I said."

How could he have blamed her for what the thieves had done? How could he have placed all of that at her feet just because she'd let a clue slip?

Of course, he knew how.

It was just as John had said. He'd used the excuse of her indiscretion to push her away so he wouldn't have to face the truth.

The truth that he'd fallen in love with her. All the way. Head over heels. Starting with the first night they met, encompassing all their tiffs, and ending with the evening of the storm. He *loved* her. Mind and body. Heart and soul.

And yet…he still loved Lily too.

"Humans are amazing creatures," his mother said. "We're made of resilience and magic and forgiveness. Go to Cami. Tell her how you feel. And if she's half the woman you say she is, she won't have any problem sharing space in your heart. Because if she's half the woman you say she is, she'll know jealousy isn't a form of love. It's a form of possession."

He shook his head. "You call yourself uncomplicated. But you know what Dad used to call you behind your back?" She only blinked for him to continue. "A philosopher. He used to tell me, 'Dalton, your momma is the human embodiment of that old saw *still waters run deep.*'"

She smiled, her eyes going soft. "And he used to tell me, 'Vera, that son of ours hasn't got enough sense to pour piss out of a boot. We'll be lucky if he graduates high school.'" She snorted. "I'm just saying, the man got things wrong sometimes."

Doc laughed. And truly, nothing felt better than laughter after tears. "In his defense, between the ages of six and sixteen I *was* dumber than a bag of hammers. How many times did I break something jumping off the roof of the barn?"

"Three." She made a face. "First your ankle, then your left arm, and finally your right wrist. I thought your father was going to kill you on the drive to the emergency room after that last one."

Doc nodded. "Lord, he was mad at me. Especially because once we got to the hospital, I kept asking the attending physician medical questions, so it took twice as long as it should have to get the bones set and the cast on. It was calving season, and Dad hated being away from the ranch."

"It was his favorite time of the year. He always loved having all the babies around."

"I miss him so much." Old sorrow turned Doc's voice gruff.

"Me too." His mother's eyes were suddenly over-bright. "Every single day."

"And you can do that and still love Randall?" He shook his head. "I don't get it."

Her mouth twisted. "That's because you're young."

He chuffed out a sardonic breath. "I'm not *that* young."

"You're still young enough to think falling in love is supposed to be angsty and tempestuous and wildly passionate." She nudged him and smiled knowingly. "And that's fine. But once you get to be my age, you realize that being crazy in love is a fool's game. That anxious, breathless, insane feeling doesn't last. And once it wears off, sometimes you're left with nothing. I'd much rather be calm in love. Understood in love. Patient and generous in love. *Content* in love."

He gave her a lopsided grin. "I think you'd get along really well with Uncle John."

"The pot grower?"

"Ha!" He nodded. "Among other things. You two have a very similar outlook on life."

She shrugged. "Maybe it's a generational thing." Then she slid him a sidelong glance. "But that begs the question, can you see yourself making a life with Cami once the fires of passion burn down to smoldering embers? Can you see yourself being more than her lover? Being her partner in life? Her helpmate? Her *friend*?"

He thought back to his dream, to Cami standing on the porch with a baby on one hip and her hand in the hair of a little boy, and nodded. "She's loud and bossy and funny and genuine. We lock horns constantly. But I've got to tell you, Mom, I'd rather be locking horns with her than sitting quietly and comfortably with anyone else. And I think I want to lock horns with her the rest of my life."

A wide smile spread over his mother's face. "Oh, Dalton. You have no idea how it warms my heart to hear you say that."

They were quiet for a long time after that, listening to the hum of the bugs, the soft sounds of the cattle, the tinkle of the wind through the chimes.

His mother had always loved windchimes.

But eventually he turned and did what he'd come three thousand miles to do. He apologized.

"I'm sorry, Mom." When a line appeared between her eyebrows, he tugged on his ear and rushed ahead. "I'm sorry I was so upset when you married Randall. And I'm sorry I held that against you all these years. It wasn't my place to judge what was right or wrong for you or for him or for Dad's memory."

She gently pulled his hand away from his earlobe. "You've been doing that since you were a baby. It's a wonder your poor earlobes aren't three feet long." Then she wrapped an arm around his back and leaned her head onto his shoulder. He placed his cheek atop her hair and breathed in the clean smell of her Prell shampoo.

"As for being upset about me marrying Randall," she went on quietly. "You were hurting. We *both* were. We just chose to handle that hurt differently."

"You handled it by being gracious and accepting and moving on with life. I handled it by being cold and disapproving and clinging to my pain."

"You're stubborn, just like your daddy. But how can I be mad about that when it's one of the things I've always loved so much about you?"

"I love you too, Mom."

She nodded and it rubbed her hair against his cheek. "I know you do, son."

CHAPTER 34

The next day
3:44 PM...

Cami sat across the table from her father and noticed how prison hadn't diminished Big Tony D's penchant for a close shave and a tight haircut. Not a shiv mark or black eye marred his face. His thick frame said he had plenty of money to buy snacks at the commissary. And the breadth of his shoulders told her he spent a lot of time with the gym equipment.

Hard time looked good on him.

Then again, the Gambino crime family had plenty of reach inside. Which meant, as long as her father kept up his end of the bargain and kept his mouth shut, he'd enjoy the best the penal system had to offer.

"To what do I owe the pleasure of this visit, Camilla?" He was the only person who never called her Cami.

His deep voice brought back a million memories of her childhood. Even though he hadn't been around all that much—he'd always been out working—when he *had* been home, she remembered cookouts and board games and camping trips planned to the Cascades.

Which was probably why it hurt so much to know he'd betrayed her. Betrayed her *trust*.

And in doing so, he'd nearly cost her her life. But worse than that, he'd nearly cost the lives of people she'd grown to care about and one person she loved with her whole heart.

"Why did you tell your cellmate about the king tide?" Her voice was hoarse from having spent the entire plane ride from Miami to New York City with a lump in her throat. Not because she'd been nervous about the coming confrontation with her father. More because she'd been sad. So unbearably sad that it'd come to this.

He made a face and crossed his arms over his chest. "Fuckin' Bernie." He shook his head. "I was just chatting. Just bragging to my cellmate about my daughter and her work, you know? Not much else to do in here but talk. And how the hell was I supposed to know that skinny tweaker had a cousin who'd try to make a run for the money?"

It was just as she'd suspected. There'd been no malice in her father's slip. Simply thoughtlessness.

Guess it runs in the family, she thought with no small amount of self-derision.

Aloud, she told her father, "I nearly died, Dad. A man *did* die."

"Pfft." He rolled his eyes. "Do the crime, do the time, right?" He held his big arms wide. "Just like me."

She blinked at him. "You don't feel any responsibility for what happened?"

A wrinkle appeared between his bushy black eyebrows. "Why would *I* be responsible? I didn't intend for any harm to come to anyone. Least of all you."

"Just like you didn't intend for any harm to come to Carlotta?"

A thundercloud as dark and menacing as Julia's outer wall came over her father's face then. "I'm no more responsible for the bomb that took out Carlotta than I am for those dumbass fishermen from Maine. If you came here to bust my balls over your baby sister, I'd rather you have stayed away."

"You might not have *intended* for anything bad to happen to Carlotta or to me, but there's a big difference between intention and impact. Your actions *impact* others, Dad. They negatively impact the people you love. Doesn't that bother you? Don't you feel just a *little* bit—"

"I never did anything but love and support you and your sister!" her father bellowed, prompting the other families and friends visiting loved ones to stop their conversations and glance in Cami's direction.

"Simmer down, D' Angelo," warned the guard by the door. "Don't make me drag your ass outta here."

"I'd like to see you try," her father muttered beneath his breath, a sardonic smirk tilting his lips as he once more crossed his arms.

It hit Cami then. There were two kinds of people in the world. Those who understood that regardless of their motivations behind or purposes for doing things, it was how their actions affected others that was important. And those who thought as long as they didn't *intend* harm, it didn't matter if someone got hurt.

Her father was the latter. Always had been, always would be.

Which meant there was nothing she could do or say to mend the rift between them. Which meant she'd always be looking over her shoulder, waiting for the next slip or the next bomb or bullet meant for him to find a home in her. Which meant it was time.

Time to sever that last tie.

"Thank you for the board games and camping trips, Dad," she told him as she pushed up from the table. "I'll always look back fondly on those times."

"That's it?" he demanded when she started to turn away.

Taking one final look at her father, she blew out a ragged breath and nodded. "Yeah. That's it."

Ten minutes later, she walked across the parking lot toward the sedan she'd rented at LaGuardia. The air outside smelled of damp concrete and motor oil. But she far preferred it to the antiseptic stench that had permeated the prison.

Checking her watch, she hoped traffic on 287 wasn't bad. The drive from Sing Sing to Staten Island usually took an hour and a half, and she was supposed to meet her mother for an early dinner at Giuliana's Ristorante before catching her flight back to Florida.

Rummaging in her purse for the rental car's key fob, she nearly dropped everything when she heard her mother call out from nearby.

"Mom?" She frowned when she saw her mother scurrying toward her. "What are you doing here? I thought we were meeting at Giuliana's?"

"I couldn't wait to see you," her mother said, pulling her in for a quick hug. Cami closed her eyes, breathing in the familiar perfume before her mother stepped back. For as long as she could remember, her mother had worn L'Air Du Temps. "How did your visit with your father go?" her mother asked with what was supposed to be a raised eyebrow. It was hard to tell under all the Botox.

The lump was back in Cami's throat. It was joined by the burn of tears. "About as I expected," she admitted wretchedly.

Her mother's left eye twitched. "You didn't blame him for what happened to you, did you? It wasn't his fault, you know."

Cami shook her head. "No more than it was my fault, I

guess, for letting as much as I did slip to you. No more than it was your fault for passing along the information to him."

Her mother sighed heavily. "Why does everything have to be someone's *fault*? Accidents happen."

"They happen a lot more when your parents are criminals," Cami muttered.

"I have never had so much as a speeding ticket," her mother sniffed, shoving her nose in the air so high Cami thought it wonder she didn't give herself a nosebleed.

"But you knew who Dad was. All these years, you knew *what* he was and what he did for a living. In my line of work, we'd call you an accomplice."

"Oh, don't be so dramatic, Camilla." Her mother waved a dismissive hand.

"Why is it I can admit that my big mouth nearly got me and all the good and decent people I was working for killed, but you and Dad can't admit to your parts in it?"

Her mother eyed her critically. "Maybe because you've always had an overinflated sense of personal responsibility?"

"Have I?" Cami blinked myopically. "Or is it possible you and Dad both have *under*inflated senses of responsibility?"

A snarl curled her mother's perfectly painted mouth. "I did *not* drive all this way to be insulted by my only daughter."

Her mother's words were like a slap in the face. "I'm your only daughter because the life Dad has chosen to lead, the life you've led with him, got your other daughter killed."

This time it was a real hand that stung across her cheek. Her mother's hand.

Cami gritted her teeth and kept from lifting a palm to the print she knew stood out in red relief across her face.

"Don't *ever* say that again," her mother hissed, her nostrils flaring wide. "It wasn't your father's—"

"How could you forgive him, Mom?" Cami cut off whatever excuse her mother had been about to make. "How could you go on living with him, *loving* him after what happened to Carlotta?"

Again, her mother's eye twitched. And a terrible expression crossed her face. "You wouldn't understand. You've never been in love."

Cami snorted and thought, *Oh, if you only knew.*

But her days of sharing personal details with her mother were over. Aloud she admitted, "If I ever do fall in love, it'll be with a man who is good and kind. A man who thinks about how his actions affect others. A man who'd sooner cut off his own arm than put the people he loves in danger."

A man like Dalton Simmons, who has more honesty and integrity in his little finger than you and Dad combined.

"Pfft." Her mother snorted. "And now we know why you're still single. Men like that don't exist. *People* like that don't exist. You're too old to be this idealistic, Cami. It's time you grew up."

Cami gritted her teeth against the nasty response sitting on the tip of her tongue.

What's the point? she thought. *Nothing will make either of them see themselves for who they are.*

She had suspected as much was true. But she'd made the trip to New York because she'd had to be sure. To do what she planned to do next, she'd had to be sure.

"I won't be calling you anymore, Mom," she said quietly.

A windy sigh left her mother's pursed lips. "And there you go being dramatic again."

"I'll never feel safe having a relationship with either of you. And I can't forgive either of you for feeling no responsibility for what happened to Carlotta."

As horrible as it was to contemplate severing her last tie to family, Cami knew she had to for her own mental health. She had to cut the toxicity and corruption from her life as surely as she would cut a cancer from her body.

"Blood is thicker than water, Cami." Her mother's expression twisted her mouth into a cruel mew. "You can't walk away from family."

"Funny." Cami shook her head. "You're the most *Catholic* Catholic I know, and yet you probably think that's actually scripture, don't you?" When her mother narrowed her eyes, she continued. "The phrase dates back to the twelfth century. To some German guy. And what he said was, 'The blood of the covenant is thicker than the water of the womb.' Covenant meaning the pledge between people who've sworn to tie themselves together. Like spouses or best friends. The phrase *literally* means that the bonds we share with the family we choose are stronger than the bonds of blood."

"And what bonds do you share, Cami?" her mother asked sneeringly. "Last I heard, all you do is work. You have no friends. No boyfriend."

The tears Cami had been holding back filled her eyes as she thought of Doc and all the men and women of Deep Six Salvage. Her tears spilled down her cheeks when she silently admitted the truth of her mother's statement.

"But I have my dignity, Mom," she said wetly. "I have my principles. And, most importantly, I have my life. If I don't set a boundary with you and Dad now, I don't know how long I'll be able to keep any of that."

"You self-righteous, condescending little—"

Cami didn't wait around to hear the end of her mother's sentence. She hit the button on the key fob and slid into the sedan's driver's seat.

As she pulled from the parking lot, she didn't allow herself to glance into the rearview mirror. She didn't allow herself to look back at her past. She made herself keep her eyes straight ahead. On her future.

Even if that future was destined to be a lonely one.

CHAPTER 35

Two days later
5:28 PM...

Cami had wondered if it was possible to die from shame and sadness. Newsflash: it *wasn't*.

Although both things, especially in combination, made a person *want* to die.

Alas, life went on. Work went on. The world kept spinning and Cami couldn't just crawl in a hole somewhere and disappear.

No matter how much she might want to.

The heat caused by the Miami sun radiating off the sidewalk hit her in the face as soon as she stepped out of her downtown office building. It made her long for the cool breezes of the Keys. But since she had no plans for a return trip, she had to satisfy herself with the thought of driving home to her air-conditioned condo, slipping into a bath to wash away the day's sweat, and sipping on a cool glass of Chardonnay while reading the spy novel she'd picked up in the airport on her way back from New York.

She'd tried the whole book, bath, and wine trick for two nights running. But she'd learned the thing about a broken heart was that it was impossible to numb it away, or wash it away, and no matter what she did to distract herself at night, it was still there in the morning.

So the key was to surrender to it. Wallow in it. *Soak* in it until her fingers turned pruney.

Someone opened the door to the pub across the street and the throaty croon of Waylon Jennings echoed out over the sidewalk.

"Fuck my life," she muttered when her eyes instantly welled up.

Doc was a fan of outlaw country—something he'd said his father passed down to him—and hearing Waylon sing about *having it all* only reminded her that she had nothing. Nothing but memories.

Memories of parents who'd turned out to be everything she thought was wrong with the world. Memories of the sister who'd been her best friend. Memories of Doc's green eyes that had seen too much of life's miseries. Memories of that single beautiful night they'd spent together.

God, I miss him, she admitted miserably as she opened her purse to root around for her sunglasses case.

She could feel the tears building and she needed to cover her eyes. The last thing she wanted was for someone to see her crying and stop to ask if she was okay since the answer to that question was *no!* She wasn't. And she didn't know when or if she'd ever be okay again.

She remembered something Carlotta had said once after meeting a man in Paris. She and the Frenchman had had a whirlwind relationship that, after two months, had ended as quickly as it'd begun.

"Our lives can overlap with someone else's for the

*briefest of times, Cami. But in those stolen days or weeks or
even months, we can grow in love and laughter and learning.
And, if we're lucky, it'll be enough to last us a lifetime."*

Unfortunately, Cami was afraid that losing that special
someone and the mourning that came with that loss might
last a lifetime too.

After sliding her sunglasses onto her face, she took
out a piece of gum and popped it into her mouth. If she was
chewing gum, *surely* she would look relaxed to any random
passersby, and they wouldn't notice if tears slipped from
beneath the rims of her shades as she walked to her car.

The *beep* when she hit the unlock button on her key fob
was a siren's call. Soon she would be home and she wouldn't
have to hide her misery. Before she could grab the hot handle,
however, she heard her name being called over the noise of
the street traffic.

"Cami!"

Her shoulders stiffened at the same time her heart sank.

She'd recognize that low, scratchy, Kiefer Sutherland
voice anywhere.

Doc.

She didn't turn around. Mostly because she needed time
to swallow down her tears, but also because she wasn't sure
she was strong enough to see him again. Not yet. Not without
throwing herself at his feet and begging him to forgive her.
To choose her. To *love* her.

And heaven knew the last thing she needed was more
humiliation. Her bosses had already raked her over the
coals for what happened on Wayfarer Island. And, more
importantly, her role in the events.

"You're lucky they don't sue!" Alex Lester, one of the
firm's partners, had yelled at her, his face apoplectic.

"They're not the litigious sort," she'd assured him.
"The firm will be fine."

Lester had huffed and puffed and folded his arms over his chest before finishing with, *"You'd better hope so."* And then he'd dismissed her with an angry wave of his hand, and she'd known, then and there, that her upward trajectory at Leeman and Lester had just hit a granite ceiling.

Of course, her stalled career was the least of her worries. Because Doc was calling her name again. And there was no way to pretend she hadn't heard him.

Dragging in a deep breath, she slowly turned. The instant her eyes locked on him, she felt like someone reached into her chest and ripped out her heart.

He was so damn beautiful. So damn familiar. And so damn dear.

Wearing well-worn jeans, flip-flops, and a T-shirt that lovingly molded itself to his broad chest, he stepped off the curb and headed in her direction. His lion's mane blew in the hot wind. His green eyes were squinted against the glare of the mercilessly setting sun. And his lean-hipped swagger brought him to her in no time.

She wanted the asphalt to open up and swallow her. Especially when he tilted his head and asked, "Are you okay?"

And there it was. The question she'd been dreading.

Of course I'm not okay! she wanted to scream. *I've lost everything. My career. My family. Not to mention, you broke my fucking heart!*

Instead, she placed a hand on her cocked hip. "Sure. Why do you ask?"

"Because your chest is all splotchy." He pointed to her V-neck blouse. "That's not because of…" He trailed off and ran a hand through his wild hair. "That's not because of me, is it?"

When she glanced down, she saw that, yes indeedy, the skin over her chest was red and mottled. Happened anytime she cried. And she'd been crying *a lot* in the last few days. Could hardly *keep* from crying, as a matter of fact.

She hoped her smile looked sarcastic instead of sad when she said, "Thank you for your brilliant portrayal as the self-centered A-hole in the movie of my life. But not everything is about you. Although…" She tapped her lip. "I wouldn't be surprised, going forward, if I *did* break out in a rash anytime we got within five feet of each other."

Mockery. Mockery was her savior. If she could just keep up the sardonic banter then maybe she'd get through this without melting into a blubbering heap at his feet.

"And once again there's that mouth your momma warned you about." He smirked.

"What are you doing here, Dalton?" She tried to sound impatient and was surprised when she actually pulled it off.

"I came to talk to you about what happened."

Her jaw tightened. "Which part specifically?"

"The part where you told your mom about the king t—"

"Stop." She held up a hand. "Just stop right there. I know I fucked up, okay? I *know* I did. And I couldn't be sorrier. I'm sorry those guys from Maine used that information to do what they did. I'm sorry Fin is dead because of that decision. I'm sorry *you* were put in the impossible position of having to shoot him in order to save the rest of us. But believe me. No one is harder on me than me. So please take whatever judgements or recriminations or indictments you have and shove them where the sun doesn't shine."

"That *mouth*, woman." He shook his head.

She didn't say anything in return, just grabbed the door handle in preparation of flight. Before she could get the door open, however, he wrapped a hand around her arm. "Wait, Cami."

His palm was warm. She felt the indents each of his fingers made in her flesh. And a million memories of just how wonderful his touch had been the night of the storm flitted through her over-heated head.

"Please let me go, Dalton." She dropped all pretense of self-possession. "Please don't make this any worse on me than it already is."

"I can't let you go." He shook his head, and her stomach sank.

"Why can't you?"

"Because I have things I have to say to you."

The man was merciless. Absolutely *merciless*.

She'd known he was tough. And stubborn. And definitely persistent. But his mercilessness surprised her.

And, yeah, okay, it pissed her off a little too.

"Hang on." She pulled her arm from his grasp and once again tapped her lip, her natural tendency toward acrimony, especially when she felt cornered, asserting itself. "I'm trying to decide if I don't give a shit or if I don't give a fuck about what you have to say."

He lifted his gaze heavenward. "Put your spurs away for five minutes, will you?"

"No." She shook her head.

"Why not?" His gaze laser-focused on her face. She felt burned by its intensity.

"Because you smell like hidden motives. The kind of hidden motives that are going to make me mad. And like I said, I'm mad enough at myself. I really don't need you piling on."

He sighed like he had the patience of Job, but she was testing it. Then he pulled her car door wide and made a grandiose gesture for her to slide inside. "Get in the car, Camilla."

Two seconds earlier, all she'd wanted was to climb into the driver's seat and speed away. But she'd wanted to do it on her own terms.

"Don't tell me what to do, Dalton." She bristled.

"Lord, help me." He shook his head. "Cami, would you please get in the car?" He lifted his hand and once again gestured toward the car's waiting interior.

That's when she saw his new tattoo. Or…it wasn't a new tattoo. It was the purple ink left behind when a tattoo artist used transfer paper to place their design onto a person's skin.

"What's that?" She pointed to his forearm. The purple outline was of a big, round flower that looked sort of like a rose. It was stamped above his lily tattoo.

"It's a camellia," he said. "From what I've been told, Camilla is an alternative form of camellia in Latin."

She blinked behind her sunglasses. "Wh-why are you thinking of having a camellia tattooed on the inside of your wrist?"

"I'll tell you if you get in the car. I'm melting out here. And we're starting to draw a crowd."

She glanced around and discovered he was right. Two of her associates had stopped to stare in her direction.

"Is everything okay, Cami?" Marcus Cole, a nice man who'd recently gone through a terrible divorce, called out.

'I'm okay, Marc," she assured him, lifting a hand to show that she truly was fine. She hoped the distance between them was enough so Marc didn't notice her fingers were shaking.

And not just her fingers. Her knees and her chin and her heart too.

Why would Doc be thinking of having a camellia tattooed onto his arm?

She wanted to jump to conclusions but didn't dare.

"We're headed across the street for a drink," Arron Rodriguez hollered above the street noise. He'd suffered a bad breakup with his longtime girlfriend, and he and Marc had taken to consoling each other with after work libations. "You want to join us?"

"No thanks!" She shook her head, hoping her smile didn't look as wobbly as it felt. "But I appreciate the invite!"

Only after both men nodded and crossed the street did she turn back to Doc.

"Now," he said patiently, "will you *please* get in the car and turn on the air conditioner?"

She nodded absently and slid into the driver's seat. She didn't realize she'd sat there numbly, her mind completely blank but also going in a million different directions, until Doc knocked on the passenger-side window.

Shaking her head, she hit the unlock button and started the car. Gloria Gaynor's "I Will Survive" blasted from her speakers as Doc slipped smoothly into the passenger seat and closed the door behind him.

She quickly switched off the radio, but not before he'd heard her song choice. He lifted a questioning eyebrow.

"I needed to feel empowered before heading into work today," she said. "Don't judge me."

"Me?" He raised a hand to his chest. "Judge you? Never."

She snorted so hard she nearly swallowed her gum. "Oh, that's rich."

He made a face of regret and he nodded. "Yeah. You're right. I've been judging you from the beginning, haven't I? Which is one of the reasons I came here today. To tell you I'm sorry. Sorry for assuming your moral compass must be skewed because you're a lawyer. Sorry for thinking that just because your father is crooked, that must mean you're crooked too. Because Cami? You're one of the straightest arrows I've ever met, and I respect the hell out of you for that. But most of all I'm sorry for placing the blame for what happened on Wayfarer Island solely at your feet when the truth is, those men were the only ones in the wrong."

Her head was spinning so fast she couldn't think straight. Or maybe her problem was that her heart was racing and sending too much blood to her head. "I—" she started and stopped, her eyes sliding once again to that purple ink stain on the inside of his forearm. "What's the other reason?" she asked desperately. Still afraid to speculate. Still afraid to hope.

"Huh?" His eyebrows drew together.

"You said one of the reasons you came here was to apologize." Why couldn't she breathe when the AC was blasting cold air into the car? "What's the other reason?"

"Oh." His face cleared. "It's to tell you I've fallen in love with you." She gasped as her heart instantly filled with happiness. Then, he kept talking, and that happiness began to fade. "I didn't want to. I fought against it. But, in the end, I couldn't help myself."

His words weren't necessarily an insult. But they sure as shit weren't the declaration of adoration and undying love she'd dreamed of.

"That's a backward compliment if ever I heard one," she said flatly. Her frown deepened when he threw back his head and chuckled.

When he finally sobered, he nodded. "Lord, I love your candor. And in the spirit of being brutally honest, I'll tell you the reason I fought so hard against my feelings for you is that I was scared of them. Scared of letting myself fall in love with you, because if I did, I knew that love might grow so big that it'd swallow me up and I'd lose myself in it."

This speech was certainly better than the one before it. But there was still something…*off*. How long could his love possibly last if it wasn't freely given? If he didn't *want* to feel it?

He saw the misgivings in her expression and sighed.

"People say the past is the past. As if it's gone because it's over. But it's never gone. We carry it with us. It's imprinted in every cell of our bodies. It echoes in the beat of our hearts. I love you, Cami. I love every inch of you. But I'm still in love with Lily too. And I'll never be finished with her."

How was it possible to feel completely elated and completely confused all at the same time? "Who says you have to be finished with her?" she asked.

The hum of the air conditioner was the only sound inside the car for a long moment. And Doc? He just sat there blinking at her.

Then a look of wonder came over his face. "My mother was right about you," he whispered, almost reverently.

She didn't want to, but she let him change the subject. "You told your mother about me?"

He nodded. "I owed her an apology too. Because how could I hold her love for Randall against her, how could I blame her for not cleaving fast to my father's memory, if I was guilty of doing the exact same thing with you?"

Usually Cami was quicker on the uptake, but she was having a tough time following his line of logic. "But I thought you just said you *are* cleaving fast to Lily's memory."

"And that's the other thing I want to talk to you about."

She considered shaking her head like a dog shaking off water. Maybe that would jar her brain around enough for his words to make sense. Instead, she simply admitted, "I'm so confused."

He turned to her fully then. When he took her hand between both of his, she felt the flutter of longing in her chest at the same time his somber expression had dread falling over her like a dark blanket. "You remember that shoebox I ran to get during the storm?"

Sweet heavens, she was suffering conversational whiplash. "Y-yes," she said haltingly.

"I keep one of Lily's silk scarves in there. And sometimes I like to take it out and hold it to my nose, because it still smells like her. At sunset, I talk to her. She was always partial to sunsets. Said they beat sunrises by a country mile." A melancholy look came over his face even as he smiled in memory. "But I think that's because she wasn't much of a morning person. I was scared to talk to her until she'd had her first cup of coffee. That woman had a mean streak that only caffeine could cure."

When he saw the line that'd formed between Cami's eyebrows, he was quick to push ahead. "Anyway, sometimes at sunset I like to go out to the end of the pier and fill her in on what's been happening with me. I buy lilies on her birthday. I keep the locket she wore when we were teenagers in my sock drawer. And I always stop and wish on the first evening star, because it was a tradition she started when we were young."

His grip tightened on Cami's hand and his eyes turned troubled. "I don't want to stop doing those things, Cami. Because if I do, I'll lose her. And I don't *want* to lose her. She was my best friend from the time I was thirteen. And yet…" He trailed off and shook his head. "I want you too. I want your wide smiles and your brilliant mind and your sarcastic tongue that always keeps me on my toes. I want your big laugh and your honest takes on life and your ability to cut through the bullshit. I want *all* of you. But how can I ask that when you won't have all of me? When there will always be a piece of my heart that belongs to her?"

Oh, for fuck's sake. That's *what all this has been about?* she thought with no small amount of frustration.

"Let me see if I have this right," she said slowly. "You've put me through all this hell and heartbreak because you were afraid I would…what? Be jealous of your dead wife? Not want to share you with her?"

He lifted one shoulder and nodded at the same time.

She sighed heavily. "You're a damn fool, Dalton Simmons. I don't know whether I want to kiss you or kill you."

"If your dead set on the latter, mind doing the former first?" He looked so earnest. But there was definitely a wicked sparkle in his eyes. "At the very least you'd make a dying man happy."

She sent him a quelling glance. "Now is not the time for jokes."

He sobered immediately. "You're right. I'm sorry."

"You say you want all of me. But you don't know how you can ask me to give all of myself to you when there will always be a part of you that belongs to Lily, right?" He nodded and had the grace to look adorably miserable. "You can ask because life isn't all or nothing, Dalton. You can ask because *love* isn't all or nothing. Loving me doesn't mean you can't still love her." She frowned. "Quite frankly, I'd find you *and* your love a little suspicious if you *could*. Because what would that say about the depth and breadth of your love?"

"Are you saying what I think you're saying, Cami?" His voice had gone so hoarse she was reminded of truck tires over a bad gravel road.

"Are you asking what I think you're asking, Dalton?"

His eyes looked overly bright when he nodded. "Will you love me, Cami? Will you let me love you?"

She was dizzy from having gone from the depths of despair to the heights of happiness so quickly. But she still managed to answer him. And even though she was a lawyer, renowned for using a lot of words, she found herself uttering only one. "Yes."

A lone tear spilled over his bottom lid. It got stuck in his beard stubble and he didn't lift a hand to wipe it away. He just let it sit there, glistening. For whatever reason, that made it more meaningful.

"Guess I can go ahead and get this thing inked." He lifted his arm with the purple camellia stamped above the lily.

"Guess you can," she told him, her heart so full she thought it a wonder it didn't burst open and spew little heart-shaped confetti all over the car.

"I'm going to kiss you now, Cami."

The way he announced it, like she needed to brace herself, had a giddy laugh burbling out of her.

"Whew. Okay." She stretched her neck from side to side. "I think I'm ready." She made a come-hither motion with her hand and then lifted it palm-out. "No. Wait. Stop. Do you want to do this with my gum or without?" She held the wad of gum between her teeth.

His smile was so wide and radiant she thought she might go blind. And yet she couldn't stop staring. This man, this handsome, brilliant, *good* man had forgiven her. He wanted her. He *loved* her.

It wasn't possible to die from shame and sadness. So she sure as shit hoped that, likewise, it wasn't possible to die from love and happiness or she'd be six feet under in about two seconds.

"Let's try without." He winked, and his gaze turned positively provocative. "We can always add props later."

CHAPTER 36

9:47 PM...

Doc was so exhausted from his third orgasm—*three!*—he could barely summon the strength to roll away from Cami so he could dispose of the condom.

Somehow he managed it. Although, as soon as the deed was done, he flopped back onto the mattress and rubbed a lethargic hand over his sweaty brow. Cami slid a silky leg over his thigh, snuggled her lush breasts against his side, and started leaving soft kisses across his pectoral muscles, stopping briefly to flick his nipples with her tongue.

"Truce," he rasped, cupping the back of her head. "I'm calling a truce."

She chuckled and stacked her fists on his chest so she could rest her chin on them. Her dark eyes sparkled in the city lights shining in through the windows and her cheeks held the lovely blush of recent release.

"Combatants call truces. Not teammates," she teased.

"Okay, how about we call it game, match, and set then?" He pushed a lock of raven-black hair behind her ear. "Because my heart might be willing but my flesh is weak."

She pretended to pout. "Sounds like we need to work on your stamina. A team is only as good as its weakest link."

He smacked her ass and loved the sound of her responding squeal. He loved more the warning in her eyes.

How is she mine? he thought in wonder. *How is this smart, beautiful,* insatiable *woman mine?*

He couldn't fathom it. And yet, she *was* his. All of her. She'd given herself to him completely and freely despite all the baggage that came with him.

It was the damndest thing.

"Okay." She laid her head on his chest, listening to the heart that was hers. "We can call it a time out. But I reserve the right to say when game play resumes."

He chuckled and snuggled her close, his eyes drifting over to the floor-to-ceiling windows and the glitter of the skyscrapers outside. Miami was beautiful at night. Like a city made of stars.

As soon as he had the thought, he was gripped by a fist of dread.

"How are we going to handle this long-distance thing?" he asked quietly, catching the ends of her silky hair and rubbing them between his fingers. "I mean, I'll hire a manager to oversee the ranch, but I'll still need to be there most of the time. I guess I could fly here on the weekends until—"

She sat up, snatching the sheet to cover her breasts.

He *hated* that she did that. Hated that she didn't think her boobs were absolute perfection. Because they were. *Lord*, they were.

"You don't want me to come with you to Montana?" Trepidation was written all over her face.

Pushing into a seated position, he rested his back against

JULIE ANN WALKER

the cushioned headboard. "Of course I do. But I didn't know if *you'd* want to. It's awfully rural there. You might be a hundred miles from the nearest Starbucks. And what about your job?"

"My days working for Leeman and Lester are numbered. After my screwup on Wayfarer Island, they'll find a way to push me out." Her eyebrows pulled together. "Are you saying nobody needs a lawyer who specializes in property disputes in Montana?"

The question was so ludicrous, he couldn't help but laugh. "Are you kidding? That's about *all* there is in Montana. Ranchers fighting each other over water rights. The state and the federal government fighting everyone over questions of eminent domain."

"So then why couldn't I hang my shingle there?" She gave him a look so direct he shivered at the thought of her in front of a jury. "Also, I like to grind my own coffee beans. And just because I've never lived in the country doesn't mean I don't love it there. For heaven's sake, some of the best times I've had recently have been on an island in the actual middle of nowhere."

His breaths were shallow at the thought of coming home to find Cami in jeans and a chambray shirt. "Won't you have to take Montana's bar exam?"

"Pfft." She rolled her eyes. "Piece of cake."

He laughed and shook his head. "Do you *ever* lack in confidence?"

Instead of answering, she posed a question of her own. "Do you *want* me to come live with you in Montana?"

He couldn't believe she had to ask. "It'd be a dream come true. *Literally.*" When she cocked her head in confusion, he told her about his dream. About the burbling baby and the boy with dark hair. About the spaghetti and meatballs and the livestock guardian dog.

Her eyes were bright with unshed tears by the time he finished. Sniffing, she said, "Well, dogs *do* belong in the house being pampered."

He pulled her into his arms then. Partly so she wouldn't see the tears that were gathering in his eyes. But mostly because it'd been at least a minute since he'd touched her and that was far, *far* too long.

She came willingly, snuggling tight against his side. And for a while they were quiet. When she finally spoke, there was hesitation in her voice. "And you're okay with that? The thought of kids?"

"Sweetheart"—he brushed a lock of hair behind her ear—"the thought of making babies with you, of raising babies with you, makes me the happiest man alive." She pushed up from his chest to search his face. There was a line between her eyebrows that he smoothed away with his thumb. "What is it?" he prodded. "I can see you've got something on your mind."

Her voice was a little raspy when she asked, "Before we start making those babies, would you marry me?"

Everything inside him ground to a halt. His heart. The blood through his veins. The breath in his lungs. Did she have any idea how the thought of taking her as his wife filled up the hollow in the center of him until it was a wonder he didn't burst with happiness?

"I would love nothing more than to be your husband, Cami. Would you be okay being my *second* wife?"

The smile that came over her face then was so soft and radiant that it kickstarted his heart. His blood followed suit, racing through him. His breaths came fast and shallow as he waited for her answer.

"Lily has your past, Dalton. I would be happy to have your future. And sometimes, when you're loving me and missing her, maybe she and I can share your present." She placed her hand over his chest. Could she feel the race of his pulse? "You have the biggest heart. Bigger than any I've known. There's plenty of room for me *and* for her in there."

He choked on a rough sob and dragged her in for a kiss he hoped would tell her all the things he didn't have the words for.

Like how amazing she was.

Like how grateful he was she'd come into his life to make him whole again.

Like how he was going to spend the rest of his life making her as happy as she'd made him.

EPILOGUE

Eight months later...

The night of the storm, Doc had lamented not being able to get away from death. And now here he was, back on Wayfarer Island, surrounded by so much burgeoning life.

All that nooky during the hurricane had resulted in Olivia getting pregnant with a baby girl. Her huge belly made it look like she'd swallowed a watermelon as she danced around the beach bonfire to the driving beats of Jimmy Buffett's "Cheeseburger in Paradise." LT watched from a nearby beach chair, his smile low and lazy and content.

Chrissy swayed next to Olivia. Her baby bump was less visible in her long, flowy sundress. Although it became more so when Wolf walked up behind her and placed his hands on her swollen belly so he could smooch the back of her neck. She spun in his arms and laid such a long, lusty kiss on his mouth that Doc had to clear his throat and look away.

Maddy cradled her and Bran's six-week-old son in her arms while Bran dug in a bag for a new diaper because young Mister Pallidino had filled the one he was wearing. And Alex was sitting on Mason's lap, cooking yet *another* marshmallow over the fire.

When she caught Doc staring at her, she scowled. "Wipe that look of judgement off your face right this minute. You have no idea what it's like to eat for two."

As if to prove her point, she flattened her graphic T-shirt across her bulging belly. The shirt read: Don't Make Me Repeat Myself ~ History.

"You ate for two when you were just one," he reminded her with a chuckle.

She flipped him the bird and then, when her marshmallow caught on fire, she howled, "Now look what you made me do! Stop distracting me!" She hastily blew out the burning confection. And then she turned to her husband, "Quick! Go get Meat before he eats any more waterweeds!"

Mason carefully transferred Alex from his lap to the chair before ambling off down the beach to go save his fat, wrinkly bulldog from himself. And Doc's eyes fell on Lil' Bastard who, like always, was pecking in the sand next to the canine.

"How's he taking to city life?" he asked Alex, pulling his toothpick from his mouth to gesture toward the rooster who'd moved with Meat, Mason, and Alex up to Boston.

She grinned and pushed her glasses higher on the bridge of her freckled nose. "He's terrorizing the neighborhood. He has the stray cats on the run. He wakes everyone up at dawn with his cock-a-doodle-doos. And he's taken to sitting on the front fence as the school kids are walking home so he can squawk and flap his wings at them. I swear he cackles in delight when they run screaming."

"So, what you're saying is he's still the same ol' pain in

the ass he ever was."

"Wouldn't have him any other way." She shoved the s'mores she'd built into her mouth, and then licked melted chocolate off her fingers.

Leaning back in his chair, Doc closed his eyes and thought of all the changes eight months had wrought. Besides all the tiny humans being cooked up, Bran had opened his Italian restaurant in Maddy's hometown of Houston. And by all accounts it was a smashing success.

Wolf and Chrissy were in the process of building six additional dive shops throughout the Keys, turning Chrissy's little business into a thriving chain. And three of Wolf's nephews had come down from Oklahoma to work in the shops over the summer.

Alex had gotten an adjunct professorship at Boston college, teaching history to dewy-eyed freshmen while Mason spent his afternoons at the Red Sox games. Since childhood, Mason had dreamed of becoming a season ticket holder, and his portion of the treasure had finally allowed him to make that dream a reality.

Romeo and Mia had made the move to L.A. Romeo's charity work was up and running and he gave the Deep Six group weekly email updates on the kids who frequented his afterschool programs.

And LT and Olivia were continuing on with the salvage business, splitting their time between Wayfarer Island and Key West as they took odd jobs hauling up sunken boats, abandoned drilling equipment, and all the random whatnot that found its way to the bottom of the ocean.

They'd heard tales of another sunken treasure and were beginning to dip their toes into the research. LT had asked the rest of the crew if they were interested in joining in this newest quest. But, to a man, they'd all declined, having had their fill of treasure hunting.

Funny, but a year ago, they'd all been as poor as church mice and beginning to lose faith in ever finding the *Santa Cristina*'s riches. And now look at them. Family men with wives and babies and businesses and days that made the time they'd spent as Navy SEALs seem like a lifetime ago.

Threading his hands behind his head, Doc breathed in the warm, moist air that smelled of sand and sun and sea life. And even though a part of him missed the endless hours of balmy weather and the gentle sound of the ocean *shushing* against the sand, he was already anxious to get back home to Montana.

The manager he'd hired to oversee the day-to-day operations at the ranch was top notch, but they were still two ranch hands short, and it wouldn't be long before fall calving season started. Also, the little medical building Doc had rented in town was undergoing renovations, and he didn't trust his general contractor to do any work without Doc breathing down his neck. But he was mostly in a hurry to get back out West because his wife was seven weeks from her due date, and he wasn't exactly comfortable with her being three thousand miles away from her OBGYN.

"Don't be silly," she'd scolded when he'd mentioned that maybe they shouldn't make the trip to Wayfarer. *"I want to see everyone. And as high as I'm carrying, there's no way I'll be going into labor anytime soon."*

"Dalton Simmons!" His wife's strident voice pulled him from his ruminations. "Get your lazy bones out of that chair and come help me!"

He opened his eyes to see her standing in the sand halfway between the bonfire and the beach house. She wore a sleeveless top that emphasized the subtle tan on her smooth shoulders and a pair of linen gaucho pants that emphasized the round wonder of her pregnant belly.

Every time he saw her, his breath caught.

She'd always been a beautiful woman but approaching motherhood had turned her into something bordering on ethereal. Of course, when she broke out her sassy pants stance, complete with cocked hip and tilted head, he thought she looked less ethereal and more witchy. Especially with her long, black hair loose and blowing in the breeze.

"You called, my sweet, loving wife?" he shot back and then chuckled when the look she sent him warned of dire consequences should he choose to keep going with the sarcasm.

"If I were you, *cabron*, I'd be hopping to," Romeo said from the chair next to him. Romeo's teeth blazed white against his black goatee when he sent Doc a shit-eating grin.

"Oh, don't sit there smiling like your wife doesn't boss you around too. We're both whipped and you know it."

Romeo shrugged and took a slow pull on the longneck bottle in his hand. "If this is what it is to be whipped, then I don't know how I ever survived being *un*whipped."

"That's a good answer, lover." Mia smirked from his other side. "The *right* answer."

Doc watched the couple canoodle for a couple of seconds before rolling his eyes. "Keep it up and you two will be in the same boat with the rest of us soon enough."

Mia shook her head. "Oh, no. We've got plenty of kids to keep us busy and happy."

Doc's heart warmed at the sight of Mia's genuine happiness. She was blooming under the radiance of Romeo's love and the life Romeo was building with her.

"You like working with the at-risk youth, don't you?" he asked her.

Her smile was shy and sweet, just like the woman herself. "More than I ever thought I would."

"Dalton!" Cami called again, sounding as if her patience was fraying.

JULIE ANN WALKER

Doc made a face. "And that's my cue." He pushed up from the chair, tossed his toothpick into the bonfire, and trotted over to his wife. Her dark eyes narrowed when he said, "Well I'm here, sweetheart. What are your other two wishes?"

"For *you* to have to carry around a twenty-pound bowling ball in your belly for starters," she sniffed. "And then for you to have that twenty-pound bowling ball spend the day kicking you in the ribs."

"Come here." He positioned himself directly behind her so he could snake his arms around her waist, grab the underside of her belly, and lift it up. Just slightly, just enough to take the pressure off her bladder and relieve her of the weight.

"Oh, that's heaven," she sighed, letting her head fall back against his chest. But she didn't rest for long. "I've made frozen virgin daiquiris for the pregnant ladies, and John and Dana have made salty dogs for everyone else. Would you go inside and help carry everything out?"

"Your wish is my command." He kissed her temple before quickly turning for the beach house. But he stopped at the top of the porch steps so he could watch her waddle toward the bonfire.

She was just so darned *adorable*. And yet, he'd learned his lesson early on that he could only refer to her pregnant walk as a "waddle" inside the confines of his own brain. If he said it out loud, he was quickly reminded what it was like to be the victim of the sharp edge of her tongue.

Pregnancy hadn't lessoned Cami's ability to wield a well-placed jab. If anything, her fecund state had honed it.

He realized he was smiling like an idiot when he walked into the kitchen a minute later and John turned to him and said, "Married life and approachin' fatherhood suits you, boy. You ain't stopped smilin' since y'all landed this mornin'."

346

"You're one to talk." He glanced meaningfully between Uncle John and Dana.

The two of them had been splitting their time between Key West and D.C., and recently they'd announced they were taking a trip to Alaska.

Doc and the others had speculated amongst themselves whether the vacation was going to double as a honeymoon since neither John nor Dana had mentioned anything about tying the knot. But when Chrissy had brought up the subject with Dana, all Dana had said was, *"We're together because of volition, not vows."* And then she had taken John's hand and John's chest had puffed out with pride.

Everyone had left it at that.

"I'm assuming this is what I'm charged with?" Doc pointed to the ice chest packed with frosty-looking daiquiris.

"Mmm." Uncle John nodded, reaching down to scratch the humungous ears of the most ridiculous dog Doc had ever seen. Dana's German shepherd/bloodhound mix had become the couple's constant third wheel. They never went anywhere without Rocko. "Dana and I will bring out the rest," John added.

Five minutes later, the group stood in a circle around the beach bonfire. The sun was a half disk as it sank into the sea to the west. The evening breeze was warm and gentle. And the smell of burning driftwood was thick in the air.

"Well, boys." LT nodded. "We did it."

"Hear, hear." Bran lifted his drink.

They *had* done it. It hadn't been easy. It hadn't been quick. But they'd not only found the *Santa Cristina* and her storied treasure, they'd also disbursed of it in a way they could all be proud of.

In the end, they'd agreed to auction off seventy-five percent of the treasure to dealers and collectors of antiquities. The rest of the collection they'd donated to various museums and institutions of learning because none of them had ever been greedy and all of them believed the historical significance of the find should be shared with the world. And even though Uncle John had fought against it, saying he didn't need their damn money because he had plenty of his own, they'd each gifted him with a share of loot.

After all he'd done to help them, it'd seemed only fair.

And now, each of them had begun the next chapter of their lives.

A chapter they had thanks to one man. The man who, with his dying words, had assured each of them had an opportunity to build a life outside the dangerous confines of the United States Navy SEALs.

"Ladies and gentlemen"—LT hoisted his glad high— "would y'all raise your glasses?"

Virgin daiquiris and salty dogs were lifted in the air. A lump formed in Doc's throat as he glanced around the gathered group and saw the curly cue lettering reading: For RL that was inked into the forearms of the men who'd become more than his partners or his friends, they'd become his brothers.

"Here's to you, Rusty," LT's voice was rough with emotion. "You were a bastard and a half, but we were able to do all this, *have* all this, thanks to you."

"To Rusty," Doc and the others said in unison before tossing back their drinks.

After he had nothing left in his glass but the salt on the rim, Doc felt Cami slip an arm around his waist. The firelight danced in her eyes and her expression was so full of love and concern that he wasn't surprised to feel his own eyes fill with tears.

"You okay?" she asked quietly.

He looked from the hot pink camellia tattooed on the inside of his wrist back to the woman for whom he'd gotten the ink. And in the cool, quiet isolation of Wayfarer Island, he gave her the only truth he knew to be absolute. "I think the Eagles said it best, sweetheart."

She narrowed her eyes. "You aren't going to start singing 'Witchy Woman' again, are you?"

"Nope." He shook his head. "I was thinking of a different song this time." When she cocked her head, he finished with, "I've got a peaceful, easy feeling."

The End

Out August 29th, 2023

BACK
IN
Black

BLACK KNIGHTS INC: RELOADED
BOOK 1

JULIE ANN WALKER

Chapter 1

"Some nights are so dark the dawn seems impossible."
The words Grace Beacham's father spoke to her that awful evening when her husband filed for divorce came back to her now as she used the outdoor spigot to wash the blood from her hands. Hands so shaky she could barely perform the task. Hands so pale the brightness shining from her lit cell phone screen made the skin appear transparent. She could see her veins snaking beneath her flesh like holding a leaf up to the sunlight.

Her father had been talking about the depths of her grief and the weight of her failure. But now she felt the simple truth of his words.

If she believed that text message, this moonless night may well be her last.

Rubbing her wet hands on her thighs, she grabbed her phone off the ground and made herself look at the screen again. Who would think six little words could have terror weighing her down until her body felt like a bag of wet concrete.

Orpheus is hunting you. Run. Hide.
"Who's out there?"

When the porch light snapped on, Grace thumbed off her phone and crouched next to the bushes. Her heart roared in her ears until it drowned out the rhythmic drone of the crickets and katydids.

Damnit!

She'd thought no one was home. The house had been dark. There'd been no cars in the gravel drive. No bark of a dog on the lookout for trespassers.

"I heard the water running!" the raspy voice called again. "I know you're there. Show yourself!"

This command was followed by a sound Grace would recognize anywhere. For as long as she could remember, her father had carried a Glock 22. The weapon made a very specific metallic *shnick* when a round was chambered.

Although, whoever wielded this weapon didn't add her father's characteristic jiggle at the end. *"To check the balance,"* he'd said when Grace asked him about the move.

"FBI! Don't shoot!" She thrust her hands in the air at the same time she stood to her full height. When the yellow porch light beamed into her eyes, she squinted and scolded herself for having stopped.

It'd take a full minute for her eyesight to adjust to the darkness after this. And on a night like tonight, a minute could be the difference between life and death.

A bent and grizzled old man wearing a ratty terry cloth robe stepped through the open front door. The few tufts of snow-white hair atop his liver-spotted head waved gently in the hot breeze.

Late August in the upper Midwest was a capricious creature. Sometimes it held onto summer with tenacious fingers. Other times it slipped quickly and quietly into fall.

This August was shaping up to be one of the hottest on record.

As if on cue, a bead of sweat slid down Grace's temple.

The warm drop reminded her of the blood she'd washed into the man's flowerbed. How hot it'd been when she first pulled the knife from Stewart's back. And then how quickly it'd turned cool and dried into a sticky crust that had stained her cuticles and coated the undersides of her fingernails. The iron-rich smell of it had made her retch anytime she'd breathed too deeply.

Which was why she'd given in to the urge to use the outdoor spigot to wash it away.

"FBI, eh?" The old coot stepped farther onto the porch. His sidearm was still aimed at Grace's chest and shaking slightly, as if the weight of the weapon was more than his withered muscles could manage. "Got some ID to prove that, missy?"

"If you'll allow me to reach into—"

"Easy there." He waved his pistol in a fast circle when Grace lowered her arms. "One hand'll do 'er. Keep that other one sky-high if ya know what's good for ya."

Grace obliged. Partly because she didn't want to take a round center-mass. But mostly because the act of swinging the gun around caused the belt tied around the man's waist to loosen. She was beginning to fear he was naked beneath that threadbare robe.

Wouldn't that be the cherry on top of this craptastic sundae? she thought a little hysterically. *Here it is, possibly my final night on earth, and one of my last visions will be of ancient, wrinkly wedding tackle.*

"You're the boss," she was quick to reassure him, keeping her right arm in the air and using her left to slowly pull her FBI credentials from the inside breast pocket of her jacket.

Unfortunately, he didn't lower his weapon even after she flashed her badge. "That real?" he asked instead.

Grace blinked. "Why would a woman in a pantsuit be

standing in your yard in the middle of the night with a fake FBI badge?"

"You tell me. What were you doin' with my outdoor faucet, eh?"

"Getting a drink," she lied. "It's a hot night."

"But what's an FBI agent doin' all the way out here?"

Running for her life, Grace thought, feeling the effects of the panic and desperation that'd been her constant companions since she'd heard Stewart shout her name from the adjoining room. The thought of spending a few minutes rocking herself in a corner and indulging in a good old-fashioned pity party complete with teeth gnashing and hair pulling sounded really, *really* tempting.

Unfortunately, she didn't have the time.

"My team and I are staying at the Moonlight Memories Motel down the road. We had a suspect escape and head in this direction. I gave chase on foot but lost his trail in the woods. When I stumbled on your house, I couldn't pass up the chance to stop for water."

Lies. All lies.

They came to her easily, but that didn't mean they didn't sit on her tongue like poison pills. Having grown up a Beacham, she'd been taught being a straight shooter—both literally and figuratively—was the only thing that mattered. Even when the chips were down. Even when her back was against the wall.

"A suspect, eh?" The man lifted an eyebrow so bushy Grace imagined some of the hair from his head must've migrated down his face. "He the dangerous sort?"

"You should go back inside and lock the door behind you," she answered evasively. "Better safe than sorry, you know?"

The well-timed *ee-oo-ee* of a siren sounded in the distance. Usually Grace took comfort in the familiar hi-lo clammer. It meant help was on the way.

Not this time. This time, and despite the stickiness of the night, she had to suppress a shiver of dread.

"Those will be my colleagues." She was glad to be able to give the codger at least one truth.

Of course it was only a *half* truth. Because those sirens weren't crying out for some mysterious missing man. They were crying out for her.

She was the suspect.

"Alrighty." He nodded. To Grace's relief, he lowered his sidearm and took a step back inside the door. "Happy hunting to ya, Miss FBI Agent. Hope ya catch the guy."

"Thanks." She offered him what she hoped passed for a smile and then didn't wait to see if he did as she instructed and locked the door behind him. Instead, she turned and sprinted for the cover of the woods.

The rubber lug soles of her sensible duty shoes seemed to find every twig and snap it in two. Spindly limbs made clattering noises as she brushed by because her night-blind eyes made it impossible to avoid them. Her labored breathing sounded as loud as thunder as she bolted…where?

Where was she going?

She had no idea.

Usually, when she was scared or in trouble, she ran home. Between her father, who was a sheriff, her two older brothers, who were both cops, and her kid sister, who was busy climbing the ranks of the DEA, *one* of them would help her find a solution to her problem.

But she couldn't leave a trail back to Buncombe County. She didn't dare drag her family into this.

Whatever *this* was.

So that left…

She skidded to a halt beside a fallen tree, pressing a hand to the stitch in her side as she tried to catch her breath and think. *Think.* If she had any hope of making it through the night she needed her wits about her.

Unfortunately, there were so many thoughts swirling around inside her head, latching onto any one of them was impossible

Breathe, Grace, she coached herself and stared hard at a patch of moss on a nearby tree that was a darker shadow in a world of dark shadows. She focused on the air moving in and out of her lungs. In and out until her heartbeat slowed and the rush of blood through her veins no longer made her deaf to the world around her.

Something moved in the undergrowth to her left. Somewhere off in the distance an owl hooted. And to her right? The snap of a twig broken by a footfall.

Tactical breathing flew out the window as instinct had her flattening herself beside the log. The rich smell of fertile soil and decaying plant matter tunneled up her nose. A stick stabbed into her cheek as she pressed it into the ground. And she bit her lip to keep from crying out when another footfall landed on crunchy leaves.

Orpheus!

Her palms were so clammy she could barely grasp the butt of her service weapon as she slowly, ever so slowly, slipped her hand beneath her body to pull the semiauto from its leather holster.

How? *oHow*

How could Russia's most notorious assassin, a man whose very existence was a hotly debated subject within government agencies the world over, have learned what she and her partner were up to? More importantly, if he *had* learned what she and her partner were up to—and the blood she'd washed off her hands would suggest he *had*—how could she possibly survive him when so many before her had not?

Run. Hide, the text had read. But run to whom? Hide where?

The forest less than a mile from the motel wasn't exactly a world away from the scene of the crime. And this fallen log wasn't exactly a safe house.

She needed a place off the grid. She needed someone who could help her disappear into darkness so deep that not even the world's brightest spotlight could find her. She needed—

The crackle of another breaking sprig had Grace squeezing her eyes shut. Her thundering heart felt like it would explode. Muscles filled with adrenaline and twitching from inaction prompted her to leap up and run. Just flee into the night in heedless flight.

Before her lizard brain could take over and push her into foolhardy action, however, she heard a flurry of movement followed by the *clomp-clomp* of hoofbeats as something four-legged dashed off to the north. Straining her eyes against the darkness, she caught a brief flash of white through the trunks of the trees.

Her breath sawed out of her. She'd been hearing the movements of a whitetail deer all along.

"You won't last ten more minutes if you keep on like this," she scolded herself.

When she pushed into a seated position, dampness seeped into the backside of her slacks. She hardly noticed. A wet ass was the least of her worries.

Before she could second-guess herself or talk herself out of it, she re-holster her Glock 19M and pulled her cell phone from her hip pocket.

She knew the number by heart. She'd opened up her contacts and stared at it hundreds of times, remembering how his hazel eyes had held such sympathy when he'd plugged it into her phone. How his beautifully stern mouth had softened with compassion when he'd said, *"If you ever need anything, even if it's just a shoulder to cry on, please call."*

It'd been years, but the sting of his pity still felt fresh.

Then and now, she hated that all he'd seen when he looked at her was a charity case. A spurned divorcee. A fragile woman who'd been rendered meek and mute when she'd come face-to-face with her ultimate failure in the middle of the Waldorf Astoria Hotel's ballroom.

She'd promised herself she would never call him.

She'd promised herself she would never need to.

And she'd hoped that one day, if they ever bumped into each other out in the real world, he'd see her for who she truly was. A strong woman. An independent woman. A woman capable of facing all comers.

And yet…here she was reaching out in desperation to the mysterious man who'd haunted her dreams. The mysterious man who'd entered her life in an instant, seemingly from out of nowhere, and then disappeared just as quickly.

Hunter Jackson.

His name was enough to make her mouth go dry.

Chapter 2

For those who knew how to listen to their senses—senses passed down through eons of ancestral memory—it was easy to detect an approaching threat.

Hunter Jackson knew how to listen.

His first warning that someone snuck up behind him were the fine hairs lifting on the back of his neck. His second warning was the subtle, nearly imperceptible shifting of the air behind him.

When a hand landed on his shoulder, he instinctively ducked and spun. His arm flew out in a semi-arc as he used his momentum to aim the hard edge of his hand at his assailant's ribs. His attacker blocked his blow at the last second by chopping at his wrist.

Pain exploded in the joint. Hunter barely gave it a thought as his muscles coiled to take a second shot.

Of course, as soon as he saw it was only Samuel Harwood, he straightened from his fighting stance. The adrenaline coursing through his bloodstream disappeared as easily as it'd arrived. And the melodic cry of Greta Van Fleet's lead singer became nothing but a tinny-sounding buzz in his hand when he pulled out his earbuds.

"What the hell, Sam?" He pocketed the small devices so he could rub at his bruised wrist. "You know better than to sneak up on a man programmed for extreme violence. I can't just shut that shit off."

Sam rolled his eyes. "Bruh, there's no one here but me, you, and Eliza. Who did you think would be coming at you sideways given this place"—Sam gestured around the cavernous warehouse that used to be a menthol cigarette factory and now fronted as a custom chopper shop—"is Fort friggin' Knox. No one gets in here without setting off a million and one alarms." He flexed the fingers on the hand he'd used to block Hunter's strike.

Hunter felt a moment's satisfaction about Sam's aching fingers since his wrist was barking like a junkyard dog.

"The effects of our training aren't just psychological, but physiological. Sometimes muscle memory takes over," he explained with a careless shrug.

Sam shook his head. "You're going to make a therapist very wealthy someday."

"You're one to talk."

Sighing, Sam admitted, "True. But the difference between you and me is that my way of coping with trauma is to employ a little gallows humor. Totally healthy. Your way is to go full-on hermit for days at a time. Ted Kaczynski ring a bell? Should I check your room for pipe bombs and triggering devices?"

Hunter hated how clearly Sam saw him. Not about being Unabomber 2.0, but about having to squirrel himself away in order to keep himself together.

Blame it on his youth. When things had gotten too chaotic, his only means of self-preservation had been to hide away in the abandoned cabin perched on the edge of town. There'd been no electricity. No running water. And the hole in the roof had let the rain and snow drift in. Even still, he'd felt better there, tucked away from everything and everyone, than he had anywhere else.

Of course, he said none of that aloud. Aloud he said, "Fuck you."

"Not even on your birthday," Sam deadpanned.

The thing about men neck-deep in covert ops, men whose job titles meant they flirted with danger on the daily, was that they tended to cut the tension by gleefully feeding each other heaping helpings of shit.

Hunter wasn't as good at it as some of the others on his team. His serious nature meant he wasn't as quick on the draw when it came to comebacks and cutdowns. But he liked to think he could hold his own.

"Because you see," Sam continued, shooting him a pitying glance, "I wouldn't know what to do with your teeny, tiny Tic Tac testies. I mean, how *do* you manage to keep the ladies coming back for more? Do you always do it in the dark so they can't see what they're dealing with?"

Hunter shook his head. "See, that would be funny except you know it's not true. You've seen them. That time in Karachi, remember?"

Sam shuddered. "Don't remind me. I don't know which was worse. The fact that we had a deathstalker scorpion living under our bathroom sink? Or the fact that when you found him, you ran out of there buck naked and screaming like a girl? I still have nightmares."

"About the scorpion?"

"About your candy stick and giggleberries bouncing around six inches from my face."

"I understand." Hunter nodded solemnly. "It must've been shocking to find out for the first time how sorrowful your own situation really was. I mean, there's that old saying about comparison being the thief of joy, right?" He clapped a hand on Sam's shoulder. "I hate that I burst your bubble of self-delusion. But if you're really worried about any of your perceived inadequacies, I've heard there's some surgical options. A silicone implant. Maybe a fat transfer. Or you could even—"

"Well, look at you," Sam cut him off, crossing his arms and cocking his head, "lowering yourself to aspersions about the size of my willy. What gives? When it comes to being a weapons-grade dingus, you usually leave that to me or Fisher."

Hunter snorted. Sam had a rare gift for words. It was probably why he liked Coen Brother's movies so much. They were filled with snappy, fast-fire dialogue.

"Blame it on us being left behind." Hunter took a deep breath of air perfumed with the competing, and yet somehow complementary, scents of too-strong coffee and grease guns. "I hate it. Makes my skin feel too tight for my body." To emphasize his point, he hitched his shoulder blades together.

Sam nodded. "You and me both, brother. But I'm trying to focus on the bright side. We may have to hold down the fort, but that's a thousand times better than playing babysitter to some politician's spoiled spawn."

Black Knights Inc. was the brainchild of the last administration. And even though the players had changed right along with the leadership, the concept was still the same.

Some jobs were too clandestine or too pressing to leave to the usual suspects. Despite the vast majority of people working for the CIA, FBI, and NSA being very good at their jobs, their hands were often tied by bureaucratic red tape. Which meant threats against the U.S. sometimes slipped through the cracks as solutions and actions were debated by committee. Throw in posse comitatus and the international resistance to certain types of government-backed exercises, and the bad guys were allowed to escape scot-free more often than anyone would like to admit.

This frustration had prompted the former president to form his own *fast action response team*, for lack of a better phrase. He'd scoured military branches and government agencies for the best of the best when it came to spycraft and those gifted in reconnaissance, unconventional warfare tactics, and the ability to counter terrorism. Then he'd found a home for these highly trained individuals in the heart of Chicago.

Behind the façade of a custom motorcycle shop worked the most elite, most covert group of spec-ops warriors the world had ever seen.

Warriors who didn't have to run their mission parameters up the chain of command. Warriors who could fly into action at a moment's notice and operate in complete secrecy without their actions being traced back to anyone inside the federal government. Warriors who sometimes got assigned bodyguarding jobs as a favor to the woman sitting behind the desk at 1600 Pennsylvania Avenue.

Three days earlier, the Black Knights had received a request to ensure the secretary of defense's daughter didn't get kidnapped or, worse, killed on her trip to Venezuela. But the job had only called for four of the six current BKI operators since there were only four extra seats on the debutante's private plane.

Hunter and Sam had drawn the short straws.

Or the long straws if one was to side with Sam.

"Oh, I don't know." Hunter shook his head. "Even a babysitting gig is better than sitting around here twiddling my dick. I'm so bored I could eat a tire iron."

Inaction made him twitchy.

Probably because when his gray matter wasn't occupied with how best to breach a position or blow up a bridge or rescue a hostage, his thoughts inevitably turned toward his future.

Or, more specifically, his *lack* thereof.

In the three and a half years since he'd come to work for BKI, he'd been watching the original crew, all the hardened operators who'd answered to the previous president and who'd left their mark behind on the world of international intrigue. But it wasn't just them he'd had an eye on. He'd been clocking their families too.

And *no*. Not in a skeevy way. More like in a shocked, amazed, *awestruck* way.

To a man, the OG Black Knights had moved on with their lives. They'd gotten married and fathered children. They'd proved that even for guys like them, guys like *Hunter*, there was something to look forward to after service.

Except...there wasn't for Hunter, was there? Not only did he not have the first clue how to build a family since he'd never been part of one, but he also lacked the basic means to begin even if he *had* known where to start.

The thought of never marrying, never becoming a dad, hadn't bothered him before. Mostly because he'd assumed it would be a miracle if he didn't end up running into a bullet with his name on it. But also because he'd had no clue what he was missing.

Then the men who'd come before him had had the unwitting audacity to show him everything he'd never thought was possible. Show him that operators who had witnessed so much brutality and bloodshed could still have the capacity to embrace domesticity. Show him just how sweet the flip side could be.

Now he was left wanting. *Wishing.*

Which pissed him off.

"Well, you're better off twiddling your dick than messing with *that*." Sam hitched his chin toward the motorcycle frame secured to the bike lift. "What the hell are you doing anyway?"

"I'm sanding off the powder coat on the engine mount so I can install the V Twin and the transmission," Hunter told him, happy to have his somber thoughts interrupted.

One of Sam's eyebrows arched so high it was nearly lost in his hairline. "Did Becky say you could do that?"

Becky Knight, née Reichert, was the wife of the former head of the Black Knights. She was also the wunderkind mechanic and motorcycle designer who made it possible for them to keep their covers intact.

Her creations were the faces Black Knights Inc. showed the world. Her bikes were more than custom choppers, they were works of rolling, roaring art, and they were sought after by collectors from Texas to Taiwan. The ultra-wealthy stood in line to drop a quarter mil on something that had only two wheels, and professional athletes couldn't seem to pass up the flash and fury of a hand-designed and hand-built Harley.

Which was all to say, Becky was *super* picky about who she let touch her babies.

"She had no problem letting me help with the last install." Hunter shrugged, figuring three and a half years of part-time apprenticeship *surely* meant he was capable of mounting an engine. "I thought it'd be a nice surprise for her when she came into the shop in the morning. You know, one less thing."

Not to mention, he'd needed a distraction from the dream that'd had him waking up covered in sweat and aching with need.

For shit's sake, it's been three years! When are you going to forget her? It was four measly days and one little kiss.

Except, it *hadn't* been one little kiss, had it?

It was cliché, but he would swear the instant his lips

touched hers, a piece of himself he hadn't known was missing had suddenly locked into place. Just *click*.

He'd felt as if he'd...*come home*.

Which was ridiculous since he didn't *have* a home. Had *never* had one.

The dozens of crappy apartments his alcoholic DNA suppliers had moved into and then been promptly kicked out of when they hadn't been able to make rent certainly hadn't counted—BTW, he'd never thought of Bert and Susan Hunter as his *parents*. That title was reserved for people who actually *cared* about their offspring.

And the twenty different foster families he'd been shuffled through those times when CPS intervened? None of those could carry the mantle of *home* either. At best they'd been temporary shelters where he'd been able to get in out of the rain. At worst they'd been prisons manned by unpleasant or downright cruel adults whose sole incentive was to cash the government checks that came their way with each kid they took in.

So what the hell was the matter with him? *Why* did he continue to dream of Grace Beacham two… three times a week? Why, after all this time, did he continue to hold out hope she'd call him?

"Be sure to wake me up before you come downstairs in the morning," Sam said, and Hunter determinedly pushed all thoughts of Grace aside.

"Why?" He frowned.

"Because I want to have time to pop some popcorn before the show."

"What show?"

"The one where Becky rips you two or three new assholes."

Hunter and Sam had grown up less than a hundred miles apart. But you'd never know it to hear them talk. Hunter had the quintessential Michigander accent, his vowels flat and his consonants staccato. But Sam? Sam's accent was pure Chicago Southsider. Especially when he got excited.

Thoughts of Becky laying into Hunter obviously excited Sam, because instead of *two or three* the words came out sounding like *two or tree*.

"Pfft." Hunter waved him off and then pointed to the chromed-out engine sitting on a nearby workbench. It sparkled like a freshly cut diamond in the single shop light he'd switched on after coming downstairs.

He'd never been much of a motorcycle guy before coming to work for BKI. Now he couldn't get enough of the machines. When he wasn't out on assignment, he could be found in the shop with a grinder or paint sprayer in hand.

"Help me lift this thing over the bike's frame rails so I don't scuff up the paint," he told Sam.

"Oh, no." Sam backed away, shaking his head. "My asshole is fine the way it is, thank you very much. And I'd prefer to keep it down to just the one."

Hunter rolled his eyes. "Becky is a hair over five feet and barely weighs a buck-ten. Don't tell me Sam the Superspy is afraid of her."

"What she lacks in physical presence she makes up for with a razor-sharp tongue that she doesn't hesitate to use. Besides, getting on her bad side is the shortest route to getting on Boss's bad side. And I don't know about you, but I've gone three and a half years without seeing that guy get angry. I'd like to keep it that way."

Boss, AKA Frank Knight, was the former Navy SEAL, ex-BKI head honcho, and current CEO of the civilian side of their operation. He was part mentor, part malevolent landlord, and *all* dad all the time to his two little girls. But he had a habit of spinning a fixed-blade KA-BAR knife atop his desk when he was deep in thought that made Hunter think

Sam was right and that there was a scary side to Boss they didn't want to meet.

"Fine." He marched over to the workbench. "I'll do it myself."

"It's your funeral," Sam warned.

Before Hunter could wrap his arms around the heavy engine and hoist it against his chest, his phone buzzed in his back pocket.

"It's two o'clock in the morning," Sam observed with a smirk after checking the time on his watch. "So that's one thing and one thing only. Booty call."

Hunter wasn't what anyone would call a monk. Recently, however, he'd been whittling down the list of lovely ladies who occasionally phoned up to ask if he wanted company.

When he'd been in his twenties, having no strings attached had been ideal. But he'd just celebrated his thirty-fifth birthday. Meaningless sex with women who were simply passing through, or who couldn't be bothered to ask him more than his name, had lost its appeal. The hit-it-and-quit-it of it all had grown tedious and dull.

He wanted more. He wanted…

What?

What was he looking for?

If he searched for the answer, he knew he'd find it. And he knew he wouldn't like it. So instead, he pulled his cell from his back pocket and told himself he would say yes to whichever woman was calling to invite him over. Told himself that the antidote to his boredom, and the best way to get over all his uncomfortable musing about what was missing in his life, was to get *under* a beautiful woman who wasn't asking him for anything more than a night of pleasure.

Except…he didn't recognize the number on his screen.

"Area code 757." He frowned at Sam. "That's somewhere in Virginia, right?"

Sam nodded. "Who do you know from Virginia?"

"Not a damn soul."

"Wrong number then?" Sam asked.

"Probably so." Hunter went to hit the button on the side of his phone to decline the call. At the last second, he hesitated. He didn't believe in the woo-woo black magic of premonition or precognition, but something told him he should answer.

Something told him it was important.

Thumbing on the phone, he held the device to his ear. "Hello?"

"Hunter?"

He nearly shit his own heart. He would never forget the sound of her sultry voice that hinted at her childhood in the South.

"Grace?" That one syllable came out strangled-sounding.

"I'm in trouble, Hunter. I need your help."

MORE BOOKS BY
JULIE ANN WALKER

In Moonlight and Memories:
In Moonlight and Memories: Volume One
In Moonlight and Memories: Volume Two
In Moonlight and Memories: Volume Three

Black Knights Inc.:
Hell on Wheels
In Rides Trouble
Rev It Up
Thrill Ride
Born Wild
Hell for Leather
Full Throttle
Too Hard to Handle
Wild Ride
Fuel for Fire
Hot Pursuit
Built to Last

The Deep Six:
Hot as Hell
Hell or High Water
Devil and the Deep
Ride the Tide
Deeper than the Ocean
Shot Across the Bow

ABOUT THE AUTHOR

A New York Times and USA Today bestselling author, Julie loves to travel the world looking for views to compete with her deadlines. And if those views happen to come with a blue sky and sunshine? All the better! When she's not writing, Julie enjoys camping, hiking, cycling, fishing, cooking, petting every dog that walks by her, and…reading, of course!

Be sure to sign up for Julie's occasional newsletter at:

www.julieannwalker.com

To learn more about Julie, visit her website or follow her all over social media:

Facebook: www.facebook.com/julieannwalkerauthor

Instagram: @julieannwalker_author

TikTok: @julieannwalker_author

Twitter: @JAWalker_author

ACKNOWLEDGMENTS

Is it weird for a writer to acknowledge her dog? Well, I don't care, because I'm gonna. Thank you Conan (aka Conan Bug, Snuggle Bug, Buggy) for being my ride or die the last three years. In that time, we've run on the beaches of Florida, climbed craggy cliffs in the Cascades, and hiked and explored dozens of places in between. You've been home for me when where we lived changed every two/three months and a pandemic shut down the world around us. Couldn't have gotten through it without you, buddy.

Serious thanks to Joyce Lamb for your insight on how to make this last Deep Six novel sparkle. Your suggestions on story arc and character development are always spot-on. This time was no different.

And big hugs to the amazing team of folks who helped me get this book into readers' hands. Marlene Roberts for making sure I dotted all my I's and crossed on my T's. Amanda Carlson for taking the time out of your own busy writing and publishing schedule to format this book. And Erin Dameron-Hill for working tirelessly with me on this cover to make sure Doc looked just right.

CPSIA information can be obtained
at www.ICGtesting.com
Printed in the USA
LVHW082041070722
722996LV00002B/225